"I'm saving your lives! Houston, go! Bruno, go!"

The two members of Team Dogma leapt in succession.

"The Chinese painted us," Sadowsky said. "Maybe they launched or the Koreans launched, we don't know. Missiles inbound, probably SA-5s. ETA: twenty seconds! Rainey, standby!"

With the news robbing his breath, Rainey got into position near the ramp, bent his knees, ready to hop out.

"Rainey, go!"

Like two giant, gloved hands, the prop wash snatched then tossed Rainey away from the transport. Rainey executed a perfect HALO roll, then righted himself, assuming the freefall position. He glanced back at the C-130, just a blurry mass with flashing lights now, and saw a figure depart the hold—

—as a bright light, a rising star Rainey knew very well was a surface-to-air missile, tore a gleaming seam in the night. The rocket honed in, the transport's heat signature waving it on.

Then the C-130's port side exploded, heaving a massive fireball.

And all Rainey could do was hang there, crucified against the rushing air as the shock finally hit him and the voices of his team broke frantically over the tactical channel . . .

Also in P. W. Storm's
FORCE 5 RECON series

DEPLOYMENT: PAKISTAN

FORCE 5 RECON

DEPLOYMENT: NORTH KOREA

P.W. STORM

AVON BOOKS

An Imprint of HarperCollinsPublishers

This is a work of fiction. Names, characters, places, and incidents are products of the author's imagination or are used fictitiously and are not to be construed as real. Any resemblance to actual events, locales, organizations, or persons, living or dead, is entirely coincidental.

AVON BOOKS
An Imprint of HarperCollins*Publishers*
10 East 53rd Street
New York, New York 10022-5299

Copyright © 2004 by Peter Telep
ISBN: 0-06-052350-6
www.avonbooks.com

First Avon Books paperback printing: March 2004

Avon Trademark Reg. U.S. Pat. Off. and in Other Countries, Marca Registrada, Hecho en U.S.A.
HarperCollins® is a registered trademark of HarperCollins Publishers Inc.

Printed in the U.S.A.

10 9 8 7 6 5 4 3 2 1

"You cannot exaggerate about the Marines. They are convinced to the point of arrogance that they are the most ferocious fighters on earth. And the amusing thing about it is that they are."

FATHER KEVIN KEANEY,
1st Marine Division Chaplain,
Korean War

"The safest place in Korea was right behind a platoon of Marines. Lord, how they could fight!"

MGEN. FRANK E. LOWE, USA;
Korea, 26 January 1952

Acknowledgments

Once again, Mike Shohl, my editor, deserves recognition and my heartfelt thanks for his enthusiasm and support of this series.

Jim Newberger, dear friend, writer, paramedic, and military enthusiast slaved over every word of my story outline and provided compelling suggestions. He then went on to read and critique every page of this sizable manuscript. And if this sounds exactly like the thank you I gave him in the first book, it is! He did the same thing all over again! His contributions are deeply appreciated.

Author's Note

While this is a work of fiction, I have endeavored to faithfully portray the Marine Corp's Force Reconnaissance community, relying upon information made public via the internet, via the many texts on the subject, and via email exchanges with the Marines themselves.

That said, there remain weapons and tactics employed by Force Recon Teams that are not described here in deference to national security. Some of what you read is the product of my imagination, but every word is meant as a tribute to those brave men who serve as the eyes and ears of their commanders.

P. W. Storm
Orlando, Florida
Force5recon@aol.com

FORCE 5 RECON

DEPLOYMENT: NORTH KOREA

01

"Third Platoon, per your warning order you will make a HALO insertion into quadrant H-Nine-Seven, which is approximately sixty kilometers northeast of Sinuiju. Intell reports three low-blow mobile radar systems operating along the Chinese border. Those radars are associated with SA-3 missiles. You will locate, photograph, then destroy those radar systems, thereby blinding the enemy's missiles. If you fail, the helos carrying our invasion force will be painted and—"

Lieutenant Colonel Richard Wilmot never finished his sentence. Instead, the fifty-year-old man with hard eyes and skin like rawhide hurled through the air amid a shower of glass, sheetrock, shrapnel, and pieces of the tactical map on which he had drawn three arrows.

In that same instant, Sergeant Mac Rainey, who had been sitting in the back row with the rest of his Force

Recon team, got blown out of his chair and slammed into the briefing room's rear wall, the wind knocked out of him. He flinched against the debris raining down and gagged as smoke poured in, carrying a metallic stench. Someone, maybe Houston or Vance, swore as other Marines closer to the front shrieked in agony.

With the explosion's thunder still booming in his ears, Rainey sat up and looked around through tearing eyes. A smoldering, jagged hole like the maw of a shark lay in the wall ahead, and through it the illuminated windows of the administrative building glistened in the rain.

"You all right?" asked Doc, his own eyes tearing, his uniform caked in dust. No explosion could stop Glenroy "Doc" Leblanc. The triple B: big, bald, black guy (though you'd best avoid that nickname) would treat your wounds even if his uniform were on fire. Kind of Navy corpsman Doc was. HERO. All caps.

"I'm okay, I think," Rainey answered, then glanced sidelong at the lieutenant colonel, now visible through the clearing smoke. The man lay supine, his head a pound of uncooked chopped meat. "Oh, God. Wilmot."

While Doc crawled among the toppled chairs toward the lieutenant colonel, Rainey coughed and waved a hand across his face, searching for the rest of his team. Corporal Jimmy Vance was already on his feet, MEU pistol drawn, sniper's instincts ushered in on a wave of adrenaline. He picked his way toward the shattered wall and window, hoping to lock his green eyes on a fleeing suspect. Lance Corporal Bradley Houston, the brown-haired dreamer and once the cockiest rookie Rainey had ever met, fell in just behind Vance. Both were alive and well, and now Rainey could breathe easy. Those guys were much more than his best shooter and radio man; they were his friends, his brothers. Sure, they were half his age, didn't understand the world the way he understood it, and sometimes Houston's bad jokes and Vance's obsession with bass fishing really annoyed him. But they were good men unaffected by an age of feminization and political correctness. They were warriors. They had the mean gene. And they had Rainey's utmost respect.

Okay, so three of his four operators were accounted for. But where was Team Dogma's newest member, E-5 Sergeant Anthony Bruno?

Faces flashed by. Marines picked themselves out of the rubble. Rainey's gaze darted from soldier to soldier as MPs charged into the room, while cries of "Corpsman! Corpsman!" echoed with chilling urgency.

A hand came down hard on Rainey's shoulder, seized his shirt, and dragged him to his feet.

"Sitting on your hands again? Just like you did in Afghanistan?" Bruno breathed like a lung-cancer patient in Rainey's ear. "You going to get them out of here? Or do I have to give the order?"

Rainey ripped out of the sergeant's grip, spun, faced the man, then seized Bruno's collar and shoved the former muscle head from North Jersey against the wall. Bruno's droopy eyes widened, and his cheeks, forever shadowed by a beard that looked more like gray sandpaper than hair, balled up as he smiled.

"You're fucking with me now, Bruno? Are you insane?" Rainey shoved the man away. "Team Dogma? Fall back outside!"

"Sergeant?" Doc called, looking up from Lieutenant Colonel Wilmot's inert form.

Rainey raised his chin.

And Doc shook his head.

Despite the chaos assaulting all of Rainey's senses, he went numb. *Jesus Christ.* The lieutenant had been murdered before his eyes. Wilmot, the man who had personally requested Third Platoon's presence, the man who had orchestrated a highly unusual transfer of personnel from Fifth Force so that he could employ the best of the best in the hottest zone on the planet, had, for his efforts, been repaid with a bomb.

Was Rainey surprised? Not necessarily. There had been eleven terrorist bombings in Seoul since Combined Forces Command had threatened to begin air strikes on North Korean targets, only a week prior. The goal was to defeat the enemy in detail. Every gun and tank emplacement along the Demilitarized Zone, every ammunitions and supply depot, bridge and crossroad, resupply and reinforcement route, airfield and naval facility, commando base and headquarters, as well as communications nodes, munitions factories, electric power girds, and government buildings were on the target lists.

Was Rainey outraged? Yes. Outraged over the breach in security. MARFOR–K Headquarters should be the safest place in South Korea. What had the bastards done? Tunneled their way directly to Seoul? The CIA and the boys in Intell would take on that headache.

Rainey waved Vance, Houston, Doc, and Bruno through the door. They hustled down the hallway and out the nearest exit, into the humid air and a relentless rain that had been falling for the past two days, a prelude to typhoon season.

"I don't know about y'all, but I didn't come all the way to Korea for this," Vance said breathlessly.

Houston, his trademark grin all but gone, drifted over to Doc. "Wilmot's dead, isn't he?"

"He bled out fast."

The lance corporal beat a fist into his palm. "I don't believe this! So what do we do now? Stand around like idiots or go kick some North-Korean ass?"

"Houston," Rainey warned.

"No, you're right, kid," Bruno said, slapping a palm on Houston's shoulder and scratching his snowy widow's peak with his free hand. "Payback is in order. And I'm going to make sure we teach them that fucking with United States Marine Corps gets you nothing but dead." He started away from the group.

"Bruno? You stay put till we get word from Major Thorpe."

The assistant team leader swung around, shoved an index finger in Rainey's face. "I didn't ask for this assignment, and I don't deserve it. You either cut me off your leash—"

"Or what?"

"Or I'll . . ."

"You'll what?" Rainey cocked a brow. There weren't many Marines, Force Recon or otherwise, who could stare him down.

After a few breaths, Bruno's shoulders slumped, then he grinned and looked away. "All right. But it's too bad these men don't know you the way I do."

Houston, Doc, and Vance glanced worriedly at

Rainey. No doubt they'd rather be dodging enemy gunfire than refereeing a war between two old soldiers.

"See, you guys don't know the whole story," Bruno went on.

Doc closed in on the sergeant, towering over the man. "All I know is, we got transferred to Korea, and they said they were giving us yet another replacement for McAllister—who's probably sitting in some sports bar while we're standing here in the damned rain. Then you show up tonight with a chip on your shoulder because you got busted down from team leader. And that, Sergeant Bruno, is the whole story."

"Nope. It's half. Rainey married Kady last year, right? But she used to be married to my brother."

"So you think Kady deserves your brother and not him?" Houston asked, turning up the sarcasm. "What happened? She left him?"

"My brother is dead. He was killed in the Pentagon on Nine-eleven."

Houston winced. "Sorry."

"That's odd. I know Kady, too," Doc said. "And she never mentioned that."

Bruno tightened his lips. "She wouldn't."

"No, she wouldn't," Rainey agreed.

Houston shrugged. "If he's dead, then what's the problem?"

"Yeah, because if there is a problem, you need to work this out before we get in the field," said Vance.

"*If* we get in the field," Doc amended.

"There's no problem here," Rainey insisted, his gaze riveted on Bruno. "No problem at all."

* * *

In the hour that followed, Rainey learned that two members of Team Reaper and one from Team Voodoo had been seriously injured in the blast. The guy from Voodoo, Private Bryan Sanchez, might not pull through. It was a small miracle that the rest of the platoon had escaped with just minor cuts and bruises. The company's XO, Major John Thorpe, a brusque man in his late thirties with a jaw nearly as sharp as a K-bar, met up with them in the borrowed conference room of an office building adjacent to the HQ. The mission was still on and had been pushed up by four hours. The North Koreans were still not allowing UN weapons inspectors back into the country and were, according to intelligence reports, still ramping up operations for an invasion of the South. Combined Forces Command would launch a preemptive strike, and it was up to Force Recon to pave the way.

"I know the platoon is down three operators," Thorpe said about halfway through the briefing. "And I understand that we're all still in shock over what happened, but we're Marines. And we've got a job to do. Now then, we're going to replace your injured operators with ROK Marines."

Several guys sighed in disgust, while a few others made faces. Rainey studied his men, making sure they lodged no protest, verbal or otherwise.

"Don't give me that shit, gentlemen. Not now." Thorpe lowered his head like a schoolteacher staring over a pair of bifocals. "You new transfers may be unaware that we train with these folks from South Korea every year during Foal Eagle. Be assured that these men are first-class operators. They've led hard lives. They are hard men."

Bruno raised his hand, much to Rainey's chagrin.

"What is it, Sergeant?"

"I just wonder, sir, if ROK Marines speak the English in the clear and most charming way."

That drew hearty chuckles from everyone—

Except the rest of Team Dogma.

"Sergeant, I understand that we can all use a laugh right now, but I don't appreciate remarks like that. In fact, I'm not sure why you ask, since everyone on your team is accounted for."

"I'm sorry, sir. I was just—"

"Suffice it to say that I've just met these men, and their English is good. Most of them learned it in high school. And not only that, one of them, a Lance Corporal Kim, grew up in the region and escaped to the South when he was a teenager. He'll make an expert guide and translator. Are you satisfied, Sergeant?"

Bruno nodded. "Thank you, sir."

"Fucking wiseass," Rainey said under his breath.

"Just for you, Mac," Bruno whispered.

"You're digging your own grave."

"No. Yours."

"Sergeant Rainey? Do you have a question?" Thorpe asked.

"Uh, no, sir."

"All right, then. Marines, it's time to saddle up. Your rides are waiting outside to take you to Osan. If this goes off without a hitch, within forty-eight hours you'll be rallying back to Extraction Point Scorpion, where a

SEAL team from the USS *Texas* will issue you dive gear and get you back to the ASDS. I should also warn you that since we are not officially at war with North Korea, you will not be treated as POWs if captured. You'll be arrested as spies. Now then. You know your codes and call signs. Don't be late for dinner, gentlemen. Good luck. God bless."

Every Marine in the room snapped to attention. "Hoo-yah!"

TEAM DOGMA
EN ROUTE TO OSAN AIR BASE
SOUTH KOREA
2215 HOURS LOCAL TIME

Inside an M998 High Mobility Multipurpose Wheeled Vehicle (HMMWV), Cpl. Jimmy Vance deliberately sat between Rainey and Bruno. He had decided that he would be the peacemaker, not because it was in his nature but because it was in his best interests. Keeping them cool might keep him alive. And remaining alive wouldn't be easy. Not where they were going.

North Korea. Mystery land. Land of tunnels and tanks. Nuclear-capable country with one of the largest standing armies in the world. Starving land. Drought. Famine. No Wal-Mart, no HBO, according to Houston. But they had a big army. Use it or lose it. Well, they were going to lose it.

The Hummer trundled forward, and Vance was thankful that Osan Air Base lay only thirty miles north. A short ride would give him less time to worry and less time for Bruno and Rainey to get at each other's throats.

"How long you been on the team?" Bruno asked Vance.

"Must be over two years now."

"Like it?"

Vance turned his head fractionally, saw that Rainey was lost in thought.

"I said, do you like it?"

"Yeah, I do."

Bruno thrust out his fat lips and nodded. "You would. You're a redneck, aren't you, Jimmy boy? Where you from? Alabama? Mississippi?"

"Florida."

"You kidding me? I bet your parents are brother and sister—"

In a flash of movement, Rainey reached across Vance and grabbed Bruno's earlobe. "They gave you to me because you need an attitude adjustment. You need to remember that you ain't no army of fucking one. You're a Marine, a member of Team Dogma. *Team* Dogma. You're giving us all a bad name."

"Oh, now I'm a member of the famous 'Force Five Recon,' and I'm the fifth member, the unlucky fifth member who always gets hurt, caught, or killed. Let's see, since McAllister left, you've had three replacements, and none of them has lasted. So they bust me down and stick me in that slot. Ain't that a fucking party?"

After a solid tug on Bruno's ear—enough to make the big guy cry out in pain—Rainey released him. They traded a look that made Vance close his eyes and sigh.

Big men with bigger egos. Vinegar and oil. Something or someone needed to shake them up.

"Hey, Jimmy?" Bruno said softly. "You got a girl?"

"Sergeant, is it okay if we don't talk?"

"I asked, do you got a girl?"

"Not exactly."

"Not exactly? What does that mean? You forgot to inflate her this morning?"

Houston, who was seated in front of them, turned back and smiled. "My kind of girl: quiet and always willing."

"Thanks for the help," Vance told Houston.

"Help? I told you to dump the bitch. But you don't listen. You blow her off, then you go back, and she just burns you, man. Every time."

"Forget those girls back home. Forget settling down. Old Bruno has a tip while you're in this part of the world. You get your asses over to Japan. There's this place in Tokyo called the Love Hotel. They got rooms with giant mirrors on the walls and ceilings. They call them 'creative rooms.' And they don't leave mints on your pillow."

"What do they leave?" Houston asked.

Bruno winked. "Condoms."

Houston clapped his hands together, rubbed them in anticipation. "Dude, we have to go there. We have to go!"

"Yeah, you do," Bruno said. "Because corrupting young minds is what I'm about."

"I wouldn't touch those girls at the Love Hotel with a ten-foot pole," Doc said.

"That's because you're married," Bruno snapped.

"No—well, yes. But as a corpsman, I've seen some nasty STDs. You gentlemen want your johnsons to fall off, that's up to you."

TEAM DOGMA
OSAN AIR BASE
37°05'N, 127°02'E
SOUTH KOREA
2245 HOURS LOCAL TIME

Osan Air Base lay only forty-eight miles away from the Demilitarized Zone, making it the most-forward deployed air base in all of South Korea. Located in a section known as the western lowlands and surrounded by rivers and rice paddies, the base was the only airfield built by the United States in Korea. At the moment, the airfield lay draped in fog, a common forecast problem that could delay the team's takeoff.

Doc, who had been glancing via penlight at his copy of the *North Korea Country Handbook*, tucked the book away as they neared the tarmac. While the other guys had barely glanced at their pocket-size reference manuals, Doc got off on learning as much as he could about his surroundings. He had already read all 432 pages and was ready to save his fellow Marines' lives with both his medical skills and knowledge of the area.

The truck stopped, and Doc shouldered his heavy Jumpers Kit Bag (JKB) and MC-5 parachute. He climbed down from the Hummer and onto the rain-slick tarmac. The JKB held his rucksack, load-bearing vest, and the rest of his gear, including his medical supplies. The bag prevented any loose items from interfering with the parachute deployment sequence, and you certainly didn't want anything interfering with that. He, like the others, had already put on his Gore-Tex jumpsuit, gloves, altimeter, and overboots. He tucked his Halo Helmet—the standard parachutist headgear—and his MBU-12P pressure demand oxygen mask into the crook of his arm, and followed the others toward the massive silhouette of the C-130 Hercules transport plane, whose four huge props were already humming and rotating.

"Hey, Doc?" Vance called, rushing up to his side. "You didn't say much during the ride."

"I was reading the handbook. And praying."

"You say one for me? I need all I can get."

"I did."

"Thanks, man. So what do you think of Bruno?"

Doc shook his head. "I'm trying not to."

"Who did we piss off to get stuck with him?"

"I got a theory."

"All I got are butterflies."

"You'll be all right."

"So what's your theory?"

"They stuck us with him because they're jealous."

"Who's jealous?"

Doc brushed rain from his face, smiled bitterly. "The pogues, man. The pogues. The world may not know it, but everyone in the Thirty-First MEU does."

"What do they know?"

"They know that you, me, Houston, Rainey, and Old McAllister are the guys who brought down Mohammed al-Zumar, the world's most wanted terrorist.

We took him down, and a year later we're still paying for our fame."

"Doc, I have to say, that sounds a little twisted. Sure, we all took some razzing, but I don't think the brass would actually punish us for what we did. I mean, the Marines took out al-Zumar. The Marines. Not the Air Force."

"Al-Zumar killed himself, Vance. How easily we forget."

"He killed himself because we were going to capture his ass. We get all the credit."

"No, we get Sergeant Anthony Bruno."

Vance shrugged. "Maybe you're right. And we also get to jump out of a perfectly good airplane."

" 'Perfectly good'? I wouldn't go that far. That One Thirty's a lot older than you, junior."

"Thanks, Doc. You made me feel so much better."

"Hey, it's good to be worried. Keeps you alert. Maybe you went to the Army Airborne School and Military Freefall School. And maybe you completed the tandem barrel jumper course and even the static line/freefall jumpmaster schools, just like me. But you shouldn't let all that training make you cocky. Up there, we should always be humble."

The jumpmaster, Sergeant Paul Sadowsky, well known for his crooked nose and the even more crooked card games he ran, greeted them at the top of the ramp. "Well, here they are to put the cherry on the shit sundae that is this jump—Big Doc, the big-time loser, and his little fishing buddy."

"Who you calling loser, you thief?" Doc asked in a mock angry tone.

"Thief?! Those charges were dropped. Anyway, I am so ready to boot your asses off this Herc at twenty-five thousand feet."

"Hey, Sergeant, why don't you come with us?" Vance suggested. "Be just like practice back at Pendleton, only when you get down there, you'll get to blow stuff up. It'll be great."

"Your party, Vance. Not mine. Now get out of my face and go strap in."

Doc frowned, as deeper within the massive hold Rainey was arguing with someone who stood hidden from view behind Houston and Bruno.

"Whoa, the sarge sounds mad," Vance said.

"Yeah, and that's strange. He's not yelling at Bruno."

Rainey's jaw had dropped the moment he reached his jumpseat. The man who would sit next to him, the man wearing his own Marine issue Gore-Tex jumpsuit and bomber jacket covered in military patches was none other than *Wolf News* reporter Rick Navarro, a self-made celebrity whose ass Rainey had saved back in Pakistan. Since then, Rainey had refused to watch the Wolf News channel, for fear that he might accidentally catch Navarro's show and be forced to pick up the TV set, hold it high above his head, and smash it on the floor. Rick Navarro, the reporter who carried a gun and routinely said that he would dodge bullets to bring the story to the American public, stood for everything Rainey hated—and then some. He was a media whore who spun stories and spread rumors like diseases.

"I say again, what the hell are you doing here?"

Navarro's eyelid twitched, and he stroked his goatee

as though he wanted to rub it off. "Maybe you haven't been watching much TV, Sergeant, but for the past year I've been the poster child for the Marine Corps. They even say that recruitment numbers are up because of my show."

"I don't give a shit what they say. I asked you a question." Rainey glanced back, waved over Jumpmaster Sadowsky. "This is a classified military operation, and I want to know who authorized your presence."

Navarro's cameraman, a hairy, heavyset geek dressed in his own Gore-Tex jumpsuit—though he had spared himself the embarrassment of a bomber jacket with patches—whispered something in the reporter's ear as Sadowsky arrived.

"What's the problem, Rainey?"

"The problem"—Rainey jabbed an index finger at Navarro—"is right here."

"You know who this guy is, don't you?"

"Of course I know who he is. What's he doing here?"

Navarro snickered. "You blind? I'm embedded, and I'm going to cover your jump. I'm going to take the American people on a behind-the-scenes tour of Force Recon operations. And it all starts right here, right now."

The reporter's dorky camera guy swung his lens Rainey's way and hit a button.

"Shut that off."

The camera guy kept shooting.

Thus Rainey tore the camera away, turned, and hurled the device like a football, sending it spiraling across the hold and onto the ramp, where it struck and went tumbling down onto the tarmac.

"Lieutenant Colonel Wilmot himself authorized this ride-along!" Navarro screamed. "And you're going to pay for that!"

"Lieutenant Colonel Wilmot is dead. And as far as I'm concerned, so are you—if you stick around any longer."

"You're threatening me, Sergeant?" Navarro looked to the others. "You guys heard that. He's threatening me."

"So am I," Vance said.

"Me, too," Houston added.

"Can I get your autograph?" Bruno asked, drawing Rainey's heated gaze.

"I think he's lying, Sergeant," said Doc. "Wilmot would never authorize something like this. Never."

"You guys are so naïve. You have no idea how much support I have—right up the chain of command. Wilmot wasn't happy about authorizing this, but he did. He had to."

Rainey looked to Sadowsky, who threw up his hands. Then, without thinking about it further, Rainey acted. Damn the consequences to hell. He grabbed Navarro by the neck and hauled the man to his feet. "Houston? Vance? Take the camera guy."

And with that, the three of them hauled Mr. Rick Navarro and his techno crony out of the hold and down the ramp. Once on the tarmac, Rainey played bar bouncer and shoved Navarro to the pavement. "You can videotape us from right there."

Houston and Vance threw the camera guy down beside Navarro. "Anything else, Sergeant?" Vance asked.

"No, Corporal. Return to your jumpseat."

"Aye-aye, Sergeant."

"I'm getting back on that airplane!" Navarro screamed.

Rainey shook his head. "You have to get past me."

"Fuck you, Sergeant."

Rainey grinned. "That's what I thought you'd say." A grinding noise from behind drew Rainey's attention: the ramp was rising. He turned and hopped up onto the platform, then paused a moment to wave good-bye to the drenched reporter.

"You're going to regret this, Sergeant! I promise you!"

The only thing Rainey would regret is that he hadn't hauled off and slugged Navarro, who, back in Pakistan, had abandoned his injured translator, causing the man to die. Life meant nothing to Navarro. The story was everything. Now he could do his reporting from the gutter.

Where he belonged.

02

Lance Corporal Bradley Houston was a tortured circus clown, painting on a happy face and joking about whorehouses, when only a month ago a call from his mother had run him over like a tank. Twice.

"Bradley, I'm afraid your father is dying."

Houston had flown home to San Diego, where Dad and Mom had created their real-estate empire, only to arrive at the hospital a mere two hours too late. As if that were not painful enough, he and his father had not spoken since Houston had joined the Marine Corps. Dad had said his son was fated to sell million-dollar properties and that the Corps was for minorities and criminals. By joining, Houston had, according to his dad's definition, transformed himself into the equivalent of a drug dealer with a rap sheet longer than his client list of junkies. Dad had no clue what Force Recon was about. Even worse, Houston had never been able to tell him about how in Pakistan he had been stabbed by the world's most wanted man, about how proud he had been to serve with great men, and about how much he missed his family. Dad would not get on the phone and would not answer email. Telling Dad to shove the whole real-estate empire up his ass had not helped, but Houston had tried repeatedly since then to make amends.

Then the man had fallen prey to cancer and had quickly succumbed, leaving Houston to wonder whether or not his father had actually loved him. The grieving had turned to dull aches, and the dull aches had turned to breathlessness. One night, after a horrible dream about his father, Houston had gone into the bathroom and suffered a panic attack in which he lost consciousness. He had never told anyone about that. Yes, he knew he had to get on with this life, but thoughts of his father, accompanied by a loss of breath, struck him nearly every day and night.

Sometimes, when he was being praised for a job well done, Houston really loved the Corps. But when his balls were being busted for a seemingly ridiculous breach of protocol, he heard his father's voice echoing as if on some sappy TV show: *Son, you should have listened to me. Instead, you betrayed me and everything I stand for. You stabbed me in the heart by joining the Marines.*

And then Houston's own inner voice would kick in: *You fucked up. You joined the Marines. You idiot. You can't do this forever. You could lose a leg, like McAllis-*

*ter. Then what're you going to do? Be poor. Because
you didn't go for the money.*

*Is that what really bothers you? Think about it. You
had a father who never loved you.*

Houston's heart raced, and suddenly there was no air
inside the C-130's hold. He trembled, looked around,
suddenly wished he were back home comforting his
mother. At least she had, for the most part, supported
him, and had tried to talk to Dad. She knew how to
make him feel calm.

"Uh, hello. I am Lance Corporal Jung Yung Kim."

Houston shuddered and glanced at the ROK Marine
to his right. He hadn't bothered to introduce himself
since the guy was a member of Team Voodoo. Apparently, the skinny Korean, whose high, tight crewcut
made him look more Western than Eastern, felt the
need to be courteous. When Houston had arrived in
Seoul, he and the rest of the team spent a few hours
touring the city. Several shopkeepers had greeted them
enthusiastically. In fact, they had been polite to the
point of making Houston feel awkward. No, he
couldn't generalize about all South Koreans, but most
seemed sensitive and eager to please—and the ROK
Marine's tone put him in that camp.

Half-heartedly, Houston reached over, took the Marine's hand. "Yeah, hey, I'm Houston, man."

"Houston? Like city in Texas?" Kim asked.

"Yeah."

"You were born there?"

"No, I was born in San Diego."

Kim frowned. "Okay."

"What a minute. I think you're the guy our major was talking about at the briefing."

"Maybe."

"How come you weren't there?"

"Our sergeant thought it better we come directly to the plane. He worried about U.S. Marine attitude, I guess. Better to get to work."

"Yeah, he was probably right. We have our own way of doing things—and we like to use our own people."

"As do we. But we are grateful for your help."

"I don't know if I'd call it help. We're just defending U.S. interests here."

A moment passed between them, and Houston realized that talking to this guy would keep him preoccupied. No thoughts of Dad or the jump. "Uh, yeah, so the major said you grew up in the North."

"Yes."

"Well that had to suck."

"My parents used to work for the South Korean underground."

"What? They were miners?" Houston joked, but Kim didn't get it. Bad joke anyway.

The Korean Marine continued: "They were spies for the government. Ten years ago, soldiers came to our house and killed them. I was sixteen. They took me to a youth camp. Three of us escaped from there. We reached the South."

"Whoa . . ." And Houston thought *he* had problems. Kim really put things into perspective. "Hey, man, sorry about that."

"It's okay. My life is good now. I learned English, and I went to United States for the Marine exchange program.

I was in some of your schools: Basic Reconnaissance course, Dive Supervisor course, and Scout/Sniper."

"No shit. Did you have old T-Rex for Basic Recon?"

Kim grinned knowingly. "Yes. He is a hard man!"

"Dude, the hardest. You should tell the other guys on your team about this stuff." Houston eyed the line of Marines seated beyond Kim. "Yeah, you should. Make them all feel better about working with you."

The ROK Marine lowered his gaze, pursed his lips. "They think we are fuck-ups."

Hearing the guy curse made Houston want to smile, but in deference to Kim, he didn't. Obviously the guy had received anything but a warm reception from his team members. Sure, they would work with him, behave like professionals, but they didn't have to like him. You couldn't blame them too much, though. They were still on edge, having just lost a few of their own. You couldn't just shove in a replacement—especially one from another country—and expect to feel the love. Trust had to be earned, and Kim and his buddies had a lot to prove. Still, it wasn't right to persecute them, and having someone like Kim who was familiar with the countryside would be a huge plus. Houston hoped that guys from Voodoo would give Lance Cpl. Jung Yung Kim a chance. The guy seemed squared away, and given the murder of his parents, he probably had an intense hatred for those from the North.

With Kim's expression growing even longer, Houston knew it was time to lighten the mood.

"Hey, Kim? You ever go to a place in Tokyo called the Love Hotel?"

Kim looked up and grinned with recognition.

* * *

Corporal Jimmy Vance took Doc's suggestion and dug out his field manual, hoping to ease his nerves and drift off into a state of utter boredom. He read about how North Koreans thought of their society as a collective whole, more important than the individuals it comprised. While most Westerners would assume that they had harsh and mechanical lives and that they hated their lives, quite the contrary was true. They didn't know any better, and were barraged by anti-American propaganda that kept them full of shit and in the dark. Poor bastards. Cogs in the machine of communism.

Vance was about to read about the NKA Army's tactical frontages and depths in defense when Doc took the book from his hand and flipped to the chapter on environmental health risks. "Read this."

The manual suddenly became a horror novel. Vance grimaced as he learned about malaria, Japanese encephalitis, Korean hemorrhagic fever, typhus, helminthic infections, and "traveler's diarrhea," which the manual's author stated was the greatest threat to troops stationed on the Korean peninsula. Vance wondered if the author had ever stared down the barrel of an AK-47. Probably not. Anyway, the point was, don't eat the food. And don't drink the water (since most of the water sources were fecally contaminated). If that weren't enough, you had pollution, extremely unsanitary living conditions, and hazardous vegetation like nettles and lacquer plants, as well as a poisonous snake called the mamushi and scorpions to contend with. The country was a men's room in a dingy bar, and you'd best wash your hands thoroughly before and after leaving.

Doc elbowed Vance. "What do you think?"

"I think I'd rather be standing on the bow of my bass boat, pitching a Carolina-rigged lizard at some lily pads is what I think."

"I'm not sure what that means, but okay."

"It means Korea sucks."

"At least the weather will be nice."

"Yeah, right. Rain today, rain tomorrow. Damn."

Nearby, Bruno, who was sitting next to Rainey, lifted his voice, and Vance pricked up his ears to eavesdrop on the conversation.

"We hadn't finished securing that position," Bruno was saying. "And you knew that. But you chose to move anyway, putting your entire team at risk."

"One mistake, man," Rainey said. "One mistake."

"Not the first. You've just learned how to cover them up."

"Don't pursue this."

"And what you did in Pakistan? You should've been busted out of the Corps for that. You ain't no hero to me. You twist your values to support the mission. Lie, cheat, steal."

"And you don't?"

"Oh, come on, Rainey. You don't know when to quit. You've played God for too long. You're a father to these guys. *The* Father. And I feel sorry for them. Because they're too close to see that you're just an old man now, getting sloppy. And that'll get someone killed. Tell you what? It ain't going to be me."

Had it not been for the C-130's thunderous engines, you might have heard a pin drop in the hold, or at least Vance thought so. Houston seemed especially taken aback by Bruno's words. Indeed, he and Houston thought of Rainey like a father. You couldn't help but admire the man's long and distinguished career, not to mention his skills as an operator. He pulled off tricks in the field that simply amazed Vance. But he did make mistakes. He did fail—because, as he liked to say, he was always pushing the envelope.

And wasn't it just grand that they had Sgt. Anthony Bruno to remind them of that?

"I've heard enough," Rainey told Bruno.

"Well, I'm not finished. You're only half the man Nick was. You know, I told Kady that before she married you. You'll never measure up, man. Never. And now I'm done."

Judging from Rainey's flushed cheeks, Vance expected him to turn, seize Bruno by the neck, and shake the pasta out of the big guy.

But Sgt. Mac Rainey just sat there, steaming, his gaze drifting off as the order to don their oxygen masks for an equipment check echoed through the hold.

As Houston put on his mask and made sure the O_2 was flowing properly, he thought about what Bruno had said. They had obviously been referring to an operation that had gone down long before Houston had joined the team, and that operation had obviously gone south. Rainey wasn't one to readily admit his mistakes or defeats, and hearing him do so left Houston feeling a little lost. One father had died, and now "the other father" seemed preoccupied, maybe even worried. Once they hit the field, Rainey might second-guess himself and put them all in jeopardy, like Bruno had said.

Nonsense. Mac Rainey was the finest operator in Fifth Force Recon, perhaps in all the Corps.

But his eyes, still visible behind that mask, told a different story, and Houston shivered at the thought that he would plummet into a foreign land with a leader who had a confidence problem.

Or was Houston the one with the problem?

Although Doc had not been close enough to hear the details of Bruno's rant, he would have ignored them anyway. Rainey was a great team leader. And Bruno was an asshole. Nothing could change Doc's assessment, and he knew that Rainey would, in his own time and in his own way, deal with the man. It was best now to fall back out of the crossfire.

Doc closed his eyes as heavy winds buffeted the transport and the fuselage rattled as though it had been constructed of recycled cans of Mountain Dew superglued together. The jump wouldn't kill them; Air Force bravado would. Leave it to the bonnet boys to fly their crate through wonton soup in order to get the job done. Doc was betting those pilots thought he and the rest were the lucky ones—they got to jump off the plane and wouldn't have to brave the weather back to Osan.

Shit. More turbulence. And the transport took a dip, sending Doc's stomach into the back of his throat. Rainey called for a radio check, and it took a moment for Doc to respond. "Dogma Two, radio check, I read you loud and clear, over."

"Dogma Team, our jumpmaster reports T-minus forty-eight minutes until we reach the drop zone, over," Rainey announced.

The sooner the better for Doc. He'd be happy to fly the friendly skies without the Air Force's "help." And sitting on his ass with a big Jumpers Kit Bag belted to his gut and hanging between his legs was not his idea of fun. Before he could bemoan his situation any further, however, Rainey called for an equipment check, and Doc made sure his nautical compass and GPS were functioning properly, along with his altimeter. The instruments were good to go. He took in another long breath, looked around at the other fourteen men, most with their hands resting easy on their JKBs. One of the ROK Marines, Doc wasn't sure which one, tapped his boot nervously, and two guys from Reaper drummed their hands on their bags. Nerves, nerves, nerves. Funny how they possessed your hands and feet. And scary how they reminded you of how fragile you were, despite all the camouflage and heavy gear. Doc had seen some of the biggest badasses in the world hesitate on that ramp. To ease their fears, he would tell them, "Don't worry, my uncle personally packed your chute, and he's the best parachute packer in the Corps!"

"Oh, really," the scared guy would say.

"Yeah. No Marine ever came back and complained that the chute didn't open!"

It was a tired joke, and most guys had heard it, but Doc liked to watch those dense few who didn't get it at first, then the lightbulb would go off a second before the jumpmaster screamed the order.

Doc looked down, realized his right leg was shaking. *Shit. Cut that out. Think about something else. Think about how this is just the beginning of another long six months overseas. Damn.* Each deployment sucked a little more life out of Doc, and each deployment seemed to age his young boys at an accelerated rate. Ask anyone who hasn't seen his kids for six months, and he'll tell you how hard it is—especially on the day you come home. There's an awkwardness at the port, a moment where—just for a second—you feel as though you're hugging strangers and you've just left your family back there, on the ship. You know these people, but suddenly you don't know them. So much has changed. You want your wife to remain frozen in time when you leave her, and it's easy to forget that she's going to church, picking up the boys from soccer, washing the car, and paying the taxes without you. You're a picture on the wall, a disembodied voice on the phone, a collection of characters on the computer screen. There's no connection of flesh and blood. For him, that was the hardest part about being a Navy Corpsman. That, and the risks in the field, risks that could leave his wife without a husband, his children without a father.

In spite of those necessary evils, he knew that once he left the service, he'd miss it more than anything. He'd probably seek out other veterans in order to rekindle the camaraderie. And that's what he enjoyed most about Force Recon. He got to work with some truly extraordinary people. Sure, the Navy and the Corps had their share of Anthony Brunos, but they were the exception. Like anything else, military life had its ups and downs. *Yeah,* Doc thought, *especially when you're making a High Altitude Low Opening drop into enemy territory to destroy some radar systems so the invasion force won't get blown out of the sky.*

Doc began playing out possible injuries his teammates could sustain on landing: lacerations, fractures, blunt trauma, and the like. He took a mental inventory of his medical supplies, saw himself rifling through them, heard the half-stifled groan of his patient. He wanted to ask all of the guys a favor: If they could, would they mind not getting hurt? He wondered which member of the team would have the best wiseass response. Houston, probably.

Glancing at the radio operator, Doc lifted a thumbs up. Houston returned the thumb. For a young man who had recently lost his old man, Houston seemed to be faring pretty well. At Rainey's request (though he would have done so on his own), Doc had sat down and talked with Houston about the loss, but the lance corporal had insisted that he was okay. Doc had thought he would teach the kid about the stages of grieving, but Houston knew the drill and was obviously doing everything he could to hide his pain. But the sheen in his eyes, the crack in his voice, and the fidgeting gave him away. He had been forced to see the company's shrinks, and they had deemed him fit for duty. But Houston was a smart character. Very smart. He knew how to fill in the cracks of his psyche, but Doc worried that the patchwork wouldn't hold. While Doc was no expert on treating mental wounds, he had seen how they could interfere with a Marine's job. At the very least, he would keep a watchful eye on his teammate. Wouldn't be the first time. When Vance had been dear Johned via email, Doc knew the pain would show up. It had taken a while, but Vance's emotions had eventually caught up with him and caused him to miss things in the field. Houston was headed down that same path, and it was up to Doc to play navigator and course correct.

* * *

Rainey's pulse bounded. For a moment, he thought he was having a heart attack. *Fucking Bruno* . . . He was one of the few guys who could push all of Rainey's buttons and make him feel foolish in front of his own men. Worse, Bruno was systematic about it, tearing into Rainey's career, character, and even his personal life.

The son of a bitch would give Rainey an ulcer, if not a heart attack.

Okay. Calm down. Once they hit the drop zone, if Bruno didn't cease and desist, Rainey would need a plan to deal with him. But it was hard to think about that. He was still stunned over the man's behavior. Marines—at least the ones Rainey respected—did not vent their frustration by making their team leader lose credibility. Bruno wasn't just hurting Rainey; he was hurting everyone.

Too bad the idiot didn't realize that their differences meant nothing in the grand scheme. They had a radar system to locate and destroy. The job would be accomplished through mutual respect and clear, decisive leadership, not through petty bickering and the questioning of every order—which was what Rainey saw coming a mile away. They should concentrate on the mission first. The mission.

But why couldn't Rainey stop thinking about what Bruno had said? Why couldn't he forget about the botched operation in Afghanistan, about the stunts he had pulled in Pakistan? Because he knew in his heart of hearts that he had stretched the truth, that he had made tactical mistakes, that the woman he had married was probably comparing him to her first husband, a man who had been characterized by all who knew him as a fine naval officer and a loving husband. The guy was a saint, and better-looking than Rainey to boot.

Maybe Rainey needed an attitude adjustment of his own. Maybe he should view Bruno's presence as a challenge, not a nightmare. It was time to stop thinking like a jealous kid with acne and start behaving like a Marine. He would not play Bruno's game. Besides, the guy had gotten his, getting busted down from team leader only to serve with a man he didn't like. The brass knew exactly what they were doing.

"Dogma One, we are now approximately thirty-nine minutes from the drop zone, over."

"Roger that," Rainey told Sadowsky. "Thirty-nine minutes."

Rainey stole a glance at Bruno, who caught the look and narrowed his eyes. Looking away, Rainey wondered what the failure rate was on the MC-5 parachute and what the odds were that Sgt. Anthony Bruno might have been issued the fateful pack, one not packed by Doc's uncle, as the medic liked to joke. Rainey sighed. No, he wouldn't play those odds.

PEOPLE'S LIBERATION ARMY AIR FORCE
RADAR STATION #4517
SOMEWHERE SOUTH OF DANDONG, CHINA
2340 HOURS LOCAL TIME

Inside a small, damp control center, Radar Officer Lee, who had just celebrated his twenty-third birthday the day prior, watched the blip on his scope with great interest. Was it yet another Combined Forces Command bomber following a diversionary path north? Two prior aircraft had done likewise, only to turn sharply right to strike the North Korean artillery corps to the south. Lee knew that the North Koreans' ability to detect such bombers had already been severely limited by prior air attacks. He wondered if Lieutenant Ho would change his mind and decide to tip off the North Koreans. A rumor had circulated that one of Ho's brothers had married a North Korean woman. While that hardly provided the motivation (having the Americans operating so close to China was motivation enough), it did make Lee wonder just how sympathetic his superior was to the Democratic People's Republic of Korea.

"Lieutenant Ho? I have another contact."

Ho stubbed out his cigarette, rose from his metal folding chair, and arrived at Lee's side. He eyed the scope, then concluded, "Bomber."

"Or transport. The CFC could be inserting special forces."

"Suddenly you are a military analyst?"

"No, sir."

"Then shut up. And get me the phone. I think it is time we talk to our friends across the border."

"Listen up, Marines! We have been tagged by a Chinese radar. No two-minute warning. This is it! On your feet! On your feet!"

The jumpmaster's cry woke Vance from a sound sleep. He realized that his reference manual had slipped from his gloved hand and fallen to the deck. He leaned down to fetch it as Sandowsky came down the line, inspecting everyone.

"We've been tagged? So what?" Bruno said over the team's tactical frequency. "The Chinese have been painting everyone."

"No talking," Rainey snapped. "Jumpmaster, Team Dogma is good to go!"

"Roger that, Team Dogma is good to go and is lead team out. Stand ready, Marines."

Vance considered how close they were to the drop zone. Surely they hadn't reached it yet. But lo and behold the ramp was already lowering to reveal a vortex of darkness chilled to a temperature of about minus 25 degrees Fahrenheit. Sadowsky was probably getting them up early: a precautionary measure because Chinese eyes were on them. Vance took a step back, dug his calves into the edge of his jumpseat. Seeing all that black made the jumpseat look pretty damned good. He tried to breathe easy, but with the oxygen mask on, he sounded like Darth Vader having sex.

* * *

"All right, Rainey, your team's up!" boomed Sadowsky, his eyes like bright beacons behind his oxygen mask. "Doc, stand by! Vance, stand by!"

Sadowsky's order left Rainey confused and shaking his head. "We can't jump yet!"

"I command the jump! Doc, go! Vance, go!"

Doc started off toward the ramp, leaned forward, and leaped into the abyss. Vance hesitated a second, then suddenly took to the air.

"What're you doing?" Rainey demanded.

"Houston, stand by! Bruno, stand by!"

"Sadowsky!"

"I'm saving your lives! Houston, go! Bruno, go!"

And the other two members of Team Dogma leaped in succession.

"What're you talking about?" Rainey demanded.

"The Chinese painted us. Maybe they launched or the Koreans launched, we don't know. Missiles inbound, probably SA-5s. ETA: twenty seconds! Rainey, stand by!"

With the news robbing his breath, Rainey got into position near the ramp, bent his knees, ready to hop out.

"Rainey, go!"

Like two giant, gloved hands, the prop wash snatched and then tossed Rainey away from the transport. The sound of his own breath loud in his ears, Rainey executed a perfect HALO roll then righted himself, assumed the freefall position, and felt the familiar and comfortable pressure on his chest. He glanced back at the C-130, just a blurry mass with flashing lights now, and saw a figure depart the hold . . .

As a bright light, a rising star that Rainey knew very well was a surface-to-air missile, tore a glowing seam in the night.

The rocket homed in, the transport's heat signature waving it on.

Three, two—

Oh, my God . . .

The C-130's port side exploded, heaving a massive fireball. For a second, Rainey stared in horrid fascination at the flames until the wind booted him sideways, leaving the ominous glow on his periphery.

A second gust struck, and he spun again, saw the shower of flaming debris growing ever more distant, pieces tumbling and winking out of existence.

And all Rainey could do was hang there, crucified against the rushing air as the shock finally hit him and the voices of his team broke frantically over the tactical channel.

03

"Dogma One to Dogma Team. Clear the channel and sound off," Rainey ordered.

Doc, Vance, and Houston reported in and gave their altimeter readings as they plunged at a terminal velocity of 126 mph.

Rainey waited for Bruno to check in. After three seconds, Rainey could wait no more. "Dogma Five, this is Dogma One, over."

Static.

"Bruno! Report your situation, over!"

"One, this is Five," Bruno said matter-of-factly. "Situation FUBAR. Isn't that obvious?"

Rainy swore to himself. "All right, they got the transport."

"And the rest of the platoon," Bruno added.

"We don't know that for sure."

"Jesus, Rainey, they had no time to get out."

Rainey steeled his tone. "Dogma Five, clear the channel, over."

"Roger, out," grunted Bruno.

"Marines, we're off our drop zone," Rainey continued. "Don't know how far yet. Keep your eyes on your gauges and keep yourself oxygenated. You get in trouble, use your rolls. And remember your landing fall. See you on the ground, Dogma One, out."

Though still badly shaken, Rainey had to focus. He had a jump to complete and a team to lead. Within two minutes he and his men would descend from 25,000 feet to 3,500—the height at which they would pull their ripcords. HALO jumps got you out of sight fast, while a High Altitude High Opening (HAHO) jump could last over thirty minutes. You used the HALO when on top of the target and opted for a HAHO when you wanted to swoop down toward a target up to forty kilometers away.

So on the bright side—if there was one—Rainey and his operators were making the "easier" of the two jumps, though that fact barely lifted his spirits. He had figured that most of the challenge lay in locating the radar site, destroying it, and then getting out alive. The insertion, once the least of his worries, should have gone smoothly. Now, if the other two teams had not made it out, and if he and his men landed too far off their mark, then the mission was already over before they set a boot on North Korean soil.

Ordinarily Vance never paid much attention to the aerospace physiology technicians, or "PTs," who were aboard the C-130s during high-altitude drops. Those guys were experts on the effects of flight on the body, and they monitored the team's condition for signs of hypoxia and decompression sickness. They didn't talk much, except when they were asking you questions to make sure you weren't wigging out from the lack of oxygen. They knew some laws of gases figured out by a guy named Boyle, something about how as you decrease pressure, volume increases—meaning you should skip the baked beans and beer before high-altitude jumps.

Which he had. He had done everything right, but still he had had problems. Moments before the jump, Vance had found it hard to breathe, and a tingling sensation in his neck was working its way toward his ears. After he shared his concerns with one of the PTs, the guy had adjusted Vance's mask and corrected his airflow. If it weren't for that PT, whose name Vance should have learned, he might have been dead before he hit the ground. And now the man who had saved his life was gone. Unbelievable.

Shaking off the grim thought, he checked his altimeter: 10,452 feet and falling fast. Far below lay a string of lights thrown haphazardly across the ground, and beyond it, a few low-lying mountains drew a wandering line across the horizon. The rest was pitch black.

He focused on his breathing: *Steady now, steady.* The wind's powerful drone and the solid weight across his arms and legs were almost comforting. Almost. Despite his Gore-Tex suit and gloves, his feet and hands had gone numb aboard the transport, but the farther he descended, the more sensation returned. He remembered reading something during his training about how for every thousand feet you ascend, you lose 3.6 degrees Fahrenheit. So the opposite must be true as you descended. He wished he could fall faster, just to get warm. It dawned on him that all of his fears concerning the jump were gone. He felt a strange mixture of exhilaration from the physical thrill and deep sadness from the missile attack. Rather than sort out those feelings, which might very well be impossible, he shut them down and thought about his training. He anticipated the feeling of the ripcord in his hand, the tremendous tug on his shoulders, and kept his gaze fixed on his altimeter.

The very first time that then Private Bradley Houston jumped from an airplane, he had had a terrible case of the flu. Told by his instructors to either make the jump or recycle, he had opted for the former since he could not bear to take the course again. Feeling as though he had cotton balls shoved up his nose and that he had just been beaten with wet towels filled with bars of soap, he had taken his position near the door. The jumpmaster had given him the "stand by" order. He had turned to acknowledge—

And vomited all over the jumpmaster and the next Marine out.

Shocked, Houston had stood there on wobbly legs while Marines down the stick either laughed or groaned.

"What're you waiting for, Private?" the jumpmaster had barked, wiping breakfast goo from his face. "Go! Go! Go!"

And he did. And somehow, that Friday, Houston earned his wings.

About a week later, he met up with the jumpmaster on a weekend of R&R, and after a particularly aggressive night of bar hopping during which the jumpmaster had been suspiciously friendly and consumed over a dozen shots, the man slapped an arm around Houston's shoulders, leaned close, and took his revenge.

Houston liked to tell that story to rookies who were worried about their first jumps. If he could earn his wings after an episode like that, then there was hope for those poor bastards.

"Dogma Three, this is Dogma Two, over."

That was Doc calling, using one of the tactical radio's privacy codes so the rest of the team couldn't hear them. *What does he want?* "Dogma Two, this is Three, over."

"What's your altimeter reading, over?"

"Nearing five thousand feet, over."

"Roger that. Thirty-five hundred is your mark, over."

Houston rolled his eyes. "Affirmative, Two. That's one number I don't forget, over."

"Just checking," Doc said firmly. "This is Dogma Two, out."

While part of Houston appreciated Doc's concern, the other part got defensive. His teammates weren't sure that he could put his father's death behind him. He wanted their trust, not their doubts. Hadn't he already proven himself—especially back in Pakistan? He had turned mistakes into successes. And when his actions really counted, he had not failed the team. Well, getting stabbed wasn't exactly the best thing that could have happened, but the distraction had bought the others enough time to pursue Mohammed al-Zumar. You just had to examine the larger picture. Sure, he was going through a rough time, but you didn't need to remind him of that by continually asking, "Are you all right?" Asking just made it worse.

Damn. He had failed to check his altimeter!

Reaching 3,492 feet and rolling down. Bracing himself, he reached up and gave a solid tug on the ripcord.

Doc Leblanc rocketed up through the air as his MC-5 parachute *whooshed* open. All seven cells of the light blue-gray nylon eclipsed the night. Now his training in canopy control would come into play. He had never been a maneuvering genius, especially during his lessons on the suspended parachute harness. He didn't particularly like being hung from a contraption of bars and ropes and then asked to perform turns as well as adjust his landing attitude and consider interference from trees, wires, and water, not to mention twists, collisions, and entanglement. And just when he had thought his instructors were done abusing him, they had strapped him into the virtual reality parachute trainer, where he had learned just how sloppy his two-riser and one-riser slips actually were. Eventually, Doc's sense of competition had motivated him to clean up his act. He had not graduated the best in his class, but his scores had put him in the top five. Not bad for a swab jockey fighting for respect among jarheads.

Breathing steadily and reacting to the driving wind, he maneuvered himself down toward a winding river, dark as black lacquer and dividing thin stands of trees. He considered what would happen once he was on the ground, and a thousand bad thoughts lined up, each one

waiting its turn to unnerve him. Had the NKA infantry
spotted him? Would they surround him the second he
hit the ground? If so, would they torture him? Ask for
ransom? Use him as a shield or a scapegoat? Would his
wife watch grainy video of him on *Wolf News*?

Doc closed his eyes for a moment and reached with
his thoughts to a man who could calm him.

Grandfather, you are still there on the island, shouting,
"Cric, crac!" to begin your tales, and healing the people
of our old village. If you could see me now, Grandfather,
you would know that although Martinique is so far away,
you're with me now. I'm going to tell you a story about a
little boy who watched his grandfather practice medi-
cine, who watched his grandfather make people happy.
You would be proud of this boy, Grandfather. Very proud.

Sergeant Anthony Bruno knew the Parachute Landing
Fall inside and out, had practiced it countless times,
could do it in his sleep or even sleep deprived, sick,
hung over, and without legs. As far as he was concerned, it was a no-brainer:

You roll your wrists, keep your elbows perpendicular
to the ground, and when the balls of your feet touch,
you execute. Don't forget to keep your chin on your
chest and your neck tense, then you move your body to
form an arc as the fall continues in the direction of the
drift. Then, it's time for a twisting-bending motion, beginning in the hips, to push the knees around, exposing
the calf and thigh as the legs give with the impact.

Easier to perform than describe, the maneuver was
designed to absorb the kinetic energy of the fall, and
Bruno wondered why they didn't cut to the chase and

tell you to fall on your side, which was basically what you did.

Figuring he had about two minutes until he executed the highly technical Fall On Your Side maneuver, Bruno glanced up at his canopy. The nylon was rustling so loudly that he heard it inside his helmet. Shit. He had never dropped in such windy conditions, and the damned rain had come on out of nowhere.

A gust struck. He struggled for control, swung several times like a pendulum, then began spiraling down like a plastic action figure strapped to a lunch bag parachute.

Welcome to North Korea, you mother . . .

Missing a heartbeat somewhere in there, he worked himself out of the spiral, realized he was falling way too fast toward a dense canopy of, presumably, pine trees, with a fairly broad clearing lying to their right.

He held his breath. Time for a turn.

Even as he applied pressure, the wind hammered him back, kicked him into another spiral, and for the first time in a very long time, Sgt. Anthony Bruno was scared.

TEAM DOGMA
ON THE GROUND
SOMEWHERE SOUTHWEST OF QUADRANT H-97
NORTH KOREA
0004 HOURS LOCAL TIME

Rainey ticked off the seconds until impact, then braced himself and anticipated the shock of hitting the ground.

No shock.

His boots connected with something spongy that the rain-slick oxygen mask made impossible to see. He turned, struggled to execute the landing, realized with a groan that he was falling into a sizable mud puddle or a muddy pond. He kicked up waves as though he had cannonballed in, then, just when he had thought the landing was over, a tremendous gust ripped into his canopy, the force dragging him through the mud. The heavy kit bag strapped to his chest rolled, pulling him over enough so that he could get his footing and detach his rigging.

With the chute free, he took a deep breath and keyed his mike. "Dogma One is down, over."

"Dogma Three is down," Houston reported.

Vance and Doc added their voices to the channel. Four of five team members were safely on the ground, but once again, Bruno wasn't talking. To hell with him for now.

With a sense of urgency so strong that only a grenade or a bullet would stop him, Rainey rose, kept hunched over, and worked frantically to remove his mask, helmet, kit bag, and chute pack. Then he began gathering the chute's rigging. Visibility was less than a hundred feet in the rain. Maybe that evened the playing field. He wouldn't be there long enough to find out. As he tugged in the chute, the heat and humidity were already getting to him. What was it? Eighty degrees at night?

Once he had the MC-5 gathered into a ball, he set it down, then stripped off his gloves and Gore-Tex jumpsuit, feeling the warm wind rush up through his dark green camouflage utilities. That done, he emptied his kit bag, removing his M4A1 carbine with attached grenade launcher, Amphibious Assault Vest, and rucksack. He stuffed the suit, parachute, helmet, and chute pack into the kit bag, then donned his vest and ruck, and shouldered his rifle.

One thing left to do now. The kit bag was filled with nearly seventy pounds of equipment he wouldn't need for the rest of the mission. Rainey drove the bag down into the puddle, sank it to nearly a meter, then, seeing that it wouldn't float, he slogged several steps up to firmer ground. Tugging on his bush cover, he took off running toward three pine trees rising near a slope about thirty yards off.

As he charged through the rain, he cleared his mind, thought only of the task at hand. Run. Don't slip. Get to cover.

He rounded the trees, paused to catch his breath, and wiped rain from his eyes. He slipped on his headset and positioned the boom mike before his lips. "Dogma Team, sound off and report your GPS coordinates, over." Even as Rainey made the request, he flipped off the protective covering on the GPS unit strapped to his wrist and activated the device.

"Dogma One, this is Two," said Doc. "Can't get a clean GPS signal. Could be weather or terrain interference, over."

Rainey consulted his own panel and confirmed the bad news, though he suspected that the interference would only be temporary. "Two, report landmarks, over."

"I'm on the south side of a river. There's an old dock here. Looks abandoned. Looks like there's some pretty good cover here, over."

"Roger that, Two." Rainey squinted beyond several more stands of trees where a sheet of darkness bubbled with rain. "I believe I see your river. Hold your position, over."

"Copy that. Holding here. Two, out."

"Dogma One, this is Three," called Houston. "I not only see the river, I'm in it. Set down in about three feet of water, over."

"Copy that, Three. Dogma Four, report?"

"One, this is Four," began Vance. "Be advised I am on the south side of Two's river. Believe I am about one hundred yards north of his dock, over."

"Roger that, Four. Stand by."

"Standing by, over."

Rainey took a deep breath, and his tone grew harder. "Dogma Five, report?"

The wind howled. The rain hissed. And Rainey leaned in closer to the trees, waiting. Waiting.

Repeating his call, Rainey closed his eyes, swore. *Stop playing this ridiculous game, Bruno. Stop it right now!*

No reply. No Bruno. "Dogma Team, has anyone heard from Dogma Five, over?"

Doc, Houston, and Vance answered in order. Again, no Bruno. Were he in trouble—and his GPS working—he could have transmitted his location by keying his mike. But Rainey doubted the man was in trouble; he was up to something, and Rainey had neither the time nor the desire to stoop to that man's unprofessional level. No one gets left behind? In Bruno's case, Rainey might make an exception.

Damn, he could never do that. But the team had to keep moving, keep communicating—

A tiny flash of light shone to the north and demanded Rainey's attention. He reached into a vest pocket, pulled out his Nightstar binoculars, used their night vision capability to scan the horizon. More flashes erupted, and Rainey realized he was staring at the distant crash site of their C-130. Infantry forces would rally on that site, and you had to assume that reconnaissance teams would be dispatched to search for and capture survivors.

All right. Game time. And the clock was ticking. He had to gather the team and have Houston see if any other platoon members had survived and could be reached on the radio. The lance corporal also needed to get Major Thorpe on the line. Presumably, the major was already aware that they'd been shot down, but Rainey needed to report their status and position, which was—

He banged the GPS. Signal error messages. So be it. Rainey had learned to depend upon courage and intestinal fortitude instead of technology concocted by cubicle-bound computer geeks. He would figure out their location with or without the gadgetry—which, as always, was only as good as the operator.

"Dogma Five, this is Dogma One," he called, figuring he'd give Bruno one last shot. "How 'bout a sitrep, over."

Rainey ground his teeth through the silence. *You'd better be hurt. Because if you're not . . .*

He shook off his anger and cleared his throat. "Dogma Team? Rally on that dock near Two's position. I'll meet you there. This is Dogma One, out."

* * *

Houston finished submerging his kit bag in the river, then he trudged off down the shoreline, toward the dock he had spied through his Nightstars. He hadn't had time for a full equipment check, but the 117 Foxtrot looked dry and functional, considering that he had done a good job of babying the long-range radio. He had made a perfect Parachute Landing Fall in water, had come up, and had prepared himself to move out in what had to be record time for him, though he hadn't checked his watch.

Lance Corporal Bradley Houston was out to prove that he didn't need grief counselors or shrinks or "time to talk" or exaggerated concern from his fellow opera-tors. He only needed room to breathe. To get on with his life. To make it down the goddamned shoreline and reach the others without anyone thinking he might have an emotional breakdown along the way. As far as he was concerned, he had only one job now: kill. He would kill the enemy to complete the mission and get back home. And he would kill any thoughts of Dad that might cloud his focus.

Sure, the enemy he could handle. But those thoughts of his father? Damn. While Houston's dad had not been the world's greatest caregiver, he had had his mo-ments. And deep down Houston had always believed that someday they would become a real father and a real son.

But time had run out.

And no matter how fast Houston ran along the shore-line, he could not escape that fact—

Or the overhanging tree limb that blocked his path.

The barrel of his carbine struck it, then drove down, striking him in the shoulder and knocking him flat onto his ass. He cursed the limb. Cursed himself. Got back on the horse. Kept on.

"Dogma Two, I'm approaching your position from the north, moving in along the shoreline," Vance told Doc. Translation: *Don't shoot me, Doc. I'm one of the good guys.*

If their tactical radios had gone down, Vance could have used one of three different signal devices that emitted insectlike calls. Everyone on the team was familiar with those sounds, and the trick itself was nothing new to reconnaissance operations. Some teams even used whistles or gunfire, especially after their cover had been blown, but Rainey wasn't fond of the latter techniques no matter what the situation. When asked why, he just made a face.

"Vance!" Doc stage-whispered as he rose slightly from behind a row of shrubs about five yards away from the riverbank.

Vance picked his way carefully toward the shrubs, kicked through them, then hunkered down beside Doc and whispered, "So, Doc. How do you like North Korea so far?"

Doc smiled lamely. "What's not to like?"

Vance shook his head gravely. "We're just lucky to be alive. You get a GPS signal?"

"Not yet."

"Anything from Bruno?"

"Squat."

"What's he pulling?"

Doc shrugged. "He wouldn't pull anything. Not behind enemy lines. Maybe he dropped hard, got knocked out. Who knows?"

"What if you're wrong? What if he—"

"Look, I don't like the guy. But don't go there. He's a Marine. He gets the benefit of the doubt."

"Sounds funny coming out of you."

"Because I'm not a Marine?"

"Because you were going to kick his ass back in Seoul."

Doc winked. "Yes, I was."

Vance grinned, then, hearing footfalls nearby, took up his Nightstars and spotted Houston hustling toward them. "Here comes Mr. Phone Home."

"How is he to you?" Doc asked.

"What do you mean?"

"You know."

"Okay, so he's a little off, but he'll be all right."

"Dogma Three, this is Two," Doc said. "Turn left, head approximately five yards up shore and keep coming. We're right behind the shrubs, over."

"Copy, Two. Dogma Three, out."

Vance watched through the Nightstars as Houston made his turn, slipped a little, but came on hard, rushing along through the mud at a good clip until he reached the shrubs. The radio operator acknowledged them with a nod, squatted, hung his head, and fought for breath.

"Dogma One, this is Two," Doc called. "Three and Four have arrived my position. No word from Dogma Five. Awaiting your arrival, over."

"Roger that," Rainey replied. "En route to your position. Dogma Three, see if you can contact anyone from Reaper and Voodoo, over."

"Dogma One, this is Three. Will attempt to make contact, roger, out," Houston said.

Vance just happened to glance down at his GPS screen. The device registered their position. "Doc?" He tapped his GPS to indicate the news.

The corpsman took note of the numbers on his own screen, then tapped several keys, bringing up the pre-loaded maps. He worked his thumb as though he were playing a computer game, then narrowed his gaze as he read something.

In the meantime, Houston spoke tersely but softly into the microphone of his 117 Foxtrot. "Voodoo Three, this is Dogma Three. Request sitrep, over."

Had the curse of Force Five Recon claimed another victim?

Rainey had not wanted to believe that there was a curse, but losing three replacements in a row gave you pause. Sergeant Anthony Bruno would not take his insubordination this far. And as Rainey charged toward the river, hearing what might be a truck engine in the distance, he at once hated Bruno and felt entirely responsible for the man. Personal differences had to be set aside. A member of Rainey's team had failed to check in and was somewhere out there. Rainey needed to know what had happened. But first things first.

He slowed as he reached the top of a small hill, then sidestepped down it, drawing closer to the river. The rain began coming down in sheets, and Rainey hit a patch of mud, lost his footing, dropped to a knee, then recovered. The last thing he needed was a broken ankle.

Taking a deep breath, he sidled his way down, past several trees, coming to within ten yards of the shoreline. There was the dock, about forty yards to his left. He started for it. Heard that vehicle getting a little closer. Picked up the pace.

"Dogma Two, this is One. I'm coming in from the south. Almost your position, over," he told Doc.

"One this is Two, roger that. Standing by, over."

"I'm hearing a vehicle behind me. Somebody get eyes on."

"Eyes on," Vance echoed, responding quickly to the order.

"What do you have, Four?"

"Searching. Okay. Pickup truck. Old pickup truck. One driver. Looks like a civilian. He's turning. Heading away from our location, over."

As Vance finished his report, Rainey reached the row of shrubs and dropped down to join his men. "All right, Boy Scouts," he said between breaths. "We've got a lost camper."

"Were that our only problem," Doc said. "GPS is working. Got our coordinates."

"Well, I know we're not in Kansas anymore, Toto. Are we still in North Korea?"

"We're about 38 kilometers southwest of the drop zone."

"Say again?"

"We dropped 38 kilometers short of the target."

Rainey smiled crookedly. "So we're only halfway there."

"A little less than halfway."

There it was: math according to Murphy and his laws. They had supplies enough for two days, which they were supposed to use for the 68-kilometer hump from the target site to the extraction point. Now it would take them nearly a full day to get to the original target. If they arrived there without incident (a huge assumption) and were able to take out their designated radar system, then they would still have 68 kilometers to cover and only one day's worth of supplies to do it with. In truth, the supplies didn't worry Rainey as much as adding those 38 kilometers.

He turned to Houston. "Any word from Voodoo or Reaper?"

The lance corporal shook his head. "Sergeant, to be honest, that's just wishful thinking. We both know there wasn't time. Those guys are gone."

"I thought I saw someone. Maybe I was wrong. Get Major Thorpe on the line."

Houston nodded, then shifted away and lifted the mike.

"Show's over, huh?" Doc said.

Rainey rubbed the corners of his eyes. "Frustrating. Damned frustrating. Come in here to make a difference. And all we get is a swift kick in the ass."

"We're too far off the mark," Doc said. "Not our fault. You know what Thorpe's going to say."

"Maybe he'll surprise us."

"After losing two thirds of the platoon? I doubt it.

And worse? This place is still too hot for a helo. We'll still have to hump it to the beach."

"Sergeant?" Houston called. "I have Major Thorpe."

Groaning through an exhale, Rainey took up the microphone. "Bright Star, this is Dogma One, over."

"Dogma One, this is Bright Star. Request sitrep, over."

"Bright Star, be advised we have four of five operators accounted for. We have received no communication from Dogma Five or other operators from Teams Voodoo and Reaper, over."

"Roger, One. Be advised we have received and analyzed your GPS coordinates. Understand you are thirty-eight-point-six-two-five kilometers southwest of designated drop zone, over."

"Affirmative, Bright Star. Your orders, over?"

As Rainey waited, he glanced at Doc, Vance, and Houston—three waterlogged warriors who deserved much more than to be screwed out of their mission and sent home. But it wasn't up to Rainey, and the inevitable sounded in the mike's receiver:

"Dogma One, helo extraction impossible at this time. You are ordered to rally due north of Extraction Point Scorpion to new extraction point coordinates. Transmitting now. Be advised that extraction window will be open for as long as possible but could close at any time. Tango Host will advise you once you near coordinates. Report in hourly or as needed, over."

"Bright Star, copy your transmission. Will rally on new coordinates for Extraction Point Scorpion. Request permission to sweep for Dogma Five before we rally, over."

"Dogma One, engage in a narrow sweep, following which you fall back immediately to the new extraction point, over."

"Understood, Bright Star. Narrow sweep, then fall back. This is Dogma One, out." Rainey tried to hide his gloom, but it wasn't easy. "You heard me, gentlemen. Narrow sweep. Then we're getting the hell out of here."

04

Master Sergeant Kwan Yong Sung held his AK-47 close to his chest as he chased the young woman. She darted left along a crumbling wall of the old machine shop, heading toward the alley beyond. The other four members of Sung's reconnaissance team had already apprehended two of the dissidents, and it was up to team leader Sung to bring in the last. Intent on showing his men how to operate efficiently, Sung poured everything he had into his legs, narrowing the gap between himself and the woman to just two meters as they reached the alley.

Splashing barefoot through the mud, the woman screamed something at him, perhaps a plea for mercy, Sung was not sure. As she attempted to veer around a broad puddle, she slipped and fell like a wounded doe, arms flailing as she tried to brace herself.

In exactly four heartbeats Sung was on her, jabbing the muzzle of his rifle against her head. The adrenaline coursed so violently through his veins that it was all he could do not to shoot her right there. *"Son-du-ro!"*

She raised her hands as ordered, then she glanced at him, her face mottled brown with dirt, her eyes burning with a familiar hatred. She was not the first member of the South Korean underground that Sung had arrested. She would not be the last.

Sung lifted his rifle, gesturing for her to stand. *"Ee-ro-na!"*

Slowly, she pulled herself to her feet and glowered at him. "One day you will understand why we do this."

He snorted. "You provide intelligence to the enemy and help others escape to the South. You do this because you are a traitor. And that is all I need to know." Sung turned his gaze ahead. *"Oom-jeek-yo-ra!"*

The woman padded resignedly back up the alley.

At last the pursuit was over, and Sung was as exhausted as he was soaked. His field uniform clung heavily, and he removed his cap to let the rain mingle with his sweat. He longed to be twenty again, a fresh recruit with knees that did not buckle after a run. Twenty, yes. No more sighing over the gray encroaching upon his crewcut. No more pains in his lower back. Two decades of service with the North Korean Army had taken their toll. But he was not an old man. Not yet.

Thunder boomed loudly overhead, and the foolish woman thought she could exploit the diversion and sprint away.

Sung stopped. Lifted his rifle. Took aim.

And shot her in the left calf.

Now they would have a bleeder on their hands. He should have bound her wrists and ankles and thrown her over his shoulder, but he had been too tired for that. Why had she made a simple arrest so difficult?

Because she hated him. He represented the government, and she hated the Central People's Committee in Pyongyang more than anything. She would raise a fist at them, even as they ordered men like Sung to shoot her. She had been corrupted by those in the South, led to believe that the people of her own country were prisoners.

Sergeant Choi, a round-faced man of twenty-five whose lack of ambition and common sense continually troubled Sung, kept close to the machine shop's wall as he rushed over. "*Sangsa?* Are you all right?"

"What do you think?" Sung snapped. "Pick her up."

Choi shouldered his rifle and went to the woman, who whimpered as she clutched her bleeding leg. Choi circled, deciding how he might lift her.

"*Lyongjang!*" Sung cried, calling Choi by rank. "Pick her up!"

"Yes, Sangsa. Right away!"

As Choi recklessly grabbed the woman, she pummeled him in the head with her free hand. If Sung had not been so angry over Choi's ineptitude, he would have laughed.

Instead, he withdrew the portable radio from his belt. "Sambyong Moon? This is Sangsa Sung. Come to the other side of the machine shop. Now!"

"Yes, Sangsa," came the corporal's voice.

Within a few seconds the rail-thin man was beside Choi and needing no further orders. Corporal Moon saw the problem and immediately assisted Choi, grabbing the woman by her ankles while Choi slid his arms beneath her armpits. They hurried off with the prisoner, and Sung fell in behind them, sensing with a shiver that it was going to be a very long night.

Moments later they met up with the others back at the truck, an old Russian-designed UAZ-469 with a boxy nose and room for only a half dozen troops. Lance Corporal Park, the shortest member of the team but the man with the loudest voice when it came to lodging complaints, had already cuffed the two male prisoners and had placed them in the UAZ's backseat, as he had been ordered.

"Good work, Ilb-yong," Sung told the man.

"Thank you, Sangsa. But there is no room to carry all of us back to the company. We're not going to walk, are we, Sangsa?"

"Not us, Ilb-yong. Only you."

The man's mouth fell open. "Sangsa?"

Sung stepped away to hide his grin. He watched as Choi and Moon shoved the bleeding woman into the UAZ, while Private Lee, a soldier with an old scar from a horrible burn on his left cheek that he would not discuss, attempted to wrap a gauze bandage around the woman's gunshot wound—even as she tried to kick him away. With three prisoners in the backseat, Park's assessment regarding room in the truck was correct. But the man had assumed that each member of the team needed his own seat and was unwilling to stand on the tailgate and clutch the truck's soft top—which was exactly what he would order Moon, Park, and Lee to do.

But first Sung needed to contact the lieutenant colonel and report the good news. He was about to turn back to Park, who served as the team's radio operator, when the lance corporal approached, proffering the microphone. "The *chung-yong* calls for you."

Sung tingled over the coincidence. "This is Red Star One, over."

"Red Star One, this is Mountain Ghost. We have new orders for you, over."

"I understand, Mountain Ghost. We have located and arrested the three dissidents, over."

"Understood, Red Star One, but a C-130 transport was just shot down, and there is a small American or UN Special Operations force on the ground in your sector, over."

An American force? Maybe even a Marine Corps force? Sung kept a white-knuckled grip on the microphone. Sung's grandfather had fought alongside the Chinese during the Korean War. According to a family friend who had been there, Grandfather had been killed by American Marines at the Chosin Reservoir. Sung kept a letter written by his grandfather in his breast pocket. The letter detailed his grandfather's experiences fighting against the Marines. The story and letter had been passed down to Sung's father, who, before he had died of lung cancer, had shared them with Sung. Since then, Sung had developed a bitter hatred for the Americans, and he had believed that he would never get an opportunity to avenge his grandfather's death.

But at the moment, a possibility presented itself.

The lieutenant colonel continued: "Red Star One, you will immediately intercept. Capture if you can. Kill if you must. Do you understand, over?"

"Understood. But what about our prisoners, over?"

In a chilling tone, the lieutenant colonel replied, "I leave that to you. Mountain Ghost, out."

Sung lowered the microphone and distractedly returned it to Lance Corporal Park, who glanced quizzically at him. "What is it, Sangsa?"

Ignoring the question, Sung lifted his voice. "Choi? Moon? Remove the prisoners from the truck."

Despite their looks of confusion, Sung's men did not hesitate. Within a minute the dissidents were sitting in the mud, rain washing steadily over them. Judging from their chattering teeth and the tears welling in their eyes, the prisoners already knew what was going to happen.

On the other hand, Choi had eyes for neither the subtle nor the obvious. His frowned deepened. "What now, Sangsa?"

Sung pulled the 9mm Makarov from its holster at his waist. He stepped up to the prisoners, loomed over them, worked the safety on his compact pistol, then extended his arm, taking aim at the first man's head.

"*So-jee-ma! So-jee-ma!*" the woman screamed.

The shot echoed off into the rain, and the traitor fell onto his gut, his head bloody but being washed clean by the storm.

Sung moved to the next man, who was already crying. "*Mom-cho-ee!*"

The woman wanted him to stop, and her defiance set

off Sung's rage. He swung the pistol on her, jammed down the trigger before she could utter another word.

Before she hit the mud, dead, Sung was already taking aim at the crying man. Wearing a grimace, Sung executed the final prisoner.

Then he glanced away, stood there, breathing, his arm still extended until he remembered to lower it. He craned his head slowly toward Lance Corporal Park. "We have room in the truck for you now."

"Sangsa," Park gasped.

"There is a Special Operations force on the ground in our sector. We are going to intercept them. Into the truck!"

Sung had never seen his men move so quickly. He tucked the hot pistol back into its holster and climbed into the front passenger's seat as Choi fired up the engine.

As they drove off, Sung pictured the next morning at the machine shop. The rain had tapered off, and an old woman, one of the local farmers, covered her mouth as she stared at the bodies. Behind her, friends of the dead traitors would arrive and begin sobbing. Inspired by fear, they would abandon their operations for the underground. They would come to their senses. They would learn to love the government.

Sung chuckled bitterly. They would do nothing of the sort. The bodies would only strengthen their resolve.

As they did his.

Lance Corporal Jung Yung Kim had bailed out of the C-130 all of three seconds before the missile had impacted. The blast had kicked him into a wild roll that had taken him nearly a minute to correct. During that time he had almost lost consciousness . . .

And the rest remained a blur.

He did not remember popping his chute or landing or even getting out of his gear and stashing his kit bag. His movements had been mechanical, a going through the motions brought on, perhaps, by the horror of it all, the echoing thunder of the explosion, the flaming bodies tumbling away from the plane, the terrifying nearness of death.

He walked in the rain, still dazed, still feeling as though he was dreaming the landscape and that at any moment his parents would come to him, rush him back into the rickety house, and hide him from the soldiers. He froze. Swung his carbine around, saw only the blurry silhouettes of trees quivering in the strong gusts. At least the rain was warm, unlike those cool rains of winter that he remembered as a child. Even the earthy smell of the place brought it all back. He was under the bed now, listening to that one soldier's harsh voice, listening to his father yell at the man, listening to his mother screaming as a loud bang struck so near that Kim curled into a ball and held his breath. A second bang silenced his mother. And the soldier with the harsh voice said something about the underground, something about spies.

Kim shook his head, trying to clear memories like cobwebs so tightly intertwined that they would never go away. He blinked hard. Turned again. Waved his rifle, wanted to gun down that soldier who had killed his parents.

But there is no soldier. Not in this place, at this time. Where are you now? Think!

Kim's disorientation began to fade, as though it were being washed clean by the rain. He realized he was walking tall, out in the open, and suddenly hunched over and scrambled toward the nearest tree. There, he kept low, kept his breathing steady and tried to organize his thoughts.

You are home. No, not home. The old home. The home you wanted to forget. Did you believe coming here would be easy?

Reality was a diamond bullet that struck him in the forehead. He was the only surviving member of his team. He had watched the others from Team Dogma jump. They were on the ground, somewhere. He had to contact them.

Kim was about to don his headset when the wind kicked up and a creaking sound drove his attention to the nearest stand of trees, about two meters back.

A Marine in a Gore-Tex jumpsuit, his helmet still on, his rigging and canopy twisted and tangled in the limbs, swung like a black pendulum in the breeze. The guy's arms hung limply, his head tilted unnaturally to one side.

After a quick examination of the perimeter, Kim charged back to the Marine. The guy dangled about three meters from the ground, out of Kim's grasp. "Can you hear me?"

The Marine was obviously unconscious. Or worse.

Kim tore off his ruck and stashed it and his rifle behind some shrubs near the tree. Placing his big K-bar between his teeth, he mounted the old, wet oak, reached the first major limb, then pulled himself up to the next. He would have to edge his way out onto that slick limb, lean over, and begin cutting the man's rigging.

But a better plan took hold. All he had to do was reach the man's rigging, use it to climb down to the Marine, and detach from there, without making a cut. Of course, both of them would drop like cluster bombs to the ground. The mud would ease some of the impact, but ankles could be sprained or broken.

A distant gunshot rendered Kim inert. He listened hard, heard another shot. Then a third one. The shots had come from the south, where, Kim knew, a machine shop and some other manufacturing facilities were located. Had the team rallied there? Were they taking fire?

With a reckless abandon inspired by those rounds, Kim shoved himself along the limb, even as it suddenly swooped, kicking him face-forward into the man's rigging. He flipped over, nearly lost his grip, was about to plummet when he reached out, snatched a piece of nylon with his right hand. He caught another line with his left as the knife slipped from his teeth. For a second he watched the blade fall to the mud, and a mere three meters suddenly became three thousand.

Measuring his movements, Kim lowered himself along the rigging, reaching the Marine after just a handful of seconds. "Hello there, buddy. I am going to get you down."

Swallowing hard, Kim checked the Marine's wrist for a pulse, couldn't find one. Then he slid his hand up, under the guy's helmet and placed his hand on the Marine's neck, trying to get a carotid pulse. Nothing there. And worse, the guy's neck crunched a little as Kim accidentally shifted his head. *Broken neck? Maybe. Dead? Probably.*

But Kim had learned back in the American schools that no Marine gets left behind. So, holding his breath, he detached the man's rigging, and the two of them dropped.

Kim hit the ground first, his boots finding no traction in the mud. He fell back—just as the Marine fell on top of him. Repulsed, Kim pushed the guy off, then rolled over and removed the Marine's helmet. Yes, the man was on Team Dogma, and he did not get along very well with the team leader. That much Kim had noticed. But Kim did not remember the Marine's name. He tried listening for breathing, but the wind and rain made that difficult. He began basic CPR, chest compressions followed by breaths, but he already feared the worst.

After a few minutes of trying, an exhausted Kim paused, glanced around. What now? Did he have time to climb back up the tree and remove the Marine's chute and rigging? And what about the Marine? The guy was dead. Was Kim supposed to carry him? Lance Corporal Jung Yung Kim was at a complete loss.

But maybe help was only a radio call away. He put

on his headset, plugged it into his tactical radio, keyed the mike. "This is Voodoo Five to any operators this channel, over. Repeat, this is Voodoo Five to any operators this channel, over."

No one replied. Was he out of range? No, he could not have drifted that far.

A ridiculous thought struck him. Had he turned on the radio? He glanced down to his waist. *Fool!* He could blame the oversight on nerves, but you were not supposed to be nervous in the field. Then again, you were not supposed to be pulling dead Marines down from trees, either. "This is Voodoo Five to any operators this channel, over."

"Voodoo Five, this is Dogma Three, wait, over."

"Roger that," Kim said, trying to temper his excitement. "Waiting for you, Dogma Three, over."

Only then did Kim remember that he, an outsider, a "foreigner" who had not been warmly welcomed by his teammates, was now the bearer of bad news. Very bad news.

05

Houston and Vance had taken the southern route along the river. Vance had been making a serious attempt to locate Sergeant Bruno, but Houston was too preoccupied by thoughts of an ambush to focus on the search. The farther they separated themselves from the others, the more edgy Houston had become. He imagined snipers behind every tree, all of them dressed in North Korean uniforms, but all of them bearing a strong resemblance to his father. No, they didn't just look like his father. They *were* his father. Houston had begun to swear aloud at the phantoms, and Vance turned back to shush him.

Thank God that call had come in from Voodoo Five, whose voice sounded familiar and diverted Houston's attention back to the here and now. The job.

"Dogma One, this is Dogma Three, over," Houston called Rainey.

"Three, this is One."

"I have Voodoo Five on the inter-team channel, over."

"Roger that, Three. Switching channel. Wait, over."

Houston nudged Vance, who was sweeping the shoreline with his Nightstars.

"What?"

"Switch to inter-team. You can hear what's going on."

"Fill me in. I think we might have something going on out there. Way out there. Truck heading this way. No headlights. Looks like NKA scouts or recon."

"Well, don't lose them."

"Then don't bother me."

Houston widened his gaze. "I won't." He placed a hand to his earpiece, listened intently to the voices coming through:

"Roger that, Dogma One. I am approximately eight hundred meters northeast your location, over."

"Roger that, Voodoo Five. Suggest you rally now my location, over."

"Negative, One. Suggest you rally my location. I have located one casualty, over."

"Voodoo Five, wait, over. Dogma Team? Rally now on Voodoo Five's GPS coordinates." Rainey fed them the numbers.

"Dogma One, this is Dogma Four, over," Vance called.

"Four, this is One, over."

"Be advised I have spotted a truck en route our position, ETA approximately five minutes. Believe NKA Army recon personnel are onboard, over."

"Understood, Dogma Four. Rally on Voodoo Five's location. We'll fall back from there, out."

Vance's expression turned grave. "This is not good."

"Why?" Houston asked.

"If we rally on Voodoo Five, we'll be heading toward that truck, not away from it."

Houston shrugged. "What do you want to do?"

Vance pushed off his haunches. "Follow orders. Come on." The sniper stole his way to the next cluster of trees and vanished behind a hogback before Houston could catch up.

Maybe I'm going to die here. Maybe I'm going to prove my father right. I'll get shot and bleed to death in the mud. And for what? There's no more mission. There's no more anything. And the guy leading us is second-guessing himself.

A piece of rubber or a fallen limb lay in the path ahead. As Houston approached, the "limb" slithered off into the brush. With a shudder, Houston scrambled up, then down across the hogback, finally catching sight of Vance as the sniper contacted Voodoo Five and reported their approach.

Two slopes and one shallow creek later, Houston and Vance found Lance Cpl. Jung Yung Kim peering out from behind some trees, with Sgt. Anthony Bruno lying beside him.

"Oh, shit," Vance moaned. "He's dead?"

"I think he broke his neck," Kim said.

"It's the fucking curse, man," said Houston, his voice

shaky. "Fucking curse. He even talked about it himself. I don't believe this shit anymore. I just can't believe it."

"Shut up, man," Vance ordered, his brows narrowed. "Just calm down."

Why Houston had vented his fear was beyond him. He rarely did that. What the hell was wrong with him? He had to get it together. Immediately. Pronto. Now. *I am a Marine* . . .

"Tell the others we're here," Vance snapped.

Houston looked at the corporal. "What?"

"TELL THE OTHERS WE'RE HERE!"

Houston jolted. "Yeah, right. I'm on it."

After shaking his head in bewilderment or maybe even disappointment, Vance jogged over to a pair of shrubs and began working his Nightstars.

"Dogma One, Dogmas Three and Four have reached Voodoo Five's position, over."

"Roger that, Three," said Rainey. "Two and I are approaching those coordinates. Stand by for our arrival, out."

Clutching his rifle, Houston waited impatiently for Rainey and Doc to get there, and when they approached, he swung his rifle on them, trembled a moment, then raised the barrel.

Doc went immediately to Bruno, while Rainey held back and stared at the body. Houston searched for some hint of satisfaction or even pleasure in the sergeant's expression, but as usual, Rainey's eyes held steady, his chin jutting out like a piece of marble.

Houston came up beside the man. "Looks like he snapped his neck in the trees."

"At least it was an accident," Rainey muttered. "For a

while there, I thought maybe, just maybe, he didn't pull his ripcord."

"Commit suicide? Why?"

"By the time you're our age, you'll understand." Rainey turned, leaned over, and hustled off. "Vance? Talk to me."

While Rainey and the sniper conversed, Houston went over to Kim, who was rapidly transferring some of Bruno's supplies to his rucksack. "Hey, man. I'll hump some of that."

"Thank you. And maybe now I am member of Team Dogma."

"Well, you got the right number: Voodoo Five, but I'm not sure you want the slot. Tends to be unlucky." Houston tipped his head at Bruno. "He's the fourth guy we've lost."

"But for me, maybe number five is lucky. I am the only one from my team to survive."

"Yeah, you are. Keep thinking that. Keep thinking that hard." Houston pulled some of Bruno's MREs from the guy's ruck and tucked them into his own pack as Vance and Rainey came charging back.

"Hey, Sergeant, you want us to try getting that canopy and rigging down?" Doc asked, craning his neck way up to the limbs.

"Forget it. They already know we're here."

Doc pursed his lips, looked to Bruno. "What do we do with him?"

The question stung Rainey, stung him hard because no one gets left behind. The injured? The dead? They all come back—

Even complete assholes like Bruno.

But the team's safety came first. They couldn't haul Bruno's body back to the beach. Doing so would slow them down and put the entire team at risk. The decision should be easy for Rainey and easy for his men to appreciate.

So why was it so hard?

Because everyone in Fifth Force knew that there was no love lost between Mac Rainey and Anthony Bruno. Some would say that Rainey had probably tampered with Bruno's chute or that the decision to leave Bruno's body behind was easy since he hated the man anyway. Had the event occurred during a training exercise, the JAG lawyers would have been all over it, and Rainey would've been squinting in the spotlight. Wasn't it convenient that Bruno had died dropping into enemy territory? Wasn't it oh-so convenient? Mac Rainey could not have planned it any better.

He exhaled loudly and glowered at the late Sergeant Bruno. *Shit, even in death you're still screwing me over, huh, Bruno? You're a piece of work.* Then Rainey lifted his head, let his gaze reach each of his men. "Marines? We have a long hump ahead. We're going down to some of that denser brush along the shoreline. We'll stash Sergeant Bruno there and mark GPS coordinates."

"You don't want to bury him, Sergeant?" Doc asked.

"Not with that recon team breathing down our necks. God willing, when the full scale invasion occurs, the infantry will come in and retrieve him. That's the best we can do now. Understood?"

"Sergeant, I'll carry Bruno out of here, if you want," Doc said. "I'll carry him all the way home."

"Doc, you and Vance just get him to the shoreline. Houston? Get me Bright Star. Kim? Finish policing up Bruno's gear, but leave his kit bag with the pack and the rest. If these bad guys are sharp, they'll figure out we got Bruno down, and they'll assume he's injured."

"Yes, and they will also assume that we are moving slower than we are," Kim concluded.

Rainey nodded. "You sound like a sharp operator, son. And I figure that before morning, you'll get your chance to really prove that." Rainy offered his hand: a welcoming to the team.

"Thank you, Sergeant."

Houston came over and handed Rainey the Foxtrot's mike. Hesitating a moment to pick his words, Rainey finally keyed up and spoke. "Bright Star, this is Dogma One, over."

"Dogma One, this is Bright Star, request sitrep, over."

"Bright Star, we have located Dogma Five, who was KIA. Repeat, Dogma Five now classified KIA. His position will be concealed and GPS coordinates marked, over."

"Understood, Dogma One. Request you transmit GPS coordinates ASAP, over."

"Bright Star, will transmit coordinates ASAP. Dogma One, out."

The storm had, if nothing else, provided the team with enough debris—limbs, leaves, and mud—with which to cover Sgt. Anthony Bruno's body. Had Bruno been wearing dog tags, Doc would have placed them in the man's mouth, but more often than not, Team Dogma operated in the field with no obvious indicators that they were Americans. While Doc and the rest finished stashing Bruno's body, Rainey transmitted the coordinates to Bright Star. With that done, he returned to the group. Doc eyed him and the others. "Does anyone want to say anything?"

Rainey opened his mouth—

But Lance Corporal Kim spoke first. "Listen!"

Doc ducked with the others and focused on every sound he could detect: the wind, the limbs scratching each other, the leaves falling, the rain splattering in mud puddles, and the faint screech of brakes.

Rainey gave Vance the hand signal for him to get eyes-on, somewhere up the slope. The sniper crawled off, keeping low along the shrubs as Rainey pointed to Houston, then Kim, sending them off to sweep left.

"Were you going to say something?" Doc whispered.

The sergeant returned an annoyed look and put a finger to his lips.

He wants me to keep an eye on Houston, Doc thought. *But I'd best keep an eye on both of them.*

For as long as Doc had known Rainey—over five years now—he had never seen the man as sensitive or sarcastic. If Bruno had served as Rainey's conscience, as Rainey's reminder of his own vulnerability, then wasn't his passing a relief for Rainey? It had to be. But the sergeant seemed even more agitated. Sure, Rainey had lost a team member, but there hadn't been a damned thing in the world he could have done. He was not at fault. And Rainey wasn't one to worry about the rumors, was he? No. He was Force Recon. He came, saw, conquered, moved on.

Doc had to believe that. For the sake of his wife and his two sons . . .

"Dogma One, this is Dogma Four," came Vance's voice over the tactical channel. "Count five NKA recon troops. They've exited their truck and are pushing toward Voodoo Five's former coordinates. We can push north from our position, over."

"Understood, Four. Dogma Team rally on the old dock. Execute!"

Rainey was up and out of there before Doc could even rise. Pulling the big Para SAW toward his chest, hoping he would not get the chance to unleash the automatic weapons' hellish fire, Doc got out of Dodge the hard way, by stepping into a knee-deep puddle that nearly sent him flat onto his gut. He pulled his leg out of the sludge with a guttural hiss, then steered himself into Rainey's wake.

North Korean water torture. That's what the rain was to Cpl. Jimmy Vance. It banged on your bush cover. Banged on your shoulders. Got into the lens of your Nightstars, streaked across the scope of your snipers' rifle. Ran down your back. Or was that sweat? That was sweat. You had to love the humidity. You had to love having an NKA recon squad on your ass, which made things interesting. Unfortunately, when it came to Marine Corps operations, the word *interesting* could be interpreted as "highly dangerous and extremely challenging."

Bitching and moaning to himself usually made Vance feel better. But not at the moment. Too many questions remained. What if the team could not reach the extraction point by daybreak? Did Rainey really believe they could move in broad daylight across a bunch of low-lying hills and farmland? Shit, an old man blind in one eye and with cataracts in the other would be able to spot them a kilometer out.

And what about the NKA force on their tail? According to the handbook, they, like any other North Korean soldiers, had been taught that laptops and laser-guided missiles do not decide wars. People who fight a "noble mission" and possess a "revolutionary spirit" will earn victory. That sounded like jingoistic bullshit to Vance, but apparently those guys really believed it to the point that their missions did not account for danger or moral values. It was all about liberating the South and reunifying the country under the current DPRK regime. While they were armed with outmoded equipment, there were a whole lot of them, and they would fight like maniacs to the bitter end. They had never had a "me" generation and weren't as selfish as Americans. In point of fact, they had nothing to lose and nothing else better to do. Which made them scary as hell.

Prior to coming to Korea, Vance had adopted an air of superiority regarding the average North Korean troops. He figured they weren't as well-trained as he was, were stuck with the aforementioned antique weapons, and, well, they just didn't *look* very intimidating—all about the same height, with the same haircut, same uniform. But he kept reminding himself that the guys back in Vietnam thought the same thing of the Vietcong, and those Marines had learned their lessons the hard way—just ask any operator who was in Khe Sanh in March 1968. It was healthy to believe that you were smarter and stronger than the enemy, but unhealthy to underestimate his ability to put a bullet in your head.

That was the military's way of explaining something Vance's mama told him every time he left the house: Be careful.

Oh, I'm careful, all right, Vance thought as he blasted his way through the underbrush like a one-man mechanized division homing in on the old dock. He had to slow a little as the path became more muddy and the splashing of his boots grew too loud. He looked over his shoulder at Houston, who was coming on way too hard. Vance paused to wait up for the lance corporal, then pointed to Houston's boots, raised that finger to his lips.

Wearing a sarcastic grin, Houston nodded, and they resumed their run.

Admittedly, Vance was being hard on the guy, but the game was on, and Vance did not feel like dying in North Korea. Call him selfish, but he didn't want Houston's "problem" to screw up everything. Yes, he sympathized with the guy, but if Houston couldn't do the job, then he didn't belong on the team. It was bad enough that Rainey was dealing with some issues that might affect his ability to lead. If those two men went psychologically south, who was left? An ROK Marine who seemed more scared than anything else? Lance Corporal Kim would probably do little more than serve as Dogma Team's translator and tour guide through the shithole. At least Doc would be there if Vance needed him. Good old Doc.

Slicing even more swiftly through the shrubs, Vance

kept on until the sagging outline of the old dock appeared at the water's edge, just fifty meters ahead. Sheets of rain drew long lines across the water and washed over everything.

"Hey, Godzilla," Houston said from behind. "Weren't you the one telling me to be quiet? You were a little loud back there."

Vance crouched down, caught his breath. "Yeah, I guess I was."

Houston lowered to his haunches, joined Vance. "So now that you're done stomping, are you going to breathe fire?"

Vance sighed. "Yeah, I get it. But this is North Korea. Not Tokyo."

"You must be right. Because I've been looking all over for the Love Hotel. All right, so Bruno was an idiot, but if we get back, let's you and me go there for him."

"For him? You want to go there for yourself, you whoremonger." Turning away, Vance pushed himself up. "We're almost there."

"Okay, but we're going to the Love Hotel. And we're taking Kim with us. He told me he knows two girls there who specialize in something, I can't remember how it's pronounced. Trust me on this one."

And speak of the horny devil. Kim, Rainey, and Doc crossed stealthily into Vance's field of view as he probed the dock and surrounding shrubs with his Nightstars. "Those guys are getting sloppy. If I can see them, so can the bad guys."

"I wouldn't say anything to Rainey. He's not having a good night."

"No, he's not. Anyway, they've reached the rally point."

If news reporting was an endless cycle of feeding the beast, then Rick Navarro was about to serve up some filet mignon that would leave his audience begging for seconds.

He flicked a glance to the monitor, where news anchor Marty Shaw, a bleached blonde with tits as round and hard as birthday balloons sat in the Wolf News Studio back in Atlanta. Navarro nearly missed his cue as he reminisced about the time he and Shaw had commiserated in the backseat of her BMW after the 911 attack.

"Rick, can you hear me?" Shaw repeated.

"Yes, Marty, loud and clear. I'm here at Marine Forces Korea Headquarters, standing in the pressroom, where, just moments ago, a spokesperson for Combined Forces Command confirmed that a C-130 Hercules was shot down over North Korea early this morning. What that spokesperson failed to mention was that I had been authorized to ride along on that flight."

"Are you serious, Rick?"

"Yes, I am Marty. Lieutenant Colonel Richard Wilmot, who I am deeply saddened to report was killed late yesterday during the terrorist bombing here at MARFOR-K, authorized and even encouraged me to record what was and still is a highly classified mission."

"So, Rick, if I understand you correctly, you were supposed to be on board that plane, that very same plane that was recently shot down."

You had to love that Marty Shaw. She knew how to arch that back, thrust out those birthday balloons, and spin that story with repetition so that even the Gomer Pyles and Forrest Gumps in the audience could follow along. "That's right, Marty. I was supposed to be on board that ill-fated flight."

"So what happened, Rick?"

"Well, I don't know if you would call this paranormal, but as I boarded that colossal transport, something tingled inside me. I didn't know what it was. At first, I ignored it. But then in my mind's eye I began to see things, you know, images of the plane flying through the night sky, images of a missile racing up from the ground."

"That's just . . . just incredible."

"I know it is. And I know this sounds unbelievable to viewers, but I have to share this with you now, Marty, because whatever it was, it saved my life. At the very last moment, as they were raising the ramp, I asked that my cameraman and I be allowed to deplane. And we did."

"Rick, again, that is simply remarkable. You know, you hear stories all the time about people who, through a series of circumstances, are unable to board a flight that crashes. But I think it's even more rare when the passenger himself has a strong premonition that this is not the place where he needs to be. It's just . . . remarkable."

"You know, Marty, I've dedicated my life to bringing the toughest and most dangerous stories to the American public. I've trekked from the frigid mountains of Pakistan, where I was held prisoner by the world's most wanted man, Mohammed al-Zumar, all the way to rain-soaked rice paddies of South Korea. And I'm thankful to report that I'll continue to do things like that because something extraordinary happened earlier this evening. Someone was watching over me, an angel perhaps, and I'd like to think that it's because we're doing something necessary and important, even life changing, and the power or powers that be saw fit to grant me a reprieve from death."

"Well, of course, Rick, everyone back here in Atlanta—and I'm sure across the nation—is breathing a collective sigh of relief. We know that the Korean peninsula is arguably the most dangerous place in the world, but we also know how committed you are to bringing us the stories from the front lines. And I just want to say thank you. Thank you for putting yourself in harm's way. Thank you for demonstrating a level of professionalism that I doubt our viewers will find on other networks."

"Well, thank you, Marty," Navarro said, acting as humbly as he could, though the strain would soon make him nauseous. "But now I have to remind you that while I escaped death, others may have not. I can't say exactly who was on board that plane, but they may very well have paid the ultimate price. However, we can still hope that some made it out. And if they did, they're on the ground, fleeing from the enemy. I suspect that in the hours to come more will be revealed, and their story will gain national and international attention. It'll be discussed at water coolers and taverns, at truck stops and diners, at gyms and political rallies and even student-teacher conferences. Because when American military forces are in peril, we're all in peril. Our patriotism attaches us at the hip. We're all brothers and sisters in liberty. And so, on this rainy early morning in Seoul, South Korea, we say a prayer for these heroic soldiers as they fight their way back toward freedom . . ."

06

Each member of Master Sergeant Sung's reconnaissance team was a politically reliable troop and a member in good standing of the Korean Workers Party. Each had served in the combat branches, and each had gone through a rigorous training process that included infiltration, mountaineering, night operations, swimming, martial arts, airborne, intelligence collection, demolition, and the usual physical conditioning. Unfortunately, each was also a human being subject to all the foibles that drove Sung mad, desperately mad.

Thus he tensed as he watched Sergeant Choi walk directly below the parachute and rigging, making the very human error of not looking up. Granted, Choi had approached the tree from the rear, where several more trees with thicker, longer limbs helped to conceal the nylon, but as he shifted in front, he should have turned and glanced up. After all, the chute flapped loudly in the breeze. That sound alone should have summoned the sergeant's attention.

But the chubby man's movements indicated that he thought only of enemy soldiers, expecting them to be on the ground and with weapons pointed at him. He had been taught to expect the unexpected, but Choi often ignored his instincts, favoring his intellect instead, and it was that intellect that, ironically, robbed him of common sense.

In the meantime, Sung had, of course, already spotted the chute and had assigned specific tasks to the other team members. Because Choi was last to arrive, Sung had decided to initiate a little field test, one that aggravated Sung more than it taught Choi anything.

"Lyongjang Choi!" Sung whispered as he scrambled up behind the man. "Perhaps you should look up?" Sung made a face and pointed at the trees, the chute, the rigging.

As Choi complied, Corporal Moon scampered out from behind two pines, carrying a bulging canvas bag. "Sangsa, I have found the kit bag. Inside is the jumper's equipment."

Sung accepted the bag, placed it on the ground, and rummaged through it. "There is nothing here to indicate whether these are UN troops or American forces."

"Does it matter, Sangsa? Both are enemies."

"I would prefer that they are Americans. Marines."

"Because of your grandfather?"

Sung frowned. "You know?"

"People talk, Sangsa. I heard that he fought valiantly at the Chosin Reservoir."

"Yes, he did."

"And that letter you keep in your pocket?"

Sung lowered his head, placed a hand over his chest. "The words of my grandfather."

"My grandfather was also a soldier, as was my father, as I am. They were not killed by Marines. But Sangsa? If we are searching for Marines and we find them, I will not hesitate to avenge your grandfather and every other grandfather who died at their hands."

"Thank you, Sambyong Moon. However, if we find these men, I hope to capture at least one. That will help the cause even more, and helping the cause will serve as ample revenge. One thing is certain though. You *will* earn your promotion soon."

Before Corporal Moon could thank Sung, Lance Corporal Park came forward, his rifle appearing too large in his diminutive hands. "Sangsa, the rain has washed away most of the footprints. There is no way to tell how many were here. Yes, we know there was more than one, but the rain"—Park scowled at the heavens—"it is our worst enemy now."

"Ilb-yong Park, we have but one enemy. Now go back there and look again. I want to know how many. And I want to know within two minutes."

"But Sangsa—"

"Go now!"

As Park drew in a deep breath and moped back to the trees, Sb-yong Lee called down from his perch on a limb just above the twisted rigging. "Sangsa, someone did climb this tree. Some small branches have been broken here."

"They could have been broken by the paratrooper as he crashed down."

"Some were, Sangsa, and they are bent down. But some have been bent sideways, away from the rigging. Also, some bark has been chipped off here . . . and here . . . I am confident, Sangsa, that someone did climb this tree."

The reserved private with that terribly disfigured cheek had done quite well for himself. Sung nodded and asked, "Why would someone climb the tree?"

Lee thought a moment. "To free the paratrooper."

"Why would he need help? Even if he was hanging from that limb, he could have reached back and detached the rigging himself."

"Perhaps he was injured, Sangsa."

"Or perhaps he was worried about the fall," Sergeant Choi said. "And he wanted to climb down the tree."

Sung leered at the man. "Lyongjang Choi, that paratrooper most certainly made a HALO drop into our country. He would not be worried about dropping several meters down to the mud."

Choi shrugged, sized up the drop once more, shrugged again.

"Sangsa?"

Sung craned his neck to regard Lance Corporal Park, who, with a weary expression creasing his face, said, "I have identified at least four separate sets of footprints. There may be a fifth, but they are all wearing the same boots, and two men might be wearing the same size, I am not sure."

"This is probably a small reconnaissance team, not unlike us," Sung said. "They have an injured member, which will work to our advantage."

"Yes, Sangsa, they will only move as fast as their slowest man. And with the truck, we can catch them."

Sung shook his head. "With the truck we will lose the element of surprise."

Park's expression grew long. Very long. "Yes, Sangsa."

"All right. Time to leave. But I wonder, where would this recon force be headed?"

His men recognized the test and carefully considered the question before speaking. Sung was constantly challenging them, seeking to know how much they knew, seeking to improve them—no matter the time, the place, the situation. His colleagues would argue that he wasted precious time in the field engaging in such activities, but Sung suspected that one day his training exercises would save his life and the lives of his men— even as they helped earn the team victory.

And for that reason, Sung hoped that at least one of his men, perhaps Lee or Moon, would suggest the logical course.

Regrettably, Sergeant Choi opened his mouth first. "I have heard rumors that the American CIA is operating behind the Chinese border, just north of Sinuiju. This recon team will head south to the outskirts of Sinuiju, then cross the border and attempt to meet their friends there."

"Nonsense," Park said. "They will find a good valley to the north and wait for their helicopter."

Sung turned to Lee. "What is your opinion, Private?"

"Sangsa, you mentioned in the truck that this team's transport was shot down. I believe they were headed north, perhaps to gather intelligence on our radar and missile sites. They never reached their destination. I also believe they had a plan to escape, but it did not involve rescue by helicopter. They know our air defenses are still in place. They are headed southwest, to the coastline, where they will escape to a submarine."

"And to do that," Moon added, "they will keep close to the river and follow it up into the mountains. Then they will move down toward the bay."

Sung widened his eyes and almost smiled. "I agree. They will seek a route with the most cover. Choi? Park? Go to the truck and gather the rest of our gear."

The sergeant and lance corporal sprinted off, while Lee climbed down from the tree and Moon wiped off the lenses of his binoculars. The corporal handed the binoculars to Sung, who raised them to his eyes and repressed a chill.

Somewhere out there, clinging to the shadows and trees along the shoreline, lay their quarry.

The hunt was on.

TEAM DOGMA
EN ROUTE TO EXTRACTION POINT SCORPION
NORTH KOREA
0130 HOURS LOCAL TIME

Rainey knew he had about five hours of darkness left, that the new extraction point was now nearly forty kilometers away, and that he and his men could not get there before dawn because the average march rate of an infantryman was only about thirty kilometers in an eight-hour period. As usual, Murphy, whose laws of combat were painfully true, was laughing at Rainey from his bivouac in the sky.

Screw Murphy. Rainey would come up with a strategy that accounted for them *not* reaching the new extraction coordinates by daybreak. They would need to hide and wait for the cover of darkness. But could they? And could the submarine remain in Korea Bay for that long? Even if both parties could wait (which seemed as dangerous as it was unlikely), where would the team hide? The original escape route had them traveling those 68 kilometers through rural terrain, hiding one night in a wooded, sparsely populated area, then moving on, all the way to the coast. According to the maps, their new path had an elevation of zero to one hundred feet above sea level, offered meager cover, and would take them toward a few small fishing villages lining the coast. Yes, the new route was more direct, but Rainey and his men might be forced to extract during broad daylight in a populated area. Pulling off something like that would require them to drain their luck, their bodies, and probably empty every magazine they had.

So what was the team's strategy?

Part of Rainey argued that he should trust himself and just shoot from the hip. As the situation unfolded, he could discover that 70 percent solution that wasn't perfect but would save their asses. Besides, some of those questions could not be answered until the situation was upon them. But that last one, the idea of extracting in broad daylight . . . Well, that bothered the hell out of him. It wasn't as though they could pose as

North Korean surfing celebrities and paddle out on their long boards to catch a submarine instead of a wave while patrol boats crisscrossed the waters. Moreover, the place was, presumably, heavily mined. Escape would be hard enough at night with all those obstacles and all those eyes on them.

What they needed to do was turn the weather and terrain into allies instead of enemies. What about Lance Corporal Kim? How could he factor into the equation? He was supposed to come from the area, supposed to be familiar with key elements that the maps failed to mention. The man jogged just ahead of Rainey, who was pulling up the rear. When point man Vance called for the next halt, Rainey would steal a moment to pick Kim's brain.

With that mental note taken, Rainey focused on the path, the mud squishing beneath his boots, foliage ripping past his shoulders. They were following the river southwest, straying no more than a hundred or so yards from the shoreline, threading their way between thin stands of pines, shrubs, and swearing over the rain.

After another hundred yards or so, Vance signaled for the next halt, and Rainey called him on the radio. "What do you got, Three, over?"

"River's taking a sharp turn to the right, heading directly west toward the border. There's a little creek that continues on. Map says for another klick, over."

"Roger that. Follow the creek," Rainey said, scrolling up on his own GPS map. "Then take us into the foothills. But stand by for a minute, over."

"Standing by, over."

Rainey caught Lance Corporal Kim's attention and waved him back. "Lance Corporal, you know we can't follow this course for too long."

"Yes, Sergeant. It is the obvious path."

"Yeah, it is. So you're supposed to know this place."

"I grew up here, Sergeant."

"Which must mean you also escaped. Care to repeat the trick?"

"You want to trick the enemy?"

Rainey realized that the man's English was good but that there were phrases he did not quite understand. "What I mean to say is, can you help us escape again?"

"I think so, and I do have one suggestion. There are some farmhouses along the way to the coast. The underground sometimes uses them, and many of the farmers are friendly to the cause because the government has abused them for many, many years. I know the frequencies some of the underground operatives use, and they monitor the NKA's military channels and can usually decrypt their signals."

"What're you saying? That we can get ahold of these people?"

"Maybe. They must know that our transport has been shot down. They might be listening. We can call them for help. They could at least slow down the recon team following us."

"Sounds like a long shot."

"We should try."

"Okay. When we reach the hills, we'll stop again, and you'll contact those people."

"I will try, Sergeant."

Rainey glanced away, pushed up his boom mike. "Dogma Three, this is Dogma One. Move out, over."

"Moving out," Vance replied. "Dogma Three, out."

Lance Corporal Jung Yung Kim had kept one secret from Sergeant Rainey, and as he followed the black man the others called "Doc," he began to feel guilty, began to worry that his promise to Rainey might fall short. He forced the secret from his thoughts, wouldn't entertain it, wouldn't allow it to plague him until the time came.

And for the time being, he would privately lament his predicament. Volunteering for the mission had been a grave error. Now the past might haunt him in more ways than one. He longed for the cool comfort of his rack, for the routine of training, and for someone to talk to who understood what it was like to have your family and home taken from you. Did any of these men know how to build a life from nothing, how to find order and meaning, and how to recognize that happiness is born in the heart, not in the mind? Maybe Houston did. He seemed like a man who listened, a man who was also troubled by something that kept his gaze very distant. Perhaps there would come another time and another place for them to talk. If they escaped North Korea, Kim would take Houston to Japan, to the Love Hotel.

But they would not find love there. Only escape.

Kim tucked his rifle into his chest, ducked to avoid a low-hanging limb . . .

And heard a single shot disrupt the rain's steady drone. As he hit the mud, his rifle slipped from his grip, and pain needled through his right bicep.

Automatic fire scissored violently through the trees just above his head, originating from somewhere behind. The tactical channel burst to life with the tense voices of his new team:

"Dogma One, this is Dogma Three. Estimate that fire from about three hundred meters east our position, over."

"Roger that, Three. Dogma Team? Do not return fire! Repeat! Do not return fire! Rally ahead north of the creek and into the foothills."

"Dogma One, this is Dogma Four. Taking fire from the north and now the south!"

"Dogma One, this is Three. Confirm that fire north and south our position."

"Damn," said Houston. "They must have flanked us!"

"Understood, Three and Four," Rainey answered coolly. "Okay. Return fire on north position and drive forward. Dogma Team, go, go, go!"

Kim's right arm was beginning to go numb, and he checked his shirt sleeve, saw the tear, a small blood stain, told himself the wound could not be that bad. He was afraid to look any further. He grabbed his rifle with his good hand, and, keeping as hunched over as possible, fell in behind Doc, who was already waving his big Para SAW like a fire hose and spraying the tree line with rounds that cut bark like butter and blasted into the darkness.

"Lance Corporal?" Rainey shouted from behind. "Have you been hit?"

"A glancing round. Nothing serious," Kim answered, not missing a step and keeping tight on Doc's heels. "I am good to go, Sergeant."

"Outstanding. Let's move! Let's move!"

And Kim did, but he felt lightheaded and a little nauseous. It occurred to him only then that he had actually been shot—for the first time ever. He tried holding his rifle, could barely feel the trigger. Then he switched hands, fingered the trigger with his left, and while that felt awkward, he could at least fire from the waist.

Within another minute, the pines, while not very tall since most of the area had been decimated during the Korean War, began to grow in number. Kim knew that their chances of escaping the ambush would increase dramatically if they managed to reach the foothills. He remembered crossing through this region during his escape to the south, remembered that somewhere up there lay the wreckage of an old Y-5 biplane, once used for bombing and to insert Special Operations forces. A large portion of the plane's fuselage had remained intact, and if the team could not shake the NKA troops on their tail, then the Y-5 would at least provide more cover than the trees. The chances that the wreckage had been cleared away were slim; air force personnel had long ago stripped the biplane of its valuable components, leaving the metal carcass to nature's wrath.

"They're on the move!" Houston cried into the radio. "Sounds like two, driving back toward our right flank."

A gaping hunk of bark exploded from a tree just a meter to Kim's right, confirming Houston's report.

Doc paused, swung his weapon around, and cut loose with another thundering salvo. Kim added his rifle's voice to the fray, though he feared his aim was pathetic.

While suppressing fire didn't have to be surgically accurate, the perfectionist in Kim argued fiercely to the contrary.

Then Doc's weapon went silent, and he turned his bright eyes on Kim. "Lance Corporal? Come on!"

Kim chased after the man, and they moved into the thicker groups of trees, the rain tapering off to the occasional heavy drop as the denser canopy shielded them.

Houston and Vance moved about twenty meters ahead, forging on into the cooler, damper forest, while Sergeant Rainey lingered a few yards behind Kim. "Little faster, Doc," Rainey called.

"The lord only gave me four cylinders, what can I tell you?" Doc grunted.

Kim wasn't sure what that meant, but the big corpsman managed to pry a little more speed from his legs. As did Kim.

Abruptly, the gunfire behind and to their left broke off into the eerie dripping of rain from the trees and the sounds of their combat boots stomping in the mud. Doc suddenly sneezed, becoming the first victim of the forest's musty stench.

Shooting a quick glance over his shoulder, Kim whispered, "Sergeant?"

Rainey caught up to him, spoke as they ran. "What is it?"

"Good cover, maybe. At the top of the hill. Turn left."

"What do we got? More trees? A hill?"

"An old plane. Better than the trees."

"Do our bad guys know about it?"

"I don't know. But its better than the trees."

"And maybe it's a good place for a little surprise of our own."

"Yes, we can leave them a gift."

"Dogma Three, this is Dogma One. Turn left at the top of the hill. There's an old plane over there. Look for it, over."

"One, this is Three. Looking for your plane. Hope we can fly it out of here, out."

Kim took a few more steps, but the mud turned to water, and there was no more footing, no legs beneath him. With a muffled thud he realized he had fallen, but there was nothing he could do to get up. He heard his name. Heard Doc answer. Heard the boots. Then . . .

NORTH KOREAN ARMY RECONNAISSANCE SQUAD
NORTHEAST OF SINUIJU
NORTH KOREA
0138 HOURS LOCAL TIME

All of the time and effort Master Sergeant Sung had spent training his men had been forsaken the moment Sergeant Choi had decided to open fire without authorization. Choi had been trained to observe, report, and follow orders. What had led up to such a grave error? Had Sung driven his men too hard?

That did not seem likely. They had found the paratroopers' trail and had pursued as quickly yet as stealthily as they could. They had become part of nature, unnoticed like the clouds, the thunder, and the rain. They had become master thieves and had spotted the rearward soldier, whose nondescript uniform and bush cover did not betray his country of origin, though Sung suspected even more that they were pursuing American Marines. His team had come close enough to smell the enemy, or so Sung mused.

Growing so excited that he could hardly breathe, Sung had sent out Park and Moon to the left flank, Choi and Lee to the right flank, while he would advance up the middle.

They had closed in. Fingers poised over triggers.

Each step carefully measured.

No communication. Not a whisper.

Just the beating of their hearts.

And then, Sung had been ready to give the order for Park and Moon to grab that rearward soldier, capture him at knifepoint, then grab the next—each soldier washed away in the rain until the final man, still unaware that his team was gone, turned, met Sung's gaze, and knew he was defeated.

The object, Sung had reminded himself, was to capture at least one man. Bringing in five dead reconnaissance men was one thing, but capturing one or more who might crack under interrogation would make Sung the envy of his recon platoon and serve to honor his grandfather's memory.

But then that shot had torn a hole in Sung's anticipation, in his confidence, and in his plan.

"I've wounded one!" Choi had cried over the radio.

Sung had opened his mouth, about to scream, when suddenly, all of his men had opened fire. That single round had been like a split-second fuse, a fuse that once lit had been impossible to extinguish.

Well, at least Choi's error had not ruined everything.

At the moment, they had enemy on the run, and Sung and his team were once more closing in. Lee and Park spearheaded the group, with Moon to Sung's left and Choi to Sung's right. There was no time to discipline Sergeant Choi. That would most assuredly come later.

"Red Star Three, this is Red Star One, over," Sung called.

"Red Star One, this is Three," Park answered, his breath coming hard and forcing static into the radio. "No sign of enemy yet. But we are still on their path, over."

"Very good. Do not stop! Keep moving! Out!"

If Sung were a younger man, a more naïve man, he would have already called for assistance. Infantrymen could be flown ahead and dropped into the forest so that Sung and his people would drive the enemy directly into the trap.

But Sung alone had been charged with apprehending the enemy, and he and his men would complete the mission without help. The decision to work alone was not born of egotism or arrogance; it was born of survival. In Sung's world, being charged with a mission and then crying for help was much more than a sign of weakness. It was a sign of incompetence. Moreover, in time of war, incompetent soldiers would be dealt with in the field in the same way that Sung had dealt with the dissidents. The only consolation Sung had was that he had chosen not to get married and raise a family. He had led his life trying to meet state-defined goals rather than personal interests. He had only his reputation and the reputation of his family to lose. But those things were very valuable, and he would fight for them until he could no longer open his eyes and raise his fists.

Lee and Park were taking them higher into the foothills, and Sung wished he could thumb on a penlight. Twice he tripped over exposed roots as thick as his arms, and twice he thought his heart had stopped. He backhanded rain from his eyes and squinted into the gloom, propelling himself on over wet beds of pines needles until Park's voice sounded from the radio at his hip. He charged to a tree and crouched down. "This is Red Star One, over."

"Red Star One, their trail leads to the wreckage of an old plane up here, over."

"Stand by," Sung ordered. "Do not advance on the plane. We will all meet you there."

Skirting around a series of shallow depressions, then winding through solitary trees rising up like grim sentinels, Sung found Park and Lee lying on their bellies on the backside of a hill, with Park studying the mangled wreckage of an aircraft half-buried in the hillside.

A panting Sergeant Choi came up behind Sung, towing along a deathly silent and strangely pale-looking Corporal Moon. "Sangsa," Choi rasped. "I am certain I wounded one of them."

"And I am certain we will discuss what you did later." Sung nudged his way between Park and Lee, then took the binoculars from Park. "I see the plane."

"It's been up there for many years, Sangsa. The trail leads up to it. They are using it for cover," said Park.

"Are they?" Sung asked, turning back to face Moon and Choi. "Are they really? And was it luck that they came upon it? Or do they have someone with them who knows this terrain?"

"Interesting questions, Sangsa," Choi said. "If they are on the run, then they would not stop and attempt to fight us from behind the plane. They would just keep moving."

"Or not. They could have assumed positions in the trees to our flanks," Lee suggested. "So that if we advance toward the plane, they can spring their ambush."

"Many questions and no answers," Sung said. "And every situation is yet another test."

Park sighed in disgust. "What are we going to do now, Sangsa?"

"We are going to ignore the plane. Choi? Moon? Take us along the right flank, then pick up their trail as it leads away."

"But Sangsa, what if they are at the plane?" Choi asked. "They might see us."

"There is no one at that plane."

Choi averted his gaze, but the challenge in his tone was clear. "It is raining. It is dark. And our binoculars are old. How can you be certain?"

"Lyongjang Choi, I welcome your opinions because they help me train you to become a better soldier. But do not dare question my orders now—not after what you did."

Sung was about to order Choi and Moon to leave when, from the corner of his eye, he saw Corporal Moon collapse to the mud. Choi gasped and dropped to the corporal's side, while Lee began frantically unbuttoning Moon's shirt—

And there it was, a gunshot wound to the chest, one that Moon had recklessly bandaged while on the run. The corporal lay there on his back, blood bubbling from the hole, his breath coming in ragged bursts. "Sangsa, I am sorry. You will . . . avenge your grandfather . . . without me."

Sambyong Moon was no longer the lean, efficient corporal on Sung's team. He was a dying boy groping for breath, for anything that would assure him that his life had been worth something.

While Lee doused Moon's wound with antiseptic, Sung got down on his knees in the mud, held the corporal's hand. "Sambyong, you have fought valiantly."

"Yes, Sangsa. I know. I know."

Sung released the man's hand and motioned for Lee to step away. "Make him comfortable. But quickly."

"Yes, Sangsa."

Park, Choi, and even Sung himself stared gravely at the fallen Moon, who was most certainly bleeding heavily inside. His eyelids began to flutter, and then, his head simply rolled to one side.

"He has lost consciousness," said Lee.

"And so will the men who did this," grunted Park. "They will lose their lives."

"Leave him," Sung ordered Lee. "Choi? Park? Take us to the left flank."

The desire for revenge got into Sung's feet, his breath, his heart. He longed to scream!

07

TEAM DOGMA
EN ROUTE TO EXTRACTION POINT SCORPION
NORTH KOREA
0155 HOURS LOCAL TIME

While Lance Corporal Kim's gunshot wound to the
right bicep had been minor, he had lost consciousness
for a moment, and that had presented Doc with a secondary challenge. Kim's blackout was not from a loss
of blood (though he had lost some), but from the mental
trauma of being shot. Doc had seen the reaction before.
Soldiers became so stressed out by thoughts of losing
an eye, an arm, or a leg that they simply passed out. A
good sternum rub usually brought them around, as it
had Kim, and for the moment, Doc kept the lance corporal at his side as Rainey, Houston, and Vance tied the
ribbon on the birthday present they were leaving for the
bad guys.

"Thank you, Corpsman," Kim whispered as he and
Doc took in the downed plane and surrounding trees
through their Nightstars.

"That's three times you've thanked me. It's okay.

And call me Doc. Please. That's a title that took me a long time to earn."

"Okay. Thank you, Doc." Kim still felt awkward around the man and felt even more compelled to make conversation. "So I guess maybe Houston was right."

"About what?"

"About the curse of being fifth member on your team."

"I don't believe in that crap, but my grandfather . . . boy . . . he grew up on Martinique. Some of those island folks are real superstitious."

"Some people in Korea are the same."

"Yeah, well, it's just a point-of-view thing. You only got nicked. And that's pretty lucky."

"I told Houston I was the only guy on my team who made it. And I was the fifth member."

"So there you go. And hey, you don't happen to see anything, do you?"

Kim panned left with his binoculars. "No, nothing."

"That's good."

"Good?"

"I mean they're not poking around the plane. They figured we'd keep moving and wouldn't bother using it for cover."

"My first thought was to use the plane as cover, but Sergeant Rainey thought otherwise. He is a smart soldier. All of you are. I wish your team could come and train more of us."

"Once the CFC launches their preemptive strike, most of your training will be on the job. Best kind of training anyway. Live fire. The works. Train as you fight, they say. And there's one thing that being in real combat teaches you that you can't learn any other way."

"What is that, Doc?"

"That there's no room for mistakes. Yeah, that's obvious, but it's way too easy to forget. You'll make a few mistakes. People will die because of them. And believe me, the next time you're in the shit, you'll remember, and you'll never make the same mistake twice."

"You speak from experience."

Doc's voice grew thin as faces from the past materialized in his mind's eye. "Yeah, I do. We've all made them. I know Rainey has a few on his own mind. But we have to get past them. You have to be a confident operator. You have to believe in yourself."

"I will remember that."

"You know, Kim, I bet you will." Doc had barely finished his sentence when he thought he saw a figure dart from one tree to the next, advancing at an unsettling rate. He spoke quickly into his boom mike: "Dogma One, this is Dogma Two. Think I got movement over here, on our left flank as predicted, over."

Rainey issued a quick whisper of acknowledgment to Doc, then tossed Vance and Houston a pair of hand signals. All three of them hauled ass back toward Doc's position atop a foothill about a hundred meters north of the plane.

In short order, Rainey would learn just how smart his opponents were. The plane had provided an old-fashioned fork in the road, one that had given the bad guys pause and had caused Rainey to second-guess not only his own team's moves but the enemy's. Presently, those NKA recon guys were on the move and would die like bad guys should—so long as Murphy was still snoring through the night.

Feeling like an adrenaline junkie who had just received a triple fix, Rainey clutched his carbine and rounded two trees, keeping within a meter of Vance and Houston. His mouth went dry by the time he reached Doc and Lance Corporal Kim.

"How many wires you set?" Doc asked.

"Three," Vance answered, and Rainey was glad the corporal did because he was jamming a canteen in his mouth.

"How did you know they'd take left flank?" Doc asked.

"Simple," Houston said. "Because the right's way too muddy. There's a whole lot of water washing down that side of the foothills."

Rainey straightened, took a long breath, replaced the cap on his canteen. "Gentlemen, it's time to punch back in. Vance on point." He swung around, faced Kim. "How's that arm, Lance Corporal?"

"I am good to go, Sergeant."

Rainey looked to Doc, who offered a solid nod.

"All right," Rainey continued. "And hey, Kim, don't worry about passing out. Happens to the best of us. Any of these guys give you a hard time about it, you let me know."

"If they tease me, Sergeant, it is only because I deserve it. I have never been shot before. My cherry has been popped, as you say."

"Hey, I like that," Rainey said. "You've definitely been hanging around with too many Americans."

"Well, I wish we could stick around for the party," said Houston, staring through his rifle's scope. "But I'm guessing they'll have a nice bang without us."

"Wish we could find some place dry," Vance said with a shiver.

"If you want to hang your skivvies by the fire, you'd best get a move on," Rainey said. "Then again, I doubt you'll find any campfires aboard that submarine."

"But they got the best food," Doc said. "Best in the Navy. I can't wait."

"Come on, you hens. Shut up and run." With that, Rainey waved on the team, and, one by one, they slinked off toward the next rain-soaked hill.

Stealing a final look down on the plane, Rainey considered a wish of his own, a wish that those men down there had grown weary and careless.

NORTH KOREAN ARMY RECONNAISSANCE SQUAD
NORTHEAST OF SINUIJU
NORTH KOREA
0205 HOURS LOCAL TIME

Master Sergeant Sung and Private Lee wove a jagged path through the shrubs and trees, reaching a position from where they could survey the back of the biplane. Sung found a particularly thick pine, rested behind it, withdrew his binoculars.

"What do you see, Sangsa?" Lee asked.

"The plane is empty."

"I did not doubt you, Sangsa."

"Yes, you did. But you will never admit that. That is

all right, Sb-yong Lee. I hope you are learning to think like the enemy."

"I am, Sangsa. They are more cunning than the dissidents we have been arresting. They are an enemy to be respected. But so are we."

Sung nodded, lowered his binoculars, and gave the signal for them to leave.

"Red Star One, this is Red Star Two, over," came Sergeant Choi's voice over the radio.

"Go ahead, Red Star Two."

"We have located their trail, over."

Sung was about to reply when a revelation struck him as though carried down on the droplets of rain: perhaps the enemy had known that he and his men would ignore the plane. They had also known that the swiftest path would be away from the muddy hills of the right flank.

"Red Star Two and Red Star Three, hold your positions!" Sung cried in a stage whisper. "Do not move."

"Red Star Two and Three, holding our positions, over."

"What is it?" Lee asked.

Sung slipped his radio back into its waist holster and rose. "The enemy knew we would take this route."

"Of course, it is the route they have taken."

"Yes, it is. Follow me now. And stay close. We have no choice but to use our penlights to search for tripwires. We will find some."

Lee's gaze did not flinch. "Yes, Sangsa."

With his own gaze sweeping hard across the muddy earth, Sung advanced for another fifty yards until he squinted and saw a thin, almost invisible line cutting across the path. "There," he said, motioning to Lee with the barrel of his rifle. "Right there."

"Sangsa, I believe that is just a limb, a very straight limb," Lee said, stepping slowly forward.

"Hold, Sb-yong!"

"It is all right," Lee said, crouching down to more closely examine the object with his own penlight. "Just a limb."

Sung clutched his rifle so tightly that his knuckles threatened to burst through the skin. He had become paranoid, and now they were wasting precious time. But should he and Lee pick up the pace? Only if they could be swift *and* cautious. "All right, Sb-yong. Keep moving. More quickly now. But keeping looking for wires."

"Yes, Sangsa. I will lead."

And, young man, you will die first if you are careless.

"Red Star One, this is Red Star Two, over."

Sighing in frustration, Sung tore the radio from his waist. "Red Star Two, this is One, over."

"Red Star One, awaiting your arrival. Is there any problem, over?"

"No problem, Two. Observe radio silence until we arrive. Out."

Lee, who strode to a position about three meters ahead of Sung, stepped on something that snapped—

And Sung froze, held his breath, and glanced away expecting to feel the concussion of an explosion.

None came.

"Sangsa, are you all right?" Lee asked, having paused to stare back curiously at Sung.

"Yes, keep moving," Sung quickly answered. He took a step forward, imagined that his leg had made contact with a wire, imagined that the claymores were blasting him from the right and left, imagined that his arms and legs were being shredded off his torso, imagined that he hit the ground and lay there, his blood forming a warm puddle around him as Lee shrieked in horror.

But there was only the cool rain and the unbearable humidity and the sounds of Lee's boots dropping lightly onto more carpets of pine needles.

You are still alive.

Keeping his eyes on Lee, Sung felt a little better about continuing, though his fear continued to rear its ugly head. He was a soldier. There was no fear. Only caution.

Then why did he feel so incapacitated?

Was his willingness to sacrifice himself for the cause beginning to wane? Was he becoming selfish? More interested in personal interests than in the mission? What was it? He was changing, and he did not like this change.

In about three minutes they reached Park and Choi, who were sitting in a cluster of trees, their rifles held at the ready. The two men got to their feet, and Sung shared with them his suspicions regarding a trap.

"This is a large forest, Sangsa," Park said. "And their trail breaks off into three, sometimes four and five tracks, even while it is spread out over as many as ten meters. Their tripwires are not long enough to cover such an area."

"Perhaps they are. And perhaps they have assumed we would follow along the center of their trail, which is what you have been doing. Any trap would be left in that area."

"So we must be cautious," Choi said, his ability to point out the obvious not lost on Park and Lee, both of whom looked away, their expressions full of contempt.

"Sergeant, you will lead," Sung said, reminding everyone that Choi was the most expendable man now. Corporal Moon's loss had hurt very much. If only Sung had been given the choice of which man to sacrifice first . . .

"Sangsa, I will lead, and I will find the tripwires if they are there."

"Very good."

They fell in easily behind Choi, with Sung taking the rear. He knew the decision to linger behind could be considered cowardly by those unfamiliar with infantry tactics, but the leader had to survive. Without him he seriously doubted that his men would complete the mission. They would, at the very least, call for assistance. Sung would not let it come to that. He would stay alive. They would capture or kill the enemy on their own terms. They would earn the honor and respect they deserved. And one day, the North and South would be reunited. Korea would be the greatest nation on Earth.

Within five minutes Choi's hand went up. While Park and Lee squatted down, Sung bent over and rushed up to the Sergeant.

"Right there, Sangsa," said Choi, pointing his penlight at the shadows ahead. "Can you see the wire?"

The sergeant had better eyes than Sung, who could see no more than grainy mist rising from the leaves and mud. "Where is the wire?"

"It is there, Sangsa." Choi looked down, carefully measured another two steps, switched on his penlight.

Sung did likewise, and the wire materialized, a once glistening piece of metal alien to the landscape; however, the wire's sheen had been cleverly dulled by mud so that it seemed to be lying across the ground instead of hovering at ankle-height. Sung's gaze followed the wire to the base of a pine, where he picked out the boxy shape of a claymore mine.

"They could not have had time to set very many," Choi speculated. "Two or three. No more. This is the first."

"Where will the others be?" Sung asked. "Along the same trail?"

"No. I believe the other wires will be to our flanks. The enemy would not set them along the same trail, especially if we tripped one."

Sung's tone softened. He actually agreed with the man. "Lyongjang, the wires may not stop us, but they will slow us down, giving the enemy a chance to escape. And that is exactly his plan. Fear and misdirection."

"Then should we abandon their trail?"

"No," Sung snapped. "If we do, we may lose them. Move on."

Sung whirled and went back to Lee and Park, notified them of the tripwire in their path. Sung held his breath as Choi stepped over the wire, followed by the others. Then came Sung's turn. He gingerly placed one leg over the wire, then blinked away that now recurring nightmare of what a claymore mine could do to delicate human flesh. Sung's other leg came over, and with his shoulders beginning to slump, he realized he had cleared the trap and could relax.

But thoughts of the next wire consumed him. And each sound louder than a footfall made him flinch. During the next few moments he heard a hundred or more explosions in his head, anticipating them so much that he occasionally recoiled and closed his eyes. He was beginning to lose his breath as they pushed through a narrow ravine between two foothills.

"Sangsa," Choi called back. "Please, come here."

Choi had not bothered to signal a halt, but Park and Lee went reflexively to their haunches.

Repressing the desire to grit his teeth, Sung raced up the line to see what was happening. When he reached Choi's side, he tried not to gasp.

The sergeant had chosen to follow the middle of the trail because he believed the wires would be positioned to their flanks. But the enemy had outsmarted him, and Choi had found the next wire, all right. He had bumped it before he had realized it was there. His boot pressed firmly against the thin cable as though he were about to kick it away like a gossamer. However, he, Sung, and any other infantryman familiar with such explosives knew that releasing the pressure might trigger the explosives.

Therefore, Choi stood there, a fey little man frozen between life and death, his eyes pleading, his lower lip quivering—

While Sung contemplated what to do.

"Sangsa, please, save me!"

Sung ignored the man.

"Sangsa, please."

Sung grabbed the man's throat. "Shut up!"
Then both of them looked down at the wire.

TEAM DOGMA
EN ROUTE TO EXTRACTION POINT SCORPION
NORTH KOREA
0235 HOURS LOCAL TIME

Corporal Jimmy Vance was not feeling very good about the tripwires that he, Houston, and Rainey had set up in their trail. Those NKA Recon guys—varmints who definitely needed killin'—should have already been smoked. Their continued survival meant that they had either 1) not encountered the wires (unlikely since they spanned the trail) or 2) had found the wires and had avoided them (which sucked, big time). There was also the possibility that one or more of the claymores had, when triggered, failed to detonate. Yes, one maybe. But all three? No. They could have bumped one, which failed to blow, and then they would have been alerted to the others. That was probably what had happened, and the damned silence kept reminding Vance that they had failed. The others were probably thinking the same thing, but no one was talking. Even Houston had become a church mouse, which was highly unusual for him. It appeared that the radio operator, like everyone else, was walking on eggshells when it came to dealing with Rainey. No one would dare point out the possibility that Operation Birthday Present had become Operation Waste Three Claymores.

Then again, could those NKA recon guys really be that good? Throwing yourself on a mine was one thing; discovering where those mines were and carefully avoiding them was something much more difficult. What if one of the claymores had not failed? If those bastards had managed to evade all three tripwires, then Vance would salute them—

A billionth of a second before he capped each man with his big old sniper's rifle.

Breathing a deep sigh, Vance decided he would no longer worry about those recon guys. Even if they were stopped, other bad guys would come. They always did. And Vance would do what he always did: reach out with all of his senses as he walked point and led the team away. If that failed, he would swing around, take aim, fire! Take aim . . . fire!

Ahead lay nothing out of the ordinary: just more foothills and, far off to the east, a few lights from maybe a town or some farmhouses or something. The Korean water torture still had not let up, and Vance's bush cover sagged heavily around his ears. God, what he couldn't give for a sweet-smelling T-shirt fresh out of the dryer.

Slowly, he drew up on a lone tree, was about to turn back to see how far behind Houston was when the lance corporal nearly knocked him over.

"Jesus . . ." Vance gasped.

"Oh, shit, man. Sorry."

"What the hell's the matter with you?"

"I said I was sorry."

"Just get off my ass and get back in position."

"Hey, man, you don't have to be nasty about it."

"Listen, bro, we got problems, you know? Just deal with them. We have to get out of here—and that ain't going to happen with you walking around in a daze."

"Yeah, right," Houston said, slipping off to Vance's left flank. "Your sympathy and support has been duly noted. Asshole."

Vance could only shake his head, and as he started down the next foothill, carefully minding his steps across a mushy ridge, an explosion boomed from behind, followed quickly by a much louder, more powerful thunderclap. He hit the deck, felt his right leg give, and suddenly went sliding down the hill. He dug the butt of his rifle into the ground, jammed it in hard as though setting a fence pole, and arrested his fall as the explosion echoed and died.

"Dogma Team," came Rainey's voice over the tactical channel. "The birthday boys have opened one of their presents, over."

"Roger that, One," said Doc. "But did that sound like just a claymore to you, over?"

As a matter of fact, the blast had not. There had been a smaller explosion just a second before the larger one. "Dogma One, this is Dogma Three," Vance called. "From my vantage point that explosion sounded more like an F-1 Frag, followed by a claymore, over."

"Dogma One, this is Four," Houston said. "I agree with that assessment, over."

Vance wondered if Lance Corporal Kim would offer his opinion on the explosion, but the ROK Marine kept off the channel. Vance held his position and waited for Rainey to give the order to move out.

Thirty seconds passed. A minute. Vance considered calling back. What was the sergeant doing?

"Dogma One, this is Dogma Two, over. Dogma One, this is Dogma Two, do you copy, over?"

With his Nightstars pressed firmly to his eyes, Rainey scanned the treetops and came upon the lingering smoke from the discharge. He had wanted to hear a detonation so badly that when one came, he had immediately assumed that only a claymore had gone off, and worse, he had announced his mistake to the entire team. Doc had good ears. Vance had even better ears. One of those NKA recon guys had triggered a fragmentation grenade, which in turn had probably set off a claymore. But why? The explosion had given up their position.

"Dogma Two, this is Dogma One," he said, finally answering Doc. "Stand by, over."

"Standing by, but I remind you, Dogma One, the bad guys must be on the move, over."

"Understood, over."

Rainey put his tactician's mind to work. Maybe, just maybe, the bad guys wanted him to believe that at least one or two of them had fallen for the trap. But so what? What did they hope to accomplish? Did they want Rainey to believe that he and his men were no longer being pursued? One explosion would hardly convince them of that. Maybe they wanted Rainey to believe they were fewer in number. Again, so what?

Or maybe they had wanted to give up their location so that they might draw fire from Rainey's team. But if they were recon, then they knew that Force Recon operators rarely carry the arms to engage in drawn-out battles. You think, shoot, move, and communicate. And when you're in enemy territory, you only fire to clear your escape route. It was all about getting out, getting back.

When you really thought about it, the enemy's deliberate triggering of a claymore seemed like a grave tactical error, and presented an intriguing mystery. Nevertheless, Rainey's men were waiting and daybreak would not. "Dogma Three, this is Dogma One, over."

"One, this is Three, over."

"Agree with your assessment that an F-1 or similar ordnance triggered that claymore. Reason unknown at this time, over."

Lance Corporal Kim scrambled up to Rainey. "Sergeant, I have one idea about what is happening down there."

"Well, Kim, I hope it's a good idea, and I hope you can tell it fast, because we have to leave."

"I know, Sergeant. So here is what I believe: That recon unit detonated a fragmentation grenade, which set off one of our claymores."

"That's all you got? Tell me something I don't know."

Kim lifted his brows. "Do you know why they detonated the claymore?"

"Do you?"

"I think so. They needed to destroy the claymore—not just avoid it."

"Why would they need to destroy it, unless . . ." Rainey's eyes widened as it all came together.

08

Master Sergeant Sung had, for a long moment, considered leaving Sergeant Choi behind so that the man could decide his own fate. The team's welfare was more important than an individual's, and Choi should be proud to sacrifice himself for the cause. That conclusion had been painfully obvious, born of a philosophy Sung had been taught his entire life. There should have been no question, no indecision, no guilt.

But Sung had found no honor in leaving Choi. A rescue had to be attempted, and such an attempt, he had reasoned, could prove a valuable training lesson for Park and Lee, who would most assuredly grow from the experience—no matter the outcome. Moreover, Sung had concluded that if he managed to save Choi, the naïve man's loyalty would strengthen because he owed his master sergeant his life. Choi might one day become a soldier who would make Sung proud.

However, freeing the bungling sergeant from a trip-wire had proved extremely difficult. Sung had reasoned that he could not gamble on relieving the pressure on the wire. The claymore would explode sideways in a fairly wide spray and not give Choi time enough to escape. Sung had imagined a thick lead wall standing between Choi and the bomb. The wall would absorb most of the blast and protect Choi. Sung had known that he needed something similar to, yet more accessible than, a lead wall in order to give Choi a fighting chance. And then an idea had finally sent a chill across his shoulders. A fragmentation grenade tossed at the claymore might blast it aside, and even if the claymore did detonate, the direction of its blast would be away from Choi.

But what about the noise? Sung knew he could not alter that consequence, and he had been prepared to sacrifice the team's location because he believed they could move quickly enough to evade fire.

Surprisingly, Choi, initially the coward and a man who had been begging for help, had found the martyr inside. "Sangsa, do not risk the entire team for me. The mission is more important than one man."

"We have already lost one man. I am not prepared to lose another."

Choi's eyes had welled with tears. "Look at me. I am here, with my leg on this wire. I am already gone."

"I will not believe that. I do believe that you, me, Park, and Lee will capture the enemy before they can escape."

"Sangsa, you are a fool if you try to save me."

"A fool?"

"If the same happened to you, I would leave you here."

"He is right, Sangsa," Park had said. "Revealing our location will put us at a disadvantage. We are uncertain of the enemy's capabilities. They could have RPGs or they could launch mortars. If that happens, we will die."

"We must leave him," Lee had said. "It is the best for all of us."

"You see, Sangsa?" Choi had said. "They know what to do."

Sung had withdrawn the fragmentation grenade from his pack, clutched the striker release, and pulled the pin. "After I throw, you will count three, then dive back toward me, keeping your face away from the blast."

Choi had mustered a defiant look that caught Sung off guard. "Sangsa, I will not—"

"Lyongjang, you will. Now." Sung had tossed the grenade, seized Choi's wrist, and together they had lunged for a mud puddle as the terrific booms stung their ears and the concussions struck solid blows across their backs.

Choi had rolled over, his face covered in mud, only his eyes visible in the shadows. "Sangsa . . . thank you."

"You were right," Sung had said.

"I was?"

"Yes. I am a fool." Sung had glanced back at a stunned Park and Lee. "Move!"

And with the smoke still billowing up into the rainy sky, Sung and the three young men in his charge had beat a path over splintered wood and tattered leaves.

A few foothills later, Sung still reflected on the foolishness of saving Choi as they once again picked up the enemy's trail.

Lance Corporal Park drifted back, proffering his radio's microphone. "Sangsa, the chung-yong calls again."

Sung jolted as though Park could read his conflicted thoughts.

"Are you all right, Sangsa?"

Swiping the microphone from Park, Sung drew in a breath to steady his nerves. "Mountain Ghost, this is Red Star One, over."

"Red Star One, our advance guard reports the sound of an explosion near your coordinates, over."

Sung closed his eyes. "Mountain Ghost, the enemy triggered one of their claymore mines. We believe they have injured. We are in pursuit, over."

"Red Star One, the weather should improve in the next six hours, but we are ready now to send another reconnaissance squad. Our Hoplites are standing by, over."

There it was. Sung's CO was prepared for the team's failure. If Sung accepted the aid, the victory would be bitter, the future even more uncertain. The team still had a chance, and he would not deny himself or his men the opportunity. "Mountain Ghost, send help at our request, over."

"Say again, Red Star One, over."

"Mountain Ghost, we will request additional support when needed, over."

The pause was unusually long. Presumably, Sung's CO had been taken aback by Sung's insistence that he would call for help only when he wanted it.

"Red Star One, acknowledged. Standing by for your request, out."

Sung replaced the microphone, then caught Park staring. "What is it?"

"Sangsa? Are you going to let them help us?" asked Park. "Because if the enemy slips away—"

"They will not."

"And if they do?"

"This is *our* mission."

"But is it not better to accept help and capture the enemy than to fight alone and lose?"

"We are hunting a small force, and we will take them ourselves. We do not need twenty-three-millimeter machine guns or fifty-seven-millimeter rockets. We do not need more troops. We need only speed, determination, and the hearts of warriors. Do you understand?"

Park did not like that answer, but he knew better than to complain further. "Yes, Sangsa."

Sung turned his gaze up, let the rain fall on his face. "And now we will charge the enemy. They will not know what hit them . . . until . . . it is too late."

WOLF NEWS CREW
MARFOR-K HEADQUARTERS PRESSROOM
YONGSAN, SEOUL
SOUTH KOREA
0240 HOURS LOCAL TIME

"Okay, Rick, so we're looking at the map now," said anchorwoman Marty Shaw from her news desk back in

Atlanta. "Why don't you explain to us North Korea's suspected plan of attack?"

As he stood in the pressroom with his stomach groaning, Rick Navarro regarded the computer-generated map of the Korean peninsula on his monitor, then he nodded to Shaw. "Marty, North Korea's primary objective is to reunify the North and South under their control. Intelligence indicates that they envision fighting a two-front war. Their first front will consist of conventional forces breaking through the DMZ and destroying all Combined Forces Command elements there. As the map indicates, they have three avenues of approach: the Kaesong-Munsan Approach, commonly referred to as K-M North, with forces pushing down from the northwest corridor. Then there's the Chorwon Approach, which includes forces attacking the middle portion of the DMZ and entering the Kumhwa Valley. And finally, we have the East Coast Approach, which has troops penetrating the DMZ and battling along the Taedong River."

"Sounds like they'll need a large force to invade in three separate areas," Shaw said, expertly setting up Navarro so he could deliver his next bit of analysis.

"Marty, the North Koreans have the fourth-largest standing army in the world, and those generals of the first echelon know that they can't compete with the technological capabilities of both South Korea and the United States. So they go back to the old ways, back to the blood-and-guts nature of war. Their strategy includes the use of surprise, shock, speed, and overwhelming numbers of troops."

"When you say surprise and shock, what exactly do you mean? Can you give us some examples?"

"Marty, one of the guiding principles of the North Korean Army is annihilation. That means that the enemy—us—is not given time to withdraw or retreat. It means they will take no prisoners. It means they will slaughter everyone in their way. It means that if we don't launch a preemptive strike, there will be a blood bath. And that's only in regard to ground forces. In addition, they'll launch SCUD and FROG missile attacks against airfields, lines of communication, and logistic facilities, and those air strikes will prove equally deadly."

"Rick, there are rumors that the North Koreans possess and will use both biological and chemical weapons. I know we've discussed this before, but I'm wondering, what's the word there? Has the CFC released any new information?"

"Marty, we haven't heard much about biological weapons, though one source said that if the North Koreans chose to use them, they would rely on infectious agents like those causing anthrax or plague. On the other hand, there has been much brouhaha regarding chemical warfare. One of our sources indicates that the North Koreans have at least eight industrial facilities capable of producing nerve gas and an assortment of other agents. They can deliver these weapons by using virtually all of their fire support systems like rocket launchers and even mortars."

"So launching a chemical attack wouldn't pose much of a problem for them, even with their older equipment."

"Word here is that they *will* employ chemical weapons in an attempt to demoralize the CFC and limit mobility. And old or not, they have the missiles and launchers to carry out such a strike."

"What's the Marine Corps saying about all this? Are they really prepared for such an attack?"

"They are, Marty. And so are the other branches of the service. Both our troops and the ROK forces have received chemical warfare gear. The Marines in particular use Mission Oriented Protective Postures gear—the so-called MOPP gear we've been hearing a lot about. They and the others train continually in how to deal with contamination, and the North Koreans have made their own preparations, even as they plan to fight on a second front." Navarro glanced down at his notes. "Multiple sources confirm that enemy special operations forces dressed in South Korean uniforms and equipped with South Korean weapons will penetrate the DMZ prior to the attack. These forces will enter via air, sea, and through tunnels under the DMZ. According to my sources, these special operations troops will attack at night, create confusion, and maybe even gain control of critical terrain."

"So how will our forces know who's who, if the bad guys, so to speak, are wearing good-guy uniforms?"

"In all likelihood, the bad guys won't be wearing luminescent tape or carrying some of the other thermal and infrared devices our troops use to identify themselves. Still, the element of surprise will be theirs."

"That's interesting—and disconcerting—Rick. And speaking of special operations forces, have we learned any more information regarding that downed Force Reconnaissance team?"

"We're still awaiting another update, Marty. But we can only presume that those men are having a very rough night, charging back to the coastline in monsoonlike conditions. We can also presume that the North Koreans have been alerted of their presence and have sent troops in to capture them. You know, Marty, it's so frustrating to be standing here with only a microphone, knowing that men I've personally met, men who possess the courage to put their lives on the line for America, are out there and need help. If I could, I'd fly in to get them myself, but I'm just standing here in this little room and wringing my hands, doing the same thing that people all across the United States are doing—just hoping and praying our boys make it back alive. Tossing it back to you, Marty."

"All right, thank you, Rick. That was Rick Navarro, our embedded reporter, who's at Marine Forces Command Headquarters in South Korea."

Navarro slumped and rubbed his sore eyes. "Could somebody get me some fucking breakfast?"

By the time he opened his eyes, his entire crew had vanished.

TEAM DOGMA
EN ROUTE TO EXTRACTION POINT SCORPION
NORTH KOREA
0255 HOURS LOCAL TIME

During his backbreaking trek up some hills of oatmeal while carrying a heavy automatic weapon, Doc tried to forget about how shitty the conditions were. In doing so, he took himself thousands of miles across the globe. What were the boys doing back home? Were they giving their mother a hard time going to bed or waking up? Were they still getting good grades? Were they still growing up too fast?

Doc choked up. God, he missed his family, missed them so much that it physically hurt. The pressure on his chest was not stress related. He should have concentrated on the path ahead.

Vance signaled the next halt as they reached the base of a mountain whose elevation Doc estimated at about a thousand feet, very small as mountains went, but significant in that part of North Korea. The team formed a tight string behind some jagged boulders and a few fallen trees that had been washed down the forty-five degree incline.

"All right, Kim, you want to try again?" Rainey asked.

The lance corporal nodded and scampered his way down the line toward Houston. The ROK Marine had already tried once to contact the South Korean underground, whom he had said were operating in the area. Maybe the second time would be the charm. Doc was going to listen in, but Vance turned to him and said, "Hey, Doc? I think we got a little problem."

"What do you got? Immersion foot? What?"

"It's not me." Vance's gaze targeted Houston. "I didn't want to say anything, you know?"

"He's all right."

Vance shook his head. "Couple minutes ago I heard him talking to himself. I'm talking a complete conversation. Like he was back in the hospital with his dad. I think he said the F word like a hundred times."

"He wouldn't be out here if he wasn't ready."

"You think he's ready because he fooled the shrinks? Give me a break. I'm just worried about the boy. I'm worried about him screwing the pooch for us all."

"You worry about you. I'm the corpsman. I'll worry about him. Besides, I happen to know one young sniper who's been preoccupied with a certain girl back home, and this same sniper got a little distracted during a previous operation."

"Point taken, Doc. Just keep your eye on him. I don't know, issue some Prozac or something."

"Marines need protein, not Prozac."

"If you say so, Doc." Vance headed off toward the last of the boulders.

Was it the rain making tensions so high? That was only part of it, Doc knew. Bruno's death still weighed heavily on all of them, though in deference to Rainey everyone kept silent about that. Doc lifted his Para SAW and worked his way back to Rainey, Houston, and Kim. "I need some good news," he told the sergeant.

"And we got it, I think," Rainey said, tipping his head toward Kim, who had Houston's microphone in hand and was still talking rapidly in Korean.

"Hey, man," Houston said, grabbing Kim's arm. "How much longer you going to be?"

"Let him talk, Houston," Rainey said.

"You'd think he was a goddamned telemarketer, the way he's going on, with us sitting here and the bad guys coming."

"Sometimes it takes longer to say things in their language," Doc said, unsure of the truth in that, but it sounded like a pretty good excuse. What didn't sound good was Houston's tone, which boarded on hysterical.

"I am almost finished," Kim suddenly said. "And I do have the good news."

"Dogma One, this is Dogma Three," came Vance's voice over the tactical radio.

Rainey turned from the group. "Three, this is One, what do you got, over?"

"Dogma One, be advised count four bad guys on the move, advancing fast. Very fast, over."

"Kim," Rainey called, interrupting the lance corporal. "Finish. Now!"

"Yes, Sergeant."

"Dogma Three, keep eyes on those bad guys, over."

"Roger that, Dogma One. Dogma Three, out."

"If he's got eyes on, why don't we call their bluff, wait until they're on us, then let me open up?" Doc suggested.

"Wish we could, Doc. But we don't know how many more are behind them. Maybe they called for help. Maybe there were already other guys operating up here. Too many variables. Think about it. If it's only those four guys, would they come charging up the hill? Or would they bide their time and drive us steadily into a trap?"

"What're you thinking? There's an entire Advance Guard behind them?"

"I'm thinking we won't be here to find out."

"Okay, Sergeant, I can tell you the good news," Kim said.

"Not now, Lance Corporal."

Doc felt a slight tremor in his boots. He thought for a moment that a nerve was twitching in one of his legs. But then his knees wobbled, and he realized the ground was rumbling. "What the hell . . ." His gaze swung skyward, where he searched for a chopper or some other source of the vibration.

"Dogma One, this is Dogma Three," cried Vance. "Rally my position! Rally my position! Looks like half the mountain's coming down!"

The mountain's coming down? Doc fixed his gaze upward, where a massive, fluctuating silhouette descended toward them, swallowing trees and shrubs as though they were toothpicks and balls of lint.

For a second or two, Doc just stood there, not horrified, not yet, just transfixed as the huge mudslide lumbered straight for him.

09

Master Sergeant Sung ignored the ground quivering beneath his boots and hollered the order to open fire.

While Sergeant Choi and Lance Corporal Park reached positions near a jagged outcropping and directed their AK-47s toward the enemy's flanks, Private Lee drove straight at the enemy, his RPK-74 light machine gun blazing.

As the chaotic popping of weapons resounded through the night, Sung repeatedly scanned the mountainside for enemy muzzle flashes while occasionally jerking his head up, expecting to find that unwelcome air support to arrive at any moment. After all, what else could make such a rumble?

However, the muzzle flashes did not appear. Neither did the air support. Instead, Lance Corporal Park came dashing straight at Sung, as though he had just witnessed some great massacre. Park's eyes resembled glassy marbles, and his face had gone pale. "It's coming this way! We have to move!" Park ran past Sung, then hesitated, pointing. "Come on!"

Directing his attention to the mountain, Sung finally saw what had frightened his man. An enormous wave of mud and debris lumbered down as five shadowy figures scrambled like insects to evade its path. Sung allowed himself a second's worth of hope that those insects—the men he sought—would be knocked down and buried under tons of rolling rock and mud. Then Sung realized that he could not stand there and watch. If he and his men did not react, the slide would cut them off, and the enemy, if not wiped out by the slide, would escape.

"Sangsa, we have to run! Now!" Park screamed.

"No! Advance!" Sung shouted. "Advance!" He charged away from Park, working up into a full sprint. "Before we lose them, advance!"

"Yes, Sangsa! But we are going to die!"

A quick look back confirmed that Park was now falling in behind Sung. The lance corporal now appeared more terrified than those dissidents Sung had shot earlier in the evening.

Choi and Lee narrowed the distance between each other as they neared the east side of the mudslide's path, a path that had broadened to nearly twenty meters as the slide consumed more of the mountainside, gorging itself on rocks, trees, weeds, and yet more earth.

Gunfire boomed again, and Sung recognized the sounds of the enemy's weapons. They were returning fire, and they were close, very close. He drove himself on, determined that he and his men would bridge that gap, get to the west side of the path as the mudslide passed within a meter behind them.

He yelled for Choi and Lee to run faster.

Screamed for Park to catch up.

Then he cursed the enemy as he jammed down his trigger, sending a salvo across two trees. Shards of bark flew into the air as the rounds narrowly missed the rearmost soldier, who ducked and darted, then turned to squeeze off a pair of rounds that sent Sung flat onto his stomach.

Choi and Lee drew closer to the slide as Sung dragged himself up and raced to join them.

"We cannot make it!" cried Choi.

"It is moving too fast," Lee added.

And both men suddenly stopped, jerked themselves back—

While Sung willed his legs into springs and catapulted himself into the air, soaring into the mudslide's path.

"No, Sangsa!" Park yelled.

"Come back, Sangsa," Choi said. "Come back!"

Were his men cowards? Or was Sung reckless? He had made the leap without thinking. Was his thirst for blood, for honor, for respect too great?

Sung hit the ground, stumbled, fell, looked up, realized he was nearly ten meters shy of the west side while behind him, his men opened fire on the enemy.

You are a fool. You have killed yourself.

Maybe not.

He started running, running for his life, then, as he was about to leap again, his legs were swept out from under him. He extended an arm, tried to brace himself, as the mud seemed to inhale him.

The ground paralleling Rainey's path came alive with
shots ricocheting off the rocks, slashing through the
shrubs, and thumping into the muck. Occasionally, a
round would whistle past his ear, prompting him to give
a nervous tug on his bush cover, as though he could
ward off the next shot.

Rainey was the last man to cross the slide's path,
gaining two meters of clearance when the giant amoeba
of mud rolled by with breath-robbing force, tossing up
globs of dirt and clumps of weeds the way a lava flow
tosses up fiery rock. Too bad mudslide evasion tactics
were not part of Force Recon's training program.
Rainey would have them added if he survived the mission. In fact, he might even author the materials himself. Rule #1: mudslides, like incoming fire and buxom
blondes, always have the right of way.

Leaning on a tree and gasping for breath, Rainey
watched with awe as the flow continued pouring down
the mountainside. He imagined that if tanks and other
vehicles of a mechanized corps stood in the slide's path,
they would flip over and get washed away. You had to be
close to the thing to really experience its power.

A fresh volley of incoming fire and a burst of static
from his tactical radio drove Rainey farther behind the
tree.

"Dogma One, this is Dogma Two, over," Doc called.

"Go, Two."

"Dogma One, we have established firing positions from our side. Be advised we are taking fire from three positions east our location on the opposite side of the flow, over."

"Dogma One, this is Dogma Three," Vance said.

"Go, Three."

"Be advised my weapon has misfired and is clogged with mud. Will use my MEU pistol, over."

"Dogma One, this is Dogma Four," said Houston.

"Go, Four."

"Be advised my weapon works and I am tired and I am wet and I'M GOING TO KILL THESE MOTHER-FUCKERS!"

Houston had barely finished screaming into the radio when the sound of his carbine reverberated across foothills. *Had the kid gone off the deep end? What the hell was going on? Were the others going to freak out, too?* No, that wouldn't happen. That couldn't happen. Marines—especially Force Recon Marines—were trained to breathe easy in the face of death. That was par for the course. And keen-eyed Marines could see through the fog of war no matter how dense, how chaotic, how insane the situation became.

Or so Rainey had believed. His own senses were already overloaded by the slide's thunder, the multiple reports of weapons, the shouts of his men, and the loudest sound of all—his inner voice, the one that now said, *You let them get too close! They're right the fuck on top of you! Right there!*

But the slide had cut them off, right? He ducked, spun around—

And the torrents of mud just a meter behind him

seemed to rise up, as though they had come alive and were morphing themselves into a figure.

"Now my fucking rifle's jammed, too," Houston cried.

"You're broadcasting, you idiot," said Vance. "Get off the channel."

"Both of you shut up!" Doc hollered.

"Dogma Team, this is Voodoo Five. Still count three bad guys, over."

Rainey blinked, backhanded rain from his eyes, and through the flecked darkness realized that he was not hallucinating. The mud had not risen up but a soldier had, a North Korean covered from head to toe in muck, his narrow eyes illuminated by the reflected light from a gleaming blade in his fist.

"Sergeant!"

Reacting to the cry from Doc, the muddy Korean lifted the knife and lunged for Rainey, who took a step back so that he could level his rifle on the bad guy.

But the soldier surprised him by breaking out of the lunge and whirling in a sudden wheel kick that knocked away Rainey's carbine.

Ignoring the natural reaction to glance at the weapon, Rainey kept his attention on the man, rain washing away the mud on the Korean's head to reveal a graying crew cut and crow's feet. Rainey might be squaring off with the recon team's leader, who had to be the baddest ass on the block, trained in tae kwon do, trained in multiple methods to kill a man with his bare hands, let alone with a knife. Somehow the guy had crossed the mudflow, a remarkable feat right there.

Rainey took another step back, and relying upon his own martial-arts training, launched himself into a sidekick, trying to knock away the Korean's knife.

While in midair, three successive rounds punched into the tree Rainey had been leaning against, the shots fired from behind, fired by one of Rainey's own men. Had they pegged him for a bad guy? Shit!

While a fourth round boomed, Rainey hit the ground and the Korean spun away, out of Rainey's reach, drew back, then advanced and slashed at Rainey, the blade coming within a finger's length of Rainey's chest.

Before the Korean could make another attack, Rainey seized the man's wrist with one hand and drove his free arm up against the guy's arm, hoping to snap it like a chicken bone.

But the Korean saw Rainey's move coming a mile away and stepped into Rainey while turning to twist free. Still, the effort had cost him. The knifed slipped, falling to the mud. The Korean dove for it.

And Rainey booted him under the chin, knocking him flat on his back.

As the guy pushed up on his hands, Rainey withdrew his MEU pistol, took aim at the guy's chest.

Then gunfire from both the NKA guys and his own men sent him ducking for cover before he could pull the trigger.

He wanted to scream, "Hold your fire!" But even if his men did, the bad guys wouldn't.

Another round. Another breath. Silence. Where was the North Korean? Rainey scrambled around a shrub near the flow, lifted his head to steal a furtive glance. Heart slamming, hand shaking, he cursed himself for losing the guy. As he backed away from the shrub . . .

. . . . a pair of hands locked onto his pistol.

Reflexively, Rainey fired, the shot ripping through the limbs as he hissed with exertion, arms taut as he struggled against the Korean's powerful grip.

NORTH KOREAN ARMY RECONNAISSANCE SQUAD
NORTHEAST OF SINUIJU
NORTH KOREA
0305 HOURS LOCAL TIME

Master Sergeant Sung knew that his opponents would be trained in the ways of foot and fist, but he had not known that their tae kwon do skills would include the chung do kwan style, with its emphasis on speed, power, and kicking. His opponent's clean technique had definitely caught Sung off guard.

But no matter. He would wrench free the pistol and turn it on the soldier. As he struggled with the weapon, another shot went off, chipping into the tree behind him.

Across the mountain, the man who had yelled, "Sergeant!" spoke no more, but Choi, in his infinite lack of wisdom and common sense, kept yelling in Korean for the enemy to surrender, and Sung wished he had left Choi to the claymore.

Still clenching the pistol, Sung jerked the man, drove the enemy soldier down onto his side, but the big man's momentum carried Sung as well, and together they began rolling back toward the mudslide.

Sung kept his death grip on the weapon as the soldier tried to force the pistol down, toward Sung's head. They came out of the roll with Sung on his back, his head less than a meter from the streaming mud. A sudden splash doused his face, the dirt stinging his eyes. He let out a cry, forced the soldier onto his back. "American Marine?" he asked, his English broken, but hopefully clear enough for the soldier to understand. He squeezed shut his eyes again, trying to free the dirt, and hollered, "AMERICAN MARINE? AMERICAN MARINE?"

Rainey shoved the man sideways, but in doing so lost his grip on the pistol. The damned rain and mud had slid beneath his fingers and palm. *Damn it!* Now the Korean had the pistol, though he held it by its barrel.

Emitting a strangled cry, Rainey drove his fist between the weapon and the man's hand. He punched the pistol free and sent it tumbling into the flow. He thought of reaching back to get Bruno's rifle attached to his ruck, but there wasn't time. He took the soldier's neck in both hands, and gritting his teeth, prepared to end the contest by crushing the man's larynx.

The Korean gasped, his dark, mud-caked eyes swelling, his breath reeking of something spicy and foreign, then—

A knee to Rainey's groin sent him up and crashing sideways—not in pain, since he had chosen to wear his cup—but in surprise over the Korean's strength.

Nearly in unison, they shot to their feet, and while Rainey stood a full head taller than the man and outweighed him by at least thirty pounds, the physical difference hardly allayed Rainey's fears. The guy had cleared his eyes, had assumed the ready stance, and wanted to go at it again, right there on the mountainside, with their men still trading fire. The Korean had more on his mind than just capturing or killing the enemy.

Rainey braced himself, closed the gap, balled his

hands into fists and lifted his right leg in a side kick meant to connect with the bad guy's chest and slingshot him back into the landslide.

The kick fell short. The Korean grabbed Rainey's boot with both hands and twisted, about to break Rainey's ankle, when Rainey jerked back, out of the Korean's grip.

And fell on his ass.

Howling, the bad guy threw himself into the air toward Rainey, phlegm leaking from the corners of his mouth.

Rainey started to turn away, but the Korean struck a solid blow to his head. Rainey's ears began to ring, and flashes of light stabbed his pupils.

Cold, slimy hands found their way around Rainey's neck. He reached up, groping to get them away, but he was too slow. By the time he found the Korean's wrists, Rainey could no longer breathe. Mustering the last of his energy, he dug nails into the Korean's veins until he thought they would pop.

"American Marine? Tell me and you live."

The pressure decreased for a second, and Rainey stole a quick breath.

"American Marine?"

Rainey's mouth worked, but the words would not come out.

"American Marine?"

Finally, from the back of his throat, the words escaped: "Fuck you."

10

The North Korean tightened his grip on Rainey's throat and shoved him down. Mud wormed into Rainey's ears and crept farther up his face. If the Korean didn't strangle Rainey, he would drown him in the muck. The guy had options. Rainey could use some himself.

He tried bringing his knee up behind the Korean where he sat on top of him, but the guy held him so closely that Rainey could barely make contact. On a second try he managed to move the Korean slightly forward—

But the shift in position was enough. Rainey freed one leg, drove his boot up into the Korean's groin (returning the favor, of course), then sent the guy staggering backward like a drunken private on his first R & R.

Rolling over onto his hands and knees, Rainey coughed and tried catching his breath, watching as the Korean tripped, fell, and began tumbling back toward the mudslide. Another meter or so, and the guy would be swept away.

"Sergeant!" came a familiar voice from behind.

Doc came sidestepping across the mountainside, his Para SAW held at the hip, his nondescript utilities covered from the chest down in mud. A pair of rounds struck like blow darts in the puddles to his left, sending him dodging toward a tree.

"Hold your position, Doc," Rainey cried.

"Holding!"

A look ahead made Rainey's heart sink. The North Korean had arrested his tumble, was already on his feet, and now came slogging back like a goddamned Korean Energizer Bunny.

If that weren't headache enough, somewhere up the mountain, branches rustled, creaked, then popped loudly.

Rainey chanced a look up. *What? More troops? No, not more troops. Please . . .*

A familiar rumble took hold as the earth sent a shiver straight up Rainey's legs. He craned his head, fought to see anything through the darkness and rain, and then . . . it emerged, a swell of mud about two meters high that surged down the mountain.

Rule #2: Marines who encounter soil anomalies due to water saturation should be wary of further ground depreciation.

Yes, that's how the pogues would word it. Rainey would just tell you that when there's one slide, there's probably another.

Not that the Korean gave two shits about it. He came at Rainey like an animal, all instinct, no fear, no other purpose in the world save to kill his prey.

And of all the men Rainey had fought against in South America and in the Middle East, this guy took the cake.

But enough was enough.

Rainey groaned and forced his bruised hide up, his legs still a little wobbly. He noted the Korean's position before he lowered his head and drove forward like a linebacker, intent on driving his shoulder into the bad guy's chest and flushing him down into the flow.

The plan worked insofar as Rainey's shoulder did make contact, and he did manage to drive the North Korean a few meters back.

But before he could reach the flow, the rumble increased with such intensity that he couldn't help but turn, look, gasp, and shit a metaphorical brick. Make that two metaphorical bricks.

Fact: He had miscalculated the second mudslide's progress, figuring he would at least have enough time to hit the bad guy, free his K-bar, gut the man, then get out of there.

Fact: The slide was upon them, just a dozen meters away. He pulled free of the Korean, spun around, started running back toward Doc's position, but another glimpse of the second slide proved that even Doc and the rest of the guys across the mountain were directly in the beast's path.

You could run all you wanted. Pray all you wanted. But the slide was coming for you. And coming for the bad guys, too. It seemed that Mother Nature had decided to exact payback on the muddy boys playing with their toys.

"Run, Sergeant!" yelled Doc. "Run! Run! Run!"

"Fall back!" Rainey ordered, his tone half-hearted because he figured they wouldn't make it.

"Come on, Sergeant!"

Hands like sledgehammers slammed onto Rainey's shoulders, jerked him back, sent him down, his ruck hitting first.

The Korean circled, straddled him, grabbed him by the shirt collar. "United States Marine?"

Rainey could hardly hear the man. The slide's roar drowned out nearly everything—except the snap of a tree off to the left as the colossal wave of mud struck.

The Korean looked up, grimaced, and probably realized he should have been paying more attention to the mountain. He released Rainey and started to rise.

As Rainey sat up, the first wave of mud smacked him onto his chest, oozed over him like a cold blanket to cover his waist, his shoulders, then threatened to cover his head.

Shouting something in Korean, the bad guy toppled across Rainey, rolled, then reached out, seizing Rainey's wrist.

"Hey, asshole," Rainey said, groaning out the words. "We can play later."

Rainey tried to pull away, but the next wave of mud washed completely over his head as the Korean's other hand found Rainey's throat.

Turning panic into rage, Rainey drove his own hand forward, found the bad guy's neck, and latched on—

Just as a third wave sent both of them jetting down the mountain amid the shattered trees and rolling rocks that pummeled Rainey's shoulders. His body screamed for air, his eyes burned in the mud, but he kept that hand tightly around the Korean's throat.

* * *

"We're not falling back without the Sarge and Doc!" Vance shouted at Lance Corporal Kim.

"Look," the ROK Marine said, pointing across the mountainside as the wall of mud approached. "They are already gone. And we cannot outrun it."

"Well, I don't know about you losers, but I'm not surrendering to some fucking mud!" Houston stomped off down the mountain. "Now come on! We can beat this son of a bitch! We're Marines!"

Vance gave a hand signal to Kim, and the two of them hightailed it after the swearing, half-whacked radio operator.

Now, bass fisherman Vance was used to being around muddy shorelines and muddy lake bottoms. Your crankbaits and soft plastics often got full of mud as you worked them along the lake bottom, so you reeled them in and wiped them off. And that was pretty much the extent of Vance's experiences with mud. You didn't give mud much thought in your daily life.

Now as he dropped onto a mushy hump, trying to guard his steps but finding bad purchase, he realized that the slide might actually kill them. He almost laughed. After all, it was just a big wave of mud and rocks and junk.

A really big wave. Moving faster. Getting closer.

"We won't make it," Vance sang in a sarcastic tone.

"We can make it," Houston shouted back as he led them down a rock-strewn furrow that had probably been carved out by the previous year's storms.

"I want to make it," Kim said between breaths.

And Vance grinned inwardly at the South Korean's attempt to chip in a word. Still, there was wisdom there.

They all wanted to make it, and maybe that singular desire would save them.

Without so much as a crack of thunder or gust of wind to forewarn them, the sky opened up, as though the clouds were giant Hefty bags full of water and someone had run razor knives across every one. Pelted by huge raindrops, Vance could barely see the men ahead as they descended farther, the ground turning to sponge beneath their boots.

"I can't see anything!" Houston cried.

"Just keep going!" Vance said as a mild pressure struck his boots, sending his gaze over his shoulder.

But he couldn't see jack. Didn't need to see jack.

Guess what was knocking at their back door?

Yup. The mudslide had reached them, but the torrential rain had thinned out the edge of the flow so that they had a few seconds before the heavier mud struck.

"I'm slipping," Kim said. "Watch out."

"What's that?" Houston called. "Is it coming?"

"Well it ain't stopping!" Vance hollered, then his boots slid out, and it was all he could do to remain seated.

Dragging his sniper's rifle along like a pathetic oar, he began riding the thing down, the mud rushing up to his waist. He tried digging in his heels for stability, but the flow carried him so swiftly that his boots just ripped across the mountainside. He felt like sewage being flushed down a dark, endless pipe, and the damned mud was rising higher, now covering his arms and lapping at his chest.

Then, through the curtains of rain, he caught sight of a dark line rushing up at him, and only at the last second did he realize that a lone, hunchbacked tree was holding out against the slide.

"Aw, shit . . ."

Vance worked his rifle, tried to shove himself to the left but wound up turning only slightly. His shoulder smacked hard into the trunk, the impact shaking through his ribs and stealing most of his breath.

As though driving a bumper car after downing a half a bottle of Jack, he spun around, tried to remain upright, but the streams of mud coming off that tree washed him onto his stomach, sending him headfirst down the mountain.

He would have muttered, "Aw, shit," if his mouth weren't so full of mud.

With arms and legs flailing, he groped for a hard surface, knowing he had to turn, get his head up. But the slide's momentum was just too great. For the moment, all he could do was spit and rocket down, down, down . . .

Doc Leblanc had assumed that death in North Korea would come in the form of a grenade or a bullet or maybe even a knife to the throat—if he was foolish enough to let a bad guy get that close. But to assume he would be killed by, of all things, mud? No, that one would not have made the list.

However, during the prior five minutes, Doc had gained a newfound respect for mud, particularly when tons of it had come rushing down the mountain, had swept away his sergeant and a bad guy, then had carried him off like a wine cork tossed into whitewater.

Getting killed by a mountain with diarrhea? Damn. It could happen, and at the moment it topped the list. What a way to go. The embarrassment of it. Sure, the corps would not disclose the details of his death, but those documents wouldn't remain classified forever, and his kids and descendents would learn that he had not gone out in a blaze of glory.

Yes, sir, Doc's legacy was literally being dragged in the mud.

Clutching his Para SAW and keeping it tight to his chest, Doc rocked himself forward and released a groan as his ass hit a pothole, then a rock scraped along his hip and jostled his pack. For once he wasn't complaining about the heavy ruck; he was using it to help keep his face up, though he now had a North Korean Shower Massage blasting into his eyes.

I love this place.

Doc's boots, once flowing freely, did a head-on with a tangled web of submerged roots. His right boot caromed away, but his left boot slid between twisted roots and got caught—

Not that the mudslide cared about that. It kept coming and knocked Doc onto his stomach, his leg still locked in the roots. He fought against the current, trying to reach his foot, the mud slapping into his face and getting quick-washed by rain.

And then a much higher mud wave broke over him, and for a pair of seconds, he was completely submerged. Repulsed by the mud jamming into his ears and nostrils and seeping between his lips, Doc wrenched himself up like a rodeo bull. His head cleared the mud. And better, his boot jerked free.

After rolling back onto his butt, Doc tried to wipe the mud from his eyes with a mud-covered hand. Then he tried his mud-covered sleeve. Then he just looked up, blinked, spat, and let the rain do its work. Though he had never felt more slimy and disgusting, the fact that he did feel slimy and disgusting reminded him that he wasn't dead yet. No, sir.

Glenroy "Doc" Leblanc was one Marine who would live.

So what if they think I'm crazy? Fuck them, thought Lance Cpl. Bradley Houston. If he stayed angry, and if they listened to him, then those losers back there might actually make it. He was going to kick the mudslide's ass, big time, really big time.

Houston showed his teeth to the mud, let the mud know who was boss, cursed the mud, and knew that within another minute, the mud would kneel down and surrender. No force of nature was a match for a United States Marine! Earthquakes? Lightning? Mudslides? Bring 'em on!

As the ground abruptly leveled off and the mud washed ahead, rising up the nearest foothill, Houston screamed and hauled himself out of the black river, envisioning himself a zombie rising from a shallow grave. No doubt he looked the part.

"Kiss my ass!" he howled.

With the more violent current pushing off to his left, Houston staggered through knee-high mud toward a rise about twenty meters off. Once there and out of the slide's path, he turned, cleared his eyes with the heels of his hands, then hocked a loogie and let it fly. "Vance? Kim? Over here! Over here!"

Damn. That was his adrenaline talking. He should

have never cried out. He had no idea were the bad guys were—and to assume they were dead was about as stupid as . . . shouting for your teammates.

Still on his hands and knees, Lance Corporal Kim dragged himself away from the river of mud. Distant lightning flickered, followed by a thunderclap, and, most curiously, a voice ahead. Was that Houston calling for them? Why would he do such a thing?

Fortunately for Kim and the rest of the team, Houston did not shout again. Kim knew that if any of the North Koreans had survived, they had surely heard Houston's call. And they would be on their way. Which was why Kim worked his arms and legs even harder to clear the mud.

Seconds later, nearly out of breath and about to collapse, he felt hands dig under his pits and lift him. He turned to find a dirty-faced Houston standing there, grinning strangely. "Yo, what up, K-man?"

Kim shushed him, slipped out of man's grip, and waved Houston back toward higher ground.

"Hey, man, we have to get Vance. And what about Doc and the Sarge?"

"You have alerted the enemy," Kim said, hurrying away. "We will take cover up there."

"Not without the rest of my team, I won't."

"Please, Lance Corporal Houston. Let them rally on us up there."

Houston coughed, shook himself off like a wet dog, then finally nodded.

II

Rainey was not sure why, but the Korean suddenly released him, and then, with an almost inhuman force, he managed to pry Rainey's fingers from his throat.

With a sudden jerk, the Korean fell back, his arms outstretched as he splashed into the mud and was swept away.

Ripping himself around, Rainey faced forward and tried to steady his breathing, which in turn he hoped would calm him. The slide funneled into a deeper ravine below, and as it did, Rainey seized the opportunity to throw himself to the right, out of the flow. And wouldn't you know? The damned stunt actually paid off. He landed flat on his gut, rose to his hands and knees, crawled forward a few meters, then yanked himself to his feet. His tactical radio's headset with attached boom mike still hung around his neck, though he suspected the thing would need a good cleaning and drying before it would function properly again.

As the rain cleared the mud from his face, shoulders, and neck, Rainey glanced around, tried to get his bearings. A groan from behind sent him to his haunches and reaching for Bruno's rifle, still swinging from his ruck.

"Sarge . . ." Panting and spitting, Doc dragged himself from the mud.

With a start, Rainey rushed to the man, took one of Doc's wrists. "I got you, Doc. I got you."

"Hey, they didn't mention this shit in the field manual."

"Thought I read that chapter."

"Hell, I'm probably the only guy who read the damned thing."

"And now you can write the chapter on mudslides, while I make sure they become part of our training."

"Good. So what happened to your friend?"

"Oh, he's down there somewhere. These guys don't know when to quit."

"Why do we always get the martyrs?"

" 'Cause somebody in Fifth Force loves us."

"Nice to be loved."

Rainey shook his head at the grimy corpsman. "So, can I say you look like shit?"

"Didn't know you needed permission, but it's granted." Doc stood, blinked hard, regarded Rainey. "Can I say you look shittier?"

"No, you cannot. You good to go?"

"Think so." Doc patted his mud-covered Para SAW. "My weapon's another story."

"Let's try to get a big lead on these bastards, see if

we can buy ourselves enough time to clean our weapons and ourselves."

"Okay. And hey, Sarge. You all right?"

Rainey knew exactly what Doc was getting at—and he wouldn't let Doc get anywhere near the answer to that question. "Don't worry about me."

But Doc's expression said he was more than a little worried. Much more.

"Listen, Doc," Rainey began, grabbing the man's shoulder. "I'll get us out of here. I swear it."

"I believe you. I just wish there was something more we could do here, you know, instead of just running away."

"Me, too, Doc. Me, too."

Together, with weapons at the ready, they took off down the mountain, beating a mushy trail toward a rise offering pretty good cover. Rainey hoped the others had noticed it, then he reminded himself that first they had to have survived the mudslide. Damn, if just one of those assholes had screwed up and gotten himself killed, there would be serious hell to pay. Rainey already feared that Bruno's ghost would show up at any moment to taunt him, to remind him that he had lost his edge, that he had no business leading men into and out of enemy territory. The glory days were over, right?

No, they're not. Just be there, boys. Just be there.

"Lord, I know I haven't been much of a God-fearing man and that I haven't spoken to you or asked for your help and guidance for a long time. But Lord Jesus, I thank you for allowing me to fight another day—and to go fishing another day . . ."

Continuing to mutter, "Thank you, Lord. Thank you, Lord . . ." Cpl. Jimmy Vance shifted on wobbly legs away from the flow. Still shaken by the rocket ride, he did manage to keep a watchful gaze as he sidestepped farther down, then climbed atop two fallen trees lying across his path. From there he spotted two men hurrying toward a somewhat rocky patch of higher ground to his right. Lightning flashed, and Vance was fairly certain those guys were Doc and Rainey.

What the Sarge and Doc didn't realize was that two men had already reached that position. Vance had seen them hustle there after first leaving the mud, though he was not sure whether those two guys had been Houston and Kim or two members of the NKA recon squad. Someone had called out for him, but the voice had been distorted by the thunder and the rain.

Crouching down near a tree about five meters away from the mud river, Vance lifted the dirty boom mike to his lips and keyed his radio. "Dogma Team, this is Dogma Three, over. Anyone this channel report, over."

He held up the small earpiece, which had fallen from his ear, and listened for a response. Big surprise: None came. The radio was working, but maybe the mike was too muddy to pick up his voice.

Quit wasting time, he told himself. *Get over to that rise and see what's going on!*

With a twenty, maybe a thirty-mile-per-hour gust of wind whipping over him and turning the rain into needles, Vance burst from the tree and into Mother Nature's carwash. As he neared the rise, he heard the familiar, insectlike clicking that came from one of his teammates' signal devices. He shifted up and over the rise to find Doc lying on his gut, Nightstars in one hand, clicker in the other. "You're late, Corporal, you're late," the corpsman said with a grin.

Houston, Kim, and Rainey huddled beneath two small trees providing meager cover from the rain. The sergeant waved over Vance and Doc.

"All right, Marines. Playtime in the mud is over. Now it gets serious."

Houston's eyes bulged. "I am a heart attack, Sergeant. I am as serious as it gets."

"Shuddup, Lance Corporal. Kim, what's our ETA to the farmhouse?"

The South Korean was already staring at his GPS screen. "It's not far. Just under one kilometer."

"Good. Vance? You and Kim take point."

"Sergeant, all I can count on right now is my sidearm," Vance said, patting his holster. "Pretty pathetic."

"Are you kidding me, Corporal? If your head's still working, then that's all you need. Now let's move out!"

NORTH KOREAN ARMY RECONNAISSANCE SQUAD
NORTHEAST OF SINUIJU
NORTH KOREA
0328 HOURS LOCAL TIME

Fearing his own death, fearing it so much that he had become a coward when the moment had come, Master Sergeant Sung had released his opponent in an effort to save himself. He should have throttled the enemy into lifelessness, then let the mud take both of them. If Buddhism had taught Sung nothing else it was that suffering is inseparable from existence. To go beyond the pain, he needed to disregard himself and his worldly desires. If he did that, he would obtain such enlightenment that pain and misery would become his brides.

Still consumed by his failure, Sung wandered absently out of the mud, the flow rushing around his ankles as he reached the base of a foothill.

A man stepped out from behind a tree, and Sung wrenched his rifle from his pack, leveled the weapon, and fired.

Click. He looked down, realized the magazine had fallen out.

"Sangsa?" cried Sergeant Choi. "Sangsa?"

With shaky hands Sung lowered the rifle, squinted through the rain, and saw Choi trudging toward him.

"Sangsa, I have found Park and Lee. I will take you to them." Choi's eyes never left Sung's rifle.

"I would have shot you, had I not lost the magazine," Sung said, only then wincing against the sand between his teeth.

"You pulled the trigger, Sangsa?"

"I did."

"Then I will never forget this night, the night you saved me, and the night you almost killed me."

"Most men would be angry."

"Yes, Sangsa. But you and I . . . We are not most men. Now let's hurry. The enemy is escaping. We must pick up their trail!"

"Or maybe we should cross the border."

Choi's eyes narrowed in confusion. "Cross the border, Sangsa?"

"Into China."

"Do you believe the enemy is headed there?"

"No."

"Sangsa? I am confused."

"Lyongjang, you are not alone in your confusion. But you are right. The enemy is escaping, and we are good soldiers. Let's go."

As he followed Choi back toward the foothills, Sung felt for his grandfather's letter. He kept the document enclosed in plastic, since he had been thrust into water and mud before. Yes, the letter was still there, still dry. The old man had instructed him to be loyal, to be patient, and to be proud of dying for something much larger and much more important than himself.

But maybe Sung could get some or all of the enemy to do likewise. Maybe he could take out some of his anger and frustration on them. Purpose finally filled his steps. And while he did not feel much better about himself, he needed to summon back his courage. For them. His men.

TEAM DOGMA
EN ROUTE TO EXTRACTION POINT SCORPION
NORTH KOREA
0330 HOURS LOCAL TIME

Doc thought he heard Houston talking to himself, so he quickened his pace and fell in just behind the man.

"I just got some anger, some hostility to get rid of,

that's all," Houston mumbled. "I'm not going crazy. I'm just under a lot of stress."

Normally, Doc made it a point not to talk much when humping toward a coordinate—especially while in enemy territory. Common sense was a thing of beauty. But given the circumstances and a solid nod from Rainey, he decided a few words with Houston were in order.

As they kept tight to the foothills, following Vance and Kim farther north toward distant lights on the other side of a broad plain, Doc came up beside Houston and said softly, "Hey, Lance Corporal. How're you doing?"

"I'm straight, Doc. A-okay. One hundred percent good to go. This is one operator who is at the top of his game, performance tuned and as extreme as it gets."

Doc nudged him with an elbow. "I was looking for the short answer."

"No, you weren't."

"You're right."

"My old man dies, and everybody thinks I'm losing my mind. Ain't so. Ain't so at all."

"Nobody thinks that. You're just angry. But you have to watch that. You have to be angry enough to kill—but not so angry that you get yourself killed, you know?"

"Gotcha, Doc. Didn't know you were a shrink, too."

"God help us. I can fix the body. Usually, that's easy. But fixing the soul? That's always hard."

"Hey, man. Thanks."

Once Vance and Kim reached the base of the foothills, Vance raised his arm for a halt. Before them lay a broad, muddy field stretching for about a quarter kilometer west toward a cluster of dark, two-story buildings.

"That them?" Vance asked the ROK Marine.

Kim consulted his Nightstars. "Yes."

"Looks like no one's home."

"Or that they are asleep. They would not want to call attention to themselves."

"And neither do we. Which begs the question: Can we really trust these guys?"

"You can trust them."

"You say that as if *you* can't."

Kim just looked at Vance, his expression unreadable.

Hunched over, Rainey came trouncing up the line of men. "Let's hear it."

"Farmhouse dead ahead," Vance said. "We just have to cross the field."

"And there's absolutely no cover," added Rainey.

Vance sighed heavily. "That's right. And those good old boys from the NKA can just lean back and pick us off."

"Not if we crawl across," Rainey countered.

"Aw, Sarge. Haven't we had enough mud? Come on. And I don't know if you got a good whiff of that field, but it is nasty."

Rainey cocked a brow. "What do you suggest, Corporal?"

"That we follow that perimeter line over there, running like bats out of hell all the way. Far as I recall, this game's about time."

"Which we're wasting right now. All right, Vance. It's your show to the farmhouse. You get us there, I'll take you to Tokyo and buy you that expensive Daiwa reel you've been talking about."

"You don't have to bribe me with fishing tackle, Sergeant."

"I know. Deal?"

"Hell, yes. Hope you got some money saved. A whole lot of money."

Rainey dropped back to alert Doc and Houston. As he did, Vance directed an index finger at Kim. "I hope for your sake that your friends treat us right."

"They will. But they're not my friends."

Once Vance got the signal, he and Kim led the charge, fresh mud splashing as high as their shoulders as they beat a line north, then turned along the field's perimeter, where the ground was a little rockier but equally muddy. The stench Vance had noticed earlier became powerful, nauseating, and made Vance imagine that they were running alongside a thousand overflowing port-o-potties.

Yes, Vance could deal with the enemy, who wanted to kill him. But the corps wasn't paying him enough for this . . .

Doc had read in the North Korea field manual that raw sewage was routinely dumped into the environment. Apparently, thirty toxic chemicals banned by the World Health Organization were still being used by North Korean farmers, and three of them whose names Doc could not remember were classified as extremely hazardous. Thus, he found Rainey's decision to have them run beside the field a very good one. They might very well have been crawling through highly contaminated soil. Damn, if the mud didn't get you, the pesticides would.

While the younger operators darted ahead, Doc and Rainey fell several yards back but still burned boot rubber at full throttle—that is, for a couple of older farts. Doc's sense of urgency had never been greater, and he could relate to Houston's paranoia. At any moment, a loud crack could echo over the thumping of his boots, the howling of the wind, and the drone of falling rain. That sound might be the last thing he or Rainey heard. Simple as that.

So, was it time to make peace with God? Nah. Better to believe the miracle would come. Better to go a little deeper into debt with the big guy above. That would be okay. Doc had good credit, anyway. If the interest rates killed him, then so be it.

Drawing closer to the farmhouse—and beginning to believe that they really would make it, Doc felt a little giddy. Maybe the mudslide had wiped out the bad guys. All was well.

Until two men dressed in drab, utilitarian garb popped up from the ground, just a few meters ahead of Vance and Kim, their AK-47s coming to bear.

"Hit the deck!" Rainey cried, even as Lance Corporal Kim began shouting in Korean at the men.

Doc plopped down hard, then pushed himself up on his elbows as he reached for his pistol.

Kim was being helped to his feet by the taller sentinel, a very young man, maybe just a teenager. "It's okay," Kim said. "Let's go. Let's go."

Turning his gaze skyward, Doc thought, *Lord, don't play with me like that.*

Covered in a fresh layer of mud that gave Doc a case of the shudders, they followed the two men past the main farmhouse, with its warped wooden roof, battered shingles, peeling paint, and several deep puddles growing along its sides. The walls sagged inward, and some of the windows had been boarded up with now rotting plywood. Damn, if the place didn't remind Doc of the squalor he had seen in Martinique.

They slipped by a tractor easily older than Doc. Several other farm vehicles lay in the distance, and they, too, had those big, funky fenders you saw in black-and-white films of the forties and fifties. Doc wondered if the Koreans had ever laid eyes on modern equipment. It was as though their government wanted them frozen in time and space.

Beyond the tractor lay the nearest barn, its walls a patchwork of repairs, its roof losing the battle against gravity. The shorter man raced ahead, thumbing on his flashlight. He reached for a rusting latch, opened the door, then motioned everyone inside. Something in the Korean's expression bothered Doc. Yes, the man looked worried, and that was to be expected, but there was something else.

"Vance?" Rainey called.

The corporal nodded and took up a position just outside the door, his pistol in one hand, his Nightstars in the other.

Rainey leaned over to Doc and whispered, "Something's wrong."

"Yeah, I get that, too."

Drawing in a deep breath, Rainey gestured with his

carbine toward the doorway, and Doc tensed before passing inside.

For the first time since being in North Korea, Doc did not hear the rain, and the barn's silence took him by surprise as he and the others engaged in a standard clearing of the room. Doc's gaze shot immediately to the corners, the niches, the places where bad guys could be hiding, but the shadows did not yield much to the dim light. He thought of donning his Night Vision Goggles, but there was no time. Still, what he could see proved as predictable as it was non-threatening. Dozens of wooden crates lay in stacks about ten high across the far wall, and above them, nearly lost in the darkness, hung a loft spanned by huge, wooden rafters. A musty, earthy scent replaced the horrors of the field outside, though as Doc shifted a little farther into the barn, he could still catch the slench of the mud on his boots.

After Rainey announced that the barn was secure, the short guy led them toward a corner workshop. Tools and pieces of farm machinery cluttered two old, grease-stained benches, and a pair of trenches had been dug in the ground by the big tires of some tractor or other farm vehicle. Still more crates lined the back wall, and from behind one stack came a wiry old man holding a rifle. He waved his weapon at Doc and Rainey, then his eyes crinkled up as he shouted at the shorter Korean.

"Houston, you called clear in this area," Rainey reminded the lance corporal.

"I know, Sarge. And I don't know where this guy came from!"

Rainey turned to Kim. "What's he saying?"

The ROK Marine didn't look happy. "He says we should not have come."

"But you said—"

"I make a deal with Chun." Kim lifted his chin at the short Korean. "He is with the underground. And so is Kwan, a friend of Chun's who lives and works here on the farm." Kim looked to the taller Korean. "But the old man is Chun's father, and he wants no part of this."

"You tell the old man we just want to clean up, then we'll be on our way," Rainey said.

Kim translated, but the old man, whose thinning gray hair and gaunt cheeks made him appear more Grim-Reaper–like than human, crossed to his son and worked his little mouth like a gunnery sergeant grilling a private. If the old man had brushed his teeth in the past decade, there was no clear evidence.

"This is just fucking great," Houston said, throwing his hands high in the air. "I need a shower. What do I get? Caught up in some domestic drama."

Rainey glared at Houston. "We'll need Bright Star on the horn in a couple of minutes. Does my Foxtrot work?"

"Okay, Sarge. I'm on it."

"Yes, you are."

"Sergeant Rainey?" Kim called. "The old man wants us to leave now."

Rainey shrugged. "Can't you have Chun talk to him?"

"I do not think that will help. Chun's father is a proud member of the Red Guard."

"Red Guard?"

"It's the Worker-Peasant militia," Doc said. "You get conscripted when you're seventeen, serve in the military for about eight years or more, then when you get out, you're part of the Red Guard—for life. I'm betting Kwan and Chun here are still members, even while they're working for the underground."

"Is that right, Kim?" Rainey asked.

"Yes."

Chun crossed over to Kim and muttered something.

Rainey darkened his tone. "What's he saying?"

"He says the radio woke up his father. He is sorry for the trouble."

"Wait a minute. Are you telling me these two guys work for the underground, and the old man doesn't know about it?"

Kim posed the question to Chun, who eyed Rainey and slowly shook his head.

"We blew their secret," Doc said.

"We didn't blow it. They did," Rainey retorted.

Vance suddenly shifted into the barn. "Sarge, we got a couple of Hoplites buzzing northeast. Doesn't look like they're headed this way, but they could turn."

"All right. Keep eyes on, keep me informed."

The corporal nodded and vanished behind the door.

Doc nudged Rainey while keeping his gaze on the old man, who was now arguing fiercely with his son. "We need to get his weapon."

"Kim, tell the old man I want to talk to him," Rainey said softly. "Then you get behind him. I want his rife—and you're going to get it."

"Yes, Sergeant."

As Kim was about to move, Chun grabbed his shoulder and rattled off something. Kim offered a clipped reply before shifting gingerly back to the old man and Kwan. He issued Rainey's request, then started to cross behind the old man. However, the lance corporal found the barrel of an AK-47 following his every step.

Doc considered making a move of his own, but Rainey's look said that he would make the grab.

The old man shouted at Kim.

Chun shook his rifle and hollered something at Kwan, who then pointed at his father, distracting the man—

Even as, in a flash, Kim leaned over, wrenched free his K-bar, and came up with it as the old man swung around.

Kim reared back with his knife, just a heartbeat away from burying it in the old man's shoulder.

Rainey sprang forward—

While Doc dove behind the Sarge to tackle Chun.

And then, the worst thing that could have happened . . .

Happened.

The old man opened fire.

12

Master Sergeant Sung and his men had picked up the enemy's trail and were about to head across the open field when the muffled yet distinctive popping of an AK-47 sent them diving onto their bellies. They lay on a patch of muddy grass as Sung studied the farm through the rain-streaked lenses of his binoculars. He saw no lights, no movement, save for a few thin trees waving in the wind.

"The enemy has awakened those farmers," Choi said excitedly.

"Where are the lights?" Sung asked.

Choi stammered. "I . . . I do not know."

Park and Lee pushed up to their haunches and looked to Sung for orders.

But Sung hesitated.

"Sangsa, they fired a weapon. Maybe they are scared

and turned off the lights. We should move in. Now!" Choi cried. "This is our chance!"

"That's right," Sung said, having to convince himself and still bothered by the farmhouse's few windows, which remained dark. "Let's go." He gestured for Choi to lead them, then waved on Park and Lee.

Although they were soaked, dirty, and tired, Sung witnessed an extraordinary sense of determination in his men. Yes, he could take credit for some of that, but their inner strength carried them now. As he jogged behind Lee, he reminded himself that he could draw on their youth and on the commitment he had made to them. He could renew his vow to be a great soldier. He could accomplish the mission, for the mission was most important.

Drawing within fifty meters of the main farmhouse, Choi gave a hand signal, then spied what he could through his binoculars as Lee, Park, and finally Sung reached the sergeant's position.

"I believe the shots came from the house," said Choi.

"But I thought they came from one of the barns," Lee said. "They are more north, and the sound did come from the north."

"Then Choi, you and Park will search the farmhouse. Lee and I will search the barns," Sung said.

"Sangsa, I have tried cleaning my rifle, but there is still a lot of mud," said Park, directing his gaze to the weapon. "I do not know if I can trust it."

"Then trust your pistol, your knife, and your heart," Sung said, trying to spark the man's confidence and his own. "Now then. I have visited this farm once before. There was an old man living here with his son. And there was another boy who helped them. There was an old woman, too. But I believe she died last year."

"We will look for them," said Choi. "But we must move. There haven't been any more shots. The enemy could already be gone."

"Or maybe they did not come here. Maybe one of those farmers spotted them near the field and tried to shoot them. The enemy could be retreating, and we would just be wasting time," Park said.

"If the enemy was being fired upon, then why didn't they return fire?" Choi asked.

Sung put a finger to his lips. "The answers will come." He gave the signal for Choi and Park to advance.

Leaving mud flying in their wake, the two recon soldiers kept their heads low and charged toward the farmhouse. For a few seconds, the wind swept in so violently that Sung saw only a blurry streak of rain, then the silhouettes of his men reappeared as they came within twenty meters of the farmhouse.

"Sangsa?" Private Lee called. "Should we go now?"

Sung nodded, confused over why he had watched Choi and Park instead of storming toward the barns with Lee.

Nearly blown over onto their sides by another blast of wind, Sung and Lee sloshed through the muck, and by the time Sung was nearly out of breath, they reached an old tractor and slipped behind its large rear wheels, which were nearly two meters in diameter. Sung checked and double-checked his rifle, as did Lee.

"There is so much mud," the private said, staring gravely at Sung's rifle.

He nodded, then whispered, "Have your pistol ready. And a grenade. Maybe two."

"Yes, Sangsa."

Rain funneled down off the barn's roof just behind them, and the water began creeping up, over their boots. Time to move. Gritting his teeth, Sung looked to the barn door. Yes, they might be walking into a trap, but they had to seek out the enemy. What was more, the promise of dryness and a bit more warmth lay within. He held his breath and signaled Lee.

At once they sprang to the door and stood on either side, then Lee raised the latch with the muzzle of his rifle while wedging his boot into the jam.

After a quick nod from Sung, the private kicked opened the door and bolted inside.

Sung should have been right behind the man, covering his subordinate's back. But he was not. He leaned against the barn door, the rain washing over his face—

Until the moment finally registered, and with a wild scream he rolled and carried himself into the musty darkness, believing that muzzle flashes from the corners would erupt, and he would fall quickly and quite pathetically to his death.

TEAM DOGMA
FARMHOUSE NORTHEAST OF SINUIJU
NORTH KOREA
0357 HOURS LOCAL TIME

Rainey lay in a narrow crawl space beneath the farmhouse's floorboards, wondering how the hell his life had come to this. All they had wanted to do was blow stuff up and go home, not wind up hiding from the enemy in some dirty hole. Fate, as Vance would say, is another varmint that needs killin'.

Back in the barn, the old man's salvo had—thank God—fallen wide, missing Houston by a quarter meter, maybe less.

Then Lance Corporal Kim had made sure that the old man would never fire again. A single thrust of Kim's K-bar had rendered the loyal North Korean lifeless. Chun had cried out a second before Doc seized him and covered his mouth.

"Don't kill him," Rainey had ordered Doc.

And the corpsman had whispered "Shush," into the young man's ear while tightening his grip.

"Fuck, fuck, fuck," Houston had groaned, while Vance had swung into the room, waving his pistol.

"All right, Marines, time to leave," Rainey had ordered.

"No go there," Vance had said. "More Hoplites to the west, and barely any cover till we get to that wooded area. They'd spot us in a second."

In the interim, Kim had engaged in a rapid conversation with Kwan.

"What?" Rainey had asked.

"He says it's better we stay here."

"You tell him there's a recon team on our ass?"

"He says they'll hide us. He says if we go, we will definitely be caught. They can misdirect the recon team."

Rainey had gone outside and glimpsed the western terrain and the Hoplite choppers for himself. Then he had rushed back and told Kim okay.

"What about *him*?" Doc had asked, still holding Chun.

"Tie and gag him."

"That's not necessary," Kim had said.

"You just killed his father. If you just killed my father, you wouldn't be standing long."

Kwan had interjected a few words, and Kim had answered. Then, regarding Rainey, he had said, "Chun knew this day would come. The old man would have betrayed him. The old man was already dead. He was murdered by the government years ago. His heart was blackened."

"That's great," Rainey had said. "Doc? Tie and gag Chun. Kim? Get Kwan here to show us his hiding places, then tell him we're going to tie and gag him, too."

"Sergeant, if the recon team comes here, there will be no one to misdirect them."

"That's right. But there will be five men who intend to kill them. Let's go."

However, by the time Rainey was slipping into the space beneath the floorboards, he had second-guessed himself, and allowed Kwan to remain free and in the kitchen.

Well, I can thank old Doc for that, Rainey thought as the floorboards creaked and Kwan shouted something to at least one, maybe two men who were entering the farmhouse.

Doc had convinced Rainey to trust Kwan. They needed to remain at the farm at least until those Hoplites left, and sending off the recon team in the wrong direction would allow them to do so. If the bad guys arrived and found no one home, their suspicions would be heightened and they'd be more apt to tear the place apart. That logic still seemed a little faulty to Rainey, but he had gone along with it—only because he had chosen to remain as close to Kwan as possible. If the young man decided to rat them out, then at least the rest of the team would have a fighting chance.

Drawing in a long breath, Rainey closed his eyes a moment, clenched his pistol, and listened as wood creaked just a few inches from his nose.

Vance lay on his belly, up in the loft of the second barn. He had smashed apart a few crates and had wriggled himself inside them like a big old farm rat just waiting to dart out and snatch a piece of bologna that fell from Farmer Joe's sandwich. Then again, most South Koreans did not go by the name of "Farmer Joe," and he seriously doubted that any of them enjoyed a good bologna sandwich on white with heavy mayo (and you had best skip the mayo if you're taking such sandwiches on a bass-fishing trip; that is, unless you're bringing along the cooler. The Florida sun ain't kind to mayonnaise—and Vance ought to know).

Just moments prior, a faint scream from the other barn had rendered the corporal inert. He had replayed that scream in his mind, had realized that it had not belonged to Rainey, Doc, or Houston. And Kim did not strike Vance as the kind of guy who would make such a noise. Even when mortally wounded, the ROK Marine would probably die in silence. After hearing that scream, Vance had remained absolutely frozen, figuring that the barn door would swing open at any moment.

No, not any moment. Now.

With his Night Vision Goggles pulled tightly over his

eyes, he watched the glowing green silhouettes of two men as they moved robotically inside, sweeping the corners as they had been taught. Knowing he had the element of surprise and imagining himself taking out both men with two carefully placed shots, Vance trembled with the desire to act.

But he could not. His job was to remain there, just some old scarecrow stuffed into the crates—even though he had them. He had both of them dead-on! His MEU pistol, meager though it was, would not fail him. He knew that. He *knew* that.

Suddenly, he was seven and tucked under his father's pickup truck during a game of hide-and-seek. He had always been the best hider on his block. Tommy Jannison was the only kid who had ever found Vance, and that was because Vance had had a cold that day, and had sneezed. Who knew then that such a skill might save his life?

The ladder leading up to the loft squeaked a little, and Vance took his pistol in both hands.

A boot struck a rung. Another boot struck, and the top of the ladder pulled away from the edge of the loft, then slapped back hard. A man grunted, continued up the ladder. And no, he did not sound like Tommy Jannison. Not one bit.

Houston was up on the main farmhouse's roof, perched beside a crumbling chimney and wondering whether the damned wind would blow him off or the damned rain would wash him away. Rainey had told him point-blank that if the situation went south, his job was to get off a second sitrep—

Then kill every bad guy in sight.

No problem there. No problem at all. And the Foxtrot radio had checked out just fine. He had made his first report from the roof, utilizing his earpiece to remain silent. He had automatically transmitted the team's GPS coordinates, and had assured Bright Star that they would soon be on the move. Then, less than a minute later, he had watched those two little mothers enter the farmhouse, where he knew Kwan would confront them. Houston had kept low, listening as attentively as he could to what was happening inside. But with the weather in his ears, the walls between them, and the foreign language, the task was, in a word, not easy (make that two words).

So Houston waited for a gunshot, either from an AK or an MEU pistol. You couldn't mistake one for the other. But in truth, it didn't matter who fired first. The moment a shot rang out, he would crawl to the edge of the roof so that he could pick off any bad guys leaving the front door. He wished Vance were up top with him. The fisherman was the better shot, and he would make crouching in the rain a bit more bearable—if he didn't cop an attitude again. Houston figured he owed the guy an apology for his behavior. An hour ago he would not have thought that, but after leaving the mudslide, he had experienced a moment of clarity, a moment in which he had reflected upon what he had said and done. It was not fair to subject the team to his issues. Shit, they had their own problems on top of the botched mission. Fair was fair, and he wasn't being the Marine he should be, the Marine he had become after the mission in Pakistan.

Okay, he had figured that out. You didn't need to be a

Jeopardy grand champion. But what about the mood swings? Had he gone manic? Mr. Good Marine one minute, Mr. Raging Fucking Lunatic the next? Why did that feeling get inside him, make him want to strike out so fiercely that he would kill anyone—friend or foe— who got in the way?

Voices outside sent a shudder through his gut. He shifted slowly around and peered past the chimney, staring down though his NVGs at Kwan and the two recon soldiers, still conversing. One of them shoved his rifle into Kwan's chest.

If you shoot him, I'm going to kill you, Houston thought.

Kwan yelled something, lifted his hands in the air.

And Houston sighted the bad guy with his pistol.

Doc and Chun sat within a narrow tunnel beneath a battered aluminum storage bin used to store various attachments for the tractors. The tunnel connected the first barn with the main farmhouse and had been dug over sixty years prior by the farm's original owners. Of course, the wooden supports lining the passageway were rotting and probably termite infested, and Doc wondered if confronting the enemy might be less dangerous than hiding in the dank, about-to-collapse hole. Kwan had suggested that the entire team hide in the tunnel, but Rainey had declined. Yes, it was better to spread themselves out, though Doc had suggested that they not leave Chun alone. So they had gagged him, tied his hands behind his back, and had Kim instruct him not to make any trouble.

Now, the boy's teary eyes, illuminated by Doc's penlight, made the corpsman even more uncomfortable. Occasionally the boy sniffled, and Doc held a finger to his lips and tried to offer a sympathetic look, but he wasn't sure if his sympathy meant anything. He felt as responsible for the old man's death as Kim, and now he guessed that there wasn't a damned thing he could do or say (in English or otherwise) that would make Chun feel better.

So they just sat there, waiting until Vance or Houston came to get them out.

Doc had just breathed a heavy sigh when someone threw back the bin's heavy metal lid. He gave Chun a wide-eyed look, then braced himself and aimed his pistol at the edge of the tunnel, where it turned up and was concealed by a piece of dirt-covered plywood.

A whisper sounded above the wind. Had the words been English or Korean? Shit, Doc couldn't tell.

Lance Corporal Kim felt even more certain that volunteering for the mission had been the biggest mistake of his life. Not only had he been shot down over enemy territory, but he had been forced to kill a civilian. And while such an act carried with it a unique set of horrors, Kim felt even more shaken because—truth be told—he had never killed a man.

During his training, he had had many discussions, both formal and informal, with his fellow Marines regarding what it must feel like to take someone's life and to live with yourself afterward. Even those men who had killed were hesitant to say that it was easy or just part of the job. They had said that everyone deals with it differently and that most Marines find the courage and peace of mind to continue serving their country. They had cautioned Kim and his buddies not to reflect too deeply upon their actions. They had said that the guilt could become unbearable.

But what else could one do while lying beneath a tarpaulin spread across the wooden flatbed of an ancient pickup truck? What else could one consider when a dead man lay within arm's reach? There was only the moment, the moment, the moment . . .

The knife had penetrated the old man's skin so easily that for a second Kim had thought he was stabbing a pillow. But then the blade had struck bone, and a sickening grinding noise had resounded as the old man had fallen and the blade had ripped free.

But Kim had not stopped there. He dropped, reared back once more, punched stainless steel into wizened flesh, into a blackened heart. And then he came up, a K-bar dripping with blood still locked in his hand. Kim's gaze had turned to Chun, and Kim had never seen a man so horrified, so consumed by helplessness and agony.

With a grenade in one hand, a pistol in the other, Lance Corporal Kim forced away the guilt, turning himself into a being with one sense—the sense of hearing. And through the rain, footfalls sounded and drew closer. At any moment they would be upon him.

And he would, without hesitation, kill again.

The guys in the barn had missed Vance. Of course they had. Did they have any idea who they were dealing with? World champion Hide-and-Seek dudes from the age of seven do not get sloppy. If Vance was hiding around wood, then he *was* wood. If he was hiding in water, then he *was* water. He was a chameleon, not a casualty. And the second his North Korean guests had left the barn, Vance had slid down the ladder, and now crossed quickly to the door. After a second's worth of inspection, he scuttled out to pause behind a rusty backhoe. He searched for the bad guys. Where were they?

After exactly three deep breaths, he sprinted for the first barn, reached it, stole his way along the wall, then paused at the corner, where he could glimpse the front of the farmhouse.

"Yeah, I know you guys," he whispered, zooming in with his NVGs. Four NKA recon guys encircled Kwan, and one of them repeatedly jabbed his rifle into Kwan's chest. Damn, where was Doc's Para SAW when they needed it? The corpsman could have dropped the entire group with a couple of salvos, though Kwan would have been cut down as well. Call it an acceptable loss, or payback for their screw-up. They should not have awakened the old man. They should have planned better.

Vance wished he could have called Rainey to report, but there was always a chance that the faintest hum or burst of static could be detected. Turning his attention to the farmhouse's roof, he scanned the chimney area for Houston. No Houston. Either the radio operator had crawled around to the other side of the chimney, or he had found another position.

Or maybe, given his instability, he had spread his wings and had taken the old LSD swan dive off the roof. Bottom line? He wasn't where he should be, and that really pissed Vance off.

But what about the others? A look to the old truck suggested that Kim had remained in position beneath the tarpaulin, and another look to the old storage bin gave Vance a chill. The lid lay open. The bad guys had searched the bin, but if they had discovered Doc and Chun they would have hauled them out or at least gone in after them. Maybe they had. Maybe there were more than four guys. Shit. Vance contemplated dashing over there to find out.

The conversation between Kwan and the recon guys continued, and though the field book contained many of the most common Korean phrases, Vance failed to remember any of them. The only thing he understood was their body language, which was harsh. Very harsh.

Kwan dropped to his knees.

One of the recon guys—the oldest, from the looks of him—raised his pistol to Kwan's head.

And Vance took aim at the veteran soldier. *Oh, shit, man. Don't do it. Don't do it . . .*

13

Master Sergeant Sung did not trust Kwan's story. The boy had told him that Chun and Chun's father had been monitoring the military channel and had learned of the downed C-130 transport. They had taken up their rifles and had stood watch over their farm. Some time later, they thought they had spotted some men on the outskirts of their field, and after calling for them and receiving no reply, Chun's father had opened fire, after which he and his son had gone off in pursuit while Kwan, a friend of Chun's who lived and worked on the farm, remained behind.

Kwan had then explained why he had remained behind, but his story was weak. Very weak. And much too convenient. Apparently, he had stayed to alert any soldiers who might come by. But when asked if he had used the radio to do so, he had said he was about to call for help when Sung and his team had arrived.

Again, much too convenient.

Moreover, would two struggling farmers, loyal or not, just happen to be up late and just happen to be monitoring the military channel? The only civilians Sung knew who frequently monitored those channels were retired military, subversives, and members of the South Korean underground, who were known to operate in the area.

Sung took a step forward so that the muzzle of his pistol touched the boy's forehead. "Tell me what you know, Kwan. And I will let you live."

"I told you the truth." Despite the rain, Sung knew the boy was crying.

Driving the pistol a little deeper into Kwan's flesh, Sung asked, "Chun and his father were awake in the middle of the night?"

"Yes."

"I do not believe you."

The boy tensed. "We heard a plane, then an explosion louder than thunder woke us up."

Sung weighed the truth in that. Perhaps they had heard an explosion, and the sound had driven them to the radio for news. But Sung was not aware of the plane's coordinates, so there was no way to verify that these farmers could have heard the explosion—especially during a violent thunderstorm.

"Sangsa, if he saw them leave, then maybe he can lead us back to them," Park suggested, breaking Sung's train of thought.

"Maybe they are still here," said Choi. "And we should search again."

"Have you no opinion, Sb-yong Lee?" Sung asked,

glancing sidelong at the private, whose scarred face shone slick and ghastly in the lightning.

"Sangsa, if they are still here, then they are watching us right now." He turned his head toward the rooftops. "And if you kill Kwan, you may be the second man to die."

Sung adjusted his grip on the pistol. "Should we find out?"

Flinching, Kwan lowered his head. "Please, I told you what I know. I am a loyal member of the Red Youth Guard. I will do everything I can to help you capture the enemy. I am only here to help—not to lie. I have spent my entire life in the service of our great country. Do not punish me for that."

After a moment's consideration, Sung lowered the pistol. "Choi, you and Park search the barns and the house again." The two men rushed off. "Now then, Kwan, I find it odd that there are no footprints where you say Chun and his father pursued the enemy."

"They headed north, toward the border. The rain has hidden most of their trail. But if you look carefully, you may find a few marks that have not yet washed away."

"Show me again." Sung waved his pistol, and Kwan got shakily to his feet. The young man led them past the barns, toward the edge of a fallow field.

"Here?" Sung asked.

Kwan nodded.

With Lee covering his back, Sung raised his binoculars and panned across the foothills, but the rain and gloom made his inspection difficult, if not impossible. He panned down, sweeping slowly across the pock-marked field dotted with literally hundreds of small puddles. Indeed, the enemy's footprints could have been filled in by the rain, and it could take literally hours of combing through the mud to pick up their trail.

Sung shoved the binoculars into the crook of his arm, then whirled and pushed his pistol into the Kwan's chest. "Are you lying?"

"No, Sangsa. I want to kill the enemy as much as you do. I am here to help." The boy stared unflinchingly at Sung. If he was lying, he had remarkable courage. Sung was not sure if he could have kept himself as composed, and the boy's stare was beginning to persuade him.

Sung glanced over his shoulder. "What would you do, Sb-yong Lee?"

"Exactly what you are doing, Sangsa. Search again. And if we find nothing, then we set out after the enemy. This man will lead us. And if he is lying, he will die."

"Yes, we will kill him, but we will have lost the enemy."

"Maybe not, Sangsa. If he is lying, he will take us away from the enemy, toward the north. At that point, we will head south."

"But we will have lost much time."

"We are losing time right now."

Sung turned to Kwan and rasped, "Do you understand what will happen if you are lying?"

"I do, Sangsa. But I know the truth. And if you kill me anyway, then I die with a clear conscience and a pure heart."

Sung lowered his pistol, started back toward the farmhouse. Out of the corner of his eye, he spotted an old pickup truck parked behind a pile of wood at the far corner of the field. "Lee, did we search that truck?"

"I did not see that truck, Sangsa."

"Do you see it now?"

Lee nodded vigorously.

"Then search it immediately!"

While the private headed off, Sung continued toward the farmhouse, saying, "I hope you have some towels and something warm to eat."

"I do, Sangsa," Kwan said. "I will warm some soup. But I thought time was your enemy."

Feeling about as wet, filthy, and drained as any human being could, Sung sighed deeply. "I will make time my ally—as I hope you are. I sincerely hope . . ."

TEAM DOGMA
FARMHOUSE NORTHEAST OF SINUIJU
NORTH KOREA
0410 HOURS LOCAL TIME

Lance Corporal Kim lay very still on the pickup truck's flatbed, the tarpaulin still pulled over his head as the thudding of boots grew nearer. He knew that one of his teammates was coming to get him—

Or one of the North Koreans was coming to kill him.

He waited for the chirp that would indicate a friendly approach.

More footfalls. And the man was almost on top of him.

No chirp! And then:

"Kim!" Vance whispered.

The lance corporal threw off the tarpaulin to find Vance, his face shielded by his NVGs. The sniper proffered a hand.

"You forgot to signal," Kim reminded the man.

"Forget the fucking signal!" Vance grabbed the old man's body by the ankles and began dragging him off the flatbed. "I think one guy's coming. He's still far enough away. Give me a hand."

They dragged the body to a pile of scrap wood from a demolished shed. Vance shoved a few large pieces of plywood over the body, then motioned for Kim to join him on the other side of the debris. Keeping as tightly as they could to some of the longer beams, they watched as one of the NKA recon soldiers poked around the flatbed, opened the truck door, then squatted to steal a peak beneath the vehicle.

Kim imagined either himself or Vance bursting from the pile and quietly knifing the man, but the soldier's disappearance would sound the alarm. It was better to keep them all alive and misdirected while Kim and the others slipped away.

Satisfied that the pickup truck was empty, the soldier started off, then suddenly halted, turned back for the pile of scraps, his gaze focused on the plywood covering the body.

Vance already had his K-bar ready, as did Kim. The sniper gave Kim a signal indicating that he would make the move, and Kim wished he could feel relief in that.

The soldier drew closer and leaned toward the pile, squinting in the darkness. Lightning picked out his features, and Kim frowned at the man's scarred face.

Drawing in a long breath, Vance pursed his lips, then mouthed the word, "Wait."

Kim nodded.

The soldier shoved aside a smaller scrap with his rifle's muzzle, then leaned down to move another piece.

Houston had slid around the chimney three times already, and each time he had feared crumbling brick would break loose and tumble to the ground. In fact, one small chunk had already rolled free and splashed into the mud, but thank God the rain had drowned out the noise. Presently, while he huddled against the chimney, two of the damned soldiers were tearing the farmhouse apart as Kwan and the oldest Korean, the sergeant probably, headed inside. Houston wondered what it must be like for Rainey, lying beneath the kitchen floor, listening to those bastards. Then again, the Sarge could have already changed his position when the others had left the farmhouse. That's what Houston would have done. Hopefully, Rainey was already outside. Had to be. *Needed* to be.

A burning scent caught Houston's attention, and he suddenly realized that someone had stoked a fire, with smoke now billowing up out of the chimney, then bending hard in the wind. The smoke smelled pretty good, and Houston's stomach growled in agreement. Damn, the enemy was inside a warm farmhouse and cooking while he was stuck up on the roof, in the rain, and feeling so damned tired that he would pay anyone a thousand bucks for a good night's sleep. With excruciating precision, he changed his position once more, looked out to the woodpile with his NVGs.

He held his breath, saw movement, zoomed in, probing deeper. And there he was. One of the recon guys was
picking through the rubble. Damn, wasn't Kim right
there, lying in the back of that pickup truck? That recon
guy was dangerously close, and Houston swore over his
inability to do something. Hide-and-seek was a kid's
game. Wasn't it high time that they acted like men?

NORTH KOREAN ARMY RECONNAISSANCE SQUAD
FARMHOUSE NORTHEAST OF SINUIJU
NORTH KOREA
0414 HOURS LOCAL TIME

Master Sergeant Sung's boot pressed hard against one
of the kitchen's floorboards. The hollow creak struck
him as curious. Most curious.

"Is this why you keep telling me to have a seat?" he
asked as he reached down and abruptly yanked up the
board to reveal a hole about two feet deep beneath the
planking. "You did want me to discover this?"

Kwan, who was holding a heavy metal bowl by its
attached handle, shook his head. "There is nothing to
see there."

Sung booted up several more boards and shone his
flashlight into the empty depression. "This is easily
large enough to hide a man."

"Not a man, Sangsa," Kwan said. "Chun's father
sometimes hid food there. Chun and I helped him dig
that hole after he had been robbed three times. Many
starving people come from the city and try to rob the
farmers."

"You have an answer for every question," Sung said. "Are there any other tunnels or holes I should know about?"

"No, Sangsa."

"Why does Chung's father no longer use the hiding place?"

"He still does."

"But you said 'he sometimes *hid* food there,' which implies that he no longer does."

"An error, Sangsa. My apology. Now please, sit. I will warm your soup."

As the boy pushed past him, Sung grabbed Kwan's arm. "Just warm it slightly. We'll be leaving soon."

TEAM DOGMA
FARMHOUSE NORTHEAST OF SINUIJU
NORTH KOREA
0418 HOURS LOCAL TIME

Peering through a slit between two boards covering a shattered window, Rainey watched the older recon sergeant, the one he had grappled with in the mud, accept a bowl of soup from Kwan. Jesus, had the guy lost it? The enemy could be lurking about, and he was sipping soup? Talk about a glaring tactical error. Or was the sergeant using himself as bait in an attempt to draw out the enemy? Was he that cunning? That clever? Maybe. Even so, Kwan's job was to get the recon team away from the farmhouse so Rainey and his men could, in fact, clean their equipment, grab a bite themselves, then get moving; however, from the looks of things, that might not happen any time soon. Kwan need to get the show on the road, and Rainey needed Kim to communicate that to the Korean.

Carefully measuring his steps, Rainey pushed around the farmhouse toward the back, then hit the wall as two of the recon guys jostled past the nearest barn's door, steering themselves back to the farmhouse. Once they passed out of view, Rainey donned his NVGs, switched them on, then did an Olympic sprint for the tractor. Concealed behind it, he waited for a moment, then shuffled along the barn's west wall, realizing with a muffled groan that rain washing off the roof had dug an ankle-deep trench that made running in silence well-nigh impossible. So he slowed down.

Which saved his life.

Had he jogged to the edge of the barn, he would have run directly into a lanky soldier whose face bore an awful scar. The man had come running across the field from the woodpile and was presumably on his way back to the farmhouse.

Rainey, catching sight of the guy's approach, hit the deck, the mud and rain swallowing most of his body. He tucked himself tightly against the barn's foundation and lay there, face covered in muck, heart thudding loudly in his ears as the soldier passed within a meter—

And Rainey increased his grip on the knife in his hand.

Then . . . the footfalls grew distant. Rainey slowly emerged from his mud puddle, rose, then started across the field, toward the woodpile.

He was about halfway there when a signal chirp sent a shudder through him. His pulse slowed, if only a little, as he rounded the pile's corner and squatted down beside Vance and Kim. He raised his NVGs and nodded to the worried men.

"Jesus, Sarge, we almost blew it here," Vance whispered. "Guy started picking through the wood. We moved the body in there."

"Yeah, I almost ran into that guy myself. Looks like they're getting ready to have a party in the farmhouse."

"Then let's frag 'em and get going," Vance said. "Those Hoplites have already moved on. We don't keep moving ourselves, we die. That's all I know."

"Yes, but Kwan is still inside the farmhouse," Kim pointed out.

"And Houston's up on the roof," Rainey added. "At least I hope he is. Vance? You and Kim go get Doc and Chun. Take them to the back barn and start cleaning your weapons. I'm going to stay tight on the farmhouse, see what's going on. I'll get Houston and rally on you, but tell everyone to be ready to move out as soon as Houston and I get there. Good to go?"

"Aye-aye, Sarge," Vance said. "Good to go."

"Sergeant?" Kim called.

"What is it?"

The ROK Marine appeared out of breath, couldn't talk, and just stared at Rainey as though he had been shot again.

"What is it, Lance Corporal?"

"Sergeant, Chun and Kwan are valuable members of the underground. Others died so that they could remain here to assist those wishing to escape to the South. Men like them helped me to escape. If they die—"

"I know what you're getting at, Kim, but you have to

put the guilt and the rest of it aside. If these boys wind up buying it because of us, then we have to accept that. No, it ain't easy." Rainey sighed. "It is what is."

"But we won't intentionally sacrifice them, is that correct? They are too valuable. The entire network could be disrupted, and during a crisis like this we can't—"

"Lance Corporal, I can't comment any further. Now get moving."

Vance darted away, with the long-faced Korean Marine turning to sweep up behind. Rainey understood Kim's guilt over having killed Chun's father, and he understood Kim's sense of responsibility to the men who were helping the team. But Rainey was still not convinced that underground guys like Kwan—and especially Chun—could be trusted. Yes, Kwan had not alerted the enemy, but the tide could change quickly. Very quickly. As much as he might regret it later, Rainey knew there would be no hesitation, no contemplation when it came to sacrificing Kwan and Chun in order to save himself and his men. And if Lance Corporal Kim had a problem with that—if he interfered in any way—then Rainey would do what was necessary. Whatever was necessary. Rainey, Houston, Vance, and Doc had fought their way through some of Hell's baddest neighborhoods, and if Rainey had anything to say about it, no individual or mission would tear them apart.

Stealing his way back to the farmhouse, and for once thankful for the storm, since it did a thorough job of concealing his passage, Rainey returned to the exact spot he had left, removed his NVGs, and focused his right eye through that crack where two warped sections of plywood met.

There were four recon guys in all: the oldest guy, the sergeant; a plump-faced, doofy looking guy; a short guy carrying a big radio; and the lean guy with the burned face. While the sergeant finished his soup, the other three cleaned their rifles, ignoring the mud dripping from their faces and shoulders. The sergeant's causal movements and long yawn stood in stark contrast to the intensity evident in the other three. Kwan stood near the cracked mantel, muttering something to the old sergeant, who seemed to dismiss him at first, then suddenly the soldier rattled off something that sent Kwan cowering and nodding.

All right, Kwan was still inside, but so were the four recon guys. And those men needed very badly to die. An executive decision was in order, and in the blink of an eye, Rainey made it. He slipped around the farmhouse, then backed away enough so that he could see Houston on the roof.

No Houston.

Rainey moved farther along the farmhouse wall for a better angle on the chimney.

Jesus, still no Houston.

Had the lance corporal climbed down? When? Rainey backed farther away from the building, thought he saw one of Houston's legs near the chimney, but he couldn't be sure, damn it.

She was the best piece of ass Houston had ever had, with the face of a supermodel, the body of an athlete, and the libido of a porn star. All of which described a woman who was not real, could never be real—

Except in Houston's dreams.

"You like Love Hotel?" she whispered in his ear as he slid on top of her.

"Oh, yeah, baby. I've been waiting my entire life for this!"

Houston was about to enter her when—

"Bradley?"

Craning his head in surprise, Houston turned to find his father standing there, shaking his head in disappointment. "This is what I raised? A killer and a whoremonger? I wanted you to be a successful businessman and a gentleman. Look at yourself. You're pathetic."

Gasping, Houston awoke to chills rushing up his spine.

It was raining? Windy? His back hurt like hell? Where the hell was he?

More chills fanned across his shoulders as he sat up, realized he was on the roof.

Lance Corporal Bradley Houston was a United States Force Recon Marine who had fallen asleep on the job.

Shit! My father was right! God, what've I done?

Carefully, he leaned forward, looked down, spotted Rainey on the ground below. The sergeant eyed him angrily, then signaled: Four enemy soldiers were inside the farmhouse. The rest of the team was inside the smaller of the two barns. Rainey wanted Houston to hop down from the roof as quietly as he could. Sure, he could reach the rear edge, where the drop would only be about ten feet into the soft mud, but the impact wouldn't be silent. Houston glanced back at the crumbling chimney and groped for an idea.

NORTH KOREAN ARMY RECONNAISSANCE SQUAD
FARMHOUSE NORTHEAST OF SINUIJU
NORTH KOREA
0425 HOURS LOCAL TIME

With a belly full of warm soup and the mud cleared from his eyes, nose, and mouth, Master Sergeant Sung rose, told his men to finish cleaning their weapons, then moved to Kwan. "Take what you need. You may be gone for a long time."

The boy nodded, even as the roof groaned and a faint thud from outside had Sung craning his head and reaching for his pistol. "Down!" he whispered to his men. They hit the deck, and Sung crawled toward one of the living room's boarded up windows. He slowly raised his head, listened attentively for any more noise outside. Then he looked to Lee and gave a signal, and the private crawled toward the front door, gently opened it, then stood and vanished outside. In the interim, Choi had already turned his rifle on Kwan, and the boy sat on the cold, wooden floor, his arms extended.

Park was beginning to pant, and Sung signaled for the lance corporal to go outside and sweep left. The radio operator bit his lip and crawled off.

But before Park could reach the door, Lee quietly returned with a muddy brick in his hand. "Sangsa, I found several in the mud."

Sung wondered if the wind and rain were strong enough to dislodge the bricks. Over time, maybe, but it seemed Kwan's story was crumbling like the chimney. Sung stood, went directly to Kwan, seized the boy by his neck. "Do bricks always fall from your roof?"

"This is the worst storm we have had all season, Sangsa."

Shoving the boy aside, Sung rushed toward the front door, slammed past it, and emerged outside, with his men trailing close behind. He paused below the chimney, scrutinized it for a moment, then let his gaze play over the ground. To the untrained eye, only clumps of weeds, mud, and mud puddles rolled out across the field, but Sung saw a pattern emerging.

Losing his breath, he charged toward the barns.

"Sangsa?" Choi cried.

Sung passed the first barn, spied what he thought were more tracks in the mud, and followed them to the second barn.

"Sangsa, those are our tracks," said Choi.

"Are they?" Sung pointed to Choi, then Park. They would lead the charge inside. Lee stood ready to the right of the door as Choi switched on his penlight.

Sung nodded tersely.

And his men rushed in, rifles at the ready, with Sung just behind, his adrenaline surging.

Choi probed the corners with his light, but they were empty.

"Sangsa, we have searched this barn twice," Park groaned. "No one is here."

"And what about Kwan? Should I go back for him?" Choi asked.

Sung lowered his pistol, glanced around, his breath growing more labored. The hairs on his neck stood on end. He sensed the enemy had been close. He sensed they had been present all along. He sensed that he had been deceived, and those sensations sent him running from the barn. He reached the edge of the field, where he staggered to a halt and lifted his binoculars. Again, the weather stole most of his view, but he thought he saw movement where the field descended slightly to the west. He adjusted magnification, blinked, searched once more for that movement—

And then, far off to his left, near the pile of wood, an engine sputtered to life. The old flatbed truck!

"Choi! Park! Lee!"

The truck cleared the woodpile and rumbled away. From Sung's vantage point he could not see clearly if anyone was present on the flatbed, but that did not matter. Even if only Kwan was in the truck, that proved the man had betrayed them. Kwan would die.

He raised his pistol, took aim—

But automatic weapons fire rattled loudly from the flatbed, and Sung threw himself onto his belly, his instincts screaming in confirmation.

Muzzle flashes shone ahead through the splashing mud, the booming painfully familiar: a squad automatic weapon. "Fire! Fire!" he ordered his men.

A quick glance to his right revealed that Choi, Park, and Lee had also dropped and could barely see through all the rain, mud, and incoming rounds. Choi shoved his rifle up, triggered a salvo, then Lee followed.

But Park kept his head jammed into the mud as he squeezed off rounds without looking.

"Park! Go back for Kwan," Sung hollered, then a thumping sound sent a shudder through him: a rifle-launched grenade was incoming!

The bomb exploded short, sending a shower of mud over Sung and his men

"Park!"

The young man crawled backward on his hands and knees, the automatic fire so dense that Sung could barely face forward. Park continued his retreat while Lee and Choi blindly returned fire.

"They are escaping!" Choi screamed.

Sung did not need the obvious reminder. He needed a lull in the fire. And as the truck sped farther away, that lull was about to come.

14

Rainey had not planned on taking the old truck. Yes, he had considered it, but there had been too many unanswered questions: Did the truck still work? If so, did it have fuel? Who had the keys? And wouldn't using it result in a very noisy escape? Furthermore, even if they managed to get out in the truck, they would have to remain on the gravel road—out in the open and quite vulnerable to air attack—otherwise, they would no doubt get stuck in the mud.

Consequently, Rainey had dismissed that option, but when he and Houston had entered the barn, Doc had charged up, dangling a set of keys before Rainey's eyes.

"No way, Doc."

"Just hear me out. I think this'll work."

Rainey had groaned through a sigh. "You got twenty seconds."

Doc had launched into a rapid fire summary. With Kim translating, he had asked Chun about the truck. It seemed the boy had the keys, the truck had nearly half a tank of fuel and, despite its appearance, the thing ran pretty well—or so the kid had said. Chun had even volunteered to drive. Rainey had balked, but Doc had convinced him that they could use the truck to gain some ground on the recon guys, then ditch it once they reached the forest to the south. After a few seconds of gut-wrenching deliberation, Rainey had agreed, but Chun had not been allowed to drive. Vance had taken the wheel, and it was a good thing old man McAllister had taught the fisherman how to drive a stick.

Lance Corporal Kim had voiced no misgivings, but Rainey had seen major disappointment in the man's eyes. Once they fired up that truck, Kwan was a dead man. Everyone had known that. But no one—not even Chun—had said a word about it.

Gripping the flatbed's warped, wooden railing, Rainey sent off another trio of rounds, his aim faulty, but at least he and the others had quickly cleaned their weapons and were keeping the NKA recon team at bay. Houston and Doc were in the flatbed with him. Vance, Chun, and Kim were jammed into the cab, with its torn-up bench seat and blocky dashboard, but Kim had pushed himself up, through the passenger side door's open window. He balanced himself there, driving his heels into the door as he spoke the good word of democracy with bullets that betrayed no accent. The ROK Marine clenched his teeth, fired intently, and Rainey just knew Kim wanted more than ever to kill those recon guys in order to save Kwan.

"There goes my first mag," Doc announced as his Para SAW went silent.

"That's it, Doc," Rainey said, as a round chipped off a piece of the railing just a few inches from his hand. "Shit. Vance? You got the pedal to the metal or what?"

"You kidding, Sarge? I press any harder, my boot's going through the floorboard!"

"Then put it through the floorboard!" Rainey pushed himself back against the cab, tried to brace himself against the bumps as he lifted his Nightstars, immediately assessing the grainy green images.

At the far end of the field, Kwan sprinted through the mud, heading for the foothills. "You dumb kid," Rainey muttered. "Why didn't you go for the tunnel?"

Rainey swept back to the NKA recon guys' last position. Two men were jogging left, while a third was charging back, headed in Kwan's direction.

"What are they doing, Sarge?" Houston asked.

"They're breaking off. One of them is going for Kwan."

"He won't make it, will he?" said Doc.

Rainey tightened his lips, zoomed in on Kwan. A shot boomed. Kwan gripped his calf, fell to the mud, started crawling like a wounded buck leaving a blood trail.

Houston opened up, firing about six shots before Rainey called for a ceasefire.

"Look at us. Fucking cowards. Running away again," Houston said.

"You want to go back there and fight them?" Rainey asked. "You get out of this truck right now."

Houston averted his gaze. "Maybe I should've stayed in the infantry."

"Lance Corporal, quit while you're ahead," Doc suggested.

Another look through the Nightstars gave Rainey a shiver. Two of the recon guys were dragging Kwan back toward the old sergeant.

Execution time.

"Hey, Sarge, we should ask Chun if our favorite bad guys can start up one of those tractors. Yeah, those old machines are probably real slow, but they're a lot faster than humping it on foot. We might want to take that into—"

"Not now, Doc." Rainey continued staring through his binoculars as the Korean soldiers dragged Kwan to his feet before the old sergeant.

NORTH KOREAN ARMY RECONNAISSANCE SQUAD
FARMHOUSE NORTHEAST OF SINUIJU
NORTH KOREA
0440 HOURS LOCAL TIME

Master Sergeant Sung, pistol in hand, was about to put a bullet in Kwan's head. He glanced to Lee, who stood stoically on the traitor's right side, both hands gripping the man's arm. Choi, who shifted behind Lee, panted, but he, too, showed no fear.

And then there was the pale Lance Corporal Park, who held Kwan's other arm. Park's left eye noticeably twitched before he looked away, anticipating the loud bang.

"Park!"

"Yes, Sangsa?"

"Take the weapon."

"Yes, Sangsa." The young man accepted the pistol as Choi moved in to switch positions and hold Kwan. "I will guard him for you, Sangsa."

"No, you will execute the traitor! Now!"

With his eye twitching more violently, Park held the pistol in both hands and extended his arms. "Why doesn't he beg for his life?"

Sung balled his hands into firsts. "Execute the traitor!"

Park turned a worried look on Sung. "We should question him first, Sangsa."

"We know enough. Kill him!"

"Sangsa, you should have the honor."

Bearing his teeth, Sung went to Park, ripped the pistol from the young man's hand, took aim at Kwan.

"I die with honor!" Kwan hollered.

And Sung fired.

Before the traitor hit the ground, Sung spun around and brought his pistol within a finger's length of Park's twitching eye. Every muscle in Sung's arm tightened.

Choi raised his hands. "No, Sangsa!"

But Sung fired again. As the vibration ran through the pistol and up Sung's arm, Lance Corporal Park hit the mud, his head hanging at an unnatural angle, his arms flailing back, his right leg jerking.

Private Lee did not move, but Choi dropped to his knees, staring horrified at his fallen comrade. "Why, Sangsa. Why?"

Sung leveled his gaze on the sergeant. "He was not a soldier. Now get up, Choi. You will be the radio operator. Switch packs with Park. And take all of his supplies. Hurry!"

"We are continuing after them?" Choi asked. "Just the three of us?"

"Yes."

"But we can call for support. A Hoplite could reach them in minutes."

"It is *our* mission to capture them!"

"Sangsa, we are making a grave tactical error if we do not call for assistance."

Sung jammed his pistol back into its holster. "We will call for help, once we have captured the enemy."

"How can we capture them now? They will be long gone."

"Stop questioning the Sangsa!" Lee shouted.

Sung faced Private Lee, put a finger to his lips, then regarded Choi. "The enemy will not ride in the truck for long. We will catch up with them."

"I am ready, Sangsa," Lee said, his tone a challenge to Choi's reservations.

"Very well," Sung replied. "We are going to run now. We are going to run until daybreak."

"Sangsa," Choi called, fumbling with Park's radio pack. "Do you wish to fail the mission?"

Sung recoiled in surprise. "What did you ask?"

"You have killed one of your own men and refuse to call for help. It seems you *want* to fail."

Choi's accusation struck a nerve. Sung withdrew his sidearm, shook it at the sergeant. "No more questions, no more opinions from you. I am like any other sangsa now. I give orders. And you obey. Or you will die. Understood?"

"Yes, Sangsa."

"Now hurry!"

As Choi frantically prepared himself, Sung's thoughts turned to the future. If the enemy escaped through his fingers, he could not go on serving. He could not go on living. As a result, he should be highly motivated. His thirst for victory should be unquenchable.

But had he already surrendered in his mind? Was he, as Choi had accused, undermining the mission so that the end might come more swiftly? Had he just grown too tired of the chase?

Master Sergeant Sung rubbed the corners of his eyes, blinked hard, and marched off into the rain. Private Lee dropped in behind him, while Choi still struggled with Park's radio pack. "It will take a while for their tracks to wash away," he said, spotting the first pair of trenches. "But it will not be long until they are in our hands!"

Sung's words might have inspired Private Lee, but as for Choi and himself? Sung was uncertain. About everything.

TEAM DOGMA
LEAVING FARMHOUSE NORTHEAST OF SINUIJU
NORTH KOREA
0450 HOURS LOCAL TIME

Corporal Jimmy Vance knew better than to feel too cocky. He and his exhausted teammates were, after all, driving in a forty-year-old, musty-smelling pickup across muddy lowlands located in a country whose government brainwashed its citizens from birth into hating everything and anything American.

But you could still find a few guys like Chun who would risk their lives to help people escape to a better life. No, Vance did not trust the guy, and even Doc had agreed that Chun should remain tied, but the kid had offered the truck's keys, even after Kim had killed his father. Vance couldn't believe that. Chun must have realized that his involvement in the underground would some day clash with his father's loyalty, although he had probably never imagined a scene as horrible as the one back in the barn. Vance hoped the guy wasn't setting them up. If he was, then Vance hoped Rainey would give him the order to draw blood. A lot of blood. But what if Chun's intentions were sincere? Damn, it was hard to relate to these people. Vance would never help the same guys who had killed his dad, but maybe Chun, Kwan, and the rest of the underground guys were all about the cause, the big picture—just like the field manual said. Individuals weren't important.

Chun pointed ahead at a sharp bend in the gravel road, where a dirt path snaked off to the left. He said something quickly to Kim, who interpreted. "Chun says we should take the dirt road. But we should do so on foot."

"Bullshit," Vance said, lifting his voice above the hum of the windshield wipers, the right one lacking rubber and simply scraping across the glass. "We're riding in this truck for as long as we can."

Kim translated quickly, and Chun grabbed Vance's arm and spoke emphatically.

"He says he will drive on the gravel road for as long as he can to draw the enemy away," said Kim.

That wasn't a bad idea—if they could trust Chun. "Ask him why he's willing to do this after what happened to his father."

"I would rather not," Kim said.

They were fast approaching the fork in the road, and Vance slowed the truck. "Sarge?"

Rainey leaned over the railing to get near the driver's side window. "What is it?"

"Chun wants us to take the dirt road into the forest. He'll keep driving until a Hoplite or some NKA regulars pick him up. Straightforward diversion. What do you think?"

"I think I don't trust this guy. Never will. But stop the truck!"

Vance brought the old pickup to a screeching, quivering halt. As the engine chugged like an old locomotive, Rainey jumped down from the flatbed, tugged open the passenger's side door. "Kim, ask him how far to the forest," Rainey said.

Kim complied, received his answer. "He says about a kilometer, maybe a little more."

"Good. Team Dogma, listen up. We're getting out. We'll keep to the ditches along this gravel road. We'll make the forest before daybreak. Vance? Shut off the engine and take the keys."

Chun and Kim began a heated exchange as Vance did as instructed. Once the engine went silent and the keys were safely tucked into a breast pocket, he swung open his door, hopped to the ground. As he crossed to the flatbed to retrieve his pack, he found Houston standing with the pack in hand. "Hey, man. We still buds?"

Vance hoisted his brows at the lance corporal. "Who said we weren't?"

"I'm an asshole, I know," Houston said, helping Vance into the ruck.

"I want to believe you're just strung out is all. You've been through a lot. You're going through a lot. But you keep yourself squared away. No more bitching. No mistakes."

"That's the plan."

Vance punched Houston hard in the bicep. "Don't just say it—"

"Believe it," Houston finished.

They joined Doc, who had hiked over to the nearest ditch and was just standing there, getting drenched, while Rainey discussed something with Kim and Chun. Suddenly, the sergeant broke away from the group. "All right! Vance, take point. Houston, when we reach the forest, we'll be needing to check in, so be ready."

"Sergeant, please, we should give him a chance," Kim interrupted. "Let him drive the truck away. Those recon soldiers will follow!"

"Lance Corporal, fall in."

"But we can trust him, Sergeant. If we just leave him here—"

"What? He's going to die? He knows he's already dead. He knows that."

"Then let him come with us. It's his only chance."

"I'm not dragging along a guy I can't trust."

"But you trusted him enough to take the truck?"

"Lance Corporal, fall in!"

"Hey, Kim?" Vance called, waving over the ROK Marine.

Kim reluctantly shuffled forward, his eyes widening. "The sergeant is making a mistake."

"No, he's not. Chun knew the risks."

"But your sergeant does not understand what is going on here. That young man just lost his father, yet he is still willing to give his life for us. Yet that means nothing to your sergeant."

"He's your sergeant now, so you'd best follow orders and keep the griping to a minimum." Vance raised his head at Houston. "This guy can tell you that's good advice."

Houston started to say something, but Rainey had already finished adjusting his pack and was jogging over. "Good to go?"

After nods all around, they descended into one of the runoff ditches alongside the road. Chun, still seated and bound in the idling truck, glared at them as they left.

All things considered, Vance agreed with Rainey's decision. Yes, it would have been helpful if Chun diverted the enemy, but the kid could not be trusted. Leaving him bound in the truck was the best thing. When he was found, he could say he had been kidnapped by the enemy, then abandoned with the truck. Kim had probably argued that the recon guys would not believe that story since Kwan and Chun were friends and Kwan had been shot as a traitor. However, other NKA soldiers could find Chun, and he could offer the lie to them. He might even be released. Okay, that was wishful thinking, and admittedly, Vance would not play those odds. As Rainey had said, the Korean was already dead. Man, Vance felt blessed that he wasn't Chun: a shitty life followed up by a shitty death.

Purging everything associated with Kwan, Chun, and the farmhouse from his thoughts, Vance kept his head low and switched into machine mode. He was a Force Recon cyborg programmed to advance, analyze, and react. Even his rhythm was programmed to the rain and the night. He was not in an on-again, off-again relationship. He did not tremble with the desire to rope in a big lunker bass. He was not scared shitless of getting shot. He was a warrior who felt really, really . . . tired.

Lance Corporal Bradley Houston would have gambled on Chun. Risky kind of guy that he was, Houston had spent enough time in Las Vegas casinos to know that if you didn't take chances, you did not win. Seemed like a no-brainer to him. Which was why he considered Rainey's decision to abandon the kid too conservative and basically lame. No, Houston would not have taken on the extra baggage, but hey, let the guy drive the truck. How much damage could he really cause? Better yet, set him up with a couple of claymores, let him lure the NKA guys to him, then ka-boom! Now that was a plan! The kid would martyr himself. The kid would've liked that. But no. Chun would just sit there, wondering how and when he was going to die. That was torture. Houston would not have wished that on his worst enemy. Well, he would have wished that on the NKA recon guys, who, for the better part of the night, had done a fine job filling that role.

As he kept within two meters of Vance, his rifle at the ready, his boots squishing in the mud and threatening to give at any second, he remembered Vance's advice. If he could just keep his emotions in check, if he could just concentrate solely on the mission, then everything would be all right.

C'mon, that's bullshit, and you know it.

Houston was too smart for mind games. He had never been one to live in denial. He simply thought too much. And all the humping in silence turned his thoughts inward—

Where Dad was waiting for him.

Shit.

All of the mixed-up emotions would come on like a migraine—and his mood would swing like a damned pendulum from professional soldier to raving lunatic. If he went ballistic again, Vance would not give him a second chance. Neither would Doc. And Houston had most definitely maxed out his second-chance card with the Sarge. Sure, they would deal with him during the escape. They had no choice. But if they all made it out, Houston doubted he would remain on the team. Rainey would turn field-goal kicker, booting Houston's ass back to infantry the second they got home.

But that would not happen. Houston was in control. He would haul his ass all the way to the Korea Bay, then plant said ass aboard a nice, cushy submarine. And when leave time came, he would go to the Love Hotel. He would have himself a good time. And not once would he look over his shoulder. The ghosts were behind him.

Weren't they?

Although Doc Leblanc had been a little surprised by Rainey's decision, he understood it. Did not question it. Realized where the sergeant was coming from. Sure, Doc could go on for hours speculating on the decision, but no matter what, he trusted the man. There was no one on the planet he would rather have leading the team. Doc's wife and boys owed Rainey big time. And when they got together, Doc always made sure that his family welcomed the sergeant with open arms. Any walls that might have existed between them—color, age, branch of service—had long since crumbled. They shared that unique bond, that military kinship that lasted a lifetime. "Once a Marine, always a Marine" were not words. They were life. And Doc never doubted for one second that Sergeant Mac Rainey would lay down that life for the team. Doc would do the same. The politics associated with serving rarely got in the way of that promise, of that duty. Sure, you could die for your country, but without people, without your brothers, your fellow Marines, countries did not exist. Hate the mission. Love your buddies. Die for them if you had to. However, the trick, as old Patton had said, was to get the other poor bastard to die for his country. *Well*, Doc thought, *you can't say we're not trying* . . .

If he had one regret about coming to North Korea, it was the same regret voiced by Rainey. After all was said and done, he wished that they could make a difference. Oh, yes, they had made a difference in the lives of Kwan and Chun, but Doc did not want to go there. Lives had been lost and ruined. Enough said. Stopping at the farm had been a huge mistake, but no one could have predicted that outcome. It was time to mend wounds and move on. And in the moving, Doc hoped that somewhere along the line they could do something meaningful. Maybe he was just putting too much pressure on himself and the team. It wasn't as though they could capture the world's most wanted terrorist every time out or stop a war between the CFC and North Korea. Doc would settle for something small. One life saved. One life changed for the better. That was all. The medic in him was getting restless.

Just ahead, Lance Corporal Kim hit a rut, slipped, and dropped hard onto his right side. Doc was on the Marine immediately, setting down his Para SAW and offering a hand.

"Talk to me, Lance Corporal."

Kim groaned, then sat up. "I'm okay, Doc."

Rainey worked his clicker, signaling Vance to a halt as Doc hauled Kim to his feet.

"Good time for a radio check," Rainey said, then gave the hand signal to Vance and Houston, who shifted up their boom mikes and switched on their tactical radios.

While Doc had wiped off his own earpiece and mike, Rainey's voice sounded muffled and full of static, though Doc could still hear the sergeant. "Dogma Team, this Dogma One, radio check, over."

The check went off smoothly, with Kim finishing: "Dogma One, this is Voodoo Five, read you loud and clear, over."

"Dogma Team, this is Dogma One. Continue to monitor tactical frequency. Now move out," Rainey ordered.

Satisfied that Kim was good to go, Doc patted the ROK Marine on the shoulder, then retrieved his Para SAW. He glanced up as the rain began to subside. Good news. Bad news. He hated getting soaked, but losing the storm's cover wouldn't help the cause.

"You hanging in there, Doc?" Rainey asked, studying the distant truck through his Nightstars.

"I'm good. Hey, at least if you're sweating you can't tell, right?"

Rainey stowed his binoculars, jogged off with Doc. "I like your attitude."

"Good. Now that I've buttered you up, I can ask the big question. We're going to extract in broad daylight, aren't we?"

"You're worried about that already? Shit, Doc, just reaching the coast will probably get us killed. Once we leave the woods, we'll have to go through at least one of those little fishing villages—and Doc, I hate to break it to you, but you're going to have a hard time passing for a North Korean fisherman."

"Me? What're you going to do? Put black shoe polish in your hair and Scotch tape your eyes? I don't think so, big guy."

"Well, there goes that plan."

"Hey, maybe the weather will clear and we can call in the Cobras for cover."

"You're dreaming, Doc. Unless war is declared within the next few hours, we're on our own."

"Then tell Houston to get the president on the horn. I need a word with him."

"Right away, Doc. You're the man."

Rainey drifted back a little, sliding in behind Doc. Thankfully, the sergeant had not lost his sense of humor. He had assumed a role that old Terry McAllister had mastered. Even during the most dire of circumstances, McAllister could deliver a line in a deadpan that would split Doc's sides. Sure, Doc's medic kit was jammed full of drugs, but there was one medicine—the best medicine—that they all needed to carry in their hearts, because if they couldn't laugh, what was left?

Lance Corporal Kim's gunshot wound ached a little since he had jarred the bandage during his fall. Still, a greater pain had spread through him like a virus, and he guessed that it would take months, probably years for him to overcome it. He should have never contacted the underground. Those boys did not deserve to die. Furthermore, their deaths would weaken the network, which could result in more arrests and more deaths. Sergeant Rainey could not see the extent of what had happened. All he considered was escape, and if he left a trail of death in his wake, then so be it. Survival was everything. Yes, Kim understood that, but there were ways to stay alive without jeopardizing everyone around you.

But was he being unreasonable? Contacting the underground had been the logical choice. As Rainey had said, Kwan and Chun had known the risks, and Kim should not feel responsible for them.

But I killed Chun's father. And our presence resulted in Kwan's death. They only wanted to help us. And what did we give them in return? Suffering and death . . .

This was the same group that had helped Kim escape to freedom in the South. Without them, he would have died. Without them, he would have become a mindless laborer toiling away in some field, or worse, a mindless soldier trained to protect a corrupt regime. The underground had saved Kim's life. How could he *not* feel guilty? How could he *not* be disturbed? He had seen more death in one night than most ROK Marines might see in a lifetime. Yes, it had become a night of death, and living through it was growing unbearable.

Trying to work out his frustration through his legs, Kim increased his pace, drove his boots deeper into the mud. How could he put it all past him? How could he concentrate on escaping when he felt tortured about remaining alive? No, he was not suicidal. He would not do anything to endanger himself or the other men. But if asked again to bring others into their escape plan, he might just decline—especially if those "others" were members of the South Korean underground (who, once again, might very well betray his secret). No one else deserved to die for them. He and the American Marines were spies who had been in the wrong place at the wrong time. They had known the risks. Sacrificing innocents so they might survive was wrong. They were responsible. Accountable. The bill was theirs alone.

But Sgt. Mac Rainey would not agree. He would accept help. If people died because they had given that help, then that was their business. He would say that he had not asked Kwan or Chun to give their lives. They had done so willingly.

So what was Kim to do, other than follow orders? If he was captured, he would be shot just like any other member of the team. His desire to escape should be as dire as theirs. And it was, though that burden must remain on them. No one else should be dragged into their nightmare. Kim would do everything he could—short of disobeying orders—to prevent that.

"Dogma Team, this is Dogma One! On the deck! On the deck!" Rainey boomed.

Confused, Kim dropped to his hands and knees, found himself swimming up to his elbows in muck. Only after a half dozen breaths did he sense a slight rumble in the ground.

And then, barely audible above the wind and rain, came the drone of an engine. A big engine. Diesel.

Rainey crawled up the trench, bringing himself to the top for a look through his Nightstars. "Dogma Three? Dogma Four? This is Dogma One. Heavy vehicle approaching. You two get across the road! Now!"

15

Sergeant Choi had been the first one to slow down, and moments later, Private Lee had joined him in a light jog that had fallen off to a brisk walk. Master Sergeant Sung had known that his men could not sprint for very long. They had been exhausted before they set out. But as always, he had pushed them to the edge, which as always would harden them for what was quite literally a long road ahead.

They had been following the old pickup truck's tracks when, in the distance, Sung spotted movement. He paused, and a look through his binoculars brought one confirmation and one surprise: the truck was out there, seemingly abandoned, but beyond it, another vehicle too distant to make out, had turned onto the road, heading west.

"The truck is there," he told his men.

"But they are not, Sangsa," said Choi.

"It could be an ambush," Lee warned.

Sung shook his head. "They would not waste time on that. Their leader assumed they would be too vulnerable in the truck. They used it only to gain a lead on us."

"But if he did not, and it is an ambush, then we will walk right into it," Choi said.

"No, Lyongjang, *you* will. Lee and I will remain well behind. The mission is too important to risk all of us."

Choi bit his lip, looked away. "Yes, Sangsa, but in case something happens, we should report in before we reach the truck. Mountain Ghost has been expecting to hear from us. He has probably tried to call several times. May I have your permission to turn on the radio?"

"Leave it off," Sung snapped.

"Sangsa, there is another vehicle far off," Lee said, peering through his own binoculars. "I can barely see it, but it is there."

"I know," Sung answered. "But first the truck. Choi? Go now!"

PICKUP TRUCK
GRAVEL ROAD SOUTH OF SINUIJU
NORTH KOREA
0516 HOURS LOCAL TIME

Chun had waited until the Marines were out of sight before contorting his small frame so that he could shove his bound wrists down, below his rump, and pass his legs through. With his hands in front, he had reached down and had slid out the spare truck key from beneath the floor mat. In recent years, his father had become exceedingly forgetful and had lost several sets of keys, thus Chun had made it a point to keep copies in all of their farm vehicles. The Marines had not counted on one old man's failing memory, and the copied key now sat in the ignition, ready to be turned.

Yet for the past few minutes, as Chun tugged at his bonds, trying to free his hands, he had been weighing his options. If he started the truck too soon, the Marines might return, believe he was somehow betraying them, and open fire. If he started the truck too late, the reconnaissance squad might be too close for him to escape.

But escape to where? He had thought it might be better to leave the truck and simply hide in one of the ditches. He could cover himself with mud. That might work for the moment, but he would never reach the next safe house before sunrise. The army would pick him up and torture him until he confessed. The downed plane had surely brought many troops to the area. Thus, he had decided to take the truck back to the dirt road and follow it for as long as he could. He would remain faithful to his original offer to divert the enemy. He would do that not because he had any particular love for the American Marines; on the contrary, he loathed them. But he knew how important the cause was, how their military and CIA supported the cause, and how helping them to escape might make his life—and his death—more meaningful. Finally, heading into the forest would at least provide him with better cover to evade a search. He was not very optimistic about escaping all the way to the coast, where another safe house awaited, but anything could happen if he was willing to take a chance.

He glanced down at the key. Checked the rearview mirror. What was that back there? A figure running toward the truck? A soldier? Yes!

Chun started the truck, and with hands still bound managed to throw it in reverse. He began backing up toward where the dirt path forked off to his left. He didn't need to check the mirror to see the familiar soldier advancing now and just a few breaths away from tucking his rifle's stock into his shoulder and firing.

Reaching the fork, Chun booted the brake pedal and clutch, then took his hands from the wheel and shoved the gear shift into first. The truck bucked a bit as he released the clutch and rolled onto the dirt path.

TEAM DOGMA

EN ROUTE TO FOREST SOUTHWEST OF SINUIJU

NORTH KOREA

0516 HOURS LOCAL TIME

Houston and Vance lay on their bellies in the little ditch on their side of the gravel road. The team now had three guys on one side, two guys on the other. They could execute a vigorous ambush of the vehicle if necessary. Houston liked the plan, but what had caught him off guard as he had crossed the road was the distant sound of the pickup truck's engine. Vance had heard it too, and they had reported the sound to Rainey while the heavy vehicle rumbled even closer.

"I thought the Sarge ordered you to take the keys?" Houston asked.

"He did. I got them right here. The little guy must've had another set. Maybe he can get away."

With his Night Vision Goggles concealing his eyes, and the road's gloom tuned to the green hue of a failing TV, Houston peeked his head up a little—

And three things occurred simultaneously:

He recognized the heavy, eight-wheeled vehicle as a missile launcher, a SCUD missile launcher to be more accurate.

He realized that his lucky bush cover had blown off his head while crossing the road; however, it was safety pinned by the chin strap to his assault vest. He reached back to grab it. No cover. Just an open safety pin.

In a panic he scanned the road, retracing his steps, and there it was, his lucky cover with the bullet hole in it, the lucky cover that wasn't so lucky anymore. The hat lay in the middle of the road. And damn, why couldn't it have fallen upside down to present a lower profile? Shit. He might as well have planted an American flag.

Okay. Maybe the driver wouldn't see the cover. Then again, he wouldn't be driving without headlights unless he had night vision capability. The North Korean Army might not waste money on equipping their average soldiers with NVGs, but you had to assume that men driving expensive missile launchers at night had been granted the ability to see.

The team's cover was about to be blown because of Houston's carelessness.

It was a nightmare made real, an impossibility made possible, an error so grave that he could barely believe it himself. He had slid down half a mountainside in the mud and had not lost the hat. But he couldn't hump it across a simple road without losing it? The pin had weakened. The stupid little pin had weakened! He should have checked it. He should have gone over every inch of his equipment.

"Vance?"

"Shut up. It's coming!"

Houston grabbed Vance's shoulder. "I dropped my bush cover."

"So what? Forget it."

"It's out there, in the road."

"Don't pull my leg now, buddy."

"I have to get it." Houston started out of the ditch, but Vance seized him by the ruck and dragged him back down. "Let me go!"

"What the hell are you doing?"

"Getting my cover! If I don't, we're screwed. Look!"

Vance took a second glance. "Oh, shit. You have to be kidding me. This ain't happening."

"Let me get it."

"No way. You're staying put."

"Dogma Team, this is Dogma One. Standby. Do not move. Do not breathe, over."

"Vance, let me go."

"You heard the Sarge, man. There's no more time! And you should thank God that—"

"Dogmas Three and Four? This is Dogma One. Is that a bush cover I see in the middle of the road, over?"

Houston sighed loudly. "Dogma One, this is Dogma Three. Affirmative on that bush cover. My pin broke, over."

Gunfire boomed in the distance as the pickup truck's engine revved several times. Three more pops, followed by another trio—

As the SCUD drew within five meters of the bush cover and came to a rumbling halt.

"Motherfucker, they got us," Houston muttered.

"Not if me and my sniper rifle got anything to say about it," Vance said.

Houston's shoulders slumped as he stared through his rifle's scope and waited for someone to exit the vehicle, his confidence already shot to hell.

"Dogma Team? This is Dogma One. Hold your positions. Dogma Three? Grab me a few images of this, out."

Houston dug into one of the many pockets on his assault vest and produced the digital camera. He'd rather be shooting bullets than pictures, but he was in no position to complain.

NORTH KOREAN ARMY RECONNAISSANCE SQUAD
HEADING SOUTH OF SINUIJU
NORTH KOREA
0518 HOURS LOCAL TIME

Once the pickup truck had started, Master Sergeant Sung and Private Lee had begun running. Choi was coming up behind the truck by the time its driver had pulled onto the dirt road and was barreling off.

Choi fired two rounds, but the truck had kept on moving, and Choi had broken off his pursuit after falling into a puddle. The truck and its driver were escaping.

Sung hiked his way across the mud, reached Choi, and without warning backhanded him across the cheek.

"I am sorry, Sangsa!"

"You should not have fired! You have betrayed our position!"

"But Sangsa, they know we are behind them. They know we are pursuing."

Sung reached for his pistol but found Lee's hand covering the weapon. "Not again, Sangsa," the private said. "Please."

"Sangsa, I did my duty," added Choi. "I did not hesitate, as Park did."

Trembling with rage, Sung swung away from his men and pounced back toward the road. The rain was growing heavier, and his binoculars did a poor job of picking out that heavy vehicle in the distance. Perhaps the enemy had inadvertently fled into a trap. Meanwhile, one or more of them had been trying to divert Sung and his men down the dirt path.

"Should we follow the truck, Sangsa?" Choi asked, arriving at Sung's side.

"Or the road?" added Lee, calling from behind them.

"We follow the road."

Choi nodded, then, unable to meet Sung's gaze, glanced away and said, "Sangsa, we should contact Mountain Ghost."

"I will tell you what we should do. And right now, we should capture the enemy! Move!"

Rainey estimated the SCUD's crew at five. Two men had
exited the vehicle (a MAZ 543 P TEL, according to
Doc's reading of the field manual) and gone around to
the back, one wearing Night Vision Goggles, the other
carrying a pair of binoculars. While Rainey had assumed
the bush cover had commanded their attention, they
seemed more concerned with the shots fired behind them
and the pickup truck off to the side of the road. The two
Koreans argued with each other while Rainey, Doc, and
Kim wormed themselves deeper into the mud. No corus-
cation, no reflection would give them up.

"Dogma Team, this is Dogma One," he said softly.
"Stand by."

The appearance of a TEL so far north of the Demilitarized Zone struck Rainey as odd. Naturally, the North
Koreans moved their missile launchers at night and
moved them very often, but this particular TEL had to
be en route to some position far south since its missile
was presumably out of range to strike targets in South
Korea. Rainey knew that the NKA's mechanized corps
lay to the south between the Third and Seventh Corps,
and perhaps the TEL and its crew were en route there,
but for what? Servicing? They would still be out of target range and still be too far north of the DMZ to do any
significant damage. Granted, Rainey was no expert on
the SCUD—and he was unsure of which type of rocket
and warhead sat piggyback on the TEL—but he re-

membered reading something about the SCUD "B" having a range of something like 300 kilometers, which from their position would barely scratch enemy targets. Still, Doc would pour through the manual and come up with some ranges that would solve the mystery.

After glancing to the corpsman and Kim, and receiving nods from both, Rainey watched as the Korean soldier with the binoculars climbed back into the TEL's wedge-shaped cab, while the guy with the NVGs crossed back toward his door—

Then stopped.

He had caught sight of the bush cover. As he walked toward the hat, he pushed up his NVGs. Then, as he got closer, he hesitated. Smart guy. Rainey had read stories about American tank crews in Vietnam who had been killed because garbage lying in the road had been booby trapped by the VC. The enemy knew that American tank crews loved to crush stuff. Apparently, North Korean SCUD crews were a bit more cautious, and as the driver got down on his haunches for a closer inspection, he stole a look over his shoulder, his paranoia mounting.

"Dogma Team?" Rainey whispered over the radio. "Stand by. Dogma Three? You got those images, over?"

"Dogma One, this is Dogma Three. Affirmative on images, over."

"Very well, Dogma Team. On my order, Dogma Three and Voodoo Five will target the tires. Dogma Two will focus fire on the cab. Dogma Four, ready to cap the driver, over."

Each of his men responded in turn. Not surprisingly, Houston's voice had sounded a little shaky. What the lance corporal did not know was that the corps no

longer shot men who dropped their hats in the middle
of the road. Those inept Marines were now stripped to
their skivvies and hung from the highest tree because
military budgets had been slashed over the years and
nylon rope was cheaper and recyclable.

Having finished his inspection, the driver finally
reached out and plucked the hat. He studied it curiously,
his index finger probing the bullet hole in the cover's
fabric for a moment. Then he rose, jerked around, his
eyes bugging. He shouted something to his men, tossed
away the cover, then dashed madly for the cab.

"Dogma Team? Stand by."

After a loud clunk, the TEL shifted into gear, its massive diesel engine issuing a startling roar as it kicked up
gravel and pulled away.

But Rainey would not allow himself a sigh. Not yet.
Shots had been fired near the pickup, and Rainey assumed that Chun had attempted an escape that had
gone badly for him. Now the recon team was closing in.

"Hey, Sarge? We came here to blow stuff up, didn't
we?" Doc asked.

"Yeah, we did."

"Then are you thinking what I'm thinking?"

"I'd love to take out this launcher, Doc. But we have
to keep moving."

"I hear that," Doc said through a sigh. "Still, it'd be
nice to get rid of some of this extra weight. We're all
dressed up with C-4 and got nothing to blow."

Rainey grinned thinly then keyed his mike. "Dogma
Team? This is Dogma One. Regroup my side of the
road. Dogma Three? Police up that bush cover, out."

* * *

As he ran across the road, Houston reached down and scooped up the cover, not missing a step. He wanted to tear the thing into a million pieces, then set those pieces ablaze. He settled for balling the hat into his fist as he leaped down, into the ditch, with Vance trailing.

"Lance Corporal, do me a favor, will you?" Rainey asked. "Make sure nothing else is going to fall off, okay?"

"Aye-aye, Sergeant."

Vance smirked, shook his head, grabbed his balls as he passed Houston.

And the last scrap of confidence clinging to Houston's gut broke off and fell to the mud.

"Hang in there," Doc said, slapping him on the shoulder. "And keep your hat on."

Houston shook his head and moved off with the others. Maybe the rain was getting to him, that's all. Maybe his failure had nothing to do with the huge mistake he had made by becoming a Marine. Maybe his father had been completely wrong.

Or maybe someone on the team was going to die because of Houston's incompetence. Maybe that's what it would take before he finally stopped arguing with his father and came to the realization that fathers know best and that sons had best listen. Someone had to die.

He violently tugged out a fresh safety pin from one of his breast pockets and got to work reattaching the bush cover to his vest.

Corporal Jimmy Vance did his best to keep the SCUD launcher in sight, as Rainey had instructed. Vance wondered if the Sarge had something up his sleeve—hopefully, a demolition job involving that missile system and its crew. If Vance and the rest of the team did die in North Korea, it would be gratifying to know that they had taken a few guys and an expensive piece of ordnance with them.

But to die without having ever caught a ten-pound bass? Now that just wasn't decent or correct. Only after catching a trophy lunker at least that heavy could Vance accept his death as a good soldier and a better fisherman. His biggest fish had been eight pounds, thirteen ounces, according to his digital scale, and before releasing the bass he had taken pictures to have a Fiberglas mount made to the lunker's length and girth. That mount hung in his mother's living room.

Thus matters of life and death involving Marine Corps work were important, but bass fishing . . . well, Vance would say there was a fine line between a sport and a religion (golfers and fly fishermen could easily attest to that), and Vance had fired up his big Mercury outboard to cross that line many years ago. Staying alive to finally catch that lunker? Was there any better reason to live?

"Dogma Four, this is Dogma One, over."

Vance's throat had grown dry during the run, and his voice came in a deep burr. "Four, this is One, over."

"Confirm TEL is still within visual range, over."

While it wasn't easy taking his eyes off the roadside and keeping pace, Vance did so and spied the missile launcher still chugging onward in the distance. "Dogma One, confirm TEL within visual range. Can laser-rangefind on your request, over."

"Negative, Four. Keep this pace. Dogma One, out."

Keep this pace? Dude, I'll try. But if it's killing me, what the hell's it doing to you old farts in the back?

Yes, Doc and Rainey had to be running on fumes, but they weren't dead yet. Knowing their luck (and Murphy's schedule), the entire team would be completely winded, and some NKA bastards would ambush them. Vance figured he would need to call a halt. And soon. No matter what Rainey had said. But how much farther to the woods? The silhouettes of trees began sprouting up on the horizon, and while a sheet of gray clouds still covered the sky, that sheet grew steadily lighter. The Lord had opted for a gloomy morning, and maybe it was fitting after one hell of a gloomy night. Damn, if he were back home, low light conditions meant the bass would hit topwater lures. And here he was, in North Korea missing out.

All right, then. Vance could get them to the forest. Drive them on. Hard. And once there, he would call for that halt.

But damn if the road didn't suddenly veer left. The shoulder rose up to within a half meter of the gravel. As Vance zoomed in with his NVGs, he saw that their path would remain elevated for a good one hundred meters. The ditches and the embankment would be gone. No cover, no problem? Unh-huh. Big problem. They would have to move faster. With a fire growing in his legs, Vance paralleled the road, digging deeply into the mud to make the two meter climb. He arrived tentatively on top, keeping his head low as he slowed for just a few seconds to get his bearings.

Oh, man, they were walking down Main Street, begging to be shot. But what choice did they have? Could they crawl all the way to the forest? Bullshit. They were going to run. Hard. Very, very hard.

* * *

Doc Leblanc had decided that Lance Cpl. Jimmy Vance was Satan himself. No mortal could maintain such a brutal pace, a pace that inflicted pain and suffering on Doc's weather-worn hide. Over thirty and no spring chicken (his wife had once referred to him as a "fall turkey"—and worse, she had made the comment just after sex), Doc usually carried his burly physique as nimbly as the kids, but you mustn't forget that he carried the heaviest weapon, and, arguably, the heaviest ruck.

So as the team drove on, up that embankment and onto higher ground, Doc found himself drifting back, past Rainey, and falling several yards behind. Rainey repeatedly glanced over his shoulder to check on Doc's progress, and Doc hated being the slowest guy, but he had already reached into his reserves—twice—and they were drained. He slowed. Fought for breath. Decided to blame it on the mud. The wind. The rain. It had nothing to do with weakness, damn it.

Come on, man. You're a Navy Corpsman! Tough as these Marines! You're the cream of the crop, best of the best! Go Navy! Go Doc!

And with that thought, Doc crumpled to his knees. By the time he looked up, Rainey had turned back for him.

"I'm good to go, Sarge," Doc gasped.

"Yes, you are," Rainey growled in his ear as he hauled Doc up. "You can do this! You can! Come on! We're almost there!"

Jogging on wobbly legs, Doc resumed his pace, with Rainey at his arm. But Doc couldn't help breathing like a woman in labor, and there was no hiding that from the Sarge.

"You will not quit on us, Doc. You hear me?"

"Yes, Sergeant."

"You got a wife and two little boys back home. You will not quit on them. Do you read me, Doc?"

"Yes, Sergeant!"

After a quick burst of static, Vance's voice sounded over the radio. "Dogma One, this is Dogma Four. Should I call for a halt, over?"

"Negative, Four," Rainey answered. "Keep pace, out."

"And I'm keeping pace, Sarge," Doc said. "I will not quit on you. I will not quit on them."

"That's right, Doc. You're the man. You got the speed. You're a Force Recon Navy Corpsman. You are the hardest of the hard. Nobody quits this gun club. Don't you forget that!"

"Aye-aye, Sergeant!"

The anger quickly swept over Doc. He was angry at his body for not being stronger. Angry at himself for forgetting how important it was to keep on. To live. And that anger toughened him. Made him truly feel like the hardest of the hard. He was going to run across the road and reach the woods. He would prove to himself and everyone else that Navy Corpsmen are and will always be first-class operators.

NORTH KOREAN ARMY RECONNAISSANCE SQUAD
HEADING SOUTH OF SINUIJU
NORTH KOREA
0530 HOURS LOCAL TIME

Master Sergeant Sung had finally identified that heavy vehicle as a SCUD missile launcher. As he and his men reached the area where the vehicle had stopped, Sung ordered Choi and Lee to search both sides of the road, while he stood off to the shoulder, peering at the shrinking SCUD through his binoculars. The stench of dirt and wet grass and weeds threatened to make him sneeze at any moment, yet that stench had tipped him off. Areas off to the side of the road had been trampled.

"Sangsa? Boot prints!" Lee called.

"And at least two sets here," Choi added, rising up onto the shoulder. "It is the enemy!"

Sung winced over Choi's "keen-eyed assessment" as he continued to scan up, across the road, peering farther into the distance. His eyes grew blurry. He paused to rub them. Then he wiped the binoculars' lenses clean of rain. A second look nearly made his heart stop. Five figures ran alongside the road. Sung doubted the image. Blinked. Looked again.

No, his eyes had not deceived him. Why would the enemy choose such a vulnerable route?

Ah, the embankment had leveled off. They had had no other choice. Sung shoved the binoculars into his ruck, screaming, "Lee? Choi? Move now! We have them!"

16

Sergeant Mac Rainey had the willies. Not the standard issue willies that accompanied getting blown out of the sky over enemy territory. These willies were much stronger. In fact, Rainey could almost feel the enemy's gaze on his shoulders. You had to assume those guys were back there, especially that old sergeant. You had to assume that he and his men had searched the area where the SCUD had stopped. You could even assume that he had spotted the team running out in the open and were in pursuit.

Worst of all, that NKA recon team was being cheered on by a ghost named E-5 Sgt. Anthony Bruno. *"Hey, Rainey, what's your plan when you get to the forest?"*

"Fuck you."

"That don't work, Rainey. I'm in your head, man. And I just keep coming. You got a fucking plan or

what? Or are you pulling this out of your ass like you always do?"

"Fuck you."

"No plan, huh?"

"I got a plan!"

"You can lie to them, Rainey. But you can't lie to me. You were a good Marine. But it's time for your paddle ceremony. Time to retire. Or maybe it'll end here."

"Fuck you."

"Hey, death ain't so bad, man. But it ain't so good, either. You feel like you're on the line for chow, but the line don't ever move. And you just keep getting hungrier and more tired. And it starts raining harder, and you just can't stand up anymore."

Was it Bruno's voice or the sound of incoming fire that drove Rainey to the deck? He wasn't sure. All he knew was that somehow he was on his gut, listening to Doc yell, "Incoming! Incoming!"

"Dogma One, this is Dogma Four, over? Dogma One, this is Dogma Four, over?" Vance called frantically.

Rainey stole a breath. They were taking fire. He was supposed to be in charge. He *was* in charge! "Go, Four."

"I make three shooters about two hundred meters out. Permission to fire, over."

Gravel spat over Rainey as two rounds fell short in the road. He ducked and grabbed his boom mike. "Dogma Four, open fire. Dogma Three? Voodoo Five? Stand by, over."

Doc, who was lying on his gut a meter off to Rainey's right, had his SAW resting squarely on its bipod. "Good to go, Sarge," he reported.

"Dogma Three? Voodoo Five? Stand by to fall back on my order," Rainey said, now staring through his carbine's night-vision scope.

As Vance had reported, there were only three muzzles flashing at ankle height. Then . . . a pause in the fire. The enemy was moving up.

"Doc, let 'em have it," Rainey ordered. "Dogma Three? Voodoo Five? Fall back with me. Now!"

While Doc's Para SAW reverberated like a war drum and coughed up enough lead to keep those AKs silent, Rainey joined Houston and Kim for a bat-out-of-hell sprint for the nearest stand of trees, now just a couple hundred yards away. They blew by Vance, a young man tuned in to his scope and his trigger, a Zen master in the zone. The sniper's rifle boomed. And he cursed.

Once they reached the trees, Rainey hunkered down, ordered Doc to retreat while Vance covered him. The moment Doc's SAW went quiet, the AK fire resumed, but Vance answered in kind.

And with his face creased heavily with exertion, Doc pounded his way for cover. Rainey wanted to close his eyes. Didn't. How many operators had he seen shot in the back or in the head while making that final run? Six? Seven?

"Come on, Doc!"

"Dogma One, this is Dogma Four. Believe I got one, over," Vance reported.

"Very well. Fall back, Dogma Four. Fall back!"

Doc rounded the trees and nearly crashed into Houston and Kim, who grabbed him, helped him to the ground. "Shit . . ."

Vance's rifle sounded again.

"Dogma Four, fall back," Rainey ordered.

"What's he doing?" Houston asked.

Down on his haunches and struggling for breath, Rainey searched the road, waiting for a dark figure to appear. AK fire popped once more. Then nothing.

"Where the fuck is he?" cried Houston.

"Dogma Four, this is Dogma One, over. Dogma Four, this is Dogma One. Report your situation, over."

"Sergeant, permission to go get Vance?" Houston asked.

"Denied."

"I'll go bring him back," Doc said.

"No one's going anywhere."

"That could be more true than you know," said Lance Corporal Kim. "I know this forest, Sergeant Rainey. And it is mined . . ."

Rainey cursed through a deep sigh. Yup. They were having a bad night. Trouble was, when Marines had bad nights, people usually died. "Dogma Four, this is Dogma One. Report your situation, over."

Vance had thought for certain that he had struck one of the shooters, but somehow he had missed—even after accounting for the wind speed, direction, and the rain. Shit, he had missed. Just like he had missed shooting Mohammed al-Zumar. Vance's marksmanship had gone to shit. He sucked. Didn't belong in the corps anymore.

Unless he proved something to those Korean bastards. And himself.

One of them broke to the left, and Vance tracked the soldier's movements, had the shot—

Took it.

He gazed wide-eyed through his scope, searching for the soldier, imagining the guy lying face down, his fingers still quivering. But there was no soldier. Just more rain. Torrential now. And the shuffle of boots growing nearer.

Damn, he had broken orders to fall back and had ignored Rainey's call. Time to get the hell out. No time to prove jack. He crawled backward, heard something, froze just as an enemy soldier jogged past him no more than five meters to his left. A gust of wind had nearly blown the guy down and had, Vance suspected, concealed him from the soldier's view.

But two more were out there, advancing as well, probably coming right at Vance. If he stood and ran, they might spot him. If he remained, they might just trip over him. And what about the guy who had passed? Once he retreated, Vance would have to take him out unless he swung wide, running parallel to the forest.

Trembling with indecision, he lay there, rain washing into a puddle growing around his chest, the water just a few inches shy of his chin.

More footfalls. Close. But off to the right. Maybe far enough away. The other two guys were passing him now. Rainey called again, his voice coming tinny through the earpiece but loud enough to jar Vance. "Dogma One, this is Four," he whispered. "Enemy advancing past my position and heading toward you, over."

"Dogma Four, this is One. Come around for shots, over."

Vance faced west, then peered up, hoping to spot one

or more of the soldiers advancing along the road, but visibility had gone to three, four meters at best.

Then again, that could be good news: If he couldn't see them, they couldn't see him. He sprang up, took off running, rifle at the ready. He was behind them. Had the advantage. One, two, three shots was all it would take. "Dogma One, this is Dogma Four. Coming around for shots. Hold your fire. Visibility near zero, over."

A blur of movement to the left grabbed Vance's attention. Hunched over but moving swiftly, one of the soldiers charged. Okay, he had one. But where were the other two? He slid down his NVGs, scanned, came up empty. He shoved up the goggles, jogged a few more steps, dropped down to one knee, took aim at the guy.

Where was he? Vance peered hard through his rifle's Night Vision Scope. The soldier had vanished behind a closing curtain of wind and rain. He swore, keyed his mike: "Dogma One, this is Four. Visibility zero now. Request I rally your position, over."

"Negative Four. Proceed one hundred meters south and rally on treeline, but do not advance. We believe the forest is mined, over."

"Confirm one hundred meters south but do not advance into forest, out."

Vance checked his GPS coordinates, marked the position, then turned himself south and raced off the road, into the muddy field, concentrating on his legs, his breathing.

Rainey was furious with Vance. And that was putting it mildly. Why the sniper had delayed falling back not only required an explanation, but it also would have resulted in a catch-22 had Rainey not ordered the sniper to another rally point. While the enemy advanced on their position, Rainey and the others had not been able to fire—out of fear of striking Vance. So the NKA recon guys had gained some serious ground.

In truth, Rainey could not take full credit for the idea to rally south. Lance Corporal Kim had picked out the SCUD's big tracks veering off the road and working toward a southern break in the forest. Kim had suggested that the launcher's crew knew of a path that was not mined. And while Rainey didn't like the idea of fleeing from one group of enemy soldiers into the trail left by another, he absolutely hated the idea of stepping on a land mine and getting dissected by shrapnel. They were too smart and had come too far to buy it like that.

Since Vance was, hopefully, rushing ahead to meet them, Rainey took a chance and put Kim on point. Yes, Houston had given Rainey a look, but Kim knew the forest, and as they picked their way along its edge, the ROK Marine called for a halt and pointed out the trip wire of an OZM-3 Antipersonnel Mine. Those little love toys had an effective range of ten meters. Yes, it had been a good call, putting Kim on point.

Within five minutes they reached a clearing where the missile launcher had turned, churning up mud, weeds, and shrubs as it wove into the forest. Kim showed them a tree that had lost a long, surfboard-shaped portion of bark, and though the scar appeared natural, the ROK Marine said it marked the path. Scarred trees would appear every twenty meters or so, he added. Rainey ordered Houston and Doc to take positions on each side of the path, while he and Kim set up in the center as they waited for Vance, whose clicker went off twice as he arrived less than a minute later.

"Long line at the drive-thru?" Rainey asked, though he was definitely not making a joke.

"Got held up, Sergeant. I'm good to go, now."

"You'd better be."

Vance sighed. "Yes, Sergeant."

"Dogma Two? Dogma Three? Anything?" asked Rainey as he pulled out a small, laminated tactical map.

"Thought I caught one nearing our original position," Doc reported. "Rain's dying down a little. They'll be ringing our bell soon, over."

"Dogma One, this is Three. Confirm two more bad guys our original position, over," Houston said.

"Kim, we can follow this path through the forest, but tell me what's not on my map," Rainey said, pointing to their current coordinates.

"There are some rice paddies just after it."

"Yeah, but are those mined, too?"

"No. Then we follow the river, where it divides here, all the way to the village of Chongsan . . . here."

"Yeah, I got that. But back up. We follow the SCUD's trail to the paddies. Any idea why they'd bring a SCUD all the way over here?"

Kim shook his head.

"What's farther south—I mean just before the artillery corps gets set up?"

"Just the mines at Ch'olsan. And a few more prison camps."

Rainey contemplated that, but nothing clicked. "All right. Forget the SCUD for now. When we get to Chongsan, we'll need help getting to the beach."

"I'm not sure what you mean, Sergeant."

"Come on, Kim! We can't walk through that fucking village in broad daylight. Next chance we get, you're back on that radio and calling for help."

"Dogma One, this is Dogma Two," Doc called. "Count three advancing. We have to move, over."

"Roger that, Two. Dogma Team? Fall back! Dogma Four? Take point." Rainey gave Kim a hard look, then pocketed his map and jogged away.

NORTH KOREAN ARMY RECONNAISSANCE SQUAD
FOREST SOUTHWEST OF SINUIJU
NORTH KOREA
0556 HOURS LOCAL TIME

"But Sangsa, how could they know the forest is mined? How could they know that?" Sergeant Choi asked as Master Sergeant Sung pointed out the enemy's tracks along the forest's perimeter. "Do you believe they discovered one of the mines?"

"It is unlikely—but possible," Sung answered.

"Sangsa, I respectfully disagree. It is not unlikely. It *is* impossible."

"No, Choi. I caught a glimpse of one through my binoculars. And he is a Korean."

"A traitor, Sangsa?"

"Perhaps a member of the underground who knows this area as well as any of the local people. When we capture the enemy, we will be sure to keep him alive for questioning. Understood?"

"Yes, Sangsa."

Sung motioned for Lee to move out, and he and Choi charged up behind the young man.

Although Sung's frustration had been continually mounting, he took a moment to appreciate his adversary. The enemy had evaded his men, had evaded the minefield, and had cleverly chosen to follow in the missile launcher's path. Sung would have made the same decisions, were he fleeing from the country. He faced a worthy adversary, and if he died at the enemy's hand, at least he had come to know that much.

The sudden thumping of an Mi-2 Hoplite helicopter drove Sung to the nearest tree. "Choi? Lee? Here!"

As the two men converged on Sung's position, the small helicopter, capable of carrying six to eight troops, wheeled overhead in the gray sky, its twin rotors clanging as though about to snap off. A break in the storm had drawn at least one curious pilot to the area—or so Sung had thought.

Sergeant Choi took a deep breath. "I am sorry, Sangsa."

"You are sorry, Choi?"

"Sangsa, I contacted Mountain Ghost. There is another recon team aboard that chopper. They are here to relieve us."

"They are here to relieve us," Sung repeated slowly, his gaze going distant as he considered the humiliation, the utter shame involved in having failed the mission. Sung glanced to Private Lee, who was glowering at Choi. Yes, Lee understood the mission the way Sung did. It was *their* mission. They were closing in on the enemy. Victory was nearly at hand.

But Choi had ruined everything.

As the chopper circled once more, preparing to land, Sung thought that maybe the mission did not have to end. He was a recon soldier, a tactician who always found an avenue of attack and an avenue of escape.

While Choi's attention was focused on the chopper, Sung withdrew his pistol. He raised his arm, took aim at Choi—

And fired as Lee knocked his arm away and the shot went wide. Choi recoiled, jerked free his own sidearm, and brought it to bear on Sung.

"Hold your fire!" Lee cried. "We cannot shoot each other!"

"He tried to kill me!" Choi hollered over the chopper's thundering turbines.

Sung was ready to fire again, but as he looked into Choi's eyes, then flicked his gaze to Lee, the horror of what he was doing struck a shuddering blow. "Choi! This is *our* mission! We will not be relieved. We will finish it now!"

"No, Sangsa. We are finished. And if you attempt to leave, I will shoot you."

"And if you do that," Lee began, turning his rifle on Choi. "I will shoot you. Stay, Choi. Be relieved. The sangsa and I will finish the mission."

"You are fools if you do that. You will be considered traitors. And our relief team will hunt you as well as the enemy."

Sung backed slowly away from Choi. "No, Lyong-jang. You will stay here. You tell them we are still pursuing the enemy. You will tell them that if they approach too loudly and in numbers, they will ruin our operation. You will tell them to hold here until we call for them."

"Sangsa, I will not."

"You will, Choi." Sung held his gaze on the sergeant until the younger man could no longer face him. "Look at me, Choi."

After a deep breath, Choi finally obeyed. "Please, Sangsa. Do not ask me to do this."

"You will. You owe me your life." Sung exchanged the hardest of looks with the young man before summoning Lee deeper into the forest.

"Sangsa? Do not go!"

But Sung was already trotting off with Lee.

"Sangsa?"

Sung chanced a final look at Sergeant Choi, who sat there, staring at the ground, as the rotor wash ruffled his uniform.

TEAM DOGMA
FOREST SOUTHWEST OF SINUIJU
NORTH KOREA
0559 HOURS LOCAL TIME

"Well, I was getting worried," Doc told Rainey as they hiked along the clumps of earth kicked up by the TEL's big tires.

"Yeah, getting worried about what?" the sergeant asked.

"About the bad guys not sending in any reinforcements. We're Force Recon. We don't want this to be too easy, do we?"

"You're absolutely right, Doc. I hope they're choppering in an entire company."

"Yeah, and I'd tell you the shit is about to hit the fan, but I believe the fan has already been destroyed by a heat-seeking missile."

"That's old Murphy and his laws again. He just loves fucking with Marines."

Doc grinned inwardly. You had to laugh over their predicament. Otherwise you'd drop to your knees, pummel the ground, and curse the heavens. Damn. The longest night of Doc's life would, he guessed, be followed by the longest day. But as they say: Sweat dries, blood clots, and bones heal. Time to suck it up.

Vance ducked behind a tree as he spied the missile launcher in the clearing ahead. Houston hunkered down behind Vance, saying, "Let's hijack that thing and ride it all the way to the coast. Wouldn't that be a trick, man? See us come rumbling up to the shoreline riding atop a goddamned missile launcher? Damn, I'd get out and take a picture. Sell it to *Newsweek* or something!"

Vance smirked at the gabber. "Lance Corporal? Stop talking."

"Just trying to give us a little boost, since we're probably going to die here."

After putting an index finger to his lips, Vance slipped out his Nightstars and through intersecting limbs observed the SCUD's crew as three men worked on the hydraulic pump controls near the TEL's tailgate. Two others remained in the cab, whose side doors hung open. After a pair of loud clicks, the big missile's cradle rose very slowly from its resting position. "Oh, no, no, no. Y'all are not doing what I think you're doing."

Houston nudged Vance's shoulder. "What?"

"Maybe I'm wrong, but I think they're getting ready to fire their missile."

"Are you serious?" Houston took a peak through his own binoculars. "Hey, maybe it's just a test."

Kim jogged up and crouched down. "What's going on?"

"Take a look," Houston said, offering Kim his binoculars.

The ROK Marine's expression turned grave as he took in the magnified view for a second, then said evenly, "They are preparing to launch."

"How do you know what they're doing?" Houston asked. "I say they're just getting the thing primed up and ready, so if the order comes in—"

"It takes about four minutes to raise the missile and about an hour to complete the launch sequence," Kim said. "Fueling is a dangerous operation, and they only do that when they are certain they will fire."

Houston frowned at Vance and cocked a thumb in Kim's direction. "Fucking guy thinks he's a rocket scientist."

"Lance Corporal Houston, I learned about mobile missile launchers when I was in California, the same as you."

Houston shrugged. "Yeah, well, I wasn't paying attention that day."

Rainey and Doc shuffled up and found cover to the group's left. Vance gave them a heads up, and when he finished, Rainey shook his head and groaned, "When it rains, it pours."

"Oh, don't joke about the rain," Doc moaned.

The sergeant huffed. "Wish I were joking. Okay,

Kim? You get with Houston on the radio. See if you can contact some of your buddies so we can rendezvous with them in Chongsan."

"I am sorry, Sergeant. It is not that simple."

"Then you make it simple, Marine. Go." Rainey regarded Doc and Vance. "You two come with me. Let's move in for a better look at that SCUD before we take off."

"Take off?" Doc asked. "Sergeant, I don't know about you or the other guys, but I got a little problem with letting them launch."

"Me too, Doc. I'm all about blowing up stuff. But we have to keep moving."

"We will. Gun and run. You know what I'm saying?"

"We could take out the crew real quiet," Vance said. "Then we set the charges in just a couple of minutes."

"We'll see, Marines," Rainey said. "We'll see."

The sergeant directed Vance to the right flank, and he took off, threading his way silently between the trees. Somewhere behind them, that Hoplite chopper lifted off, leaving Vance to wonder just how many bad guys were now on the ground. Repressing a chill, he picked his way a little closer to the missile launcher, and from his new vantage point he spied a dirt road that had been cleared to the rear. The road wove off toward two huge mounds of dirt about three meters high and four meters apart. They could be machine-gun nests or something worse. The ground beyond the mounds grew strangely dark, as though an oil slick had spread across the forest floor.

"Well, well, well. What do we have here?" Rainey muttered as he pressed his Nightstars to his eyes. "More surprises."

"What is that dark spot, Sarge?" Vance asked.

The faint whine of a truck engine grew abruptly louder.

"Hit the deck," Rainey ordered.

"That's a Russian-made truck," Doc said, having shoved himself into a bush. "The old UAZ-469." He eyed the vehicle through his binoculars. "Looks like a hardtop jeep, drives much worse. And it's got a real thin skin."

"Where'd it come from?" Vance asked.

"From the tunnel out there," answered Rainey. "That black patch on the ground? That's a tunnel entrance, kid. What did you think it was, a bass lake?"

Vance shook his head as the UAZ drove up to the launcher and two soldiers emerged, both wearing the service uniforms of NKA desk jockeys. They spoke rapidly with one member of the SCUD crew, then walked around the TEL, inspecting the entire operation.

"Gentlemen, I think I know what we're looking at," Rainey said. "Most SCUDs are reloaded from a towed resupply trailer, right, Doc?"

"That's right."

"But this SCUD's got no trailer. Once they fire the missile, they drive the SCUD underground, where it's hidden from view and resupplied. But you know what's really bothering me? The fact that they're launching from here. That missile must have one hell of a range."

"Meaning we ain't looking at the old SCUD B," Doc said. "And it doesn't look like a SCUD C. Whatever it is, it ain't in the field manual. Could be Russian. Could be Chinese."

"Could be nuclear," Vance added.

"Don't go there, Corporal," Doc snapped.

"Shit, man. We could be looking at a first strike by the North Koreans," Vance said, feeling a chill twist up his spine.

"Or maybe we already hit them," Rainey said. "There's one way to find out."

Lance Corporal Kim could simply lie. The American Marines did not know his language, thus Houston, who was listening to him speak over the radio, would never know what was really said. Kim could report that he had spoken with a member of the underground and that they could not help in time. The Marines would be on their own. The lie would prevent other members of the underground from sacrificing their lives. Most of all, it would preserve Kim's secret.

But when Kim heard Yoon's voice over the radio, he knew that no matter the consequences he needed to do the right thing. Marines were Marines—no matter the country of origin. Rainey, Houston, Vance, and Doc had become his brothers, and he could not turn his back on them. He had thought he could be selfish. He had thought he could protect the underground and himself. But his selfishness could cost all of them their lives. And so he had surrendered to his fate.

"How'd it go?" Houston asked when Kim had signed off.

"Good. We will have help when we arrive in Chongsan."

"Fuckin' A, dude."

The ROK Marine cocked a brow.

"It means good," Houston said.

"Yes, good."

"You don't sound very positive," the lance corporal said.

Kim shrugged, imagining that all of his fear had been compressed into a small, silver coin that he tucked deeply into his pocket. "I am positive, Houston. But we must reach Chongsan first."

Sergeant Rainey came rushing through the brush, eyes full and wide. "Hope you got good news, Lance Corporal."

Kim nodded. "We will have help in Chongsan."

"Outstanding. Give me the details later. Houston? Call Bright Star. I want to know if Combined Forces Command has already launched an air attack on North Korean targets."

"Wouldn't we have heard something?" Houston asked.

"I don't know. Just find out."

"Aye-aye, Sergeant."

"Kim? Vance? Get eyes back on that missile. Doc? You and me will fall back a little to establish a defensive position until I decide if it's gun and run—or just run."

NORTH KOREAN ARMY RECONNAISSANCE SQUAD
FOREST SOUTHWEST OF SINUIJU
NORTH KOREA
0604 HOURS LOCAL TIME

Sergeant Choi rose to his haunches as Master Sergeant Han came rushing over and crouched down. Han, a man slightly older than Sung, with rubbery lips and a flat nose, looked confused. "Lyongjang Choi? Where is Sangsa Sung?"

The rest of Han's recon team jogged past the master sergeant and established a perimeter. The others were young, clean, well rested, ready to capture the enemy.

But who was the enemy now? Or rather, was there more than one enemy? Yes. Choi knew what he had to do. Lance Corporal Park had not deserved to die. Master Sergeant Sung was not acting or thinking properly. Choi cleared his throat and spoke slowly, "Sangsa, Master Sergeant Sung and Private Lee have gone off after the enemy."

"And you remained behind to rendezvous with us?"

"I did. But . . ."

"But what? Do you have something you want to tell me?"

Choi began to lose his breath. "Sangsa, Master Sergeant Sung asked that your team remain here until he calls for you."

"But you called Mountain Ghost and requested assistance."

"Yes, I did, Sangsa. Because I cannot follow Sung anymore."

Han's hand went for the pistol at his waist.

"No, Sangsa, it is not what you think. Sung killed Lance Corporal Park, and he has refused to call for help."

"He killed Park?"

"Yes, because the lance corporal would not kill a traitor."

"Then Park was a traitor himself."

"Sangsa, you do not understand. Sung's behavior has been very strange. He has allowed the enemy to get this far. I do not believe he wants to complete the mission."

"Do you know what you are saying, Lyongjang?"

"Yes, I do. I think Sung may want to die. And he wants all of us to die with him. That is why I called Mountain Ghost. That is why you are here. I only want to serve my country in the most honorable way. However, Sangsa Sung has lost his honor."

"Sergeant Choi, I do not believe you. Sung is an old friend. A soldier of great honor. He would not do as you say."

"Sangsa, you must believe me."

"Perhaps it is you, Choi, who have lost honor."

"No, Sangsa. Please . . ."

Han gazed thoughtfully at Choi. "Sergeant, we will find Sung. And you will help. And then the truth will be known." The master sergeant craned his neck toward his men, gave them the hand signal to advance. "Now, Choi. You will stay close to me. Where I can watch you."

Though the delay might give the enemy an even greater lead, Master Sergeant Sung could not help but pause for a moment to see what Sergeant Choi would do. Sung had observed the conversation through his binoculars, had seen that Choi had joined the group, and now observed the advance of Han's team.

Sergeant Choi, a man whom Sung had saved from certain death, had betrayed him.

"Private Lee, do you see what he has done?" Sung asked.

"Yes, Sangsa. Choi has disobeyed your orders. But he still does not deserve to die."

"For a man with a hard face, you have a soft heart, Lee."

"No, Sangsa. You do not know me very well."

"Tell me, what will you do if Han's team comes for us?"

"Sangsa, I do not know. But I do know this is our mission. Let us complete it."

Sung nodded quickly, then charged off for the next cluster of trees.

17

Lance Corporal Bradley Houston had, when keying his mike, automatically updated Major Thorpe as to their whereabouts. He had gone on to explain that Sergeant Rainey was busy with surveillance and had asked if the CFC had launched an air attack. No, they had not. The president of the United States had issued the North Korean government an eleventh-hour ultimatum, and presently all forces were on standby. Not a single bomb had been dropped.

"Bright Star, be advised we have eyes on a SCUD–type launcher that is currently fueling its missile. Believe it may be part of a preemptive strike, over."

"Roger that, Dogma Three. Request GPS coordinates on launcher, over."

Houston rattled off the coordinates, then added, "Bright Star, request sitrep regarding Extraction Point Scorpion and dinner engagement, over."

"Dogma Three, be advised the dinner party is still on, over."

"Roger that, Bright Star. Request we make this a breakfast or a brunch, over."

"Negative on breakfast or brunch, Dogma Three. Dinner party is tentatively set for twenty-one hundred local time. Can you attend, over?"

"Roger that, Bright Star. Have received invitations for twenty-one hundred and will attend. Confirm that the house staff will greet us at the front door, over."

"Affirmative, Dogma Three. The house staff is standing by, over."

"Roger that, Bright Star. Request orders regarding missile launcher, over."

With the rain and wind tapering off, the forest had grown very silent, and while he waited for Bright Star's reply, Houston swung his head this way and that, believing he had heard footsteps or the snap of a twig. He stiffened, held his breath, swept his gaze once more over the nearest trees.

"Dogma Three, you are ordered to eliminate the target, then continue rallying toward Extraction Point Scorpion, over."

Lowering his voice, Houston replied, "Roger that, Bright Star. Eliminate target and rally on Scorpion. Will update as necessary. Dogma Three, out."

Houston listened a moment to the rain dripping from the limbs and to the beat of his heart. A tingle worked across his neck and the instincts he had spent many hours honing came alive. Someone was out there, watching him. And when he moved, that someone would open fire.

"Dogma Three, this is Dogma One, over," Rainey called.

Not bothering to swing up his boom mike, Houston whispered, "Dogma One? This is Three, wait, over."

As he focused in on two thin trees about thirty meters off, Houston thought he saw a man crouched down, only half his face visible from behind the tree. But when Houston blinked, the man was gone.

He's out there, ready to make his move when I make mine. He wants me to move. Fuck it!

Bounding up with reckless courage, Houston took off through the forest, not bothering to look back, ready to flinch at the sound of incoming fire, ready to dive for home plate as the trees exploded.

Nothing followed. No sounds save for his breathing, his boots, his mind screaming, *Go! Go! Go!*

He reached Vance's position near the missile launcher, not remembering the run, his mind still flashing with the image of that man's face. Dizzy with adrenaline, he squatted, took in air as though he'd spent the last four minutes holding his breath.

"What're you doing here?" Vance whispered. "The sarge is back there."

"Thought I saw a bad guy. They're moving in on us. We gotta get the fuck out of here."

"No shit. You get with Bright Star?"

"Yeah. And it's all bad."

"The sub ain't coming?"

"It's coming. But not until tonight."

"You'd best call the sarge right now."

Houston nodded, and only then remembered that he

had told Rainey to wait. "Dogma One, this is Dogma Three, over."

"I've been waiting, Three. Go."

"Be advised I have rallied to Dogma Four's position. Have contacted Bright Star. CFC has not launched an attack. Our extraction time twenty-one hundred, not before. Bright Star updated regarding new target of opportunity. We have orders to destroy the target and continue rallying on Extraction Point Scorpion, over."

"Roger that, Dogma Three. Stand by, over."

Rainey darted from his position to Doc's, behind a thick shrub. The corpsman leaned into the stock of his Para SAW, the bipod jammed firmly into the dirt. "I got movement out there, Sergeant."

"How many you think?"

"With just one Hoplite? Maybe another small team. But you never know. They could've piled those guys in there. I can't confirm."

Rainey nodded. "All right, help me out, Doc. Five-man crew working the TEL. Tunnel beyond, with who knows how many bad guys inside. Enemy recon troops coming in from our six o'clock."

"You don't need help with that one. It's all about friendly fire—or what are they calling it now? Fratricide?"

"You read my mind, Doc. We'll rally on Vance and get set up."

"Aye-aye, Sergeant." Doc rose, began folding up his weapon's bipod. "It'd be interesting to see what they got inside that tunnel, huh?"

"Don't push it, Doc."

"Hey, these guys have been digging tunnels for over forty years."

"Forty years? Four hundred years. It doesn't matter to me. We're not going."

"Sarge, we could be standing on an entire regiment right now and not even know it."

"And you want to go down there?"

"No one's ever gathered intell on these tunnels."

"Doc, nailing the world's most wanted terrorist wasn't enough for you? Now you want to play tunnel rat in North Korea? Where's the conservative Doc Leblanc I used to know?"

"I'm right here."

"Yeah, here stands a guy with a wife and kids."

"Yeah, I know, I know. I just want all of this to mean something."

Rainey tipped his head toward the path. "Maybe it will. We're out of here." He flicked up his boom mike. "Dogmas Three and Four? This is Dogma One. Dogma Two and I are rallying on your position, out."

"Oh, man this ain't good," Vance whispered as another UAZ truck rolled out of the tunnel and veered right, taking a secondary path that came gut-wrenchingly close to their position. The truck continued on, then suddenly stopped. An NKA soldier hopped out of the passenger's seat, while the driver remained inside. The soldier stood there a moment, then started into the brush, coming directly toward Vance, Kim, and Houston.

Kim put a finger to his lips, unsheathed his K-bar, and motioned that he was ready. Vance was a little surprised that the ROK Marine had volunteered to take out the soldier, should they need to, and no, Vance wasn't arguing. In fact, he couldn't. Kim had already crawled away.

Vance assumed that the recon guys who dropped in via the Hoplite had radioed ahead to the boys in the tunnel, who had in turn alerted the missile crew. Those guys at the TEL kept close to their vehicle, gazing warily over their shoulders as they worked. The sarge needed to get things moving. Yesterday. Where the hell was he?

The NKA soldier took another step forward. Lance Corporal Kim rose behind the man, drove his K-bar into the soldier's heart as he covered the guy's mouth in a textbook kill. With the faintest of thuds, the two hit the dirt as Vance and Houston crawled to assist.

But Kim did not need help. He removed his K-bar, sheathed it, then began dragging away the body. Houston shifted over, rose, and tried to grab the dead soldier's legs, but Kim was moving too fast.

Vance slung his rifle over his shoulder and shifted his attention back to the UAZ, where the driver, a puffyeyed soldier slightly older than the first guy, had stepped out and glanced worriedly around. He opened his mouth, then thought better of calling out. He withdrew his sidearm, started around the front of the UAZ—

And that's when Vance sprinted for the truck's tailgate. He reached the UAZ, came around the driver's side, and neared the front fender as the driver risked a few more steps toward the tree line.

With K-bar in hand, Vance charged up behind the driver, slid his hand over the driver's mouth, brought his knife hand down—and found the driver's arm there to block. Vance shoved the knife closer to the diver, but the man squirmed, bit into Vance's hand as he tried to stifle the man's scream.

Suddenly, the driver went limp, and Vance turned to find Houston there, nodding curtly as he wrenched his knife from the man's back. Together they dragged the driver into the forest and set him down beside his buddy.

"Good or bad," Houston said breathlessly. "It's done."

"They already know we're around," said Vance. "Losing contact with these guys won't matter."

"And we have a truck to take us to Chongsan," Kim said, beginning to unbutton his shirt. "I will wear the driver's clothes."

"Give this guy a dollar," Houston said. "He's a fucking genius."

"Yeah, I'll pay up," Vance said. "Soon as we blow that SCUD to hell."

Two clicks came from the trees behind them, then Rainey and Doc hustled forward. The sergeant glanced at the two NKA soldiers, then shifted his gaze to the UAZ. "Getaway truck?" he asked Vance.

"Kim's idea."

"Keep those ideas coming. All right, then. Kim, you'll hang back with the truck. Houston? Vance? You'll set up behind the TEL and lay down fire to points along the line. You know what I'm getting at here?"

"I do, Sarge," Vance said. "Been there, done that. We get 'em to fire on each other. And while the missile crew's busy defending themselves against their own army, we take 'em out one by one."

"But it won't go down that easy, will it, Corporal?"

"No, Sarge. We got the tunnel to think about. And it's one hell of a wild card."

"I will recon the tunnel," Kim said. "As soon as the firing commences, I will drive the truck inside."

"I don't think so, Lance Corporal," Rainey said. "I need you to get us help in Chongsan."

"But I am the best one to go, Sergeant. I am Korean."

"Which is exactly why I need you out here."

"We could kill two birds," Doc said. "Keep a couple of crew guys alive, rig the TEL to blow, then have them drive it back into the tunnel. It'll blow underground, taking whatever they got in there with it."

"That's pretty risky, considering we don't know what they have underground. It's a hell of a lot easier to just blow it where it is and move on. Bright Star has GPS coordinates on the tunnel. Let them drop a couple of bunker busters on it."

"Yeah, that is the easy way out," Doc said, and there was no mistaking his tone.

Rainey spun around, sighed in disgust, then spun back, facing Doc. "Marines, if we get greedy here, odds are none of us will make it back."

"Sergeant Rainey, do you know that the missile they are preparing to launch is a Chinese-made M-11 with a plutonium nuclear warhead?" Kim asked.

Rainey looked to Doc for confirmation.

The corpsman shrugged. "It's not in the manual. He could be right."

"I am right. And if they fire it, tens of thousands in my country will die."

"We're taking out the launcher," Rainey said.

"They did not come to the tunnel by accident," Kim said. "This could be much more than a resupply site. There could be another launcher waiting in case this one is destroyed. We should confirm what is down there. We will not get this opportunity again."

"I'll go with him," Vance said.

"So will I," Houston added. "And I'll snap a few pictures while I'm at it."

"Come on, Sarge," Doc said. "We're never about the easy way. Let's do this."

Vance had never seen the sarge more torn up over something. He paced a moment, whirled, looked at Kim, Houston, Doc, and then Vance. "Gentlemen, if we do this, we're fucking crazy."

Houston chuckled under his breath. "Sarge, we're all definitely fucking crazy. What's your point?"

"Sergeant, we're good to go into that tunnel," Vance said. "Just say the word."

Rainey hesitated. Doc slapped a palm on Rainey's shoulder, nodded. The sergeant cleared his throat. "Three fucking stooges. That's what you are. Get in that truck. Go tell me what's in that fucking tunnel. I want a running narrative as you're going in. Channel open, you hear me?"

They answered in unison, then Vance ran off, leading Houston and Kim to the truck.

Once there, Kim plopped into the driver's seat while Vance and Houston took up positions in the cargo compartment. Shielded by the truck's canvas top, the two men kept low, shoving themselves between several footlockers sealed by padlocks. While Houston fished out his digital camera, Vance inspected his sniper's ri-

fle, then lay on his back and practiced sitting up quickly
to fire out the open rear.

Kim shoved the idling UAZ into gear, wheeled the
truck around, and headed straight back for the tunnel.

Rainey watched the truck pull away, then he stowed his
binoculars and turned to Doc, breathing a deep sigh.
"I'm responsible for those boys. And I feel like I just
sent them to their deaths."

"No, you didn't, Sarge. You did them a favor. You did
all of us a favor."

"What the hell are talking about?"

"I just had one of those moments when it all comes
together. I want you to think about this. We know it'll
take a while before they're ready to launch that missile.
And the bad guys coming in from our six will be here
soon. Screw the friendly fire idea. While those guys are
in the tunnel, we dig in, hide real good. And the bad
guys just walk on by."

"Because they know we're heading to the coast. And
no one would be crazy enough to hang around here and
try to recon a tunnel and blow the launcher," Rainey
said.

"Bingo."

"But Doc, after the big bang, we have to head down,
directly toward the enemy."

"I think when the charges go off, they'll all come rushing up here, figuring we're still in the area. We just have
to make sure we don't pass them in the rice paddies."

"Doc? I'm putting you in for a nickel raise. Come
on, we need to hide ourselves—and these two dead
Koreans."

"There are a couple of fallen trees over there, about twenty meters out. Looks pretty good."

"All right. You take the guy in his underwear. I'll take the other one."

Doc made a face. "I get the guy in his underwear. Figures. This is what I get for joining the Navy instead of the Marines."

NORTH KOREAN ARMY RECONNAISSANCE SQUAD
FOREST SOUTHWEST OF SINUIJU
NORTH KOREA
0621 HOURS LOCAL TIME

For the past five minutes, Master Sergeant Sung had been staring at the missile launcher and the surrounding forest through his binoculars. Other than a UAZ truck passing by and then driving out of view, there had been no other movement, nothing else out of the ordinary. Had the enemy already slipped by the TEL? It had seemed so. They would not delay their escape by interfering with the missile launcher's crew. Survival to them equaled stealth and speed, not attack. And if Sung and Lee were to continue evading Han's team, they needed to keep moving as swiftly and quietly as they could.

Private Lee returned from the launcher's right flank. "I see nothing but the crew, Sangsa. It must be true. The enemy has already advanced down, into the foothills, heading toward the rice paddies. They will try to reach Chongsan and the coast. What are your orders?"

"To follow, of course. But Private Lee, before we

go, I want you to have something." Sung reached into his pocket and produced the letter written by his grandfather.

"Sangsa, please, I am not worthy to accept that."

"You know what it is?"

"I have heard the rumors."

"Your loyalty is fierce, Private Lee, just like my grandfather's."

"My loyalty is what burned my face, Sangsa. I was captured by the underground and tortured, but I would not talk."

Sung had never asked about Lee's scar, and he had assumed the man would never share the story because it was, presumably, too miserable to recall. "Yes, Private Lee, you are loyal. And this is the most I can do to thank you." Sung pushed the letter into Lee's palm, folded the man's fingers over it. "Keep it in your pocket. Then, perhaps, one day, give it to your son."

"Yes, Sangsa."

"All right. We push on for the rice paddies."

"One more question, Sangsa. Do you believe they will really launch the missile?"

"If they do, they will bring darkness and death to our country."

Sergeant Choi crouched beside Master Sergeant Han, who was busy speaking to one of his men over the radio. Two members of the team were closing in on the missile launcher and had reported no sign of Master Sergeant Sung or Private Lee, let alone the enemy recon team. The security force located inside the tunnel indicated a loss of contact with one of their scouts, but such communications problems were as routine as rain during the summer months.

"Is there something you want to share with me?" Han asked.

"What do you mean, Sangsa?"

"I am wondering if perhaps you have intentionally diverted us to the missile launcher. We have not found Master Sergeant Sung or this enemy recon team."

"They have probably moved on, Sangsa, down into the foothills. We must advance now."

"Or maybe they have traveled farther south, away from Chongsan?"

"Why would they do that? Such a course would delay their escape."

"I do not know, Choi. Maybe you can tell me?"

"Sangsa?"

"Choi, I have heard stories of soldiers who have been influenced by the underground. Soldiers who have been promised new lives in the South. Soldiers who were once politically reliable but who have succumbed to treachery. Have you heard of such stories, Sergeant Choi?"

"Yes, I have, Sangsa. But I am telling you that the enemy moved in this direction, toward the missile launcher. I am telling you that Master Sergeant Sung and Private Lee followed them. I am telling only the truth."

"Then where are they?"

"I do not know, Sangsa. But we should keep moving."

One of Han's men hastened over and crouched down. "Sangsa, we have picked up at least one trail near the launcher. The footprints belong to someone wearing our boots."

Choi released a deep sigh.

"Excellent," Han said. "We will push on to the launcher, quickly question the crew, then proceed through the forest and into the valley."

"Yes, Sangsa." The soldier tugged free his radio and relayed the orders to the rest of the team.

Han raised his brows at Choi. "You look as though you are expecting an apology."

"No, Sangsa."

"Good. I do not have one."

"I would have thought the same, were I you, Sangsa."

"You are a good liar, Choi. Just remember, you are a part of a team that, as far as Mountain Ghost is concerned, already failed its mission. He alone will decide whether you live or die."

Choi closed his eyes. "Yes, Sangsa. But I hope you might convey my loyalty to him."

"And what loyalty is that?"

Frowning, Choi answered, "My loyalty, Sangsa."

"Do you mean your loyalty to Master Sergeant Sung? You obviously have none. Do you mean your loyalty to your country? I see only weak evidence in support. Do you mean your loyalty to yourself? Well, then, in that case I will share with Mountain Ghost your desire to do what ever it takes to stay alive."

"No, Sangsa," Choi said, opening his eyes to stare emphatically at Han. "I only want to serve. I only want what is best for the people of our country. I have sworn to give my life for them."

"And you may, Sergeant Choi." Han grinned darkly. "The day has just begun."

TEAM DOGMA
TUNNEL COMPLEX SOUTHWEST OF SINUIJU
NORTH KOREA
0623 HOURS LOCAL TIME

"Dogma One, this is Dogma Four," Houston began, his voice a little shaky. "Nearing the tunnel, over."

"Roger that, Four," Rainey answered. "Continue reporting. Cannot reply at this time, over."

"Roger that, One. Will not expect reply."

"Okay, defensive positions ahead. Be silent," Kim warned.

Two machine-gun nests had been established within the mounds of dirt on either side of the tunnel entrance. Each nest was manned by several NKA soldiers. They had a couple of 7.62mm belt-fed, air-cooled SMG machine guns, along with at least two mortars and another, lighter machine gun that Houston did not recognize. He relayed the information to Sergeant Rainey, then continued peeking out from between the canvas and the cargo compartment's lip, wondering if at any moment they would be stopped and searched.

"The guard gate will be farther inside," Kim said, waving to the guys in the machine-gun nests. "They don't want to call too much attention to the tunnel from out here."

"But they're ready to defend it, all right," Vance said.

"Any ideas how we're getting past the gate?" Houston asked.

"We may not have to," Kim said. "I am hoping that we can see enough from there."

Houston jostled forward as the UAZ lurched, then suddenly descended down the dirt path. Kim switched on the headlights, and the sheer magnitude of the tunnel made Houston gasp. The shaft stretched off, reaching far beyond the headlights. Thick, wooden support trusses bridged across the tunnel's roof every five or six meters, making it appear like an Arizona mine shaft. The grade shifted again, dropping much more sharply as the walls grew farther apart and the ceiling rose to nearly five meters. The air became thicker, colder, and the truck's exhaust made Houston want to gag. He covered his face with a hand and issued his next report:

"Dogma One, this is Dogma Four. We've passed the machine-gun nests and have entered the tunnel. The place is huge. Voodoo Five suspects guard gate somewhere inside. Will follow up if we reach that point, out."

"Oh, shit, here comes another truck," Vance said. "Get down."

Houston ducked as a pair of headlights shown into the cargo compartment.

"No stopping to ask for directions, all right, Kim?"

"If I ask for directions, that would betray my identity," the ROK Marine said in earnest.

"Just don't stop," Vance said with a nervous laugh.

"Of course not, Corporal," Kim answered as the other truck rumbled on by.

Realizing that he had been holding his breath, Houston suddenly exhaled, went to take another breath—

Couldn't.

He tried again. No air!

What the hell was wrong? He slapped a palm across his chest, tried to fill his lungs. Nothing. Then he wheezed loudly and grabbed Vance by the shirt collar. "Can't . . . breathe!"

With the two dead Koreans camouflaged beneath the fallen trees, Rainey and Doc had hidden themselves in the mud along a narrow creek about twenty yards south of the bodies. Just when Rainey had thought he was finished playing in the mud, the whole game had started again. By now, though, he had grown used to being as filthy as was humanly possible. He lay there, covered from head to toe in mud, only the whites of his eyes showing.

A faint breeze ruffled the nearby leaves, and as it faded, footfalls grew louder.

Rainey took in a deep breath, held it.

The old NKA sergeant and the soldier with the burned face rushed by. Not more than two minutes later, four more NKA troops whom Rainey did not recognize charged forward.

Then another older Korean wearing the insignia of a master sergeant, along with the pudgy-faced guy from the original NKA team, trailed that group. As Rainey watched them go, he expected Houston to check in at any moment. But several moments came and went, with only static filling the airwaves.

"I think we're clear," Doc whispered.

"Wait."

The voices of the TEL's crew sounded faintly in the distance. Water continued trickling along the creek. Rainey's stomach groaned. And the radio continued to hum. No Houston. No report.

"We can move," Doc whispered.

"Something's wrong in the tunnel," Rainey said. "Fuck."

"Easy, Sarge."

"I sent them in there. Me. No one else."

"You did. And I'll admit it was the wrong thing to do."

Rainey eyed the man in surprise.

"That's right, Sarge. You should've sent *me* in there. Not those clowns. *Me.*"

"No one should have gone, Doc. I'm doing just what Bruno said. I make it up as I go. Use my gut. Fail to calculate all of the outcomes. What if those boys are captured?"

"Then we'll go in and get them."

Rainey shook his head, imagined what would happen if the others died and only he and Doc returned. "They'll call this a tactical error. Not what it is. A fucking death sentence for those boys. Why did I listen to you idiots?"

"Because you always do. That's why you're a first-class team leader and operator. Now that's all the stroking you'll get out of me."

"It's falling apart, Doc. And I let it happen."

"No, you didn't. We're still in control. Fuck Bruno. Fuck all the second-guessing. Fuck North Korea."

Doc was right. And in his heart of hearts, Rainey knew that, but it was damned hard not to believe that he was screwing up, that Bruno had been right about him, that his career as a Force Recon team leader was already behind him, and that a decision he had made was about to cost three men their lives. It was all about control—control of the situation and control of his mind. Time to focus on the positive, push the "what ifs" aside, and concentrate on the solutions. Find the essence. Orient to speed and complexity. Match strength to weakness. Surprise and disorient the opposition . . .

"Fuck North Korea," Rainey repeated. "I'm in control. We're in control. Yeah. Those guys will make it out. We'll all make it out."

"You're damned right we will, because Force Recon penetrates deeper and lasts longer." Doc mustered a weak smile over the familiar saying.

Rainey drew in a long breath, nodded. "All right. You and I will take control of the TEL before those boys get back."

"Yes, we will. We'll keep at least the driver alive, maybe one other guy who knows how to launch the missile. And we kill the other three."

"Still want to drive that missile into the tunnel?"

"They didn't dig that hole for nothing."

"So when you said 'penetrates deeper,' you weren't kidding."

Doc winked. "Penetration is serious business."

"Yes, it is. But what if we kill the wrong guys?"

"I remember what the driver looks like. We'll get eyes-on for a minute before we move. I think I can figure out which one is the launch controller. That is, *if* these guys are in control of the actual launch."

"Whoa, what do you men 'if' ?"

"Sometimes the target selection and firing happens from a separate command-and-control vehicle."

"And you point this out now?"

"Look, I'm pretty confident that they control the launch. But even if they don't, we just have to get the cradle low enough to drive the TEL into the tunnel."

"How do we do that?"

"They'll do it for us."

"I hope you're right, Doc."

"I hope those guys in the machine-gun nests don't spot us. They don't have a clean line of sight, but if one decides to go for a little walk with his binoculars . . ."

"That will not happen," Rainey said, flicking his gaze to the heavens.

"No, it won't," Doc reaffirmed.

"All right, but before we do this . . . thanks."

"For what?"

"Just hearing me out."

Doc pulled himself from the mud and gazed innocently at Rainey. "I didn't hear anything, Sergeant." The big corpsman offered his hand and drew Rainey to his feet.

18

"Houston, what's wrong?" Vance asked as the lance corporal's eyelids fluttered. "Oh, man, don't be doing this."

"Is there a problem?" Kim asked from the driver's seat.

"Big problem, buddy," Vance said as Houston suddenly went limp. "Shit! Houston's passed out."

"Should I stop the truck?"

"I don't know, man! I don't know." Vance put his ear to Houston's mouth, tried to listen for breath sounds, but the damned truck was too loud. He grabbed Houston's wrist, searched for a pulse, couldn't feel anything, so he reached up for Houston's neck and—thank God—found a carotid pulse. "Maybe the exhaust got to him, I don't know. I'm not sure if he's breathing."

"Do you have a pulse?"

"Got one."

"Then listen again for his breath. I will slow the truck."

Shuddering, Vance blinked hard, cleared his thoughts,

remembered his training. He put his ear to Houston's mouth, then stared down the lance corporal's chest, looking for the telltale rise and fall. There it was. Houston was breathing.

"Come on, buddy, what's wrong with you? Ain't no time to be sleeping on the job."

"I think I see the guard gate," Kim said. "We may have to stop the truck."

Vance grabbed the digital camera lying beside Houston. "Here!" he said, tossing it into Kim's lap. "You'll have to take some pictures." Vance balled up a fist, about to give Houston a sternal rub the way Doc had taught him. But the lance corporal's eyes fluttered once more, then opened.

"Hey, man. Hey!"

"Where am I? Where's my buddy? Where's the enemy?" Houston mumbled, the old questions from Basic Training still resonating in his brain.

"You're in the truck. I'm your buddy. I'm right here. And the enemy is just ahead," Vance said. "You all right?"

"Fuck, what happened?" Houston sat up, rubbed his eyes.

"Get back down," Kim snapped.

Vance pushed Houston onto his back, while he dove forward, catching a glimpse of an enormous wooden gate, replete with concertina and barbed wire, along with several guards and a pair of old motorcycles that seemed lifted straight out of a World War II movie. Vance thought he saw several parked launchers and the nose cones of more missiles, but he couldn't be sure. He pushed a little farther down as Kim stopped the truck and opened his door.

"Where you going?" Vance asked.

But the ROK Marine did not answer as he jumped out.

"Kim!" Vance slowly lifted his head, caught another glimpse of the guard gate, saw two NKA soldiers jogging toward the truck, saw a wider chamber beyond where, indeed, a row of six or seven more SCUD missile launchers sat, all of them carrying missiles identical to the one outside.

"Fucking jackpot," Vance muttered. He lowered his head, regarded Houston. "I hope you're good to go, buddy."

"You hope I'm good to go?" Houston asked. "Dude, I think I just had a panic attack."

Vance cursed, pushed himself up on his elbows so he could sight the soldiers through the truck's windshield. "Lance Corporal, the word 'panic' ain't in a Marine's vocabulary. You'd best grab your rifle and think about that second word—because in about three seconds, it's show time."

The two North Koreans standing by the hydraulic pump controls never saw their attackers. With K-bars clenched in their fists, Rainey and Doc came up behind the men and erased them from the equation with a pair of perfectly executed punches to the heart. The men collapsed like marionettes and were left to bleed out beneath the TEL's tires. A third crew member who was, quite remarkably, standing up near the launcher's cradle and smoking a cigarette, might give them some trouble—if he and his cigarette didn't ignite the fueling missile first. Doc put a finger to his lips and ascended a small ladder, while Rainey kept his attention on the passenger's-side rearview mirror, which reflected an image of the driver and launch controller inside the cab. Those two looked busy enough.

As Doc went up top, the magnitude of the operation suddenly struck Rainey with a cold shudder. Here they were, seizing control of a nuclear weapon, in broad daylight, and well behind enemy lines. He knew other small, special forces teams had been dropped into the country—SEALS, Rangers, Berets, and perhaps even members of Delta Force—but Rainey doubted those teams were having as "good" a time as he and his men.

Rainey shot a glance up to Doc, who had already killed crew member number three and was lowering the guy's body over the side. Throwing the bloody man over his shoulder, Rainey rushed around the TEL and dropped the guy near a tire. Doc descended the ladder, crawled beneath the launcher, and began dragging the guy into the shadows.

Making tempo a weapon, they finished hiding their third victim, then Doc took the driver's side while Rainey took the passenger's.

On three, they climbed up into the cab and pointed their MEU pistols with attached silencers at the driver and controller, both of whom jerked in surprise at the two mud-covered phantoms.

"*So-ree-nae-jee-ma*," Doc ordered softly, putting a finger to his lips.

The controller lifted his hands from a control board and nodded.

"You," Rainey said, waving his pistol at the driver. "You are going to drive." Rainey mimed holding a steering wheel. "You are going to drive there." He pointed in the tunnel's direction.

The driver looked at Rainey, then at the course. Then he screamed at the very top of his lungs.

"What the fuck is Kim doing?" Houston whispered as he lay there in the truck, concentrating on his breathing: long breath in, long breath out.

"That little maniac is either going to get shot in the head, or he's going to bullshit his way out of this," Vance said. "Or worse. Maybe he's not who we think he is. Maybe he's going to hand us over to them."

"No way. I refuse to believe that," Houston said.

Kim marched right up to the two soldiers, waved a hand and shouted at them.

The two troops stopped, listened to Kim a moment, then one offered a few words. Kim responded, then abruptly both troops spun on their heels and raced off for the gate as Kim steered himself quite assuredly back to the UAZ. Once he had climbed into the driver's seat, Houston asked, "What you'd tell them?"

"I told them I have two American prisoners in the back of my truck and need to deliver them to the master sergeant here."

Vance shoved his rifle into the back of Kim's head.

Houston reached out for the rifle. "Vance."

"It is a joke," Kim said, raising his hands. "A joke."

"Don't fuck with us, Kim," Vance warned.

"I break the dreadful feelings with a joke."

"Well, your timing sucks," said Vance. "What did you say?"

"There is a platoon here. They have been waiting to

be relieved for four days. I told them to open the gates because the relief crew is on its way."

"Yeah, that's cool," Vance said. "We're going to relieve them of their duty all right."

"Lance Corporal, I fear these tunnels stretch all the way back to the mines at Ch'olsan. What we are seeing here is a small part of the ordnance they have hidden, but at least we can destroy this much."

"Shit, if we set the TEL to blow down here, you think we'll trigger the nukes?" Houston asked.

Kim shifted the truck into gear and made a tight U-turn. "That is unlikely. We will, however, be able to destroy those launchers and damage most missiles."

"If we gain control of the TEL outside," Vance said.

Kim suddenly flinched and grabbed his shoulder.

"You okay?" Houston asked.

"I tore my bandage. But I am okay."

"We need to call the sarge," Vance said, then tugged up his boom mike. "Dogma One, this is Dogma Four, over."

Although Vance's voice came through clearly in Rainey's earpiece and put him partly at ease, he could not acknowledge. He had just shot the driver in the hip, had slammed the man back into his seat, and had locked a hand around the bad guy's throat. "Listen, motherfucker, you scream again and you die."

"He doesn't understand you," Doc said.

"I think he gets my body language."

"And I think we got a problem." Doc raised his head at the approach of two soldiers, who had obviously left their machine-gun nest to investigate the scream.

"Dogma One, this is Dogma Four, over."

"Dogma Four, wait," Rainey ordered.

"Roger that, One. Will wait and report. We're heading out of the tunnel. Be advised we have multiple TEL vehicles inside, along with missiles and a platoon-size force. No obvious signs of any chemical or biological weapons. Our ETA your location, approximately four minutes, waiting."

The soldiers shifted to the driver's side of the TEL, where Doc stood ready with his pistol.

Rainey adjusted his grip on the driver's throat, then turned his pistol on the other guy. "How fast are you, Doc?"

"You want me to tell you—or shoot these guys?"

Rainey grinned inwardly. "Shooting them is fine by me."

Once the soldiers drew within five meters of the TEL, Doc abruptly leaned past the open windows.

The soldiers spotted him, their mouths opening, their eyes growing big and round as they snapped up their rifles.

First shot. Second shot.

Doc's rounds tore through their chests, killing them instantly.

"To answer your question, yeah, I am fast," Doc said with a wink.

"But how long till their friends get nervous?" Rainey asked, sighing into that fact. "Dogma Four, this is One. We need you out here, now!"

Hearing Rainey's urgent cry to Vance over the tactical frequency, Lance Corporal Kim slammed his boot against the accelerator. They sped so swiftly through the tunnel that Kim sideswiped a wall as they ascended the final stretch. The morning light cut a deep wedge across the path ahead, and Kim worried that once they bridged that light and started past the machine-gun nests, their velocity might incite the men manning those guns. He backed off the accelerator.

"Don't slow down," Vance said.

"I'm worried about the machine guns," Kim answered.

"Let me worry about them. Dogma One, this is Four. En route your location. Request orders in regard to machine-gun nests, over."

"Just pass them and get here," Rainey answered. "We'll deal with them in a minute."

"Keep low now," Kim warned as they neared the exit. His arms stiffened, and his knuckles grew white as he turned the truck slightly—

And they crossed into daylight.

He was about to hold his breath as they passed the nests, but it all happened so fast that he forgot. The truck roared on by without incident, though out of the corner of his eye, Kim saw the gunners sweeping their muzzles to follow the truck's every move. He flicked his gaze to the mirror, watched the mounds of earth shrink behind them as he veered right, onto the path leading to the TEL.

"Guys, do me a favor?" Houston asked. "Don't say nothing to the Sarge and Doc, all right?"

"You passed out," Vance said, his tone as serious as Kim had ever heard it.

"Just a little lightheaded."

"Lance Corporal, you lost consciousness. You said you had a panic attack."

"I was just exaggerating. It's a California thing. You

know everybody out there is always saying, Oh, I just had a panic attack."

"But I think you did," Vance said. "Fact is, you could not breathe."

"Houston, you want us to lie for you?" asked Kim.

"You know what? Fuck it. Turn me in. I fucking passed out. I'm a liability. I don't belong here."

Kim stole a glance in the rearview mirror. Houston hung his head and muttered something to himself. Given the night they had had and the recent loss of his father, it was no wonder that the young man was having problems. While Kim sympathized with the young Marine, he would not lie for him. Kim was, however, an expert in *not* volunteering information, especially information about his own past.

The TEL came into view through a stretch of thinly spaced trees, and Kim pulled over, shut off the engine. Vance and Houston were already out by the time he reached the path's edge. With Vance taking point, they fell into a line and zigzagged toward the launcher.

After seeing those weapons of mass destruction waiting below, sleeping like some great demons, Kim knew that he would do whatever it took to destroy them. He would not just be doing his duty. He would be avenging the murder of his parents and protecting future generations from having a childhood like his.

Yes, they would bring justice. And that thought brought extreme joy to his heart. However, part of him hoped that he would not return from the tunnel. Survival meant confronting Yoon and facing the truth at Chongsan. Dying would be so much easier.

Then again, he was a Marine. And as Doc had said, Marines do not choose the easy way.

"Hold this guy," Rainey ordered Vance as the corporal, Houston, and Kim climbed into the cab. "Kim? You tell this guy to start lowering the missile. Then tell the driver to get ready."

While Kim translated, Rainey looked to Doc, who nodded and turned to leap down from the TEL. Rainey did likewise, and once on the ground, they dropped their packs and removed the blocks of C-4 they had brought to destroy the low-blow radars. They got busy rigging the TEL to blow sky-high via remote detonators. Rainey and Doc had practiced demolition techniques so many times that they could sleepwalk through the procedure. But this wasn't just a radar system, and Rainey found himself checking and double-checking his work. He figured Doc was doing the same. They could afford no mistakes.

When he was done, Rainey peered beneath the TEL to Doc's side of the vehicle. "You set?"

The corpsman ducked and flashed a thumbs up. "My remote is active. We've set enough to take out the TEL and maybe a couple of others. If there are biological or chemical WMD that they didn't see down there, we should still be okay—unless they got the warhead open and they're out in the open."

Rainey nodded and checked his own remote, saw the three LED indicators flashing three times in the green.

"All right, how you want to play this?" Doc asked, coming around to Rainey's side.

"By the book, Doc. Simple but flexible. Kim takes

the lead in the truck. Houston and Vance in the TEL's cab with these guys. You and I wait until they reach the gate, then we take out the machine-gun nests. Kim drives the getaway truck for all three, they clear the tunnel, then we blow the TEL."

Doc glanced up to the huge missile. "That thing's taking a long time to come down."

"Looks low enough to me," Rainey said. "What's the worse that can happen? It snaps off and detonates?"

"Hell, yeah . . ."

"Don't worry, Doc. I guarantee that no matter what happens, you'll get what you want."

"And what's that?"

"For this to *mean* something, right?"

"So long as it doesn't *mean* my death."

Rainey waved Doc up into the TEL's cab. "All right, gentlemen, we're taking this show on the road." Rainey relayed the plan to Houston, Kim, and Vance. Once he finished, he asked if there were any questions.

Vance, who had gagged the driver, shook his head. "We're good to go, Sergeant. But I can hold the driver here in the cab. We don't need this controller guy anymore. We can either tie him up and leave him inside the cab, or dump him in the forest. Either way, he's got the missile coming down. Kim can take the UAZ and I can take the TEL, while you, Doc, and Houston focus on the nests. The fewer guys in the tunnel, the better, huh?"

"He's right," Doc said.

Rainey looked to Houston, whom he expected to launch into one of his usual protests. However, the lance corporal kept silent and never lifted his gaze to meet Rainey's. "Houston, you hold back with us."

"Aye-aye, Sergeant."

"But first you tie up this controller guy, then stow him in that side compartment beneath the hydraulic pumps."

"Lock him in the trunk. Just like the Mafia. I'm on it, Sergeant." The lance corporal reached into his ruck for some tape.

"Vance, you and Kim stay in close contact. This driver gives you any problems, Kim will tell you what to say."

"Yes, Sergeant," Kim said. "I will. And now I will go to the truck and await your orders."

Rainey grabbed Kim by the back of the neck and squeezed. "Lance Corporal? Good luck."

"And good luck to you, Sergeant."

NORTH KOREAN ARMY RECONNAISSANCE SQUAD
RICE PADDIES OUTSIDE CHONGSAN
NORTH KOREA
0735 HOURS LOCAL TIME

Master Sergeant Sung and Private Lee were wading up to their hips in the rice paddies. They kept their rifles held up, across their chests, and, hunched over, slogged as quickly and as quietly as they could. Sung probed their course, looking for signs of the enemy's passage: a torn weed, a trail of cloudy water, anything that would betray them. However, since they had left the missile launcher, they had found nothing—not even a small puddle of mud that would have dripped from an enemy uniform. Had Sung made a terrible error? Could the enemy still be at the missile launcher? No, that was not possible. They had been shot out of the sky. They were trying to escape. They would not waste time. They would not make such an error. Sung would stand by his decision. He and Lee had simply not found the enemy's trail, but they would. Soon. At least they were heading in the correct direction.

"Sangsa, perhaps we give the enemy too much credit," Lee said.

"Because we have found no signs of their path through here?" Sung asked.

"They are cunning, yes. But they are only soldiers, like us. They must move like us. They will trample grass and weeds, stir up the soft bottom here. And yet we find no evidence."

"Because they are trained to be ghosts, Private Lee."

"Yes, Sangsa. I know, but—"

"Does a ghost leave behind such evidence?"

"No, Sangsa. But it is impossible to pass through here in such a fashion. We are trained to be ghosts as well, but there is always evidence. Our task is to make that evidence is so small that the enemy will overlook it."

Sung was about to qualify Lee's remark when a faint chirp from far behind sent his neck craning, his gaze probing the foothills. "It is Han's team, closing in," he said. "Quickly, to the edge over here. Remember, Lee, it is our mission. We must reach the enemy first!"

Lee's reply came half-heartedly. "Yes, Sangsa."

TEAM DOGMA
TUNNEL COMPLEX SOUTHWEST OF SINUIJU
NORTH KOREA
0736 HOURS LOCAL TIME

"Dogma Team? This is Dogma One," Rainey announced. "Sound off, over."

"Dogma One, this is Dogma Two," Doc said. "I have the left nest in my sights, over."

"Dogma One, this is Dogma Three," said Houston. "I am in position and targeting the right nest, over."

"Dogma One, this is Dogma Four," Vance called from within the TEL's cab. "The engine is running and we are standing by to move, over."

"Dogma One, this is Voodoo Five," Kim said from behind the wheel of the UAZ. "I am ready to go, over."

Rainey swung his carbine from the right nest to the left, zooming in with his scope to pick out the machine gun and even the occasional head of a gunner. Damn, that was a big gun, the same caliber they used on the M1 Abrams tank. He panned back and across to the UAZ and the TEL. Everything looked in order. The time had come.

Then why was he hesitating to give the order? One simple word: Execute. He just had to say it.

"Dogma One, this is Dogma Five, over."

"Dogma Five, be advised you were KIA, meaning get the fuck out of my head, over."

"Dogma One, be advised that you are just an old man now, getting sloppy. And once you give that order, someone's going to die. You know that. And I know that. So what's it going to be, over?"

*"Dogma Five, you are dead. You are going to stay
dead. That is all, out."*

Shaking off the radio voice from hell, Rainey cleared
his throat, muttered "Fuck you, Bruno," then added,
"Dogma Four? Voodoo Five? Execute!"

Inside the UAZ, Kim checked his rearview mirror, then
put the truck in gear. He was no expert with a clutch,
but he managed to keep the truck from jerking violently. He carefully measured his speed, keeping the
TEL just a handful of meters behind. "Dogma Four,
this is Voodoo Five, hold steady now."

"Five, this is Four," Vance answered from inside the
TEL's cab. "I'm slipping my headset on the driver's
head. Give instructions in Korean, over."

"Roger that, Four. Instructions coming now in Korean." Kim issued orders to the man, then told him that
if he did not obey, the muddy young man standing behind him would put a bullet in his head. The driver, still
gagged, could only hum his agreement.

I should be in that cab with Vance, Houston thought as
he freed up a pair of grenades, then propped himself on
his elbows to get a clean bead on the machine-gun nest.
The truck and TEL came within the enemy's sights.

*If I were a real Marine I'd be in there. Fucking poser,
that's what I am.*

Houston began to lose his breath.

"What's he doing?" Doc muttered to himself from behind his Para SAW.

One of the gunners had left his nest and was running

down to the road just as Kim's truck approached. Doc swung his SAW around, his reticle sliding over the soldier's head. "Dogma One, this is Two. Bad guy in the road, over."

"See him, Two," Rainey answered. "Hold your fire."

Doc wasn't sure, but he thought Kim shouted something to the soldier, whose head turned toward the TEL, then he nodded and jogged back for his nest. Doc sighed deeply as the UAZ vanished into the tunnel. Three seconds later, the TEL followed without incident.

What the team would have done were it not for the ROK Marine Doc did not know. Had to be fate that Kim had wound up with them. Had to be fate that they had crossed tracks with the missile launcher. And it had to be fate that they would blow it up along with the others, then get back home safe and sound. Fate would allow them that much.

But old Murphy? He was untouched by fate, worked around it, didn't care about it, had his own agenda, the bastard.

"Voodoo Five, this is Dogma One. Awaiting your rendezvous with the gate, over."

"Dogma One, this is Voodoo Five. En route to gate, five-by-five. Will notify you of arrival, over."

"Roger, out. Dogma Two, standing by, over?"

"Dogma One this is Two, standing by, over."

"Dogma Three, this is One. Standing by, over?"

While there was plenty of oxygen to go around, Houston couldn't get his share. He panted, wanted to catch his breath, needed to answer Rainey. "Dogma . . . Dogma One. This . . . this is Three. Standing by, over."

"Roger, Three. What's your status, over?"

That was just great. The sarge already suspected something. Of course he did. Houston's voice had sounded as shaky as a victim of hypothermia. He screamed in his mind, ordered himself to calm down, to breathe, to answer, to remember that he was a Marine no matter what anyone said—including his father. "Dogma One, this is Dogma Three. In position. Standing by for your orders, over."

"Roger that, Three. Stand by . . ."

There. He had done it. If he could only keep his hands steady on his rifle, he would be okay.

A horrible screeching noise resounded from somewhere behind the cab. Vance couldn't look back for fear the driver would make a move, though the corporal suspected what was happening. The damned missile had just barely cleared the tunnel and was now scraping along the ceiling, smashing into crossbeams and maybe even dislodging a few. Sand and rocks began falling onto the TEL, and for a long moment it seemed as though they were driving through a hailstorm—

And then . . . it was over, as the ceiling rose.

The driver groaned against his gag. Vance shoved his pistol harder against the guy's head. "Don't worry about that. You just drive. Maybe you're driving us both to our graves, but I hope not. I really do."

A glimmer of light shone at the corner of Vance's eye. He chanced a look back at the control panel, where a long bank of displays labeled in Korean had suddenly lit up. What was happening was anyone's guess, but the guy with the best guess—other than the controller—

was Kim. "Voodoo Five, this is Dogma Four, over."

"Go ahead, Four, over."

"The control panel back here has just lit up, over."

"Say again, Four?"

"Repeat, the control panel has just lit up, over."

As Rainey listened to the tactical frequency, he remembered what Doc had said about the missile being controlled from a secondary vehicle. If that were a fact, wouldn't that secondary crew need to be in close contact with the TEL's crew? They would not initiate a launch unless they were certain that all systems were go.

Or should Rainey assume nothing?

"Dogma Four, this is Dogma One. Get that driver talking to Voodoo Five right now, over."

"Roger that, One. Stand by."

Rainey felt as though he aged ten years in the moment it took for Vance to remove the driver's gag and get him speaking with Kim over the tactical channel. The driver's voice, much deeper than Kim's, cut sharply over the channel. The guy sounded as angry as he was winded. Kim answered calmly, then added in English, "Dogma Team? Be advised the driver indicates that missile launch sequence has been engaged, over."

"Voodoo Five, this is One. Was the sequence engaged remotely, over?"

After a few exchanges in Korean with the driver, Kim answered, "Negative. The driver believes that the controller never shut it down. When the missile is lowered, the launch sequence should be automatically terminated, but the driver does not know why the launch is still active, over."

But I bet the controller knows why, Rainey thought. *He probably figured we'd kill him, so he decided on a little payback the best way he knew how.*

"Dogma Four, this is One," Rainey called. "We need estimated time of missile launch, over."

"Roger that, Four. Uh, we're going to get that right away, over," Vance said, now a scared-shitless fisherman sitting atop a ticking nuke.

Once again, the driver and Kim spoke rapidly with each other, and when the channel went silent, Rainey braced himself, rolled his wrist, readied his watch's chronograph.

Then Kim spoke. "Dogma One, this is Voodoo Five. We have confirmed that the missile will launch in approximately seven minutes, over."

After lowering his head and cursing, Rainey composed himself. "Confirm approximately seven minutes, out." He set his watch, then opened his mouth, about to order Vance to kill the driver. The corporal could probably handle driving the TEL, and killing at least one of those bastards would make Rainey feel a little better about being set up.

But it wasn't about feeling better. He began calculating times and distances, remembering how long it had taken Kim, Houston, and Vance to reach the guard gate the first time. The numbers did not add up.

"Voodoo Five? Dogma Four? Stop those vehicles. Repeat! stop those vehicles!"

"Dogma One, this is Voodoo Five. We are approaching the gate, over."

"Roger that, Five. Just get out of there!"

19

The TEL's driver turned his head and hollered through the open window, trying to draw the attention of the guards at the gate. Vance flinched and fired his silenced pistol, capping the Korean before the man could hit the brakes.

Vance looked up. *Oh, shit—*

The damned TEL plowed into Kim's truck, just as Kim hit the brakes. Then, realizing there was no way in hell he could slow the missile launcher and that his own truck's tires were about to be crushed by the TEL's massive wheels, Kim opened his door and leaped away, hit the ground, and tumbled.

The UAZ began skidding sideways as the TEL steamrolled onward, blowing out one of the UAZ's tires as the rear quarter panel crunched down. Then the shattered truck spun out of the TEL's path.

"Lord, I could use a little help now!" Vance cried in confusion.

Should he search for the breaks? Bail out? Stay in the cab to ambush any soldiers who came near once the thing smashed into the other launchers ahead?

Or should he just wet his skivvies, which was what he really felt like doing?

A small guardhouse, maybe ten meters by ten, had been constructed near the gate. From it emerged a half dozen troops bearing AKs as the TEL barreled on.

Vance tugged free a grenade, lobbed it at the house, tugged free another, lobbed it at the soldiers—

Just as the TEL crashed through the gate with a tremendous boom that echoed even louder than the big launcher's engine.

As the grenades' four-second fuses ticked down, Kim's rifle resounded. And that was Vance's cue to cross the cab, reach the open door, and leap to the ground.

With his attention torn between the still rolling TEL and the sudden explosions whose concussion nearly knocked him off his feet, Vance lifted his rifle, then turned and sprinted for the wall behind him, where Kim had dropped behind a long row of sandbags.

"The truck was our only way out," the ROK Marine said gravely. He ducked as three rounds tore into the dirt wall behind them. "The missile will launch, and we cannot get out in time."

Vance slumped as he realized he had capped the driver too soon. The guy's screaming had unnerved him, but he should have remembered that the driver was still in control of the TEL. He swore under his

breath not once, not twice, but five times before he
ripped out another grenade and gave it a solid toss back
toward the rubble of the guardhouse—

Just as the TEL smashed into the row of launchers
and finally came to a steaming halt, its engine still
droning, the missile sitting on its back at about a twenty
degree angle and ready to burrow its own tunnel. Four,
maybe five troops shifted out from behind the wreckage, one shouting, another rattling off a reply.

Kim pitched a grenade in their direction, then
ducked and asked, "Should we try to run?"

Vance was about to nod, about to surrender to the
fact that there was no way in hell they could escape in
time—

When his gaze fell upon those two ancient motorcycles.

In the woods outside the tunnel, Rainey lobbed his
grenade, and it dropped squarely into the left machine-
gun nest. With a simple bang, the three men posted
there gave up their ghosts. But to be sure, Doc raked the
nest with his Para SAW.

The right machine-gunner's nest was another story.
The big gun beat a terrible rhythm, and Rainey could not
understand why Houston had not answered all that fire.
"Dogma Three, this is Dogma One! Take out that gun!"

Doc redirected his bead on the right nest, keeping the
gunner there momentarily at bay. Rainey was about to
write off Houston, about to use his grenade launcher to
send in a frag of his own, when he spotted the lance corporal running through the forest, coming in from behind
the machine-gun nest. "Jesus Christ, what's he doing?"

* * *

Houston was either a Marine or he was not. He would charge the enemy and kill them all—or he would die. The world was black and white, cut and dry. He reached the nest and came up behind the mound, where a meter-high wall of sandbags protected the rear.

There were a half dozen easier ways to take out the nest. Houston had chosen the hardest, most dangerous: point-blank kills. He was locked. Loaded. And at the moment, calling him a human being would be generous. He bared his teeth, drooled.

"Hey, motherfuckers!"

The three Koreans turned their heads. The nearest guy began to raise his rifle. The guy manning the gun reached for a pistol holstered at his side. The third guy, who had been handling the ammo, started to raise his hands.

Houston emptied his clip, his weapon growing hot, his eyes burning until they blurred. When it was over, he cleared his throat. "Dogma One, this is Dogma Three. The right machine-gun nest has been secured, over."

Rainey didn't answer. He didn't have to. As Houston turned, he found the sergeant standing behind him.

Rainey glanced to the dead Koreans, their bodies riddled with bullets, then back to Houston, who looked away. "I'm good to go, Sergeant."

"Yeah," Rainey said softly as Doc ascended the mound toward the nest.

"Bad guys should be turning tail and headed this way," Doc said. "Wish we had more time to be subtle."

He caught sight of the Koreans. "Whoa. This your work, Lance Corporal?"

Houston nodded.

"Damn waste of ammo."

"Sorry." Houston shrugged.

Rainey rubbed his jaw in thought. "All right. Let's take control of this gun. If the bad guys show up before Kim and Vance, at least we'll have a solid defensive position."

While the keys were in both motorcycles, Vance could not get his bike started, and the muscles in his leg already felt like they were ablaze. Kim, who was covering him with suppressing fire, fell back, shouted for Houston to cover him, then lifted the other bike, and, son of a bitch, got the thing started with his first kick. "Come on, Vance!"

Literally shooting from the hip, Vance shifted across the tunnel, reached Kim, then ceased fire, held his breath, and jumped onto the back of the bike behind Kim. The ROK Marine nearly popped a wheelie as he dug it out. Vance used his free hand to grab Kim's shoulder, and it was a good thing he did. The little Korean could hold his own against any of those guys Vance had seen during Daytona Beach's yearly Bike Week festival.

"Where'd you learn to ride a motorcycle?" Vance asked.

Kim was about to answer, but gunfire raked parallel to their path and sent him veering closer to the left wall. The motorcycle's ancient headlight did a piss-poor job of lighting the path, and Kim barely evaded several ruts. He turned slightly right, followed the tunnel's curve, and revved out of the gunfire. Vance allowed himself a sigh.

"Oh, shit," Kim cried. He hit the brakes, leaned left, started skidding—

As a section of crossbeam that had fallen from the ceiling materialized from the shadows.

"We have to blow our charges before that missile launches," Doc told Rainey. "You know that, Sarge. Right?"

"Yeah, I know that," Rainey said, checking his stopwatch: three minutes left on the clock.

"And you can't cut it too close."

"I know, Doc. I also know that there's no guarantee that our C-4 will disrupt the launch sequence."

"How deep is that tunnel?" Doc asked.

"You worried about radiation? Hell, if it's too shallow, the initial blast will kill us all." Rainey swung up his mike. "Dogma Four, this is Dogma One, over."

Vance heard the sergeant's call as he hurtled through the air, then struck the dirt on his right side, his elbow smacking hard. He rolled over, looked back at Kim, who lay beneath the idling motorcycle where they had struck the crossbeam. Vance got shakily to his feet, reached Kim, and dragged the guy out. "Can you walk, man?"

"I think so. But we're not walking. Come on!" Kim leaned over, grabbed the bike's handlebars, and lifted the machine. "Help me get it over the beam."

The sound of an approaching truck engine drove them frantically forward. They bridged the crossbeam, and Kim climbed back onto the cycle. Vance resumed his seat in the back. "Born to be wild, buddy! Let's go!"

"Roger that," Kim cried.

"Dogma Four, this is Dogma One, over."

"Dogma One, this is Four," Vance answered. "Be advised we are riding a motorcycle and are exiting the tunnel. We'll be up there in a minute."

"Roger that, Four. It had better be only a minute. Standing by in right machine-gun nest to detonate charges, over."

"Don't wait for us," Vance said. "Dogma Four, out."

"Why did you tell them not to wait for us?" Kim asked.

"Because if the sarge don't blow that launcher, the missile could go off."

"It may launch anyway."

"Yeah, I guess you're right. But at least we got light at the end of our tunnel."

In fact, they did.

But they had barely reached the line where shadows turned to sunlight when a terrific rumble made it feel as though they were driving on Jell-O.

"What is that?" Doc asked.

Rainey felt the tremors working up through his legs. He checked his stopwatch. Still more than a minute to go. "I didn't trigger the charges."

"It's the missile!" shouted Doc.

"Shit, it must've launched early. Set off the charges," Rainey ordered, thumbing his own remote, while Doc did likewise.

"I think it's too late," Doc said.

A tinny-sounding engine caught Rainey's attention. He rose slightly from the gunner's nest, saw Kim driving the old motorcycle, with Vance hanging on the back. Suddenly, the ground heaved violently, and Kim lost control of the bike. Vance bailed out, and Kim released the handlebars a moment before the motorcycle slid out from beneath his legs.

Rainey stood up, waved both of them over, shouting, "Move it, Marines! Run! Run! Run!"

While Rainey had appreciated the quake produced by the mudslide, it paled in comparison to the incredible force rumbling beneath him. The tunnel entrance began to cave in, and the ground around it began to crack. Huge pieces of earth started dropping as the tunnel's ceiling collapsed in a domino effect, digging enormous trenches in the forest. Whether they were experiencing the launch of the missile, the detonation of their charges, or the actual detonation of the warhead, Rainey wasn't sure, but it felt like the damned world was coming to an end.

NORTH KOREAN ARMY RECONNAISSANCE SQUAD
RETURNING TO TUNNEL COMPLEX
NORTH KOREA
0752 HOURS LOCAL TIME

Upon hearing the gunfire behind them, back at the missile launcher, Master Sergeant Han immediately recalled his men, and Sergeant Choi realized that his former team leader, Sergeant Sung, had miscalculated the enemy's plans. Choi felt thankful that he was now in the hands of a more skilled, if not more threatening sangsa. As they charged back for the launcher, reaching the forest's edge and wondering why the ground was rumbling so violently, Choi's gaze locked onto a line of mud-covered men fleeing about one hundred meters to his left.

"Sangsa!" he cried. "The enemy!"

"Yes, there!" Han answered, waving over the rest of his men. "There they are!"

Choi took a step forward, but the ground began shaking so intensely that he could barely keep his balance—

And then . . . there was no ground. He was falling straight down into a tunnel that had been dug under him. Han was falling, too, along with the others, and the dirt kept coming down as they plunged nearly eight meters. Choi heard something snap in his ankle, and he was about scream in pain—

When a wall of soil crashed down, slamming him to the floor. He could not move. He could not see. He could not breathe.

Despite Lee's arguments, Master Sergeant Sung had chosen not to return to the missile launcher. While he now felt certain that the enemy was there and that he had underestimated their cunningness to strike, he also knew that Han would take his team back to investigate. Thus, Sung had held his position, waiting, watching, feeling the ground quake so hard at the edge of the rice paddies that it knocked both he and Lee to their rumps.

"It is a great underground explosion," Lee said. "Something terrible has happened."

"We continue on along the river, to Chongsan and the coast. If the enemy reaches there, we will be waiting for them."

"Sangsa, I am . . . worried."

For the first time since he had known the man, Sung saw genuine fear in Lee's eyes. "Lee, listen. The ground is beginning to settle. This explosion could simply be part of an enemy diversion. They are on the move. But we will reach Chongsan and the coast before them. Follow me."

TEAM DOGMA
EN ROUTE TO CHONGSAN
NORTH KOREA
0818 HOURS LOCAL TIME

The Hoplite chopper swooped down and flew over Rainey and his men as they submerged themselves up to their necks in the rice paddies. Rainey doubted the pilot had spotted them. Still, he ordered the team to remain there until the Hoplite disappeared behind the distant line of trees.

"Dogma Team?" he called over the radio. "Move out."

"Dogma One, this is Dogma Three," Houston said. "Bright Star requests sitrep, over."

Rainey knew that military satellites had detected the explosion and Thorpe was probably standing by in his command post, demanding to know what the hell was going on. Rainey swam back to Houston, who held the Foxtrot's mike above the water. "Bright Star, this is

Dogma One. We are en route to Chongsan and intend to keep our dinner engagement, over."

"Dogma One, this is Bright Star. Eyes in the sky detect a subterranean explosion your area. Request sitrep, over."

"Bright Star, be advised we have terminated our target and are moving on, details to follow, out." Rainey regarded Houston. "He thinks we got time to chat."

"They always do."

"How you doing?"

"I'm good to go, Sergeant."

Rainey wasn't convinced, but he wouldn't press the issue. He, of course, knew all about confidence problems. "You hang in there. We're going to make it."

Houston nodded and stowed the microphone.

"Sergeant?" Vance called from up front.

"What do you got?"

"Check the mudflow and water clarity. You have to look real close, but there's a trail right through here. See it?"

"Only a bass fisherman would notice that."

"A bass fisherman and a Force Recon Marine. Take a look. The trail keeps going. Not like the other ones, where we could see they stopped and turned around. These guys are heading into Chongsan."

"How many?"

"I'm good in water, but I'm not that good. I guarantee at least one."

"Probably more. And I thought we had just pulled off the greatest diversion of all time."

"Hey, Sarge. That warhead didn't go off, did it?"

"Trust me, Vance. We wouldn't be having this conversation if it did. But that C-4 must've set off a whole lot of rocket fuel. Really brought down the house."

"Yeah, it sure did. And I'm glad to be a green Marine, just not a glowing one. So what now?"

"Let's follow their trail. The hunters become the hunted."

By the time they reached the outskirts of Chongsan and the farm where Kim had promised they would receive help, they had lost the enemy's trail. Vance had tried in vain for nearly two hours as they picked their way along the narrow river, but as he put it, he was a hound dog with a clothes pin on his nose. Instead, Rainey had him focus on traversing the open stretch of flooded fields without being spotted by the many aircraft that rumbled overhead, all heading toward the tunnel site. Vance found an irrigation trench that was completely submerged and would provide wet but adequate cover.

So they paddled. Hard. Harder than any of them ever had. Rainey was certain of that. It was breakfast time in North Korea, and there they were, four Americans and one South Korean fleeing for their lives. Rainey almost longed for the cold, arid caves of Pakistan. Almost.

They came like dripping wet zombies from the trench, stole their way across a rocky yard, and reached a long, broad barn much newer and larger than any of the ones back at Chun's farm. After stringing themselves out along one wall, Kim said he would go alone to the farmhouse and return with a man named Yoon who would arrange to have them smuggled to the coast.

Rainey told the ROK Marine to be back within five minutes, otherwise they were coming after him. Kim agreed and took off.

"Sarge, I'm not one to complain, but ain't we putting all our eggs in one basket?" Vance asked softly, switching his gaze from the field to the corner of the barn.

"Marines, we are wet. We are strung out. But we are not finished. We're going to give Kim a shot to get us to the coast. If his contacts fail, then we'll do it ourselves. Now hold tight."

Only a minute later, a faint chirp sounded from Kim's clicker. He rounded the corner and waved them over. They followed, reached the barn door, and slipped inside. Kim led them to the back of the barn, where he pushed away an old, dusty tarpaulin to reveal the heavy metal doors of a storm cellar. They descended into a narrow basement cluttered with very old, very dusty electronic equipment, some of which actually had vacuum tubes for amplification and switching. Rainey's father had once owned an old stereo that had had the big tubes inside. "This is their radio room," Kim explained, then nodded to a young Korean man of no more than twenty, wearing tattered clothes and a headset. "We can rest a moment here."

"Look at this crap," Houston said. "It looks like World War II surplus."

"It is," Kim said. "And many men died to obtain it."

Houston sobered. "Sorry."

"All right, gentlemen. Take a load off. Vance, you got the door. Kim, where's your buddy?"

"He's on his way. He should arrive soon."

* * *

Twenty minutes later, after Rainey and the others had barely had enough time to catch their breath and soothe their weary muscles, a faint thumping from the staircase had all of them sweeping their rifles in that direction. An unarmed Korean man with a graying crewcut, hard eyes, and broad shoulders dropped into the cellar. He slapped Vance's rifle out of the way and kept coming, heading directly for Kim.

"This is Yoon," Kim said. "He is the man who will get you through Chongsan and to the coast."

Without a word, Yoon reached Kim, locked gazes with the Marine, then suddenly pulled a pistol from inside his shirt and put it to Kim's head.

"Whoa, whoa, whoa," Rainey cried, as all rifles suddenly trained on Yoon's head. "Kim, what's going on?"

Yoon barked a few words in Korean, then leveled his index finger on Kim, who averted his gaze.

"Kim? Start talking *now*."

"Yoon and I have worked together before. We are like you and Sergeant Bruno were. Maybe worse."

"Why's that?"

Yoon shouted a few words at Kim, who answered quickly and in a much softer tone.

"What's he saying?" Rainey demanded.

"He wants me to tell you the truth."

Rainey glanced to Yoon. "I'm liking this guy already."

"Sergeant Rainey, I cannot tell you everything. All I can say is that I worked with Yoon. We tried to help some people reach the South, including Yoon's daughter and grandson—"

"And what? The plan went south and this guy blames you?"

"The plan failed because I deserted them. I left Yoon alone. He was nearly captured, and his daughter and grandson never reached the South."

"You deserted?"

Kim hesitated. "Because I was a coward."

"And now you bring us here and expect this guy to help? Jesus, Kim, what were you thinking?"

"He drove a long way to meet us here. And he will help you. He is loyal to the South."

"Now wait a minute. He'll help us. Does 'us' include you?"

Kim sighed, rubbed the corners of his eyes. "For me, the mission ends here."

"Fuck that," Houston said from behind them. "Sarge, this guy's been loyal to us all along. We ain't leaving him here so this asshole Yoon can take revenge!"

"Kim, what are you saying?"

Yoon spoke rapidly, the words making Kim flinch.

"Lance Corporal Kim, you are coming with us to the coast, and you are getting on board that submarine," Rainey said.

"I made a deal with Yoon," said Kim. "I must pay for my cowardice."

"With what? Your life? Bullshit," Rainey snapped. "And now I know why you've been so iffy when it comes to dealing with the underground."

"I feared that Kwan and Chun would know who I was, but Yoon never told them."

"Yet you called Yoon yourself?"

"I had to, Sergeant. He is the best. He has the resources and the contacts. He will get you to the coast."

"He'll get *all of us* to the coast," Houston said.

"You ain't staying with him," added Vance, who moved up to Kim and grabbed the ROK Marine's shoulder. "You saved my life in the tunnel. I choose to save yours now."

"But in saving me, you choose to die. Because the NKA has troops posted throughout Chongsan. You will never make it."

Repressing a curse, Rainey scrutinized Yoon a moment. If there was room for negotiation, the old Korean's expression gave no indication. "Kim, tell Yoon I want to cut another deal."

Kim did. Yoon looked at Rainey, shook his head, muttered something to Kim.

"He says the negotiations are already over."

The younger Korean at the radio shouted nervously to Yoon, who regarded Kim with widening eyes.

"A regiment has arrived at the tunnels," Kim said. "Several squads are moving this way. We have to move now."

Doc hoisted a brow at Rainey: What would it be? Sacrifice Kim and get help? Or go it alone?

20

When Master Sergeant Sung and Private Lee reached the garrison headquarters at Chongsan, they immediately commandeered a truck and some ammo for their rifles from a corporal who insisted that they report to the lieutenant before leaving. Sung had told the man they were part of a highly classified special forces operation. There was no time for routine check-ins. They had to leave immediately. When the corporal had balked, Sung had shoved his pistol against the man's chest while Lee obtained the keys. With a parting threat, Sung left the stunned corporal and hopped into the truck.

While Private Lee drove, Sung threw his head back on the passenger's seat and closed his eyes.

"Sangsa, what are we doing here?"

"We are going to the beach road. We will set up an ambush along the shoreline."

"I was posing a philosophical question, Sangsa. Not a literal one."

"I see. We are here to complete our mission. There is nothing philosophical about that. It is quite literal."

"And if the enemy never comes? What will happen to us, Sangsa? Will we be shot?"

"The enemy will come. And we will capture them."

"Sangsa, do you truly believe they have escaped our forces back at the tunnel and will make it through Chongsan?"

"They have a Korean working with them. They have contacts with the underground. They will make it. And you and I are the only ones who know they are coming."

"But Sangsa, how can you be so sure?"

"Because I no longer underestimate the enemy. They are fierce opponents."

"So fierce that they will escape us again? Surely they outnumber us now. Perhaps we can recruit some of the Red Guard here. Mountain Ghost would never know about it."

"Sb-yong Lee, it is too late for second thoughts. We are soldiers who have been given an assignment, an assignment we will complete alone. When the battle comes, there is only death or victory. I would rather be killed fighting our enemies than at the hand of another Korean."

"Yes, Sangsa. I feel the same."

"You have had a hard life, Lee. And so have I. It has all led up to this. And we must be prepared to meet the challenge."

"Yes, Sangsa. But we are both very tired. We need to eat and to rest."

"And we will do that. I do not expect the enemy to make their move until nightfall. They would not make it past the NAMPO LCPs patrolling the coast if they tried to extract earlier. I am sure that their submarine is already out there, waiting to launch a rescue crew."

TEAM DOGMA
CHONGSAN FISHING VILLAGE
NORTH KOREA
0910 HOURS LOCAL TIME

Inside the storm cellar, the standoff continued, with Yoon still pointing his pistol at Kim's head while Rainey and his men kept Yoon in their sights. In the meantime, the enemy squads were still coming.

"Kim, ask Yoon if he still wants to smuggle out his daughter and grandson," Rainey said.

"Sergeant, I'm not sure—"

"Just ask him!"

Kim nervously complied. "He says he does."

"Perfect. How old is his grandson?"

"About ten now."

"Good. Tell Yoon we have a submarine coming to extract us. Ask him if he can get his daughter and grandson to the coast before nightfall."

"I know what you're thinking, Sergeant, and it will not work, because—"

"I gave you a direct order, Lance Corporal!"

Kim grudgingly obeyed, then listened to Yoon utter a curt reply. "He says he can get them to the coast."

"Very well. You tell him you're coming with us. You

tell him we'll take his daughter and grandson, too. Maybe you failed once, but we'll finish the job together."

"Whoa, Sarge, are you kidding?" Doc asked. "You want to take two civvies on a sub extraction?"

Rainey gave Doc a knowing look. "Doesn't sound easy, does it?"

Doc shook his head, and Rainey knew the corpsman would not protest further.

Kim made the offer to Yoon, who kept silent a moment, then said, "*A-nee-o.*" Rainey knew what that meant.

"Tell him again, Kim."

"He already says no deal."

"Tell him again!"

After a quick exchange, Kim said, "He wants to know why you're willing to risk your entire team to do this for me."

"Tell him we owe you our lives. Tell him we'll save his daughter and grandson. Tell him he has my word."

Kim shut his eyes and translated. When he was finished, he looked up at Yoon, who slowly nodded and lowered his pistol.

Rainey sighed loudly. "Let's go."

Yoon muttered a few words, then led them outside, around the back of the farmhouse, where a Self Reliance 68, a half-ton light utility truck with a canvas top arcing over its flatbed, sat idling.

When they reached the back of the truck, Yoon slid aside one of the flaps—

And three NKA soldiers armed with AKs jumped out as Kim cried, "Hold your fire! Hold your fire!"

Good thing. Houston, Vance, and Doc had their weapons leveled on the men.

Two more soldiers climbed down from the cab, and one of them shook his head and made a face at the team. He said something to Kim, then barked orders to the other three, who fanned out, crouched down, and assumed defensive positions.

Yoon climbed into the truck, then waved emphatically for them to follow. Inside, he began distributing NKA uniforms and helmets that he pulled from an old, wooden crate. The gambit was, in a word, unsophisticated.

"So this is the plan?" Houston asked. "I saw this movie. All the good guys *died*."

"And the brother got shot first," Doc said, setting down his Para SAW. "Because they knew right away he wasn't a Korean."

"These things smell like my grandmother," Vance said, crinkling his nose.

"Put them on, Corporal. You've just been drafted into the North Korean Army," Rainey said.

"Yeah, the few, the smelly," Vance groaned.

Rainey turned to Kim, who also began changing. "So we're just going to drive through town?"

"Yes."

"And if we're stopped?"

"We will be, but these men know what to do."

"And so do we."

"Let them do their job, Sergeant. If we interfere—"

"We won't. But if things go bad, tell Yoon it'll be ba for everyone."

"Yes, Sergeant."

With preparations completed, the other three diers climbed into the flatbed. They weren't p larly pleased with their cargo, but for the m they kept their contempt in check. Yoon issued a few more orders to them, then sealed the canvas flaps. Kim said Yoon would meet up with them at the docks, where they would hide inside a fish-packing warehouse managed by Yoon's brother-in-law.

About a half hour into the ride, Houston felt the truck begin to slow, then the brakes squeaked.

Then it became hard to breathe. No, he could not let this happen, not in front of the sarge, who sat right next to him. He had to concentrate. Had to overcome it. Had to filter all of the stress away.

But how, when at any moment the canvas could part to reveal the muzzles of enemy rifles?

"Get ready," Rainey ordered softly, then turned to Houston. "Easy, Lance Corporal."

"I'm all right, Sarge. I'm all right."

Vance listened to the voices outside the truck. If only he had studied the field manual more carefully, he would've been able to catch a word here, a word there. Then again, he would hang on those words, perhaps misinterpret them, perhaps get excited over nothing. Bullshit. Not knowing was even worse. He sat there, nodding to himself, his nerves creating a rhythm to comfort him, a rhythm not unlike the one he casting his line out and retrieving it. If he very, very calm, then he could snap that action. He needed to become a river clearly, unaffected. No nerves.

the shaking.

* * *

The first motherfucker who pokes his head past that canvas is a dead man, Doc thought. He steadied his SAW, the big gun's muzzle just a few inches away from the flaps.

"Daddy, have you ever killed anybody?"

"Yeah, Daddy, tell us."

When first asked that question, Doc had answered, "No." Which was a lie. But in the past year, the lie had fallen apart, and Doc had had to admit that he had taken lives. The boys knew very well that murder was wrong, and Doc had had to explain that sometimes bad guys had to die so that they didn't hurt good people anymore.

"So killing is like helping?"

Questions like that made Doc thank God for the diversion of the Disney Channel. *"Come on, the show's just starting!"*

The voices outside didn't bother Rainey. It was the voice inside that made him want to scream.

"Dogma One, this is Dogma Five, over?"

"Dogma Five, this is One. Clear the channel, out."

"Clear the channel? These are mental airwaves, buddy. They don't ever clear."

"What do you want?"

"Oh, I just want to laugh at this completely fucked-up plan you've devised. You actually think you're going to get some Korean woman and her little kid to extract to the sub? Tell me, Rainey, have these civilians been trained in dealing with ASDS operations, including lock-out and lock-in chamber protocols? Or are you, once again, pulling this out of your ass?"

"Tell you what, if we escape, you get out of my head forever. You want to play those odds?"

"You're damned straight I do. Because you're just kidding yourself, Rainey. I'm here till the day you die, and when that happens, I'll be standing at the gates of hell to wave you home. Then we can finally finish this . . ."

While everyone else seemed extremely tense, Lance Corporal Kim felt calm, almost at peace. A huge burden had been lifted. And he could hardly believe that these men, these Americans, were willing to risk so much to save his life. He could not be in the company of better men. He glanced at Rainey and now felt nothing but admiration. Kim would die for the man. Without question. Rainey caught him looking, then cocked a thumb over his shoulder, in the direction of the voices. Kim lifted his palms and mouthed, "It's okay." A few seconds later, the truck jerked into gear.

After another thirty minutes of nerve-rattling travel, the truck came to a halt once more. But this time the driver killed the engine, and the sickly sweet stench of fish began to permeate the air. A voice from outside brought the three Korean soldiers to their feet.

"We are here," Kim said.

"Smells like it," Rainey answered as the driver opened the canvas flaps, allowing the three Korean soldiers to exit. Next came the team, and Rainey climbed out last.

The truck was parked inside a small garage/loading dock. Off to their left lay a warehouse entrance shielded by heavy plastic flaps of the kind used to contain commercial cooling rooms, though Rainey felt no cool air leaking out from beneath them.

"There hasn't been power here for a few days," Kim said, pointing to a dark light bulb dangling above them. "All of the fish is beginning to spoil."

"God, this is where we have to stay until tonight?" Houston asked.

"I'm afraid it is," said Kim.

"Gentlemen, let's set up in the back, beneath the ramp. Kim, will these guys stand watch outside?"

"Yes, they will."

"Very well. Break out some MREs. Even they have to smell better than this place."

"I don't know about that," Doc said. "I got stuck with the Salisbury steak again."

NORTH KOREAN ARMY RECONNAISSANCE SQUAD
CHONGSAN FISHING VILLAGE
NORTH KOREA
1800 HOURS LOCAL TIME

Master Sergeant Sung and Private Lee had established an observation post among the dunes overlooking a beach lying about a quarter kilometer south of Chongsan's docks and piers. Although they could see for literally hundreds of meters in each direction via their binoculars, Sung feared they might miss something. And even if they did spot the enemy rushing to the water, they might be too far away to intercept. It had been up to Sung to reason exactly where the enemy might rendezvous with their rescue team. How the enemy would accomplish that task was simple. The rescue team would come ashore and radio their GPS coordinates. If only Sung could intercept that communication. But he could not. He needed to use instincts. His intuition. His training.

The submarine's captain would observe the coastline through his periscope, and he would choose a section of beachfront that would provide the most cover. The dunes were the obvious choice, and they were why Sung had chosen them in the first place. He simply had to reassure himself that he had made the correct decision.

Robbed of both a sunrise and a sunset, Sung watched the gray sky grow darker. He would awaken Private Lee very soon. They would clean and inspect their weapons. They would review their plan of attack. Sung would order Lee to kill as many as he could, but there was one man, the man Sung had fought at the mudslide, that he wanted to capture alive.

TEAM DOGMA
CHONGSAN FISHING VILLAGE
NORTH KOREA
2030 HOURS LOCAL TIME

"Roger that, Tango Host. Have received intended GPS coordinates for dinner engagement and are prepared to move out, over."

"Very well, Dogma One. Rodeo Team will greet you at the door, out."

Rainey handed Houston the Foxtrot's microphone. The skipper of the USS *Texas* had sounded very confident that his Navy divers and SEAL team could get Rainey and the others out. Sure, after Rainey had said that they would be accompanied by two civilians, there had been a long pause in communications. Then the skipper had simply acknowledged and said he would convey the information to his people.

Yoon had arrived several hours prior with his daughter, Min, and his grandson, Sam, which in Korean meant "achievement," according to Kim. Min was about twenty-five, thin as a reed, with short, coal-black hair that framed suspicious eyes. Sam, an equally thin nondescript boy, clung to his mother's side like a boy half his age. Rainey worried that if they met any resistance on the beach, the kid might panic. So, as the others finished gearing up, he waved over Kim and went to the boy. He crouched down, locking eyes with Sam, then asked for Kim to translate. "When we get to the beach, you're going to put on a mask that will help you breathe. Then we're going to swim underwater to a small submarine that will take us back to a very big one. The water might be a little cold, but we'll be okay. You just have to remember to hang on. Do you think you can do that?"

Kim spoke to the boy, Sam thought it over a second, and then nodded. He eyed Kim, then mumbled something. Rainey recognized one word: *Gameboy.*

"He wants to know, if he does what you say, will you buy him a Gameboy? He saw a colonel's daughter playing with one."

"Tell him I'll buy him a Gameboy and a dozen games to go with it."

Kim did. And surprisingly, Sam bolted from his mother's hip and hugged Rainey around the shoulders. Rainey glanced at Kim, who shrugged.

Yoon stepped over, said something to Kim, then faced Rainey as the boy returned to his mother's side. Yoon extended his hand. "Thank you," he said in English.

Rainey took the hand, shook it vigorously, then turned to the others. "All right, Marines. It's time to go home."

NORTH KOREAN ARMY RECONNAISSANCE SQUAD
CHONGSAN FISHING VILLAGE
NORTH KOREA
2048 HOURS LOCAL TIME

The sky had opened up on Master Sergeant Sung and Private Lee. Despite the downpour, Sung probed the beach about two hundred meters north, where he spotted two figures rising up from the waves. They rushed onto the beach, carrying large packs, presumably filled with diving gear. Two more figures followed with similar packs, and all four reached the base of the nearest dune, where they hunkered down.

Lee, who had also been watching through his binoculars, gasped, "Sangsa."

"Yes, Lee. That is the rescue team. And the enemy is coming. The darkness and rain are our friends now. We will move right up to them and wait."

The truck paused along a seaside road, where everyone hopped out. A few small shacks stood in the hills, their windows dark, the nearby trees bowing to the wind and rain. The area seemed desolate and far enough away from the village to give them a head start, should the garrison there get tipped off by any of the locals. Yoon's men covered them as they hit the sand and began their descent toward the bay, but just moments later, they abandoned their positions and rallied back on the truck. Rainey and his men were on their own now.

"Rodeo One, this is Dogma One, over," he called to the SEAL team leader over the designated tactical frequency.

"Dogma One, this is Rodeo One, standing by at extraction point, over."

"Roger that, Rodeo One. En route your position. ETA about four minutes, out."

Rainey could barely believe that everything had fallen into place. The planets had aligned or something, he didn't know. Didn't care. Even the rain felt good, and the sound of the breakers was something he had anticipated hearing for many hours.

Vance led them over the final stretch of dunes, where, below, the four-man SEAL team, pistols drawn, were waiting. Vance worked his clicker, and the men lowered their weapons as the team scrambled down to the meet them.

A man with a gray moustache, black face paint, and dressed in a black wetsuit hurried over to Rainey. No doubt he was the SEAL team leader, code name Rodeo One. "We'll save the introductions for later, Sergeant."

"Right," Rainey said, then pointed to Sam. "I wear his tank. He's riding piggyback and wearing the mask."

"You got it." As Rodeo One helped Rainey get into his gear, he added, "So how'd you like North Korea?"

"It sucked. We should've stuck with our tour group."

Rodeo One grinned and finished buckling Rainey's harness. "All right, let's see if we can get the kid to breathe." The team leader turned to Sam, who once more kept close to his mother's hip. Doc, who was already wearing his Draegar, a closed-circuit system that prevented any exhaust bubbles from surfacing, gestured for Min to take his mask. She would be riding piggyback with Doc. While he slipped his mask over Min's face, Rainey slid his over Sam's and adjusted the strap. Kim hurried over and told both of them to breathe normally.

A couple of yards down the beach, Vance and Houston flashed a thumbs up, their masks slid up on their foreheads, their boots replaced with fins.

Rainey motioned for Sam to climb onto his back. The kid nodded, took a step—

Then three rounds of AK-47 fire exploded from nearly on top of them.

Rainey spun around, grabbed the kid, and slammed both of them into the wet sand.

21

Propped up on his elbows, Vance cut loose a half dozen wild rounds that momentarily suppressed the snipers' fire. Nearby, two of the Navy SEALs were already directing their pistols toward one of the dunes above, though Vance guessed that the enemy had already moved. A muzzle flash to his right confirmed that and had him switching hands and jamming his rifle's stock into his left shoulder to get a better shot. He fired once, twice, couldn't tell if his rounds had hit their mark. He glanced right, saw that the SEAL team leader lay inert on the ground as Doc crawled toward him.

A look to his left stole Vance's breath. Houston lay face down in the dirt. "Houston!"

The lance corporal did not move.

"Doc? Houston's down! Houston's down!"

Multiple rounds sewed a muddy path just inches

from Vance's face. He flinched, added his rifle to the SEALs' booming pistols.

They needed Doc's Para SAW for cover, but the corpsman was tied up. He had already left the SEAL team leader and was edging toward Houston.

Vance waited for the next round of AK fire. Without a good visual on the bad guys, the team would remain pinned down. Heady with adrenaline, Vance peered hard through his scope. *Where are you, you bastards?*

Surprisingly, the boy Sam did not freak out. His mother, however, screamed to the high heavens, and Rainey could not help himself. "Shut up! Shut up!" he hollered back as he shielded Sam with his body. One of the SEALs got to his feet and dashed over to Min. He dropped to all fours, threw himself over her as Rainey keyed his mike. "Dogma Four, Voodoo Five? Break for the flanks. Now!"

"Sergeant," cried one of the SEALs. "Call from the ASDS. Patrol boat en route. ETA nine minutes. We have to go!"

Kim had already toed off his swim fans, and it felt good to charge barefoot up the dunes. He thought he saw Vance sweeping in from across the beach, but he couldn't be sure. The wind had really picked up, and the sand began cutting into Kim's eyes as the abrupt popping of two AKs betrayed the enemy's new position. They were smart to keep moving. They had shifted some dozen or so meters south and had descended a few more meters.

Wait. There it was—a fresh muzzle flash. Kim realized he had climbed above the enemy's position. Perfect. He would sweep in from behind.

"Voodoo Five? This is Dogma Four," called Vance. "Hold position, over."

"Four, this is Five," Kim responded, dropping down onto his belly. "Holding position."

Three, two, one, and one of Vance's grenades exploded below. Kim strained to hear something more above the breakers and rain. Three, two, one, and the AK popping resumed. Vance had missed.

Those two enemy soldiers, whomever they were, would continue to fire and move, and it was too difficult to spot them among the rain-swept pockets of gloom. Kim had to get closer. Muzzle to muzzle.

Rising to his knees, he tugged at the clasp of his oxygen tank's harness, let it and the tank fall to the ground. He was light and ready to move in for the kill, unburdened by everything except his own fear.

Yet he answered that fear aloud, "It is your time now. It is your time!"

And when the next round of AK fire erupted, he rose and charged toward the sound.

Streaked by rain, Vance's night scope presented a marred image to the sniper. He thought he spotted two men hunkered down, was about to fire, but only a black patch of ground shone behind his crosshairs.

"Dogma One, this is Dogma Two," Doc called over the channel. "Seal Team Leader is KIA. Dogma Three is unconscious, but I cannot find a gunshot wound, over."

"Roger that, Dogma Two. Revive Dogma Three if possible and hold your position. Rodeo Team, hold your positions as well, out."

No sign of gunshot wound? Vance thought. Fucking Houston had probably had another panic attack. *Jesus* . . . Vance should've notified the Sarge instead of keeping the lance corporal's secret. Now, if Doc couldn't bring Houston around, how were they supposed to get an unconscious Marine aboard the ASDS for the trip back to the sub? The guilt was already setting in as Vance swept his rifle to the right—

Just as three rounds blasted sand on him. He cursed, held his head down. "Voodoo Five? Where are you, over?"

"Stay with him!" Rainey shouted to one of the SEALs as the man slid next to Sam to cover the boy. "I have to get up there!"

"Better make it fast," the SEAL warned.

Rainey crawled away, then broke into a mad run, taking himself twenty meters up the beach, then turning sharply up, into the dunes. Strangely—but thankfully—no enemy fire tore into his wake. "Dogma Four? Voodoo Five? I'm advancing from the north, about twenty meters above, over."

Static answered.

Getting ambushed had surprised Rainey. Getting ambushed by only two combatants surprised him even more. There was no way in hell the NKA Army would deliberately plan such an attack by only two operators. If those men had been stationed at, say, an observation post along the coast, they would still not have attacked.

They wound have notified the garrison and continued monitoring.

As Rainey staggered down the backside of the next dune, he wondered if the attack was an independent operation initiated by that NKA reconnaissance squad they had evaded. Had that son of a bitch master sergeant and one of his cronies followed the team back to the coast?

No, it couldn't be.

Then who were those guys, and why hadn't they called for help?

Well, whether the bad guys wanted help or not, it was coming. That garrison back at Chongsan was already receiving a report of shots fired on the coast, be it from an observation post or from a civilian. Squads would arrive within fifteen minutes.

And that patrol boat was still on its way.

"Voodoo Five, report your position, over."

Vance continued to call Kim, but the ROK Marine had yet to answer. Rainey feared the worst, but he forged on, rounded the peak of another dune, and paused to look down into the darkness.

The kick from behind came on so swiftly that Rainey hit the dirt, his right hand pinned beneath his chest, along with his rifle. His breath would not come. As he fought for air, an arm slid beneath his neck, hauled him back, onto his rump. He fumbled with his rifle. His attacker kicked away the weapon. "You are prisoner of North Korean government," the man rasped into Rainey's ear.

And that voice, that horrible voice in broken English, took Rainey back to the mudslide. My God, the man holding him was that same master sergeant. The guy was unbelievably determined, maybe even obsessed to come this far. And even worse, he was operating independently, a patient hunter who wanted to capture his trophy alive.

"Sangsa!" came a voice to Rainey's right. He looked up, saw the soldier with the burned face come bounding across the dune. The soldier's gaze snapped to the right. He turned, dropped to his knees, brought up his rifle—

"Sergeant!" cried Vance.

The burned soldier fired.

And nearly in unison, Vance's sniper rifle sounded somewhere behind.

Rainey shuddered, forced his head back, but the master's sergeant's grip tightened as he shouted something to his subordinate.

Houston's head jerked to the left, and Doc removed his fist from the lance corporal's sternum. "Lance Corporal?"

The kid blinked hard. "That you, Doc? What happened, man?"

He began to sit up, and Doc shoved him back. "Stay down. We got ambushed." Doc directed his penlight into Houston's eyes: pupils equal and reactive to light. "Did you hit your head?"

"I don't think so. And I know we got ambushed, Doc."

"Do you know you passed out?"

"Bullshit." Houston rolled over and seized his rifle. "I don't know what happened. Just tell me where they are, Doc. Up there?"

"Think so. But don't fire. Don't move. Don't do anything." Doc keyed his mike. "Dogma One, this is Dogma Two. Have revived Dogma Three and are standing by with Rodeo Team, over."

In his struggle to pull away from the master sergeant, Rainey's earpiece had been yanked away; it now dangled near his ear, and Doc's voice buzzed once more.

"*Mom-cho-ee!*" someone shouted, and it took a moment for Rainey to recognize the voice. "*So-jee-ma!*" Lance Corporal Kim added as he ran straight at Rainey and the master sergeant, his rifle trained on the sergeant's head.

The burned soldier, who had escaped Vance's earlier round, swung his AK toward Kim and said, "*Jop-goon-ha-jee ma!*"

"Drop your weapons!" Vance said, jogging to the right, then hitting his gut.

"*Hang-bok-ha-ra!*" the burned soldier yelled back.

"They want us to surrender," Kim said, coming to a halt and holding steady on the master sergeant, who now had a knife poised over Rainey's heart.

Rainey found the man's wrist, but his first attempt to pry away the hand resulted in another round of choking that sent him to the brink of passing out. He relaxed his hand, and the master sergeant loosened his grip a little.

Kim took a few steps closer, out of the shadows, and as the burned soldier uttered a warning, something in Kim's eyes told Rainey that the ROK Marine was going to fire.

Several pairs of headlights shimmered from the road in the distance, their beams cutting through the rain and billowing mist. "Oh, shit," Doc muttered. "Dogma One, this is Dogma Two. Be advised we have vehicles approaching from the north. ETA five minutes, maybe less, over."

"You're wasting your time, Doc," Houston said. "The sarge ain't answering."

"Shut up."

"I can't, Doc. The sarge could've been hit. We have to go up there and help those guys. Come on, man!"

"We're holding our position—as ordered. Rodeo Team, this is Dogma Two. Hold tight, over."

"Dogma Two, this is Rodeo Two," replied one of the SEALs. "Will hold as long as we can, out."

"Jesus, Doc. They stopped firing! Something's going down. We have to get up there!"

Doc glanced at the dunes, at the headlights, then at the bay, where somewhere out there a heavily armed patrol boat was cutting through the chop. "We're holding position right here with the SEALs until we hear from the sarge."

"Like I said, what if he can't answer? What if he's dead?"

After silencing Houston with a dirty look, Doc spoke tersely into his boom mike, deciding that he would give Vance a shout to see what was happening. "Dogma Four? This is Dogma Two, over."

All of the sensory input was overloading Vance's ability to comprehend the moment and react to it. Instead of disconnecting entirely, it was time for a selective shutdown, and Doc's voice was the first to go.

Ignoring the corpsman, he steadied his aim on the guy holding Rainey. *I can cap him before he stabs the sarge. I can do this. I can make this shot.*

No, you can't. What if you hit the sarge? Are you ready to live with that?

"Dogma Four, this is Dogma Two, over."

Shut up, Doc!

NORTH KOREAN ARMY RECONNAISSANCE SQUAD
BEACH OUTSIDE CHONGSAN
NORTH KOREA
2107 HOURS LOCAL TIME

Master Sergeant Sung had not anticipated a standoff, nor did he believe that he and Private Lee could survive such a confrontation.

Thus, capturing the enemy alive meant nothing now. He would kill his honorable opponent, and then take a bullet himself—so long as that bullet did not come from the Korean. He glanced at Private Lee, wondering if beneath that burned and menacing face was a frightened young man already blaming his master sergeant for his death—

Or perhaps not. Perhaps Lee still admired Sung, and in what could be Sung's final minutes, he needed to believe that the young man's loyalty had not faltered.

If nothing else, Sung and Lee had seen the mission through—on their own. They had saved face. No matter what stories Sergeant Choi chose to tell Mountain Ghost, their commander would know that Sung had never lost sight of his mission and had done everything he could to complete it. Sung had never shrank from his duty.

Now the time had come to complete the mission. For good. For bad.

He held his breath, readied the knife.

Private Lee's eyes widened as Sung gave the barest of nods.

TEAM DOGMA
EXTRACTION POINT SCORPION
NORTH KOREA
2108 HOURS LOCAL TIME

Lance Corporal Kim knew that if he pulled his trigger and killed the master sergeant, the burned soldier would shoot him before he could get off his next round.

But it was Kim's time to act. The premonition he had received after first contacting Yoon, the one he had repressed until this very moment, was coming to pass: He would not leave North Korea, the place of his birth. He did not need to leave. He was already home.

Scarcely feeling the cold, wet metal in his hand, Kim smiled thinly at Sgt. Mac Rainey of the United States Marine Corps—

Then embraced his fate.

All Rainey could do was blink as the shot rang out.

Then he recoiled as a second shot of AK fire broke into the first round's echo, followed by a third crack from Vance's rifle.

In the next blink, the master sergeant slumped, spreading himself across the sand like wet cement.

Kim dropped to his knees, clutching his heart.

And the burned soldier toppled onto his back, his legs flinching.

There it was.

Kim had shot the master sergeant in the head. The burned soldier had returned fire, hitting Kim in the chest. And Vance, who had probably been watching it all, capped the burned guy. Rainey pushed himself away from the sergeant and scrambled toward Kim, whose lips were ringed red as he coughed up blood.

"I got you, Lance Corporal," Rainey said, seizing one of Kim's arms, then hoisting him over his back.

"No, Sergeant," Kim said, his voice coming in a gurgle. "I'm dying. Let me go."

"Sergeant?" Vance called.

"Fall back to the beach," Rainey ordered. "Now hang in there, Kim. Doc might smell like an ape, but he's the best in the Navy. He'll fix you up, then we'll all take a little swim."

Rainey wished he hadn't joked and lied to Kim, but telling him the truth just wasn't fair. Kim needed hope because maybe, at the very end, that hope would grant him peace.

As he carried Kim down to the beach, he felt the lance corporal's body go slack. And he knew. But he wasn't ready to admit it. Not yet. Like a dying man himself, Rainey clung to hope, wished for peace, wished for a miracle.

Once he reached Doc, the corpsman examined Kim's wound, searched for pulse.

"Don't say it, Doc."

The corpsman put his fingers on Kim's eyelids, pushed them down. "It's okay. I won't. And if you want, I'll carry him back."

"No, you stay with Min. Let Vance take the boy. I'm taking Kim."

"I understand." As Doc turned, a grenade exploded about one hundred meters down the beach.

"All right, Marines!" Rainey yelled. "In the water! Let's go! Let's go!"

Vance could barely talk to the Korean boy. The language barrier wasn't the real problem; it was Kim's death.

When Vance had learned that the ROK Marine was gone, he had choked up and had begun replaying the standoff over and over in his head. He should *not* have targeted the master sergeant. If his aim had been on the burned soldier, he could have killed the man sooner and saved Kim's life. Instead, he had chosen to target the sergeant—when Kim already had that man covered.

He saved me. And how did I thank him? I got him killed.

With burning eyes, Vance placed the mask over Sam's face, then motioned for the kid to breathe. With Rainey's training, the kid was already an expert. Vance gestured for Sam to climb on his back, then, with gunfire beginning to ring out behind them, he donned his own conventional mask and snorkel, and stepped clumsily into the water.

Before the waves reached Vance's waist, automatic fire ripped a path of fountains on his right. Then the gunner adjusted his aim and discharged another salvo whose line came within a meter.

"Get ready," he told the kid, forgetting that English was no good. "We're going under!"

Following the first two SEALs, Vance swam hard and away, working the fins with everything he had, his hamstrings literally shaking under the effort. Doc and the boy's mother were just behind him, with Rainey and Kim next, followed by Houston pulling up the rear. One of the SEALs had already swum out with the body of the team leader, and he had reported back that their taxi, technically known as the Advanced Swimmer Delivery System, was hovering in about fifteen feet of water. All they had to do was reach it, pass through the lower hatch, and they'd be inside a warm, dry cabin for the battery-powered ride back to the USS *Texas*.

A searchlight wiped across the waves ahead, and Vance took a deep breath and drove himself and Sam deeper, the kid beginning to squeeze Vance's shoulders hard. The drone of the patrol boat's rotor spurred Vance into a fit of kicking. He craned his neck, thought he saw something at his eleven o'clock. Had to be the patrol boat. Right there!

The dark, cylindrical profile of the ASDS appeared before the swimmers ahead, and Houston saw the two lead SEALs swim under the sixty-five-foot-long sub, then pause there to help the others. Just as the enemy patrol boat passed overhead, Vance and the boy made it through, then came Doc and the mother. Finally, Rainey, carrying the lifeless Lance Corporal Kim on his back, reached the sub, where the SEALs quickly unclasped the body. Then, while one SEAL helped Rainey inside, the other maneuvered Kim's body into place. Once the hatch was clear, the remaining SEAL waved on Houston, who froze as rounds fired from the patrol boat streaked through the water between him and the sub. Then came another string of fire, cutting him off.

A team of four Navy divers was in charge of operating the ASDS, and though Rainey could not see the ASDS's skipper, he knew the man directed operations from the tiny, two-man bridge on the other side of the airlock. The transport compartment was not as cramped as Rainey had assumed it would be; in fact, about eight men and their equipment could fit comfortably inside.

"Two operators still outside," the skipper reported over the intercom. "That patrol boat has opened fire. And there's another sub moving into the area, Romeo class. Ramirez? See if you can get them inside!"

The SEAL named Ramirez rushed out of the crew compartment and passed into the airlock. Rainey, though exhausted beyond belief, realized with a start that Houston was still out there. He rose, about to lend a hand, when one of the SEALs pulled him back down. "Buckle up, Sergeant. We'll get them in."

Though he hated it, Rainey obeyed, dropping down hard next to Doc. All eyes turned to the sub's ceiling as the patrol boat wheeled around for another pass.

A panic attack while under water was the last thing Houston needed.

And damn it, he would not let that happen. He swam down until the pressure in his ears was unbearable.

He saw the ASDS up there, saw the incoming fire bubbling nearby. Picked his path.

Then he just went for it, hands at his sides, a torpedo with legs homing in on the ASDS. Something nicked his thigh, but he was working too hard to care.

The SEAL was there at the hatch, waving him on like a dive-school coach. Tuned in to his breathing and shutting out all other sounds, Houston made the swim of his life.

Ten meters to the hatch. Five.

But his legs slowed. His vision narrowed. And suddenly there was no up, no down, no water.

No anything.

Doc sprang to his feet as the SEAL dragged Houston's motionless body into the cabin. Doc prayed that the kid had just passed out again. That's right. He had just passed out.

Pressing his ear to Houston's mouth, Doc checked for breath sounds. Heard them. Saw his chest rise. Then Doc spotted a gunshot wound to Houston's thigh and fresh blood running down the Marine's leg. A quick examination made his heart sink: the round had probably struck Houston's femoral artery, and the lance corporal was bleeding out bad. Very bad. Doc ripped off his belt, began sliding it around Houston's thigh. "I need your medical kit. A trauma dressing! Now!"

Once of the SEALs raced across the cabin toward a bay of overhead compartments and began opening one.

"Wasn't getting stabbed in Pakistan enough?" Doc asked the unconscious radio operator. "You had to go and get yourself shot?"

"Is he going to make it?" Vance asked. "We can't lose three guys here. Not three. No fucking way."

"Doc," Rainey began slowly. "You're the man. You can save him."

"Sarge, he's lost a hell of a lot of blood already. Don't know if I can stop the bleeding."

"You can, Doc. You can," Rainey said. "We've come too damned far for this!"

The air grew hotter as Doc received the medical kit and got to work. The ASDS lurched, then suddenly listed to port as enemy fire drummed along its thick skin. Surprisingly, the Korean woman Min pushed herself in beside Doc and began opening the trauma dressing with practiced hands. She smiled weakly, pointed to herself, and said, "Doctor."

22

By the time the ASDS had reached the USS *Texas*, Doc and Min had stopped Houston's bleeding, though Doc had repeatedly warned Rainey that the lance corporal was still in critical condition. Overwhelmed by the events of the past hour, Rainey could only sit there unthinkingly as the mini-sub had locked on to the *Texas*'s Dry Dock Shelter. The DDS was a nine-foot-wide, nine-foot-high, thirty-eight-foot-long chamber located just aft of the sub's sail structure. Divided into three interconnected compartments, the DDS included a hyperbaric chamber, a transfer trunk, and a hangar. The mini-sub was housed in the latter compartment, and Rainey and the rest of the team had passed through the transfer trunk, then through the after hatch leading into the sub. Houston had been rushed to sickbay while Rainey spent a few moments talking with the captain and executive officer and expressing his condolences regarding the loss of the SEAL team leader.

Ironically, Rainey had learned that the North Korean government had only hours prior agreed to dismantle their weapons of mass destruction and allow United Nations weapons inspectors back into the country. The Combined Forces Command invasion had been canceled and all special forces still inside the country were being immediately extracted. And although Rainey and his men had failed their original mission to knock out those radar systems, they had prevented the launch of a nuclear weapon and a wider nuclear conflict. Not too many Force Recon teams could include that on their resumes.

As he lay in his bunk in the ship's guest quarters, he decided that he would a write a letter to the men in Lance Corporal Kim's unit. He would tell those Koreans of Kim's bravery without, of course, revealing classified information. He hoped that Kim's life might inspire those ROK Marines to greatness. People—and not just the few operators who had served with him—needed to remember that young man. Every ROK Marine who wore the uniform needed to know that one of their own had found the courage to do his duty and make the ultimate sacrifice.

TEAM DOGMA
MARFOR-K HEADQUARTERS
YONGSAN, SEOUL
SOUTH KOREA
2 DAYS POST MISSION
0800 HOURS LOCAL TIME

"The good news is we're getting four weeks leave. Count 'em, four weeks," Vance said, sitting on the edge of his cot, already imagining himself standing on a bass boat, trolling around a crystal clear Japanese lake, and using the new Daiwa reel that Rainey was going to buy him.

"Is that all you can think about?" Doc asked from his own bunk. "You go to work for two days, and now you need a month off? Man, your generation sure is lazy."

Vance snorted. "You ain't much older than me, Doc."

"Old enough to know I don't need a month off."

"You're complaining?"

"No, I'm getting up and going over to the hospital to see Houston. Coming?"

Rainey entered the billet, an envelope jutting from his breast pocket, a Gameboy and two games tucked under his arm. "Where you going?"

"To see Houston," Vance answered.

"Let me get this Gameboy stuff to the kid, then I'm coming with you."

Vance nodded. "And Sarge, speaking of the kid and his mom . . . what's going to happen to them?"

"I guess Min and her boy will start a new life here in the South. At least something good will come out of this."

Vance lowered his gaze. "Yeah."

"Hey, before we leave, can you listen to something?" the sarge asked.

"Better not be a victory speech," Doc said.

Rainey withdrew the envelope from his pocket and slipped out a typed letter. "Wrote this for Kim's unit." The sarge cleared his throat and read, "Gentlemen—"

"Wait," Doc said, raising a palm. "If you don't mind, I can't handle something like this right now."

"But you're the best writer, Doc. That's what the fisherman here says. I need your help."

"I'll help you. Just give it a few more days."

"I just want his guys to know what he did."

Doc took the letter, glanced at it. "His guys will. Then again, if they knew Kim like we did, then they already know the kind of Marine he was . . ."

Houston pretended that he was asleep when Rainey, Doc, and Vance entered his room. He had heard them in the hall outside and wasn't in the mood to have his spirits forcibly lifted. He had labored so hard during the past two days to depress himself, and he didn't need them ruining all his work.

"Look at him," Vance said. "Faking it again."

"Maybe we should come back later," said Doc.

"Lance Corporal, if you're not asleep, then you'd best open your eyes," Rainey said.

Houston knew and hated that tone. He cracked open an eyelid. "Where am I? Where's my buddy? Where's the enemy?"

"Yup, the boy has lost his mind, his buddy, and the enemy," Vance said. "Happens to all them guys from California."

"You got a little more color," Rainey said.

Doc picked up Houston's chart and scrutinized it. "Says here that he's scheduled for a sex change."

"Yeah, that's right," Vance said. "They're finally going to turn him into a *man*."

"How much do I have to pay you to leave?" Houston groaned.

"On your salary?" Rainey asked. "It might take a couple of hours to work out the financing."

Houston closed his eyes, clutched the sheets. It was time for the bullshit banter to end. Time get it all out in the open. He couldn't stand keeping it in anymore. "Guess I'm out of Force Five now, huh, Sarge?"

"What're you talking about? You're going to make a full recovery."

"Physically, yeah," Houston answered, slowly opening his eyes and lifting his chin at Vance and Doc. "But these guys know that I still got problems."

The corpsman and sniper backed away from the bed, neither wanting to get involved or own up to the fact that they had reported Houston's panic attacks to Rainey.

The sergeant leveled an index finger on Houston. "Maybe they certified you fit for duty a little too soon. Not your fault. You'll get through this—because you're not alone. As a matter of fact, there's someone flying all the way from San Diego to see you."

About twenty-four hours later, Houston was sitting up in bed and chatting with his maternal grandfather, the former Marine who had inspired him to join the service. Grandpa still wore his hair "high and tight," emphasizing his uncanny resemblance to the great Marine Chesty

Puller. His blue eyes sparkled as he took Houston's hand in his own and said, "Your mother's not here because it's my fault. I made her stay home. It's been rough on her."

"I know."

"Now Bradley, I didn't drag my old, worn-out butt all the way to South Korea to shoot the fucking breeze."

Houston grinned. It was funny to hear Grandpa curse. He was usually quite dignified. "Is there something you want to talk about?"

"Your father."

Houston tensed. "Next subject?"

Grandpa squeezed Houston's hand. "I want to talk about your father."

"The dead guy."

"Don't fuck with me, kid. You weren't there when he was dying."

"No shit! You come in here to lay some guilt trip on me? If you did, then I'm sorry, Gramps, but you have to go."

"Listen, I was there. I heard him talking to your mother. And you know me, I'm all business, no bullshit."

"Can we talk about something else?"

"Son, I came all the way out here to tell you that in the end, your father was proud of you. He told your mother."

"No, he didn't. That's my mother lying again."

"Bradley, I listened to him for a long time. He knew what he did was wrong. And when he realized that, he realized just how much he loved you—and just how proud he was to have a Marine as his son."

"So my mother told you to fly out here and tell me this shit to make me feel better in my time of need," Houston said sarcastically. "But the truth is, my father died hating me. There it is. There it will always be."

"What do I have to do to make you believe? Give you this?" Grandpa withdrew a piece of yellow notebook paper from his pocket and handed it to Houston. Frowning, Houston unfolded the paper to reveal a handwritten letter. He immediately recognized the penmanship as his father's. With now trembling hands, he began to read and broke down before he reached the third sentence.

"Your mother found that and was going to mail it to you," Grandpa said. "But I told her not to trust the fucking mail. Bringing it here was the least I could do for a fellow Marine."

"I guess he was proud of me," Houston said as he reached the second paragraph. "I guess he really was."

"We all are, kid. Now stop that fucking crying—otherwise these nurses will think you're in the Air Force or something."

Houston wiped his face. "Thank you, Gramps. Thank you."

When Doc called home to say he'd be returning soon, he learned that his boys were doing fine but that his wife was in the middle of a "major" crisis: She had decided to paint the master bedroom herself, had chosen what she believed to be a light shade of blue, but when she had rolled it out and began some kind of faux technique, the paint had dried "too crinkly and much too dark." She practically lost her breath as she told him that she had "ruined the bedroom walls."

Though he tried to stifle it, Doc's laughter escaped.

"Don't you laugh at me, Glenroy."

"I'm sorry, honey."

"I don't know if I can fix this!"

"We got the money. Pay somebody to do it."

"Why are you still laughing at me?"

"I'm not laughing. I'm happy."

"Then you're a fool. Because when you take one look at these walls—"

"Honey, it's okay. It's just good to know that life's still going on out there. And sweetheart, you put it all into perspective."

"I don't know what you're talking about."

"That's okay. Because I still love you—even if you ruined our bedroom walls."

"Glenroy!"

"I have to go now, sweetheart!"

THE LOVE HOTEL
TOKYO, JAPAN
I4 DAYS POST MISSION
2205 HOURS LOCAL TIME

Houston and Vance stood outside two grand wooden doors with gold door knobs. Vance had never seen doors as nice as those, except maybe at one of the Baptist churches back home. The Love Hotel was one classy whorehouse, all right.

"So we finally made it," Houston said, lifting his brows and limping toward the doors. "You think they really leave a condom on your pillow?"

"Who knows?"

"Well, let's find out. I am so good to go." Houston was practically salivating.

"Yeah, but I'm standing here, trying to figure how screwing some overpriced hooker is going to pay tribute to Bruno and Kim."

"I don't feel like paying Bruno any tribute, but Kim deserves it."

"We don't need to do this," Vance said. "We're wasting our money and our time."

"But we have money and time to waste. Don't tell me you're feeling guilty. Come on, bro. Cindy never answered that email you sent before the mission, and she never answered any of the other ones. Far as I'm concerned, you're a free man. Free to get laid. Now come on."

"Maybe something happened. Maybe—"

"Don't kid yourself."

Vance turned, waved Houston over. "This isn't right. Let's go someplace else."

"And do what? Get drunk as usual?"

"Drunk? No way. We'll find some cheap hotel, go to bed early, because tomorrow morning, my friend, we're going bass fishing on a Japanese lake."

Houston started back for the Love Hotel.

"Houston," Vance warned.

"Don't worry. I'm not going to get a hooker," the lance corporal groaned in disappointment. "I just want to find out if they really put that condom on your pillow."

"No, don't. Because if you go in there—"

Houston reached the doors, yanked one open, and disappeared.

"Aw, shit." Vance charged after his buddy and reached the door, which suddenly opened.

And there stood a familiar man with a goatee and wearing a photographer's vest. The guy took one look at Vance, then rushed past the door and onto the sidewalk.

"Hey," Vance called back. "I know you! You're Rick Navarro! Wolf News! What a coincidence, man! Come back here!"

"You got the wrong guy!" Navarro lowered his head and broke into a jog.

Vance turned back toward an ornate entrance foyer, where a young, lithe Japanese woman wearing a red bustier and matching garter belt suddenly seized his wrist. "Your friend already inside. Come on, G.I. Don't be shy. Welcome to Love Hotel."

Sliding out of her grip, Vance squinted into the shadows. "Houston? Fall back, Marine. Fall back right now!"

CAMP LIBERTY BELL
FIFTH FORCE RECONNAISSANCE COMPANY
THIRD PLATOON HEADQUARTERS
NORTHWEST FRONTIER PROVINCE
PAKISTAN
15 DAYS POST MISSION
0945 HOURS LOCAL TIME

Rainey wasn't due back to the company's headquarters for another two weeks, but he had figured that since Kady couldn't leave her post as Platoon Radio Operator, he would fly to Pakistan and spend most of his R &

R with her. Wishing there were a better way, he had given her the news of Sergeant Anthony Bruno's death via phone, but he had said that he would share the details with her in person when he got back.

Now he and Kady sat on their favorite slope overlooking Camp Liberty Bell, an olive drab military city rising out of the dust. Rainey wondered how much longer Fifth Force would be stationed there. The Northwest Frontier was a cruel place that got under the skin of even the most callous Marines. Too hot. Too cold. Too many terrorist snipers. Too many starving children.

"What're you thinking about?" Kady asked, her hair a little lighter than Rainey remembered, her skin a little darker.

"I'm thinking about nothing. Or trying to."

"You want to tell me what happened?"

After a thoughtful pause, Rainey said abruptly, "Popped his chute. Bad landing. He was in a tree when we found him."

"And that's it? You make it sound like you got him killed."

"In a way I did."

"How?"

"Being assigned to me pissed him off more than anything. He wasn't thinking straight when he came down. He was trying to prove something."

"Well, he did. He proved what an asshole he was. Even his brother said it. And believe me, Mac. Anthony was nothing like his brother."

"Doesn't matter anymore. Both of them are gone. Damn. I'm getting too old for this shit."

"Excuse me? Is this the same cocky bastard Marine I married? I can't believe I'm hearing this."

"Believe it."

"If you left Force Recon, it would kill you."

"Staying in is what'll get me killed."

"You got those boys through North Korea. I don't know how you did it, but it wasn't luck. It was skill. And if you don't keep sharing that talent, then you're cheating yourself and everybody else."

"Hard men. That's what we're supposed to be. I just don't know if I'm as good as I was in the beginning."

"You're better."

"You'd think experience would do that. But the more time I spend in the field, the more ghosts I make."

"Fuck the ghosts."

Rainey glanced at her in surprise. "Whoa. Listen to this woman."

"That's right. Listen to me. Fuck the ghosts. And the what ifs and the maybes and all the other bullshit doubts, because in the end, they mean nothing. It's all about confidence. It's all about going out there and do- ing your job and coming back home to your wife . . . and your baby on the way."

"My what?"

"Your baby. That's right, Mac. I'm six weeks. You're going to be a daddy."

Chills shot up Rainey's spine. They hadn't been try- ing, but they hadn't been worried if Kady had become pregnant. "Oh, my God. Geez, you just blurt it out like that." He slid his arms around her. "I'm just : . . it's like . . . amazing."

"It is. So you go out there and do it for us."

"I guess I will."

"No, don't guess. Being the best is going to get you home. So just keep saying, I'm the best. Because you are."

"Force Recon," he whispered as he moved in for a kiss. "Hoorah . . ."